HONZA

In the Heart of Prague

Andrew Pratt

Copyright © 2020 Andrew Pratt

All rights reserved

The characters and events portrayed in this book are fictitious. Any similarity to real persons, living or dead, is coincidental and not intended by the author.

No part of this book may be reproduced, or stored in a retrieval system, or transmitted in any form or by any means, electronic, mechanical, photocopying, recording, or otherwise, without express written permission of the publisher.

ISBN: 9798551086321
Imprint: Independently published

This book is dedicated to Pavla

We met one spring weekend in Prague and so you are the true inspiration for this novel

Thank you for your love and for showing me the true heart of Prague

CONTENTS

Title Page
Copyright
Dedication
1	1
2	10
3	21
4	28
5	35
6	43
7	52
8	70
9	77
10	86
11	93
12	101
13	108
14	116
15	125
16	135
17	143
18	150

19	157
20	166
21	176
22	184
23	191
24	200
25	208
26	217
27	225
28	233
29	242
30	250
31	258
32	268
33	277
34	283
35	291
36	299
37	310
38	316
39	324
40	329
41	334

1

Old Town Square, Prague

Monday, 15th March 2010

The afternoon sun bathed Old Town Square, Staroměstské Náměstí, in warmth, creating near-perfect lighting fit for a picture postcard. Tourists ambled slowly across the cobbles, lost in their leisure and absorbing the fine architecture, only interspersed by the few local businessmen striding across the square, briefcases in hand and heads down at the beginning of the working week.

Jonny stopped at the restaurant, pausing to savour the view, and sat down at his usual table in the corner of the terrace with a good vantage point. His usual table implied some long-standing relationship to the restaurant, but this routine had materialised quickly, with five visits in as many days since his arrival in Prague. Jonny was a creature of habit, deciding what he liked quickly and then sticking by it.

The restaurant wasn't as busy as it had been the previous day, the attraction of a city break as the weather was improving having swollen the crowds in the centre over the weekend. Everywhere in Prague seemed to have suddenly become busy with the start of the season. But deep down, Jonny was also quietly content. Whereas the tourists milling around would mostly be in and out of Prague in a few days, he had three months to explore this famous capital. He was looking forward to learning the ebb and flow of the city: the best methods and times to travel, how to avoid the crowds and, of course, developing his own list of secret haunts. The Old Town Square was central to one of the most picturesque and popular tourist attractions in Europe, if not the world. Now that he had finally visited Prague, he wanted his relationship with it to be more exclusive, not overshadowed by hordes of Japanese tourists blindly following a guide waving an umbrella.

Without even realising what he was doing, Jonny automatically started scanning the restaurant, his seemingly inbuilt radar system always on full alert.

Three Englishmen in their mid-thirties were sat on the far side of the terrace finishing their lunch, relaxed friends enjoying time away. One of them was proudly wearing a football shirt, as seemed to be expected of any Brit abroad these days. Jonny didn't recognise the team strip but assumed it was a Czech team, probably purchased here whilst on holiday. The only other people on the terrace were an elderly couple Jonny recognised as German. They were huddled together for extra warmth despite the beautiful spring weather; the lady had a blanket on her lap, and they were sharing some hot chocolate and apple strudel.

Inside the main restaurant, through the folded patio-style doors, he could see only a few tables occupied for a late lunch. A young family were seated along one wall, the parents trying hard to entertain their pre-school children. In the corner a young couple were holding hands across the secluded table, away from prying eyes. Two middle-aged Scandinavian looking couples had just arrived and were being shown to a table in the centre of the restaurant, near the open doors.

Jonny sighed, knowing he would probably never lose the compulsion for assessing his surroundings. The job had taught him so much about spotting potential dangers before they materialised, nurturing his innate talent and honing his detection skills. His successful police career had provided him with mostly good experiences. But it was the bad incidents which were etched on his memory, especially the cruelty one human being could inflict on another, and they had left a firm imprint on his natural reactions. Sometimes, though, he just wished he could relax and switch off like other people.

Sitting there on the terrace, he knew nobody would mistake him for anything other than a tourist. And probably a British tourist. After all, the UK was where he was born and, apart from summer holidays abroad, was where he had spent all his forty-four years. Average height, medium build, thinning dark hair and pale skin weren't exactly distinctive, certainly not identifying him as the outdoor type, but he had been told over the years that he had smiling eyes and an attractive thick-set jawline. Even his holiday attire was universal and modest: plain blue shirt, chinos and a linen jacket. He had never stood out. In fact he'd never wanted to, instead feeling more comfortable blending in with the crowd. The irony was that he had become an expert in assessing everyone and everything else around him in search of the guilty.

Feeling comfortable and anonymous, as he liked it, Jonny gazed out across the square, noting the expanding group of tourists waiting for the hourly strike of the astronomical clock. The square was both a hive of activity, with the mix of enthusiastic tour promoters and acoustic buskers, but at the same time the space was large enough to be quiet and calming. This perfectly matched the requirements of the supplementary reason for his extended visit: to recover from the significant events of the past year, and try to release the hold that his last case still had on him.

Lost in the scene, he was just starting to contemplate how one can get used to something so easily, when he was interrupted by an approaching waiter. Standing to attention, the waiter stood dressed for admiring comments in a bohemian costume of patterned white shirt, velvet waistcoat and black trousers.

"Dobrý den," the waiter greeted him.

"Dobrý den."

The waiter suddenly recognised him. "Sir, hello again. What can I get for you?"

Jonny took a deep breath. "Ja si dam kavu s mleku. Děkuju."

The waiter smiled at Jonny, impressed. "You have been practising your Czech."

Jonny shrugged off the complement. "It's not impressive, really. I just remember some Czech words from my mother."

The waiter finished writing the order on his pad and looked up, expecting Jonny to continue.

"Well…" Jonny was going to explain, but clocked the waiter's watchful gaze. "Actually, it's rather a long story. Maybe another time."

The waiter nodded and smiled warmly. "No problem, sir. I'll attend to your order. White coffee coming up!"

As the waiter walked away, Jonny couldn't help feeling a bit awkward. He didn't want to be categorised as a show-off, but he felt he needed to try out the Czech words he remembered. He felt he owed it to his mother, or at least his memory of her. The trick was to find the right balance, demonstrating a willingness to learn whilst also showing respect for the complex language. With a little help from the phrase book, of course.

Jonny picked up the newspapers he had bought and considered them, one in each hand. For some reason he'd decided to buy both a British newspaper and a Czech newspaper at the Kiosk near the square. He'd always fancied himself as a newspaper reader but, even at weekends, when many people relaxed by reading the newspaper over brunch, he was rarely off duty and there just never seemed to be the time. For the choice of Czech newspaper, he had been completely lost. In the end he'd picked a tabloid with plenty of pictures and shorter words. Whilst probably not the best written newspaper, he hoped it might help him learn some conversational Czech during his stay.

Having put the newspapers on the spare chair for later, Jonny again looked out across the sunlit square. It was certainly worthy of its majestic label and he was already aware that the simplistic beauty of the space had a hypnotic pull. The astronomical clock was rightly the central attraction, but he was becoming very attached to the imperial Gothic church, The Church of Our Lady before Týn. The church's two steeples imposed over the square from behind the main buildings lining its perimeter. Whilst he definitely wasn't an expert on architecture, even he knew this regal building must be one of the most perfect sculptures in the world; the balance between grandeur and exquisite detail up the height of the towers made it hard to take your eyes away from them.

"Your coffee, sir." The waiter carefully placed the coffee on the table, turning the saucer so the logo on the cup faced Jonny.

"Děkuju," Jonny replied, followed by a slightly apologetic, "Thank you."

"Prosím." The waiter smiled and walked back into the restaurant.

Jonny took his notepad out of his jacket pocket and, using the pencil stored in the pad, wrote himself a reminder to find out if visitors were allowed to climb the towers of the church. The written prompt filled up the last line on the page, completing his first full page of places he wanted to visit in Prague. He knew it was time to get his act together and start exploring the hidden secrets of the city, rather than just strolling around the city centre all day.

Staring at the notebook in his hand halted all notions of leisure activities. To be precise, it was the remaining stubs from the torn pages which caught his attention. Never one to tolerate waste, he had taken the almost new notebook with him when he'd left the Metropolitan Police at the end of the previous year, pulling out the few used pages and putting them through the office shredder for security. Now the notebook was his only remaining personal possession from nearly twenty-five years in the Force. Jonny smiled to himself at the haphazard nature of prized possessions and their hidden meanings.

Jonny had promised himself he would not think back over his last case, but the notebook suddenly brought back a flood of memories. Having spent hours in counselling at the end of his service, he believed he'd managed to suppress the hopeless feeling of having failed the last victim's family. But even though he had talked to the counsellor for hours, opening himself up more than he'd ever done before in his life, he still sometimes thought he saw the dead woman's face in a crowd. She seemed to appear from nowhere when he least expected it: turning the aisle in the supermarket, or maybe getting off a train. The face belonged to Alison Bryce, the last victim of serial killer, Bill Sutherland. Sure, Jonny knew he had caught Sutherland in the end, but he also knew that if the case had been resolved quicker, Alison would still be alive. Nobody else had spotted the clue to Sutherland's identity, but this point was irrelevant; Jonny knew he had taken too long and he'd have to live with it for the rest of his life.

Raised voices from the table of Englishmen snapped Jonny out of his self-torture. A relaxed lunch between friends seemed to have escalated into a bitter feud. The smaller, stocky man, wearing a denim jacket, was talking loudly and gesticulating across the table at the taller, muscular man in the football shirt. Jonny discreetly craned forward to hear, his senses heightened, but couldn't make out exactly what was being said across the table.

Attempting to assess the dynamics, he noticed the third man was trying to act as peacemaker. Looking concerned, he was talking calmly and extending his arms, using hand signals to try to pacify both men. The call for a truce seemed to be working, the verbal contest subsiding although words were still being exchanged. Jonny watched them, trying to read the facial gestures and determine their intentions. He was dismayed to realise he had unconsciously shifted his position, ready to step in and defuse the situation. *Why can't I just have a peaceful life?*

Just as other people in the restaurant, including the waiters, were starting to notice the stand-off, the situation escalated with a battery of noise. The smaller, angry man raised himself from his chair and leaned menacingly over the table, his finger jabbing the air between him and his adversary. The scraping sound of his chair being pushed back was followed by a volley of abuse.

"You're a bloody liar! Always cheating everyone. You need to be taught a lesson!"

The target of the abuse sat motionless in his chair, the smirk on his face intended to ridicule the argument and belittle his aggressor.

After a brief staring match, the man in the football shirt said, "I've had enough of this." He stood up, knocking his chair backwards, and stormed off through the terrace into the restaurant. He walked through the open patio doors and towards the restrooms.

Everyone in the restaurant had watched the drama unfold, but calm soon descended once the man had disappeared from view. Jonny noted the assured way he had strode off, evidently annoyed but still in command of the situation. His two other friends remained at the table, the seated man attempting to coax his angry friend back into his chair. The man eventually sat down when he realised everyone in the restaurant was looking at him, the feeling of embarrassment overcoming his sense of injustice.

Jonny was sure the show was over and relaxed his body position. His experience at reading body language and facial expressions told him the angered man felt aggrieved or wronged, but was unlikely to take the matter further. If he was right about the dynamics of the small group, this man, the one who first shouted, was weaker than his antagonist and would probably be the first to apologise when the other man returned from the restrooms.

Finally picking up his coffee, Jonny reflected on how pleased he was to be away from it all. He had loved his career, well, most of it, and was proud to have achieved the rank of Detective Chief Inspector. He was also proud to have been instrumental in putting some downright disgusting people behind bars. He also knew that his temperament and unconventional policing techniques had tried the patience of many colleagues, and was abhorred by some of his superiors. He'd been hard to work with and even more difficult to live with.

He'd known from early in his vocation that he had the ability to think like a criminal, something that was difficult to instil into a police officer. Sometimes his instinct and gut feel were the only way he had got one step ahead of the villain. He was as diligent as any detective, following up any and all leads, but he knew the breakthrough in a case was often only possible if you could look at the evidence from a different perspective. He wasn't sure what it said about him as a person, but it had made for a successful career.

His decision to take early retirement turned out to be as easy as it was unexpected. One year before, he was basking in the glory of solving numerous, high profile cases, the next he was doubting everything: his reasons for dedicating his life to catching criminals, his own perceived failure to catch Sutherland before he had killed all his planned victims, and the incorrect balance of work with the important relationships in his life, especially his only daughter. *I am only killing myself, and for what?* Now the big decision had been made, he was free to look ahead with fresh eyes and enjoy the next chapter of his life. And he felt he was in the right place. This was a country he'd been aware of all his life, it being his mother's birthplace. She had never wanted to come back and he'd never felt the inclination to visit before, but now the time was right.

Jonny's contemplations were broken by screaming from inside the restaurant. Expecting some intensification of the previous episode, he turned but saw only the same two men still sitting at the table, talking calmly. It was a woman screaming. Following the sound, he saw a young woman standing in the middle of the inside restaurant, looking distraught and screaming uncontrollably. Focusing his sights, he recognised the same woman who, minutes earlier, was looking flushed with love and enjoying a romantic lunch. Jonny instinctively stood up and scanned his field of vision. The young man rushed over to his girlfriend, as the other customers and staff looked on, concerned but unsure how to react.

The young man didn't know what to do, either. The relationship was clearly new and he didn't have the knowledge to understand the signs of her distress nor how to deal with them. He tried patting her arm and providing soothing words. She just screamed again. After trying to comfort her without success, he resorted to the only action he felt could help and tried cuddling her. She still screamed, her body shaking uncontrollably. A waiter approached them cautiously, aware of the impact the scene was having on the ambience within the restaurant.

"Madam, are you hurt?"

The young woman wailed. "No!" she shouted, gulping for air, trying to breathe between screams. "Someone's been murdered!" She pointed dramatically in the direction of the restrooms and buried her face into her boyfriend's chest, crying loudly.

Jonny had watched the scene unfold with incredulity and familiar contempt. He wasn't a police detective any more. He was trying to move on with his life. And he was only here for a quiet afternoon coffee. All he could mutter to himself was, "Oh shit."

2

The Oddball Couple

Jonny felt like he was in a bad dream. Firstly, his holiday plans had been hijacked by events outside of his control, and then he found himself in the middle of a murder scene. And to make matters worse, he was a potential witness. What had he done to deserve this?

Although he had been an experienced DCI for years, the truth was that he hated murder scenes. The murdered body or bodies, to be exact. And of course, the blood. His seniority in rank always allowed him to arrive at the crime scene later, once it had been secured, and, importantly, after he had been briefed. This precious preparation time allowed him to detach himself from the gruesome reality. But there was no getting away from the grisly details when the forensic pathologist arrived, the obvious questions and answers about the cause of death making his stomach churn. But he knew it was a vital and unavoidable part of the job, the murder scene holding so many clues. He was relieved when it was over, though, his preference being for what followed in the investigation: the subsequent chase to find the murderer, with all its mind games and mental challenges.

Jonny also felt uncomfortable because he was sitting on the witness bench. He was usually on the other side of the fence, the one in control, barking orders to ensure evidence was found and preserved. Surveying the first facts, he would be piecing together what he knew so far, starting to prepare in his head the briefing he would give to his team back at the station. A successful prosecution was largely dependent on the state of the physical evidence at the time it was collected and the findings in the first forty-eight hours of the investigation.

One aspect of the crime scene that was standard for the job was the tape across the front of the restaurant terrace, confirming to all passers-by that something serious had happened. Two police cars and one van were parked on the square outside the restaurant terrace and a barrel-chested Czech policeman was standing guard, controlling access in and out of the cordon. The patio doors of the restaurant had been closed, only one door now open to allow the police officers to move around.

Inside the restaurant all the potential witnesses were sat in a semi-circle: the customers, waiters and kitchen staff. Jonny had purposefully chosen the seat on the end, keen to maintain his distance. The seating arrangement led to an odd game of eye contact that Jonny had never considered before, witnesses eyeing each other and coming to their own guilty conclusions. Only the family were seated behind the semi-circle, the parents careful to shield the children from seeing or hearing too much.

The conversation between the potential witnesses was stilted. The two English tourists, friends of the presumed murder victim, were in shock. Both looked pale, sitting slumped forward, elbows on their knees. One shook their head and uttered out loud, "I can't believe it, he only went to the loo," expecting and getting no response from his companion. The young woman was also in shock, crying softly into her boyfriend's chest for comfort, her hair shielding her face.

Everything had happened very quickly once the restaurant staff had understood the enormity of the situation. A waiter had rushed to the restrooms and come back with his hand over his mouth, close to retching, before composing himself and briefing the head waiter. The first police officers had arrived in minutes, ushering all the restaurant customers and staff to the furthest side of the indoor area as they explored the restrooms. Further police assistance arrived minutes later, the cordon was established and procedures put in place to keep the area around the restrooms clear to ensure pertinent evidence was not contaminated.

Jonny had been impressed with the speed and organisation of the police reaction. He assumed a police station or base must be close by due to the historical significance of Old Town Square, however a murder would surely not be their usual call. More standard would likely be a local homeless person straying into a tourist area or the unavoidable late-night, drunk holidaymakers on stag parties, making too much noise or picking fights. He surveyed the scene from his position on the unaccustomed witness bench and all the police officers seemed well organised, aware of their jobs, and working as a team. Protective sheeting had been laid down as a walkway and two men were already in protective suits, goggles, masks and gloves, scouring the floor of the restaurant for evidence, whilst another was taking photographs of the restaurant from every angle.

The police staff at the crime scene were being marshalled, impressively, by a uniformed, female officer, who Jonny assumed must be the sergeant. Tall and slim, her blonde hair tucked under her police hat, she had an unassuming, almost natural, air of authority for a relatively young officer, probably still in her late twenties. She had swiftly shepherded all the customers and staff over to where they now sat, taken their names and informed them all, in Czech and then in impressive English, that they had to remain here until they had been spoken to individually and given statements. Only the elderly German couple needed further reassurance because of their limited understanding of both Czech and English.

Jonny was just starting to wonder where the big boss was when an unmarked police car pulled up in dramatic fashion. The arrival caused a big stir, all the uniformed officers stopping what they were doing and acknowledging the boss, as he was led through the cordon, with a nod of respect and a greeting of "Pane". Jonny was impressed, it was certainly an imposing entrance. His own arrivals, by contrast, had always been brisk and business-like on his insistence.

The boss strode through the restaurant, all eyes on him, and up to the female police officer. His assistant, the driver of the car, trailed a few metres behind, struggling to keep up. The huddle of officers exchanged some hurried words and all walked off to the restrooms, the boss leading from the front in an exaggerated style.

This boss was certainly a character, both in mannerisms and dress sense. He was wearing an immaculately-pressed, tweed three-piece suit with a matching wide-brimmed hat and black cane. The shirt and tie were a colourful pink paisley combination and connected to the waistcoat button was what looked to Jonny like the chain of a pocket watch. His attire would have been eye-catching in any situation, but his expressive face and overstated gestures further hinted at an eccentric personality. By comparison, his sidekick was younger but scruffy, wearing a poorly-fitted suit, a white shirt that had seen better days and a large tie knot slightly askew.

Jonny chucked to himself. This could be fun! The pair of detectives made an oddball couple, displaying evident touches of some famous detectives from historic crime fiction.

After fifteen minutes the trio of senior officers returned to the main restaurant and the boss stopped theatrically in the middle of the restaurant. Slowly and deliberately he took off his hat and, in his own time, assessed all the seated witnesses across the room. After scanning the group, his eyes locked with Jonny, who felt himself being examined up and down. The boss whispered to the female officer and pointed across the room at Jonny before turning on his heel, tapping his cane, and heading off into the kitchen through the serving door. The sidekick looked at the female police officer, shaking his head in exasperation, before scampering to keep up with his boss. The female officer smiled to herself, clearly happy to be in her position, not his, and calmly walked over to Jonny.

"Mr Fox, can I please ask you to come this way?"

She then turned to reassure the other witnesses. "The detective leading this case has arrived and will now speak to you all individually. Please wait your turn and I will let you know when you are needed." The German gentleman started to get up from his chair, but the female officer kindly motioned for him to sit down and remain waiting.

The female officer led Jonny into the kitchen, which was deserted but still smelled of food, and then returned to the main restaurant. The two male detectives were sat at a makeshift interview table waiting for him. The boss stood to greet him, gave him a wide welcoming smile and gestured to the empty chair opposite. The hat and cane were perched on the edge of the table, next to a single sheet of paper with handwritten notes. The assistant sat pensive in his chair, notepad and pen in hand.

Sitting down, Jonny could see that the boss's tweed suit was as perfect and well-fitted as he had initially thought. Clearly, he liked to look dapper and took his image very seriously. Whilst he had looked younger from a distance, with his wiry, energetic frame, Jonny could see now, close up, that he was older than his youthful movement suggested, probably close to retirement age. The thinning hair and facial lines supported Jonny's age assessment, but his bright eyes shone pure vitality and delight at the world.

The assistant detective was younger, in his midthirties, probably half the age of his boss. If he was the young protégé, he still had a lot to learn from his commanding officer regarding his dress sense. Whilst well groomed, and appearing organised, his care for and choice of clothes left a lot to be desired. He gave off an air of someone struggling to keep up with the rigours of everyday life. And his boss.

Jonny settled in his seat, feeling relaxed. He wasn't startled by the interview approach having himself tried many unconventional interrogation styles in the past. But he was intrigued why he had been chosen first.

"Mr Fox," started the boss in a heavy accent, "My name is Felix Mikeš. I am the Chief Warrant Officer on this case. It is the same as a Detective Chief Inspector in UK. This is Chief Sergeant Boukal, Marek Boukal." Mikeš gave Jonny an expansive, proud smile. Boukal nodded his head towards Jonny in greeting.

"First I must apologise," Mikeš continued. "My English is not very good. Marek is of the younger generation and much better than me." Boukal blushed under the praise from Mikeš.

"Also, I am sorry for talking to you in here," Mikeš gestured around the kitchen. "It may not look very professional, but I am an experienced detective and I believe it is vitally important to talk to witnesses as soon as possible."

Jonny nodded his understanding.

"Before we start, Mr Fox, I would like to explain about my surname. 'Mikeš' is spelt with a hacek above the 's', making it a 'sh' sound. It's very important to the correct pronunciation of the word. We have a lot of this in our Czech language."

"Yes, I know," replied Jonny. "I am aware of the larger alphabet."

"Excellent," Mikeš continued warmly. "But you will not be aware that my name is also famous in Czech Republic. 'Mikeš' is the name of a black cat in a famous set of children's book. The cat has lots of adventures with his animal friends…"

Jonny interrupted politely. "Actually, my mother used to read them to me when I was young."

Mikeš looked impressed and turned to Boukal with raised eyebrows. "You have surprised me, Mr Fox. Maybe there is more about you that I do not already know."

Jonny looked confused. "I'm sorry, I do not understand. What do you already know about me?"

Mikeš raised his hands in an expressive, almost magician like gesture. "Mr Fox, I believe you are also a police detective."

Jonny looked between Mikeš and Boukal, trying to understand if there was an underlying motive to this strange line of questioning. A quick assessment of the situation reminded him that he was in Prague on holiday, was only ordering a cup of coffee in the restaurant at the time of the murder, and nobody else in this city knew him.

Jonny shrugged his shoulders. "I am not following you. Is this a test?"

Mikeš started laughing. "No, it's just me, Mr Fox. I apologise. Many people tell me I have a strange sense of humour." Mikeš turned to look at Boukal for confirmation, but his assistant maintained a blank face, unsure how to respond.

"Anyway," continued Mikeš, "in addition to making bad jokes, I also have a gift for recognising another police officer. There is something in our souls that give us away, don't you think? You can see it in our eyes."

"Very impressive," Jonny acknowledged. "Actually, I'm retired now. Hence why I'm in Prague, taking some time off."

"I knew it, I knew it." Mikeš laughed loudly and whacked Boukal on the shoulder. Boukal recovered his composure, smiling falsely at his boss, and Jonny suddenly had a sympathy for what the younger detective must endure every day.

"I was a Detective Chief Inspector in the Metropolitan Police," Jonny added. "All my life I worked Homicide and Serious Crime."

Mikeš suddenly changed back to serious investigation mode. "So, please tell me, Detective Chief Inspector Fox, what were you doing in a restaurant in Prague when a murder was committed?" He folded his arms and sat back in his chair, pleased with his unexpected change of tact.

Jonny paused to gather his thoughts. Although the interview was amusing him, he was keen to take back some control. "Mr Mikeš—"

Mikeš interrupted swiftly. "Please, call me Felix."

"Ok, Felix, I arrived in Prague last Wednesday and I'm

planning to stay for a few months. I am staying in rented accommodation in Prague 2. I found this restaurant on my first full day here, when exploring Old Town Square—"

"Staroměstské Náměstí?" Mikeš interrupted again.

"Yes, indeed," Jonny confirmed. "I've stopped here, at this restaurant, every afternoon since Thursday. I arrived today at 2.45pm and ordered my usual coffee. The table of three Englishmen were here when I arrived. About 3pm the conversation became heated. The man in the denim jacket stood up and shouted at the man in the football shirt, the one who subsequently left the table but did not return."

"And you, Mr Fox?"

"I was seated on the terrace with my coffee all the time. Until the young lady started screaming, of course."

Mikeš consulted the paper in front of him. "Can you remember exactly what the man in the denim jacket said?"

"When I arrived their conversation was friendly and I couldn't hear what they were talking about. But then the situation escalated. I looked around and heard him say loudly, 'You're a bloody liar, always cheating everyone. You need to be taught a lesson'. The two men stared at each other until the man in the football shirt walked off with a smirk on his face. I assumed he was going to the restrooms."

"Those were his exact words?"

"Yes. As you have clearly already twigged, I was a detective for a long time. My brain has been trained to remember. Like yours, no doubt."

"I see, and yes, as I expected," Mikeš confirmed. "But what is this 'twigged'?"

Jonny laughed softly and put his hand up apologetically. "I'm sorry, it's slang for 'understood'."

Mikeš repeated "twigged" a few times, rolling the words over his tongue. "Interesting. Thank you. It's good to learn something new every day." Mikeš seemed pleased with himself.

"I think it's an old Irish word," added Jonny.

With the lull in the conversation, Boukal stepped into the conversation with near perfect English. "Mr Fox, did you sense anything else about the group of Englishmen?"

Mikeš patted Boukal on the arm. "Boukal is very keen, but maybe a little raw. I am trying to teach him. To mentor him, I think you say. I'm trying to help him develop into a top detective like both of us."

Jonny smiled back at Mikeš, momentarily stumped by this eccentric detective. Not knowing how to respond, and certainly not wanting to get involved any more than he already was, he instead turned to Boukal. "All I would say is that it felt to me like the argument between the men was deep-rooted, something from their past. They were definitely friends, probably here on a short holiday. But there was real passion to the argument. The man who walked off seemed more disgusted than angry."

"Thank you, that's very useful," Boukal replied, making some notes.

There was a momentary silence as Mikeš consulted the paper to see if there was anything else to cover. Eventually Mikeš looked up, directly at Jonny. "Mr Fox, I like you a lot. You are a good, honest man. Like me. I think we have a lot in common and will, how do you say… get on well together."

Jonny started to interrupt, "Well, I'm only here for—"

"Nonsense," insisted Mikeš. "You have to live in the present. We must keep in contact whilst you are here and talk some time over a beer. You like Pilsner Urquell?"

"Well, of course, but—"

"It's agreed then. We might even need to talk to you again about the case."

"But I am retired now."

"A good detective never retires, Mr Fox." Mikeš nodded knowingly. "Please leave your contact details with Sergeant Dvořáková and I will call you."

Boukal stepped in to explain. "Sergeant Dvořáková is the policewoman who brought you in here."

"Thanks," Jonny replied.

Thinking the interview was over, he started to get up from his chair but Mikeš continued. "Your full name is Jonathan. So like John, or maybe even Jack?"

"Correct. But I've always preferred Jonny. Only my mother called me Jonathan."

In apparent inspiration, Mikeš clicked his fingers and pointed at him. "I'm going to call you Honza."

Jonny looked confused and started to protest, "Well—"

"Many people in Czech Republic called Jan, like your John, are called Honza by their friends. It's a kind sort of insult, my friend."

Jonny stared at Mikeš, confused and stunned at how his peaceful day and now this interview were turning out.

Sensing the confusion, Boukal tried to clarify. "It is like a nickname. But unfortunately I don't know any good examples in English."

"Yes, exactly," Mikeš agreed excitedly and again whacked Boukal on the shoulder.

Jonny was still speechless.

Abruptly Mikeš pushed back his chair and stood up, hand held out for Jonny. "We must continue the interviews now. Time is valuable. Thank you, Honza, and yes, we will talk soon."

Jonny stood up and shook hands with the two detectives, before walking towards the door. Well, that was the strangest interview ever, he thought. He stopped to confirm his contact details again with Sergeant Dvořáková, who then led him towards the exit out of the police cordon.

"Is Detective Chief Inspector Mikeš always like that?" Jonny asked her.

Dvořáková stopped at the cordon and smiled at him. "He is certainly a character. And a very good detective."

Jonny nodded in acknowledgement. "Goodbye," he said and walked through the cordon onto the square, still busy with tourists. He stopped and closed his eyes against the sun,

breathing deeply.
"I think I need a drink," he muttered to himself.

3

Two Left Feet

Jonny decided to take a long walk from Old Town Square to clear his head; he needed to collect his thoughts first, the drink could wait until later.

He couldn't help feeling resentful. His mission on this trip was to relax and discover Prague, helping in turn to restore his vigour and outlook on the future. But for some inexplicable reason this quest had been hijacked by events outside of his control. Deep down he felt great remorse for the victim in the restaurant; it was something he had always taken very personally in his job and the primary reason he had been so driven to bring criminals to justice. Right now, though, he just wanted to get back the sense of calm and control he'd had earlier in the day when leisurely walking the streets of the city.

The weather was helping him recover his composure. The late afternoon sun was still shining, hardly a cloud in the sky, as he stretched out his legs. His landlady had told him about the lack of rain here, and especially the sunny winter days, but it was hard not to expect rain after living in UK all his life.

After leaving the restaurant he had felt the pull of the River Vltava, winding its way elegantly through the city. He set off past the crowds at the base of the astronomical clock and followed the winding, cobbled streets to the famous Charles Bridge. The bridge was busy with meandering tourists, strolling through the relaxed atmosphere. Small crowds gathered around the stalls selling paintings and drawings of the city's sights, and a jazz band were playing to an enthusiastic holiday crowd.

Jonny stopped midway across the bridge and gazed out over the river, white water spray crashing over the weir to regulate the river's flow. He could see pedal boats on the river, large white swans and colourful cars floating slowly over the water as people pedalled furiously inside. He had been fascinated by water since he was a young boy, strong memories still remaining of his first day trips to the seaside when he would spend all his time close to the sea, mesmerised by the changing tide and the breaking waves.

Lost in the moment, his childhood memories stirred thoughts of his mother's early years in Prague. It was hard to imagine her leaving behind such a beautiful city to go to the UK, never to return. She had been a strong woman and had always dismissed him when he asked questions about her family, instead telling him only that the UK was her home now. Whatever had happened must have been serious and he'd felt it strongly from his earliest memories. Her untimely death had taken the answers to his questions with her, her story probably never to be told. As an only child he had always been intrigued by her lost family, not knowing about her parents or siblings, but he reminded himself that his journey here was driven by the desire to see her birthplace, not dig up her past.

When she had died a few years ago, he had been sadly alone in sorting out her estate. No brothers or sisters to help, and a father only in name, he having left before Jonny had the chance to know him. What Jonny did discover relating to her Czech background was sparse and old; her old Czech passport and residence documents were out of date, having been replaced by her British equivalents. Unlike many other personal items, he had been unable to throw them out and had felt compelled to dig out the folder from a box with his mother's effects before travelling to Prague.

The warmth on his face had restored his good mood and also his appetite. Having already walked up the hill to

Prague Castle the day before, he decided to retrace his steps back across the bridge. He soon found a small café in the streets of the old town where he finally had a relaxed coffee and a traditional open sandwich.

As Jonny sat relaxing, he found himself reflecting on DCI Mikeš. He was certainly a peculiar character, very different to what Jonny was used to in the Force, his strong mannerisms and eccentric personality making him hard to ignore. He was, however, oddly charming and persuasive, someone who got under your skin. Jonny smiled to himself recounting the supposed interview. 'Honza', indeed! It was as if Mikeš believed they were detective brothers reunited. Whilst Jonny had been irritated by the unwanted imposition of the afternoon's events on his own agenda of a calm and tranquil day, Mikeš' words had certainly hit a soft spot. Maybe a good detective never retires, he thought. Jonny rolled his eyes fatefully, letting the nightmare thought creep up on him of a murder being committed every time he went for a coffee for the rest of his life.

Refuelled and more relaxed, Jonny wound his way through the cobbled streets of the old town, pleased with his improving navigation skills, and easily found the bottom of Wenceslas Square. During his limited time in Prague he had come to enjoy the hustle and bustle of this, more modern square, the shops and hotels intermingled with the many terraces providing al fresco dining on the wide walkways. Halfway up the largely pedestrian square, trams cut across at regular intervals providing a flash of red and recollections of the past. He made a mental note that he still hadn't been on a tram, but in this weather the walk was too good to miss, much better than a crammed tram at rush hour.

The top half of the square was dominated by the watchful splendour of the National Museum, home for some of the most famous scientific and historic collections. Standing grand and proud on the hill, the museum building was solid and rectangular in structure with a rising central column leading to a main tower with a large, gold-edged dome and lantern. Two matching, smaller domes were situated at either end of the building, providing elegance and balance. Jonny stood on the pedestrian central reservation of the square, next to the imposing bronze statue of King Wenceslas on his horse, and felt the emotional strain of the day fade away as the lowering sun bathed this impressive building in golden light.

***

The accommodation he had chosen online had been a bit of a stab in the dark, but had turned out to be more than adequate for his needs. He planned to stay in Prague for three months and knew he could easily change accommodation if he either didn't like it or wanted to experience a different part of the city. His landlady, Ivana, had a spare room in the attic with a great view over the church on the nearby square, Náměstí Míru. His en-suite room had a desk, TV and chair, all he really needed in addition to the view, and he was welcome downstairs in the living room whenever he wanted. Ivana had even offered to wash and iron his clothes.

As he pushed open the front door of the top floor apartment and stepped into the hall, the living room door opened and Ivana stepped out smiling at him. She was either nosey or keen to make sure he was comfortable (probably both he had already concluded), because she seemed to sense him arriving or leaving and always popped her head around the door to have a word. He really didn't mind, though; whatever her motive, it was nice to have someone to talk to when he didn't know anyone else in the city.

"Hi, Jonny!" Ivana exclaimed, looking surprised to see him. "Have you had a good day?"

Jonny took his time to select the right words. "Well, it was certainly quite eventful."

Ivana waited for him to elaborate, but he wasn't going to get drawn into a long discussion about what had happened at the restaurant. For all he knew, the murder may have already been on the news and he wasn't in the mood for a catalogue of questions.

"Sounds intriguing," she giggled.

It was only then that Jonny noticed she was dressed up. She was confidently wearing a knee-length dress when he'd only ever seen her before in casual clothing. With make-up on and her hair curled, it was quite a transformation. The dress showed off her figure, complementing her curves, with a low-cut neckline.

Ivana caught Jonny looking. "I am going out tonight with my girlfriends. Do you like it?" She twirled suggestively in front of him

"Yes, the dress really suits you."

"Thank you." Ivana fluttered her eyes at him. "Maybe you will take me dancing one night?"

Jonny stuttered, slightly taken back by the forward approach. Ivana laughed, leaning slightly into him and putting her hand seductively on his arm.

"Well, I am not much of a dancer," Jonny explained. "We would say in English that I have two left feet."

Ivana laughed. "We say the same in Czech: 'dvě levé nohy'. Maybe a drink one night instead?"

Jonny was cornered now, with only one way out. "Yes, that would be good. Let's agree a date." He blushed slightly, immediately realising what he had said. "Sorry, I mean let's agree what night we go."

Ivana laughed and put her hand on his arm again. "It's okay, Jonny. I don't bite."

She continued to smile flirtatiously at him as he racked his brain, trying to work out the best way to get away, back to the solace of his room. He needed some peace and quiet after his trying day.

"Actually, I wanted to ask you, Ivana. Which local pub would you recommend? I was thinking of going for a quiet drink later. It's time I finally tried some Czech beer."

"The best local pub is called Hloupý Honza. It is only five minutes away and my friend is the manager. They have great beer and homemade food."

"Hloupý Honza!" Jonny exclaimed, shaking his head, unable to believe the coincidence.

"Yes, Honza is a popular name in Czech culture."

"I know. I found that out today."

Again, Ivana waited for Jonny to explain, but instead he made for his exit. "Thanks for the recommendation, Ivana. I'll check it out later. Have a nice evening." Jonny smiled and walked off down the hall.

Ivana's suggestive words floated over Jonny as he started to climb the stairs to the attic. "You too, Jonny. I'm looking forward to that drink."

Up in the safety of his room, Jonny took off his jacket and shoes and sat on the edge of the bed. "Honza" he repeated to himself in disbelief, as he reflected on the coincidences of his busy day.

He knew what he needed – some music to relax. About the only constant is his life since school had been Bob Dylan, the music having found him in his teens and seen him through all his major life events. In fact, the reason he was here in Prague was as much to do with Mr Dylan as it was his own inclination. One minute he was struggling to book tickets online to a UK concert on the Never-Ending Tour, the next he'd noticed another up-coming concert in Prague and only one hour later he'd not only booked the concert tickets, but also flights and paid the deposit on accommodation for a three-month stay. He'd had notions of visiting Prague before, especially in the years since his mother died, but this trip was truly booked on a whim. With a guiding hand from the modern bard, of course.

As he sat there he felt a pang of longing for his extensive record collection left in the UK; there was a personal relationship with vinyl and he missed flicking the album sleeves to select what to play. The iPod wasn't the same; it lacked a connection with the recordings, but it at least allowed him to access all the songs on his travels. Scrolling through the menu list he selected *The Freewheelin' Bob Dylan* and connected the portable speaker on the desk.

He slumped back on the bed as the acoustic guitar began on 'Blowin' in the Wind', followed by the familiar nasal voice. Before he knew it, lost in the music, sleep started to consume him and his eyelids closed for his first late afternoon nap in Prague.

4

Hloupý Honza

Ivana had been right – Hloupý Honza was indeed a good pub. Although a Monday night, the pub was reasonably busy, most customers being locals, and had a warm atmosphere. The Honza theme gave the pub charisma and a special charm: numerous photos, illustrations and eclectic artwork adorned the walls. The decorated bar was particularly striking and, being positioned directly opposite the entrance door, was an impressive and welcoming feature for both Czech people and interested tourists.

Having looked up 'Honza' online after his nap, he now understood more about the affectionate term and its importance in Czech culture. It was a popular character name in many fairy tales, revered by families and passed down from generation to generation. Hloupý Honza (Daft Honza) was one of the most popular name variations, another being Chudý Honza (Poor Honza). Honza was often taken to represent the national character, rising up from his working-class roots and making something of himself through his honesty, kindness and wit. Jonny found the history fascinating, recalling memories of the Czech fairy tales his mother used to tell him when he was very young.

The fairy tale he remembered most fondly was *Honza málem králem* (Honza Almost King), a famous movie from the 1970s. Reading the online synopsis of the film brought back vivid memories of laughing with his mother on the sofa. The fun, slapstick tale follows Honza on a bizarre journey across the kingdom during which he meets many characters, including the king and princess, but demonstrates his huge heart and moral compass to follow the path back to the village girl he is in love with. Although unable to recall exact scenes from the film, Jonny knew the film would definitely have appealed to his innocent, younger self.

Jonny felt relaxed and quietly contented, sitting at a table close to the bar with an excellent Czech beer. As every book on Prague he had ever read insisted, the Czechs really liked their beer. He had scanned the pub and, apart from two elderly ladies sharing a bottle of wine in the corner, all the women were also drinking beer.

He hadn't been particularly hungry after his late afternoon sandwich – on arrival he had ordered just a beer – but the irresistible wafts of goulash soup soon made their way to him from people eating at another table and the temptation was too much to resist. He had eaten it before but this was something special. Scraping the spoon along the bottom of the bread bowl, releasing breadcrumbs drenched in the dark, meaty sauce, was a pure delight.

The beer was also going down well, the local method of pouring giving the beer a full head and appetising life. Now he was enjoying his third glass and flicking through his Prague guide book. He knew he probably looked like the archetypal tourist, but he wanted to look up some Czech words he'd heard during the day. Before his visit he had innocently believed that he'd be able to pick up conversational Czech fairly quickly. The experience in the restaurant had however severely dented his confidence; all the police officers around him had been speaking rapidly to each other and he hadn't understood a single word.

Jonny's thoughts were broken by his mobile phone ringing loudly. Looking at the screen he saw it was Susan, his ex-wife. Knowing these calls never ended well, he took a large gulp of beer for courage.

"Hi Sue," he answered.

"Are you abroad?"

"Hello, Jonny, and, how are you?" he replied, sarcastically.

"Hi Jonny. Are you abroad? The ringtone is strange."

"Yes, I am. Just taking a little break."

"It's alright for you. Some of us have responsibilities. We can't just fly off when we want."

Jonny rolled his eyes. Why is it always like this?

"Look, what do you want me to say? I've finished with the police as you know and I can't work anywhere else for six months, so I thought I might as well travel a bit."

"Lucky for you."

Jonny decided to play the silent card.

"Are you coming on Thursday?"

"Thursday?"

"I can't believe you've forgotten again. You always forget!"

"I'm sorry, I'm not in UK this week."

"It's Charlotte's Parent's Evening this Thursday. The important one before her exams in the summer. Remember now?"

"Look, I'm really sorry. I don't remember having the date written down."

"It was in that book I gave you with all the important school dates."

Jonny heard a loud sigh at the other end of the line.

"I'm sorry. I forgot about it."

"I can see that!"

"I can't do anything about it now. Is Charlotte there, I'd like to explain."

"Jonny, don't bother. She told me earlier she didn't think you were going to come anyway. She's upstairs now, doing her homework."

"I'm sorry. Please tell her I'll make it up to her."

"Tell her yourself."

Jonny heard a sharp click and knew she'd cut him off.

He looked at the screen forlornly, hoping for a miracle to save him again. Being a father was his weak spot, the role never coming naturally to him. The police job he'd had for half his life hadn't helped; the unsocial and unpredictable hours hadn't allowed him to get into the groove of fatherhood. The lack of a role model father hadn't helped much, either. But neither were decent excuses, and he knew it. He lifted his beer glass and took another, larger sip to dull the pain.

Sat at the next table was a jolly old, moustached Czech man with saggy, watery eyes that undoubtedly could tell a lifetime of stories about the occupation during the war, the subsequent Communist era and the velvet revolution. He had a small dog for company, sitting obediently at his feet. Other than ordering a new beer and having a quick word with the waitress in the process, he seemed content with his own company. That wouldn't be a bad life, Jonny thought. It was certainly appealing after what seemed like a lifetime of work phone calls, constantly being chased for information about his cases, as well as trying and failing to juggle work and family life. Out of pure instinct, Jonny raised his glass to the old man and said "Na zdraví." The old man beamed a smile back and raised his beer glass, returning the toast. Even the dog at the old man's feet barked, roused from his nap.

Jonny returned to his guide book, mentally plotting his walking route for the next day. Without him noticing, the barman had walked over to his table and placed a shot in front of him. The barman then placed another shot glass in front of the old man. The waitress walked over with two more shot glasses and handed one to the barman.

The barman turned to Jonny. "A toast for our new guest."

Jonny looked bemused. Deciding to be polite and play along, he smiled warmly at his host. "What is this?"

"The name of the drink is Slivovice. It's a Czech plum brandy."

The barman raised his glass to the small group, preparing to clink glasses with the waitress, Jonny and the old man. Jonny knew the custom of clinking everyone's glasses and saying 'Na zdraví' before downing the shot. He raised his glass confidently to the others, carefully following the others in the ritual. However, before the toast was concluded the barman called a halt to the celebration. "You have to look into the other person's eyes when you say 'Na zdraví'," he said encouragingly to Jonny.

"Oh, right. Sorry, I didn't know."

The barman started the toast again and Jonny made sure to look into each person's eyes as he clinked their respective glass. Even though he was concentrating hard, careful to not make a mistake this time, he still managed to notice how deep blue the waitress' eyes were. In only a few days, Jonny realised Czech women had the gift of catching him off guard with their beauty.

Jonny downed his shot in one swig, but he immediately winced and started coughing, the strength of the alcohol hitting the back of his throat. The others started laughing.

"Wow," started Jonny, pausing to pat his chest and recover his voice. "That was strong."

"I think in English you say it will put hairs on your chest. Over here we just say you need another shot for the other leg."

Jonny laughed. "Both of those are true," he coughed again. "But I will need some time to recover before having another one."

The barman and the waitress laughed as she collected the glasses and returned to the bar. The barman stayed and spoke to the old man in Czech, who turned to look at Jonny with a smile.

"I was just telling Štefan that you are staying with Ivana."

"Ah," said Jonny, shaking his head. "Now it makes sense."

"Yes, she phoned me earlier. She told me to look after

you."

"Well, thank you. I feel very welcome." Jonny looked around the pub. "You have a great pub, I really like it here."

"Our pleasure. Hope you see you here again soon."

The barman extended his hand. "I'm Jaroslav, but my British friends call me Jerry. I'm the manager." Jerry gestured towards the bar. "And this is Monika." The waitress, again busy behind the bar, waved at Jonny.

"I'm Jonny. But you probably already know that from Ivana. However, given the pub's name I think you should call me Honza."

Jerry laughed again. "Perfect. Honza it is!"

Štefan asked a question to Jerry. "Jak se jmenuje?"

"Honza," Jerry answered Štefan before turning back to Jonny. "Unfortunately Štefan doesn't speak English, but he does know the uniform pub language of the world."

Jonny smiled, nodded his understanding and raised his beer glass again to Štefan. The dog at Štefan's feet stood up and barked, clearly feeling left out.

"Oh, and we can't forget Viky," Jerry introduced. "He's our canine local. Viky is short for Viktor."

Viky barked again just as Monika arrived carrying three new beers, giving one to Jerry, one to Jonny and one to Štefan. Jonny instinctively looked at his unfinished beer on the table and then towards Jerry with a quizzical look.

"It's another Czech custom," Jerry stated with an apologetic smile. "You have to tell us to stop bringing the beers otherwise they keep coming."

"Thanks for the good advice."

Jerry quickly finished the last mouthful of his old beer and raised his new beer glass for the toast. "Na zdraví" they all said as the beer glasses were clinked once more.

Before taking a sip of his beer Štefan looked at Jonny and added "Popojedem!"

Jonny looked at Jerry. "What did he say?"

"It's a word you will need to know if you are drinking

in this country," Jerry explained. "It's slang for 'let's get drinking'."

Jerry laughed and Štefan joined in, understanding the joke without the need for words.

"I think it could be a long night!" Jonny exclaimed, before taking another sip of his beer, the imprint of his strange and eventful day slowly fading away in the gaiety.

5

Back to Work

Tuesday, 16th March

Jonny was knocked out, fast asleep and dreaming heavily after one too many the night before. His mobile started ringing on the bedside table, but his only reaction was to turn over and pull the sheet over his head. His most frequent dreams were about his time on the job; either people were chasing him for updates on a case, or he was chasing a murderer. Often they just merged into a random sequence of scenes involving anyone he knew. A ringing phone was therefore nothing unusual, but this one seemed particularly loud and the pounding was starting to hurt his head.

The phone continued to ring unabated, eventually rousing him sufficiently from his sleep to open an eye. For a few moments he felt lost, not sure where he was, the surroundings of his rented room still not familiar. As the shrill sound continued, he grappled with the twisted bed sheets and blindly reached over to search the table for his mobile. Once in his hand, he squinted at the screen and saw an unknown number starting 00420, the code for the Czech Republic.

"Bloody hell," he mumbled angrily, trying to think of who would be calling him so early.

He pressed the green button. "Hello."

An excited voice started talking loudly on the other end, too fast for Jonny's sleepy state; he couldn't understand a single word. "Stop, stop. Who the hell is this?"

The voice boomed back down the line. "Mr Fox, it's me, Detective Chief Inspector Mikeš."

Jonny pressed his eyes together, both still not fully open, as he tried to focus. "Who?"

"Honza, it's me – Felix Mikeš. I am at the police station early. We need your assistance."

Jonny rubbed his face with his spare hand, trying to awaken his senses.

"Hang on." Jonny pulled the phone away from his ear and looked again at the screen. "But it's 7:30 in the morning!"

"Well, I think you British say, the bird must get the early worm."

"No, no," said Jonny, exasperated but being pulled unwittingly into the conversation. "The saying is 'an early bird gets the worm'."

"Exactly, that's what I said."

Jonny pulled a face and shook his head in irritation.

"Now listen," Mikeš continued. "We need your expert help. Time to get back to work, Honza. I'll send Boukal to collect you by car at 8. See you soon."

"But…" Jonny started, but stopped immediately as the phone line went dead.

Jonny stared at the phone screen in disbelief. He threw it down on the bed and slumped back onto his pillow, unable to believe what was happening. With eyes wide open now all he could do was stare at the ceiling and listen to the hammering in his head, knowing he had only thirty minutes to get ready.

***

Half an hour later Jonny heard a knock on his room door, but ignored it. He was hurriedly getting dressed, still slightly wet from the shower.

The knock on the door came again a moment later, a little louder this time. "Jonny, are you awake?" Ivana called,

"There's a man here. He says he's come to pick you up."

"Thanks. Tell him I'll be down in a few minutes."

"Okay." He heard Ivana turn and descend the stairs from the attic.

He finished tidying his shirt and trousers, put on his jacket and looked in the mirror, more in hope than anything else. He grimaced on seeing his dishevelled hair, circles under his eyes and bloodshot eyes. He looked rough. He quickly picked up a comb and ran it through his hair again, retrieved his wallet and keys from the table and went to the door. "Chewing gum," he remembered and quickly popped back to retrieve a packet from the desk.

Ivana was waiting for him in the hall, looking concerned. Her tousled hair and tightly wrapped dressing gown implied she had also been woken up after her girl's night out. "Is everything okay, Jonny?"

"Yes, fine." Jonny smiled half-heartedly, trying to compose himself. "Sorry if you were woken up."

"No problem." She stifled a yawn. "Are you going anywhere nice?"

"Well, that's a good question." Jonny paused. "To tell you the truth, I'm not sure myself."

Ivana went to ask another question but before she could, Jonny was walking away from her, towards the front door of the apartment. "See you later," he called over his shoulder.

"Bye, Jonny."

Outside the apartment building, Boukal was waiting by a black Skoda Superb with the driver's door open. Jonny walked over and shook his hand.

"Good morning, Mr Fox."

"Good morning."

Boukal got into the car and lent over to open the passenger door from the inside. As they buckled up, he turned to look at Jonny. "You smell of our famous cherry brandy."

Jonny blushed. "Oh, is it that obvious?"

Boukal smiled, nodding in confirmation.

Jonny felt the need to explain himself. "I've never really been a morning person. But today is worse. Last night was my first night in a Czech pub—"

"And one you will never forget," Boukal interrupted, laughing softly.

"Yes, something like that."

"Well," Boukal smiled, pleased with himself. "I took the liberty of buying you a caffe latte and a croissant." He pointed to the coffee cup and paper bag between them.

Jonny looked down between the front seats. "You may have literally just saved my life."

Jonny picked up the coffee and stole a profile look at Boukal. He was dressed as untidily as the previous day, wearing the same badly fitting suit, an old white shirt and loose tie. But as Jonny watched Mikeš' assistant drive off competently, he couldn't help thinking that maybe there was more to him than first appearances might suggest. Boukal seemed more confident on his own, without the eccentric, overbearing presence of Mikeš breathing over his shoulder. Given his relatively young age for a senior detective, Jonny knew he must have something about him to have risen through the ranks so quickly.

Jonny knew more than anyone how important it was to impress and earn your stripes at each level. Degrees and higher education honours were useful for entrance into the police force, but to make it you needed to be streetwise, learn to understand how the criminal mind worked, and be able to deliver. He had started straight from school, with no helping hand, and had literally done every job imaginable.

With the coffee and croissant starting to help, Jonny felt more relaxed. "So, Marek… I can call you Marek, can't I?" Boukal nodded. "I am confused why I am even in this car with you?"

Boukal smiled across at his passenger. "Detective Chief Inspector Mikeš is a very persuasive man."

"Yes, that's true," Jonny took another bite of his croissant.

"And a great detective," Boukal added.

"You know, you're not the first person to say that to me. The sergeant..."

"Dvořáková?" prompted Boukal.

"Yes," confirmed Jonny. "She said the same thing to me yesterday."

"Detective Chief Inspector Mikeš is older now and has probably become more eccentric with his celebrity status. But in his prime he was the best detective in the Czech Republic. He solved many famous cases."

"I see," Jonny nodded, impressed.

"He still gets results and is very well respected. But he prefers the old ways of doing things, not all the technology we have these days. He likes younger people around him now, to help and advise him."

"He sounds like me," Jonny confirmed. "'Old School' we call it."

"He's been very good to me," Boukal affirmed. "He has taught me a lot. But sometimes his methods are quite old fashioned. It is not always easy."

Jonny was now starting to understand the chemistry connecting the detective duo. "I suppose in return you help him stay ahead in the modern world of policing," Jonny added. "But I still don't understand why he wants me involved."

"Well, he definitely likes you," Boukal explained. "I've worked for him for two years and he always seems to know quickly what he likes. But I think there is another reason. He has always disliked criminal cases involving tourists because they are so hard to work out. The language is an obvious barrier, but it's also the culture differences. With this case I think he is hoping you will help us determine what was going on between the three Englishmen in the restaurant."

Jonny nodded in understanding. "I see." He finished the last bite of the croissant. "Thank you again. I feel much better."

"Prosím," Boukal smiled as he drove.

Jonny watched out of the passenger window as the car made its way around the Náměstí Míru square, circling the church and heading for the exit down the hill towards the centre. The ride was bumpy, the roads a mixture of cobbled stones and smoother tarmac, and the traffic was heavy with the lingering morning rush hour.

Jonny found himself looking up at the architecture as the car was stationary at the traffic lights. He had sat on a bench on the square most days and studied the range of architectural styles, consistent in design but varying in colour and facade. Even the functional, or residential buildings were resplendent, blending together into a perfect perimeter for the south-facing church, with its expansive square seemingly always in the sun.

The most impressive building on the square, always drawing his attention, was the Vinohrady Theatre. The stone building was grand, impressively wide with four pillars and three large arched windows in the centre. Above the entrance were two plinths, each with a statue seven metres tall. The sculptures were monumental symbols of bravery and truth, one statue with a raised sword in her right hand and the other with a mirror held up in her left hand. Whilst the sculpted figures were impressive enough, the sword and mirror were finished in gold, imposing a message over the square as they glinted in the morning sun.

As the lights changed and the car turned off the square onto the street called Anglická, Boukal broke the silence. "By the way, I have prepared a statement for you, based upon our interview at the restaurant yesterday." Boukal took a folded paper out of his jacket pocket and passed it to Jonny. "The statement is in English, with a Czech translation underneath. If you are happy with it, please sign it and give to Sergeant Dvořáková when we get to the station."

Jonny nodded, impressed with the efficiency. "No problem, thanks."

Jonny opened the paper and scanned it quickly. "So Marek, where exactly are we going now?"

"We have set up an Incident Room at the police station in Prague 1. It's close to Old Town Square. We have stations around the city, but this was the closest location to the restaurant. It is also not far from the hotel where the English witnesses are staying."

"Right. And have they been interviewed yet?"

"We spoke yesterday to all the people in the restaurant and took statements. The two other English men in the restaurant, the friends of the murder victim, were still in shock so we returned them to the hotel and confiscated their passports."

"So you plan to interview them again today?"

"Yes. There was no obvious reason to us why the victim was killed. Yesterday, everyone was being very 'nice'." Boukal emphasised the last word for effect and Jonny laughed.

"That sounds about right for the British."

"So," Boukal continued. "Detective Chief Inspector Mikeš wants you to sit in on the interviews. You know the culture so maybe you can help us build a better picture."

"Right," Jonny nodded. "And do you have a potential suspect?"

"Not yet," admitted Boukal with a shrug.

The rest of the short journey was quiet, Boukal navigating the traffic whilst Jonny reflected on the developing situation. It was easy to blame Mikeš for railroading him, but in truth Jonny was his own boss. He'd been called stubborn often enough in the past to know there was some truth in it. All Mikeš was doing was using the situation to his own advantage and Jonny was a resource that could maybe help solve the case. In similar circumstances I'd probably do the same, he thought. Catching the killer was always the top priority, above any individual or selfish motive. Accepting the circumstances for what they were, Jonny decided to go with the flow and enjoy it, hopefully use the experience to understand more about Prague. But he had to be careful not to be pulled in too deep, becoming immersed in the investigation and taking on responsibilities. Mikeš was clearly a very persuasive person.

6

The Engine Room

It was the smell and noise that hit Jonny first as he followed Boukal through the back entrance of the police station. There was nothing like the buzz of a homicide case in full flow. The fragrance wasn't yet unpleasant, but Jonny recognised the hint of body odour in the air mixed with the early morning coffee on almost every desk. Some officers had no doubt worked around the clock to set up the Incident Room. The sound was dominated by voices, people talking hurriedly, some in conversation around desks and others on the phone. The background sound of the photocopier and footsteps, as officers walked papers from desk to desk, completed the picture so familiar to him.

The scene reminded him of every station he'd worked in; so much for cultural differences, the engine room of a police murder investigation was probably the same the world over. The stress of his last case and his hasty retirement decision had pushed so many memories, good and bad, to the back of his mind. But standing in the open plan office amongst the energy of the investigation, he realised, whatever happened next he'd made a good decision to follow Boukal.

"Honza, we need to sign you in," Boukal stated.

Jonny took a slow, sidelong look at Boukal. The formality of the earlier pick-up was clearly gone, nicknames seemingly the order of the day within the police station. "Of course," he consented reluctantly, still not convinced about his given label of endearment. He stepped forward to the desk in the corner of the room, greeted the administrator and signed next to his name.

Boukal led the way through the open-plan office to a large, glass-fronted meeting room in the far corner – clearly the Incident Room. Through the window, Jonny could see Mikeš and his team about to start a morning briefing. Mikeš stood at the front of the Incident Room alongside Dvořáková, in front of a large white board with photos pinned up, accompanied by names and other words scribbled underneath. Various arrows showed a potential timeline and possible connections between the victim and the other photos on the board.

Mikeš stood out from the group with his unusual dress code, not looking anything like a policeman. He was wearing the same tweed suit as the previous day, matched with an elegant light blue shirt/tie combination. The other four members of the detective team were by contrast dressed in the usual, non-uniform standard dress code of dark suit, white shirt and dark tie. Almost identical to Boukal, just not as scruffy. Only Dvořáková was in uniform, which Jonny knew was probably standard for the role of sergeant, the key link between the detective team and the uniformed staff.

Mikeš waved heartily on seeing Jonny, then whispered a command to Dvořáková. Understanding the plan immediately, Boukal explained for Jonny. "The morning briefing is about to start. I need to go in, but Sergeant Dvořáková will look after you."

"Ok, thanks," replied Jonny.

Dvořáková approached Jonny and shook his hand with a curt smile. "Good to see you again, Mr Fox. Would you like a coffee?"

"Well, I've had a coffee already. But somehow I think it might be a long morning so, yes please, I'll have another one."

Dvořáková gave him with a stern, quizzical look. Again in uniform, although without her hat inside the station, she looked younger, her blonde hair in a short ponytail. Her outward persona, however, was older, more serious, and Jonny knew as an outsider he was going to have to work hard to prove himself worthy of the invitation into the team.

"Early mornings are always tough for me," offered Jonny, smiling, by way of explanation.

"Please, follow me," she replied.

"Thank you."

Jonny watched Boukal enter the Incident Room. Mikeš started the briefing in an exaggerated fashion, waving his arms around and pointing at the board. Jonny smiled to himself, remembering how animated he himself had been in briefings when things were not going his way.

After making him a coffee, Dvořáková led Jonny to a breakout area in the corner of the office. "This is certainly better than the machine coffee I am used to in UK," Jonny complimented her, sipping his coffee.

"There is a machine round the corner, but I leave it to the men who can't taste the difference between mud and coffee."

Jonny laughed, carefully assessing the sergeant. She was friendly and pleasant, but he detected a tough interior, without which she would probably never have made it to her grade. He had worked with many female detectives in recent years; in fact, he would usually select them first for his team given a choice. They had had to work extra hard and make many more sacrifices than their male colleagues to gain the respect they deserved. Dvořáková came across as totally dedicated to the job and very ambitious, but her guard was held high.

Jonny decided to tempt her. "I've noticed there aren't many women in the office."

Dvořáková scanned the office slowly as she spoke. "Yes, sadly not. We have many female officers in uniform and the police force here is slowly changing. But in the detective team it is still male-dominated."

"We had the same in UK a few years ago," Jonny concurred, "but it has started to change now. I'm sure it will change here soon as well."

Dvořáková looked directly at Jonny. He knew she supported his words, but she retained the steely, unconvinced look; she'd obviously heard it all before, the pace of change being slow, and wasn't going to hold her breath.

"Anyway, Mr Fox…"

"Please, call me Jonny."

"I think it is too late for that," she stated, coldly. "Detective Chief Inspector Mikeš has told everyone to call you Honza."

"Okay, then, call me Honza," Jonny relented easily.

Dvořáková studied his face closely, trying to read his intentions.

Jonny felt encouraged with the developing interaction. "And what shall I call you?"

"Well, that is more difficult. As you have indicated, the world is not equal, and so it is important to keep it formal."

Jonny nodded his understanding and waited, allowing Dvořáková time to decide on her terms. "I have no problem telling you my name is Lucie. But I think it is best if you call me 'Sergeant' when we are working."

"Understood," he confirmed with a smile.

"Anyway," Dvořáková restarted. "As I was starting to say, the English men are being driven from the hotel to the station now and we are preparing to interview them upstairs. We will put them into five separate interview rooms—"

"Five?" said Jonny, surprised. "I thought there were only three in the restaurant yesterday, and one of them was killed."

"Well spotted. The total group was six. Three of the men, who you didn't see, had gone for a walk. The three you saw had stopped for a late lunch at the restaurant."

"Ah," nodded Jonny, "interesting."

"Yesterday we got statements from all five men, but today we are going to cross-examine them in formal interviews and record the conversations. The interviews are not under caution, the men have agreed to come along willingly.

We have informed the British Embassy here in Prague and will continue to liaise with the UK Police, as required."

"Sounds like you have it all under control. Very organised."

"Thank you. We have a good team here."

Someone called across the office and Dvořáková looked up. Jonny followed her gaze to see Mikeš standing outside the Incident Room, holding open his pocket watch and beckoning them over.

"The briefing has finished," Dvořáková said. "I think it's your turn now."

"Okay. I nearly forgot," Jonny remembered. "I have signed the statement Chief Sergeant Boukal gave me." He took the statement out of his jacket pocket and handed it over.

"Thank you. I'll add it to the file."

Mikeš was waiting for them at the door of the Incident Room, arms wide open as if greeting a long-lost friend. "Honza!" Jonny saw Mikeš' eyes bursting with sparkling energy as they shook hands vigorously.

Mikeš motioned Jonny inside the room to stand next to him in front of the white board. "Thank you for coming to help us. In my experience any serious crime involving tourists, especially a murder, is difficult to solve. It is better to get expert assistance from someone who has lived the language and the culture."

"Yes, I understand," Jonny acknowledged. "I will help as much as I can."

"This case is tricky, I think you say," Mikeš added. "We have no suspect, no motive, only a body."

Jonny studied the board, but it made little sense. He needed to be briefed. "My only advice is to follow every lead, however small or seemingly irrelevant."

"Exactly," bellowed Mikeš, smiling. "That's what I always say, follow every lead."

Mikeš patted the seat next to him for Jonny, Dvořáková sitting on the other side. Only Boukal was standing. "Now

Marek, take us through what we know," Mikeš instructed.

"Right," Boukal started, pointing to the board. "The group of six Englishmen are from a town called Bishop's Stortford."

"I suppose they flew from Stansted?" Jonny interrupted.

"Correct," Boukal confirmed. "The group are friends and come to Europe once or twice a year for a trip. They choose a different city each visit and plan it around a football match they can get tickets for. On Sunday they went to see our big derby match, Sparta Prague versus Slavia Prague."

Mikeš turned to Jonny. "It's a big match. There can be lots of hooligan trouble."

"Yes, I know about it," confirmed Jonny. "I presume he bought the football shirt there?"

"Probably. We need to check." Mikeš nodded at Boukal who made a note on the board.

"The group arrived late on Friday after work," continued Boukal. "They were due to be flying back Monday evening, going back to work Tuesday. From what they have told us, their trip was quite reserved. They are all in their thirties, some with children, and they say they've mostly been to restaurants and bars."

"We need to press them on this point." Jonny added with a sceptical look. "A group of six guys in Prague? It depends on your definition of 'reserved' I suppose."

"Exactly," scoffed Mikeš. "I don't believe it either. We need to push them… I mean press them."

"How do they all know each other?" asked Jonny.

"The group are a mixture of friends," Boukal continued. "The three men who were in the restaurant have known each other for a long time, since school we believe. The other men in the group are friends from the local pub. One of the group owns the pub."

"And what did the men say about the argument at the table?" questioned Jonny.

"The two men said it was something trivial, not important. Anyway neither of them could be the killer because they were both still sitting at the table when it happened."

Jonny interrupted gently. "My suggestion is to treat these interviews as a fresh look. Let's take them back over their statements and try to find out all the links to the victim."

"Yes, very good," Mikeš jumped on the thought. "Excellent idea, Honza. This is what we will do."

"Tell me about the victim," said Jonny.

"His name was Neil Robson," stated Boukal, pointing to the photo in the middle on the board. "He was stabbed in the back of his neck. It seems from the initial forensics that he was stabbed from behind because he collapsed onto the sink in the restrooms and then fell down sideways onto another sink, ending up lying on the tiled floor on his back. The weapon is a knife with a blade about 5cm long but we are waiting for the autopsy. The incision hit a main artery so he bled out quickly. No murder weapon has been found, but we're still searching the surrounding area."

"And could it have been a random attack?" suggested Jonny.

Mikeš stepped in. "There were no signs of a robbery. His wallet and mobile phone were still in his trouser pockets."

Jonny thought. "But he was wearing a football shirt?"

Mikeš shook his head. "I don't think it is relevant. It was the day after the match and anyway there was no major trouble on Sunday."

"And what about access?" said Jonny.

Boukal looked confused.

"I'm sorry," added Jonny. "I mean is there any other way into the restaurant's restrooms."

"The restrooms are exclusive to the restaurant," Boukal explained. "They are at the back on the left-hand side. However, the restaurant is quite big, as you know, and the terrace outside is open at the sides, under the arches, connecting it to the neighbouring restaurants and cafés. It is quite easy to walk into the restaurant without using the main entrance from the square. The restaurant staff we interviewed did not notice anyone else entering, but they did admit they were quite busy after lunch. Unfortunately the restaurant does not have CCTV anywhere and nor do the other restaurants and cafés on the square. All we can check is the main CCTV for the square. We've also asked around the other businesses on the square, including shops, to see if anyone remembers a person hanging around, and we will repeat it again today at 3pm, the time of the murder."

Jonny paused to process the information. He knew he hadn't been watching intently when he was sitting on the terrace, but he believed he'd have noticed if someone had tried to sneak through to the terrace into the restaurant.

"And the young lady who found the body?" Jonny added.

After a nod from Mikeš, Boukal continued. "Like many restrooms in Prague, there is one door leading to a shared area with sinks. Inside there are separate doors, to the ladies' and men's toilets. The young lady walked through the main restroom entrance door and found the victim lying on the floor. All the witnesses in the main restaurant have confirmed she left the table less than one minute before."

"And nobody else was in the toilets?"

"No," Mikeš confirmed. "Forensics are examining the victim's clothes for DNA and also looking for fingerprints. But in a restaurant restroom it is going to be very difficult to get unique matches. We will check anything we find against the witnesses in the restaurant and also against the other men in the victim's group."

"And I suppose you have checked calls and messages on his mobile?" Jonny asked Boukal.

"Yes," confirmed Boukal. "All the calls and messages made from Friday night to Monday were to UK numbers. We are in the process of checking them. There were messages to the other friends on the trip over the weekend, but none on Monday. The call history before the weekend was deleted and I suspect that some older messages have also been deleted."

"And what about the three men from the group who weren't in the restaurant?" Jonny continued to probe.

Dvořáková stepped in. "We are waiting for confirmation of the movements of all the men. We need these routes before we can try to trace them using CCTV. There are however many smaller back streets, in the old town for example, where there is no CCTV."

Jonny nodded and an awkward silence descended on the room.

"So when we hold these interviews, how are you going to introduce me?" Jonny asked, intrigued.

"Translator?" suggested Boukal.

"No, no," said Mikeš, shaking his head vigorously. "It needs to sound more important."

"Interpreter?" offered Dvořáková.

"No, no." Mikeš paused, trying to find the right word. "I have it! Honza can be our konzultant." Mikeš slapped Jonny lightly on the back. "Yes. Konzultant. That's perfect."

Jonny caught Boukal's look and smiled, remembering their conversation in the car.

Jonny shrugged. "I have been called lots of things in my time. It's your show, call me what you want."

Mikeš stood up quickly, indicating the meeting was over, and led Jonny to the door with his arm across Jonny's back. "So Honza, are you enjoying your stay in Prague?"

Jonny laughed, finding it hard to resist the enthusiasm of this likeable, if oddball character. "Well, it's not turning out to be a quiet holiday, that's for sure."

Mikeš just smiled, giving Jonny an intense, knowing look. "As I told you, my friend, great detectives never retire."

7

Interview 1 – Group of Friends

The following are transcripts of the recorded interviews conducted on the morning of Tuesday, 16th March 2010.

Present at each interview were Chief Warrant Officer Felix Mikeš (FM), Chief Sergeant Marek Boukal (MB) and Consultant Jonathan Fox (JF). The reason for the presence of JF was explained at the beginning of the interview: he is assisting the Czech Police team on this murder investigation. JF was also by coincidence a customer at the restaurant on Old Town Square, the scene of the murder, the previous day. This has no impact on the murder investigation.

<u>Adrian Scott (AS)</u>

MB: Interview commenced at 09:03. Please state your name for the record.
AS: Adrian Scott. But people call me Ade.
MB: That is noted, but we would prefer to use your full name, Adrian.
AS: Okay.
MB: How did you know Neil Robson?
AS: We went to school together and have been best friends since.
MB: Have you always lived in the same town?
AS: Well, after going to separate universities we shared a flat in London. After a few years living together we met our partners and both moved back to Bishop's Stortford.
MB: What job did he have?

AS: Neil works, sorry… He worked in a large Pharmaceuticals company with a base in Hertfordshire. He had been there over ten years and had developed a good career.
MB: And you?
AS: I've had various jobs but I work in event management now.
MB: How often did you see him, talk to each other?
AS: We talked or sent messages almost every day. We are both married now, settled down, but we tried to see each other every week.
JF: And you were still close?
AS: Yes. I like to think I knew him well. He certainly knew everything about me. We were like brothers.
JF: Thanks.
MB: Can you describe Neil?
AS: To me he was fun but he could also be serious. Some people took a dislike to him because he was very confident, some would say arrogant. He just liked to have a good time. And he was a good father.
MB: He had two children?
AS: Yes, two young boys. His wife, Carly (Robson), is flying over tomorrow. It is just being organised with my wife, Lizzie (Scott), and also Martin's (Wilson) wife, Sophie (Wilson). The girls are close friends. Lizzie and Sophie want to support Carly. I mean she has got to identify Neil's body.
MB: Do you have any children?
AS: No, not yet.
MB: And does your wife work?
AS: Yes, she is a Trainee Solicitor.
MB: You mentioned Martin Wilson. Can you describe the relationship between you, Neil Robson and Martin?
AS: Martin went to the same school as us. We were all close at school but Martin didn't go to university. Instead he started working for a bank in London. He is a 'steady eddie', doesn't like taking a risk. Anyway, we, that's Neil and I, didn't really see much of him for a few years, but we reconnected when we both moved back to Bishop's Stortford.

JF: We know there were six people on the trip. Why were only the three of you having lunch together on Monday afternoon?
AS: No real reason. We'd all been together over the weekend. The others wanted to do something different for their last afternoon. Martin, Neil and I just thought we'd relax and have lunch in the Old Town Square.
JF: And didn't you want to see more sights before you left?
AS: We've all been to Prague before, for stag nights. Plus, last year the three of us came over with our wives for a romantic weekend. So, we've seen most of the sights.
MB: When was the romantic weekend?
AS: I would need to check, but probably May last year. Yes, it was definitely after Easter.
JF: And why come back to Prague so soon?
AS: It was because of the football. We've wanted to see Sparta versus Slavia for a long time and we just happened to get tickets.
MB: Can you explain what you have done whilst you've been in Prague this weekend?
AS: Okay. Well we arrived very late on Friday, probably didn't get to the hotel until midnight. We just went to bed because everyone was exhausted after a week at work. On Saturday we had brunch on Wenceslas Square and then walked around before going for dinner. I'll need to check the names of the places if you want.
JF: And after dinner?
AS: We went to the famous pub called Lucerna. We had some drinks and then went into the 80s/90s Party in the Music Bar. When we left there about 2am (02:00), I went back to the hotel. Neil and a few of the others went to a strip bar, I mean cabaret.
JF: Who else went with Neil?
AS: Definitely Darren (Kozma) and Gary (Needham). Not sure about Richard (Weston). Martin went back to the hotel with me.
MB: Okay, we will ask them. Did you have separate hotel

rooms?
AS: Yes.
MB: And what did you all do on Sunday?
AS: Again, got up late, had brunch. Then we went to the football match. Afterwards we had dinner and a few drinks. But not many because we'd all drunk too much on Saturday night.
MB: So, did you all go back to the hotel together?
AS: Yes, probably about midnight.
MB: And Monday?
AS: Again, late up. Had a short walk together and then decided to split up. The three of us walked to Old Town Square for a late lunch.
JF: And what were Neil and Martin arguing about at the table?
AS: Neil can be a prick sometimes. He was just winding Martin up, but probably took it too far. As I said before, Martin is a bit of a prude and easy to wind up.
MB: Martin was heard saying 'You're a bloody liar. Always cheating everyone. You need to be taught a lesson.'
AS: It was about nothing really. Neil was teasing Martin about how cautious he is. Neil just pushed Martin too far.
JF: And why did Neil have a smirk on his face before he left the table?
AS: Because he'd beaten Martin in the argument. It was just a game to Neil. He found it easy to get under Martin's skin.
JF: Did he often try to get under the skin of people?
AS: Yes, he could annoy people. He would say out loud what other people were thinking. He was straight and honest. Anyway, Neil's murder has got nothing to do with the argument. Martin and I were still sitting at the table when Neil was killed.
FM: Can you think of anyone who might want to kill Neil?
AS: No. As I said, he could wind people up, but nobody would want to kill him.
JF: Can you think of anyone who had a grudge against him?
AS: No. He'd have told me if he was in trouble.
FM: What about you? Did you have a grudge against him?

AS: No. Bloody hell, this is stupid. He was like a brother to me.
FM: Calm down. We have to ask you these questions.
MB: Can you please write down the names of the places you visited with Neil over the weekend, or at least descriptions if you cannot remember names. Our Sergeant will help you with this after the interview.
AS: Okay. I want whoever did this to… oh, I don't know. Just catch them, please.
MB: Okay, thank you. Interview terminated at 09:27.

<u>Martin Wilson (MW)</u>

MB: Interview commenced at 09:41. Please state your name for the record.
MW: Martin Wilson.
MB: How did you know Neil Robson?
MW: I have known Neil since school. We lost touch a bit after school, but when he and Ade (Adrian) moved back to Bishop's Stortford we all became closer again. Even our wives are close friends now.
MB: Please use Adrian's full first name when talking about him.
MW: Okay.
MB: What is your job?
MW: I work at a bank in London. I've worked there for over ten years.
MB: And you are married to Sophie?
MW: Yes. We have a young daughter.
MB: Does Sophie work?
MW: She used to manage a florist's, but she hasn't worked since our daughter was born. She's trying to organise the flights tomorrow with Carly and Lizzie.
MB: Yes, we are aware. We would like to talk to them, especially Mrs Robson.
JF: Adrian has told us a little about Neil. How would you describe him?
MW: Well, I liked Neil but often found him difficult. He was

loud and fun to be around, always the centre of attention. He was also very generous, always paying for more than his share. But sometimes he would just pick on people and keep going on. It could be very annoying.

JF: Like the argument in the restaurant yesterday?

MW: Yes.

JF: What was the argument about?

MW: We were having a nice lunch at the end of a really good trip, but Neil just wanted to talk about the past. He kept talking about how I'd wasted my life. I didn't want to go to university and I'm quite a home bird. But just because I haven't travelled so much doesn't mean I've wasted my life.

JF: But your reaction was very strong. You said 'You're a bloody liar. Always cheating everyone. You need to be taught a lesson!'

MW: Yes, I know. It was wrong. He just wound me up.

JF: But Martin, they are very aggressive words to say to a friend.

MW: Well he started attacking me, so I attacked him back. He wasn't perfect, you know.

JF: What do you mean?

MW: I started talking about the affair he had. He was making it seem like he was an angel, with his exciting, perfect life. I just got angry. I shouldn't have said it.

JF: What affair?

MW: Is this relevant?

FM: Please just answer the question. We will decide what is relevant.

MW: Neil had an affair with Richard's ex-wife. Well, it was claimed it was a one-off. Richard found out anyway. It was about five or six years ago now and Richard has moved on from it.

JF: But Richard and his ex-wife split up over it?

MW: Yes, divorced now. Neil was banned from Richard's pub for a while, but it all blew over. They are fine now, Richard has a new girlfriend.

JF: Thanks. We'll talk to Richard.
MB: We understand you organised most of this trip?
MW: Yes. I am the boring, reliable one so everyone tells me. I've been landed with the job of organising all our trips.
MB: Why did you pick Prague when we understand you were here with Neil, Adrian and the wives less than a year ago?
MW: We had a list of football matches in Europe we wanted to see, including Sparta versus Slavia. I have a friend from school who now lives in Prague and he knows someone who can get tickets.
MB: Who is this person?
MW: James Hopkins.
MB: He lives here?
MW: Yes. He is a science teacher at one of the International Schools.
JF: So, if James went to school with you, he also knows Neil and Adrian?
MW: Yes. But they were not close friends. James is a quieter type.
JF: Is there anything else about James and Neil?
MW: James started work on the same graduate scheme as Neil after university, at the pharmaceutical company Neil worked at. But something happened and James left the course quite suddenly after only a year. Neil said James couldn't hack it and that's why he went into teaching. Anyway they weren't friendly, James felt aggrieved about something Neil did.
FM: We need to talk to James Hopkins.
JF: And did you all meet up with James on the trip?
MW: Yes. James came along for a drink on Saturday night. He arrived late, about 10:30pm (22:30), just to give us the tickets. We were in the Lucerna pub.
JF: And did anything happen?
MW: James only stayed for an hour or so. The others said Neil and James argued, but I didn't see it because I'd gone to the toilet. It wasn't a big problem. James had said he was only staying for a while anyway and he left soon after.

JF: What was the argument about?

MW: I don't really know. Adrian told me Neil was just winding up James as usual.

MB: Can you please give James Hopkins' contact details to the sergeant after the interview.

MW: Sure.

JF: Back to the football, did you have any trouble at the match?

MW: No. The atmosphere was edgy but there wasn't any trouble. After the match we decided to walk back to the centre because it was busy and stopped at a pub on the way.

MB: Adrian is going to give the sergeant a list of all the places you visited on your trip. Can you help him with this? You may have a better recollection.

MW: Okay.

JF: Can I ask why you went back to the hotel with Adrian on Saturday night rather than going to the cabaret?

MW: Adrian was really drunk, the worst of all of us. I wasn't keen to go to the cabaret anyway. But it was clear the bouncers were not going to let Adrian in. So we headed back to the hotel.

JF: And were there any other stories from the cabaret?

MW: No, just the usual. They were all quite drunk, I don't think they stayed a long time.

JF: And there were no other issues on the trip between the people in your group?

MW: No, none at all.

FM: Can you think of anyone who would want to kill Neil?

MW: No.

FM: Did you have a grudge against him?

MW: No, definitely not. He acted like an idiot sometimes but he was still my friend.

JF: Can you think of anyone else who had a grudge against him?

MW: No.

MB: Okay, thank you. Interview terminated at 10:06.

Darren Kozma (DK)

MB: Interview commenced at 10:15. Please state your name for the record.
DK: Darren Kozma.
MB: What is your job?
DK: I work for an advertising company in London.
MB: How did you know Neil Robson?
DK: I have known Neil probably about seven years. I moved to Bishop's Stortford for a local job, then got my current job in London after a few years, but decided to stay living in the town and commute to London. The Mill Tavern is my local pub and I've got to know Richard, the owner, and the regulars.
JF: So all the people on the trip were regulars?
DK: Yes, off and on. Some of them are married with children. But there's usually someone there to talk to. Often everyone is there on Friday.
MB: You are not married?
DK: No.
MB: But you know the wives of Neil, Adrian and Martin?
DK: Yes of course. They come along to the pub as well sometimes. But they're more likely to go out on their own to a wine bar.
MB: What did you think of Neil?
DK: I thought Neil was a lovely guy. Great fun. Very generous. He seemed to annoy some people but he and I never had a cross word.
JF: But do you understand why people got angry with him?
DK: No, not really. I always thought he was just telling it straight, direct but honest. Maybe some people didn't like it.
JF: Did Martin get angry with Neil on the trip before the last day?
DK: No, I don't think so.
JF: We understand Neil had an argument with James Hopkins in the pub on Saturday night?
DK: Yes, but it was over very quickly. More like harsh words I would say. I had never met James before, but he seemed to

dislike Neil from the start. James seemed to think Neil was involved in him losing his first job. Neil made him angry by laughing and James left pretty quickly.
MB: And then you went to a cabaret?
DK: Yes. I went with Neil, Richard and Gary. Adrian was too drunk and Martin was never going to go.
MB: Did anything significant happen?
DK: No, just drinks, a few dances. It wasn't good. We all left together about 3:30am (03:30).
JF: And Neil?
DK: Neil was drunk, but okay. We stopped for food on Wenceslas Square and went back to the hotel.
MB: Can you tell us where you went for a walk on Monday afternoon, whilst the others went to the restaurant?
DK: Well, we didn't know they were going to eat. Richard, Gary and I wanted to go for a longer walk, so we walked towards the Charles Bridge.
MB: But you split up?
DK: Yes. Richard and I walked over the bridge, Gary said he was going to walk through the old town. I decided to go to The Lennon Wall again.
JF: Why?
DK: I just like it. We don't have anything like it really in UK.
MB: And Richard?
DK: He walked across the bridge, said he was going up towards the castle again.
MB: What time did you leave The Lennon Wall?
DK: Probably about 2:30pm (14:30). I walked back across the bridge and then through the old town, exploring as many old streets as I could.
MB: After the interview can you please show one of our detectives which route you took.
DK: I will try.
MB: And what time did you get back to the hotel?
DK: I arrived back about 4pm (16:00). I was first back. I collected my small suitcase from the concierge and was having a

coffee when I got the call from Martin.

MB: And what time did Richard and Gary arrive back at the hotel?

DK: They were back by 4:30pm (16:30). I called them. We waited at the hotel for Adrian and Martin to return.

JF: Did you know Neil had had an affair with Richard's ex-wife?

DK: Yes. Although I was told it was a one-off.

JF: What do you know about it?

DK: Neil and Natasha, Richard's ex-wife, bumped into each other at some conference. I don't know where. Anyway, they slept together. I was told Neil wasn't interested in seeing her again, but Natasha kept messaging him. That's how Richard found out.

JF: And what did Richard do?

DK: Richard blew his top. Confronted Neil, I understand. He also barred him from the pub for a while.

JF: How long?

DK: My guess, four months. It must be over five years ago now. Natasha moved out and Neil finally grovelled his way back into the pub. Richard now says his marriage was on the rocks anyway and Neil did him a favour.

JF: And it hasn't been an issue for either of them?

DK: No, I don't think so. Neil had settled down properly since, had two kids. Richard has a new girlfriend.

JF: Okay. Anything else?

DK: No.

JF: Finally, we understand Neil, Adrian and Martin came over to Prague last year with their wives. Do you know if anything happened on the trip?

DK: I know about the trip, but I didn't hear of anything happening on it.

FM: So you didn't want to harm Neil?

DK: No. Of course not.

FM: You had no problem with him at all?

DK: No.

FM: Can you think of anyone else who would want to harm

him?
DK: No.
JF: You seem very sure.
DK: He was a nice guy.
MB: Okay, thank you. Interview terminated at 10:46.

Richard Weston (RW)

MB: Interview commenced at 10:55. Please state your name for the record.
RW: Richard Weston.
MB: What is your job?
RW: I own the pub, The Mill Tavern, in Bishop's Stortford.
MB: How did you know Neil Robson?
RW: Neil was a regular, along with the other guys on the trip.
MB: Did you see him outside of the pub?
RW: Only if I bumped into him in town.
MB: What was Neil like?
RW: He was always the centre of attention. Fun, yes. But also a bit of a loudmouth.
MB: Have you got any examples?
RW: Not really. But if there was ever an argument, you could bet your bottom dollar it would involve Neil.
JF: This is a bit sensitive, but we understand Neil had an affair with your ex-wife, Natasha.
RW: It was a long time ago.
JF: But it would help us if you could explain what happened.
RW: Why? How can it be relevant?
JF: Look, Neil gets killed on a trip abroad with his friends. If he did have an affair with Natasha it creates a motive. We just need to understand so that we can rule you out of our enquiries and get you back home as quickly as possible.
[Pause]
RW: Okay. But I want to make it absolutely clear I am now totally fine with what happened. It's all in the past.
JF: Noted.

RW: My marriage was not going well. Natasha and I were arguing all the time. My guess is we'd have been divorced within a year anyway.
JF: But?
RW: Natasha worked part-time as a waitress at conferences and banquets. It was extra money for us during the winter season when trade could be low. It turned out she was working at a dinner which Neil was attending. Anyway, the facts are that he was staying in London, she made up some story to also stay in London, with him, and I found out.
JF: How did you find out?
RW: I saw a message on her phone. It was clear.
JF: Did you confront her?
RW: Yes. She claimed it was a one-off, but the messages I saw implied more than that.
JF: And you confronted Neil?
RW: Yes. I went to his house and we argued. Carly, his wife, was also there. It was a bit of a scene. He claimed it was a one-off as well, but said Natasha was chasing him.
JF: What did you do?
RW: I chucked Natasha out. I banned Neil from the pub. And I tried to get on with my life.
JF: It must have been difficult.
RW: It was at the beginning. But to be honest, I was pleased to see her go. I was happier after a while. After about three months Neil came to see me, to apologise again. He said he was sorry and that he'd changed. Carly was also now pregnant. I confess I made it difficult for him, made him beg a number of times to be let back into the pub, but actually I was okay with it.
JF: Sounds all a bit easy.
RW: I knew you'd say that. But I really can say he did me a favour. Over five years ago now and there has been no issue between us.
JF: And you are in a new relationship now?
RW: Yes. Hana started working at the pub a few years ago. Now

we are together.

JF: Okay. Thanks for telling us your version of what happened.

MB: On Monday afternoon Neil, Adrian and Martin went to the restaurant. Where did you walk to?

RW: I walked with Gary and Darren for a while and then we split up. I walked across the Charles Bridge with Darren and headed up towards the castle.

MB: Why?

RW: We'd actually already walked up to the castle on Saturday morning. However, when I was talking to Hana on Sunday night she suggested an observation deck near the Strahov Monastery. She said you get great views of the entire old town.

MB: Yes, I know it.

JF: How did Hana know about the observation deck?

RW: She is actually Czech. She comes from outside Prague, but worked here for a few years before coming to the UK.

JF: That's a strange coincidence, isn't it?

RW: Yes, I suppose so. I'm supposed to be coming back in the summer to meet her family.

JF: Good luck with that. Where is Hana now?

RW: She is running the pub whilst I'm over here. I've spoken to her every evening to check the pub's okay and there haven't been any issues.

JF: Okay, thanks.

MB: What time did you leave the observation deck to start walking back?

RW: Probably about 3:15pm (15:15). I walked back to the hotel a different way, across the bridge where the Dancing Building is?

FM: The name of the bridge is Jiráskův most.

RW: Sorry, I don't know the Czech names.

MB: What time did you get back to the hotel?

RW: About 4:30pm (16:30). Darren called me when I was walking back.

MB: After the interview can you show one of our detectives the route you walked?

RW: Okay. I also have some photos I took from observation deck.
MB: Thanks. They will be useful.
JF: We understand James Hopkins met up with you all on Saturday night, and he and Neil argued.
RW. Yes. I had never met James before and I hardly talked to him, just thanked him for helping get the tickets. But like I said before, if there was an argument you would bet a lot of money on it involving Neil.
MB: And from your perspective, there were no issues within the group over the long weekend?
RW: None.
MB: Nothing happened at the football match?
RW: No. We didn't see any real trouble. We were led to believe it was going to be much worse.
MB: And nothing else happened involving Neil over the weekend?
RW: I didn't noticed anything.
JF: On Saturday night it seems everyone was a bit drunk.
RW: We are all used to drinking together so there was the usual jokes, but no trouble.
JF: And in the cabaret?
RW: We were all quite drunk. Darren was looking after Neil because he was worse. It was a bit of a blur really, but we all came out together.
FM: Can you think of any reason why someone would want to kill Neil?
RW: No. Unless of course he's been playing away from home again.
FM: What do you mean?
JF: It means Neil could have been having an affair with someone else's wife.
FM: Ok, right.
JF: Are you thinking of anyone specific?
RW: No, of course not.
[Pause]

RW: Sorry, it was a bad joke.
JF: Well, if you think of anything please let us know.
RW: Do you have any idea who did this?
JF: No. But we are keeping an open mind.
RW: Right.
MB: Okay, thank you. Interview terminated at 11:26.

Gary Needham (GN)

MB: Interview commended at 11:38. Please state your name for the record.
GN: Gary Needham.
MB: What is your job?
GN: I run a local building firm based in Bishops' Stortford.
MB: How did you know Neil Robson?
GN: I've known Neil for years. We went to different schools but we played football together. Like all the guys here, we now meet down the pub regularly.
MB: Did you see him outside of the pub?
GN: Not much. I have done some building work for him and Carly over the years.
JF: And you've never had any problems with him?
GN: No, he's a good mate.
JF: What did you think of Neil?
GN: Surely you don't think I did this.
JF: Just answer the question.
GN: I just don't like what you're insinuating.
JF: I am not insinuating anything. We are asking everyone. This is a murder investigation.
[Pause]
GN: I always got on well with him. He was fun to be around. He was generous which I liked, always the first to buy a round. Also...
JF: Yes?
GN: Well, I've been going through a difficult time recently. My marriage has broken down and work has been tough. He al-

ways asked how I was. He was interested and I appreciated it.
MB: So you are separated?
GN: Yes, going through the divorce now. Grace and I split up about six months ago.
JF: How was Neil generous?
GN: Small things really. He's doing well at work so helped pay some of my costs for this trip. As I say, he looks out for friends.
JF: I suppose this hasn't always been the case with the other friends.
GN: I suppose you are referring to Neil's affair with Richard's ex-wife. That's way in the past now. As a matter of fact, Neil always said I'd helped him during that time. He was feeling low when he was banned from the pub. So he said it was right he helped me now.
JF: How did you help him?
GN: Nothing really. I just keep in contact with him when he was barred from the pub and I had little words with Richard to help smooth the situation.
MB: Back to this weekend trip, were there any issues involving Neil?
GN: Well I'm sure the others told you about James Hopkins.
MB: Yes. What did you see?
GN: It was nothing really. James is an odd person, I know him from when we were all younger in Bishop's Stortford. He always had a chip on his shoulder about something or other. He blames Neil for what happened at the firm they worked at, but that's all I know.
MB: Anything else?
GN: No. It was a good trip. I really needed it with all the stress I've had recently. And everyone was getting on well, no arguments.
MB: On Monday afternoon you went for a walk whilst the others went to the restaurant. Where did you go?
GN: I walked with Richard and Darren to the Charles Bridge, but didn't fancy walking across. I carried on walking around the old town. I was feeling a bit down because it was the last

day. I didn't fancy much going back to the reality of life in the UK. So I walked around the quiet streets for a while and then popped into a pub.
MB: What pub did you go to?
GN: I can't remember. It didn't have a catchy name. I'm sure I could find it on Google though.
MB: Okay. After the interview can you show one of our detectives where the pub is, and also the route you walked? What time did you leave the pub?
GN: I was in there for about an hour and a half. I left about 4pm (16:00) and had just started to walk back to the hotel when Darren called me.
JF: Do you know anything about the trip to Prague last year, when Neil, Adrian and Martin came over with their wives?
GN: No, not really. I think the guys organised it and it seemed a big success.
FM: Can you think of any reason why someone would want to kill Neil?
GN: No. There's no way it has anything to do with anyone on this trip.
FM: No way?
JF: He is saying it can't have anything to do with the other men on the trip.
FM: Okay, but someone killed him.
JF: Is there anything else you know related to Neil that might help us?
GN: No, sorry. I would tell you if I knew about something.
JF: Well please let us know if you remember anything.
GN: I will.
MB: Okay, thank you. Interview terminated at 12:08.

8

The Murder Board

Jonny, Mikeš and Boukal sat in the Incident Room, each silently dwelling on the output from the interviews. Mikeš was agitated, full of nervous energy, restlessly shifting in his chair. By contrast, Jonny was calm and still, looking straight ahead into space, deep in thought. Boukal sat respectfully, awaiting instruction, marker pen in hand.

"A busy morning," Mikeš said aloud. "But I don't think it has helped us at all in terms of suspect or motive."

Jonny didn't take the bait. Instead he sat thinking, occasionally glancing up at the photos on the white board seeking the inspiration of a connection.

Scanning around the room for a distraction, through the glass window Mikeš saw Dvořáková approaching the Incident Room. Behind her was an older lady in a housecoat, pushing a trolley of refreshments. Mikeš jumped up to greet them, a big smile on his face, opening the door wide with a flourish.

"Perfect timing!" boomed Mikeš. "Just what we need."

The older lady smiled affectionately at Mikeš and wheeled the trolley into the room. Slowly she moved the refreshments from the trolley onto an empty table.

"Děkuju, Katka," Mikeš thanked her.

"Prosím," Katka replied, nodding respectfully to Mikeš and Jonny, before leaving the room.

Dvořáková automatically played hostess, arranging the coffee mugs, bottles of water and glasses, and plate of sandwiches.

Jonny had returned to his study of the characters posted on the board. "Honza, come now," Mikeš tried to rouse Jonny from his internal deliberations. "Honza, my friend, you need some fuel for your brain."

Mikeš walked over to Jonny and placed a mug of coffee in his hands. "Eat, Honza. Every Czech grandmother says you must eat. We even have Czech versions of English sandwiches. Not to be missed."

Jonny looked up at this likeable character and smiled. Mikeš had the natural ability to put people at ease and keep the energy levels high. Despite what Boukal had told him, Jonny believed the staff had a strong affinity with Mikeš and trusted him implicitly. But he seemed to have a tendency to get distracted, easy bored and, as shown in the interviews, he could be very direct at times. Jonny wondered how Mikeš would react if he didn't get it all his own way.

Jonny accepted the plate from Dvořáková and took some sandwiches.

Boukal also took some sandwiches, but before he could even take a bite Mikeš snapped him into action. "Right, it's now a working lunch! Marek, you have the pen? Please make notes on the Murder Board as we talk."

Boukal put down his plate with a hungry sigh and jumped up in front of the board, the marker pen back in his hand.

Mikeš turned to look deliberately at everyone in the room, including Dvořáková who had now taken a seat. "Right, what do we know? Let's get everything we know on the board. As Honza suggested earlier, we need to follow every lead, big or small. But we first need to identify all the potential leads."

"Sir," started Dvořáková, "the five men are working with the team right now to document their walking routes on Monday afternoon and also the places they visited in Prague over the weekend. Once we have confirmation we will check the city CCTV cameras to verify their movements. We will also follow-up by checking the internal CCTV systems of the pubs, restaurants and cafés they visited if we need to."

"Excellent," enthused Mikeš.

Mikeš studied Jonny. "Honza, you are being very quiet."

"I'm still trying to work out this group of people. They have all known each other for quite a long time, some since school. The men claim to be friends and are saying mostly positive things about each other. But there also seem to be lots of underlying issues and arguments – the victim even had an affair with the wife of his friend. There is something not quite right here. I just can't put my finger on it."

Mikeš looked confused. "What is this with your finger?"

"I'm sorry," Jonny said, smiling. "It's slang again. It means I can't work out why it doesn't feel right."

Mikeš still looked confused. "I was always told that the English language was easy, but there were lots of sayings I didn't understand in the interviews. Something about 'steady eddie' and 'betting bottom dollars'. Crazy language!"

"Don't worry sir," Boukal said. "I followed what was said and I can brief you later after we get the interview transcripts typed up."

"Great," Mikeš acknowledged. "Honza, please continue."

"I think there are a few things we are not being told and I am not sure why. The only person I really believed was Richard Weston. The person who was definitely lying or holding something back was Darren Kozma. Did you see his defensive body language when he was answering questions about Neil Robson? He had his hands clasped tightly on his lap, like he was afraid he was going to give something away. At times in the interview he was also biting his lip."

"What does it mean?" queried Mikeš.

"It can be an indication the person is scared of not being believed. Or possibly scared of being caught lying. Usually the first one in my experience."

"You know a lot about this subject, Honza. Is it like studying body language?"

"Not really," corrected Jonny. "There are a growing number of studies on human behaviour, mostly for people skills training in the business sector. These studies try to help business leaders to influence other people in the workplace. The science is based around human facial expressions. I have read some books and find it fascinating. I started to use it in interviews, to identify when people felt uncomfortable with the questions they were being asked."

Dvořáková interrupted keenly. "I studied some behaviour science in my Psychology module at university."

"Very good," Jonny commented. "Studying facial expressions can be really powerful if you can record interviews and play them back in slow motion. There are a small number of micro expressions, such as contempt, fear and disgust that can give away how the person is feeling. And because they are natural expressions, it is very hard to hide them. I found it more useful when you have a suspect and know what you are looking for. It is difficult to use these techniques at this stage, early in an investigation, because we are still trying to piece together the background information."

Mikeš clapped loudly. "Very impressive. This is exactly why I surround myself with younger, brighter minds. You can't beat science."

"Yes," agreed Jonny. "But first we need to do our background work, find out as much as we can. We need to build a picture of the lives around these men. We also need to meet James Hopkins and find out what his story is and why he argued with Neil Robson on Saturday night."

"I will organise the interview," confirmed Dvořáková.

"I would like to analyse the calls and messages Neil Robson made over the past few days," Jonny continued. "I know they were all to UK numbers, but there may be something we are missing. We should also check the messages and calls from the friends' phones just in case they have been in contact with any Czech numbers whilst they have been in Prague."

"I'm co-ordinating the phone information," stated Boukal, continuing to make notes on the board. "I'll make sure we get the mobile phones from the friends before they leave today."

"And…" Jonny continued, "…I presume we still have Neil Robson's belongings?"

"Yes," Dvořáková stated. "Forensics have the small suitcase he left at the hotel and also the belongings and clothes he had on him when he was found. They are checking for DNA and fingerprints."

Jonny paused to think. Mikeš gave him a hand signal, encouragingly waving him on to continue leading the review. "Good. I would like to look at them when they come back. Also, I assume his room was cleaned because they had all checked out?"

"Yes," confirmed Boukal, "but we checked with the hotel and the cleaner has confirmed she did not see anything strange in Neil Robson's room. Also, we have secured the rubbish from the rooms serviced by the cleaner. The rubbish is from all the rooms serviced she cleaned so there are multiple bin bags, but we have it if we need to check it."

Mikeš nudged Jonny with a wink. "See, Honza, they have been trained well."

"I am impressed," Jonny stated. "You have a good team. The basics are being done well and at the moment I think we have all the key areas of the investigation covered. But, and this is very important, I know from my last case that a small detail can easily get overlooked. If that small detail is not noticed, or maybe the link to something else in the case is missed, it can give the killer more time to cover their tracks. Or worse still, time to kill again."

Mikeš looked carefully at Jonny, trying to read him. "This last case you mention, I think it made a big impression on you. Am I right?"

"Yes," Jonny confirmed, taking a deep breath. "I blame myself for the death of the last victim. Other people said I was being too hard on myself, but I know I took too long to find the key links in the evidence. It was staring me in the face. I took it personally. The last victim was a young woman, a girl really, only 15 years old. Same age as my daughter."

"I didn't think you were a family man." Mikeš looked surprised.

"Divorced a long time ago. My daughter lives with her mother." Jonny paused to make sure he chose the right words. "The killing of the last victim was just too close to home."

Mikeš smiled and put his hand reassuringly on Jonny's forearm. "The other people are right. You should not feel guilty. I am sure you have saved lots of people over the years and put many bad people in prison. You should think of them and be proud, my friend. This job has a fine error of judgement and we cannot always get it right."

"Thank you," Jonny replied, sincerely.

"And Honza," Mikeš continued, "the best way to bury the skeletons is to solve another murder mystery. Catching killers is why you joined the police, to give some peace to the poor victim's families. It is what I have always believed in, anyway. I think it is why you were here, in Prague, when this murder was committed. It is your destiny, Honza."

"You could be right. It certainly feels like I have no control over it."

Mikeš laughed loudly and patted Jonny's forearm again.

"Okay everyone, show over," Mikeš stated, appearing keen to move the meeting on. "We have a killer to catch, remember. What else do we have?"

As Boukal recapped the key points on the board and the potential leads to be followed up, Jonny reflected on what Mikeš had said. It was certainly true that he'd never allowed himself the time for redemption, having taken some time off after his last case and then, almost immediately, decided to take early retirement. He generally preferred the old-fashioned way of just pushing on and keeping busy, trying not to overthink things. But the counselling had helped him understand the benefit of analysing the internal impact of a traumatic event.

His last case was less about the severity of the killing, rather the timing of the case alongside his own feelings at the stage in his life. His mid-life crisis, perhaps. He also knew it was influenced largely by the difficult relationship with his daughter. Sitting there, watching Mikeš emit positive energy over the team, Jonny knew that he would see this case through and he resolved to accept it for what it was and for all the emotions it was going to bring out in him. He had been told in counselling to seek out his own healing and maybe this case was it.

Once Boukal had summarised, he turned his focus to next steps. "The autopsy is booked for 2pm with Dr Králová. Sir, are you going?"

"Of course," boomed Mikeš, turning to address Jonny. "Honza and I will go. The morgue is only a short walk across the square, towards the river."

Jonny nodded. "It will be good to stretch the legs. Actually, I'd also like to have a look at the crime scene. Yesterday I only saw it as a witness, or maybe a suspect."

Mikeš laughed loud. "Very good joke, my friend."

"I would like to see the restrooms where the murder was committed," Jonny added. "And also take a look at the access to the restaurant from the walkway."

"Good idea," Mikeš added with a smile. "We can kills two flies with one hit. 'Zabít dvě mouchy jednou ranou'."

Jonny laughed. "It's amazing how the sayings across the two languages are so close, but so different. In English we say, 'kill two birds with one stone'."

Mikeš smiled affectionately at Jonny as he stood up, checking the time on his pocket watch. "We have a lot of Czech to teach you, Honza. Now let's rock n' roll."

9

Retracing Steps

Walking away from the police station, Mikeš bounded in front, hat on and his cane snapping energetically at the cobbled streets. Jonny was lagging behind, struggling to keep up. Despite his further years, Mikeš clearly kept in good shape, evident by his wiry, strong physique and the spring in his step. Jonny thought he had been doing well with his daily walking since arriving in Prague, but this substandard performance was making him reappraise the need to workout more regularly.

Realising he was ahead by a few metres, Mikeš suddenly stopped and turned on Jonny. "Going too fast for you, Honza?"

"Well," wheezed Jonny, catching his breath, "you are setting quite a pace."

"Important for the heart, my friend. Seems like we need to get you fit. Do you know that many police officers have heart attacks within one year of retiring? We don't want this happening to you. You are a young man, so much to look forward to."

Mikeš restarted walking, relaxing his speed to allow Jonny to step in next to him.

"So how do you keep fit, Felix?"

Mikeš smiled. "I like that."

Jonny looked confused. "Like what? I don't understand."

"You used my first name."

"Why wouldn't I?" Jonny queried, still confused.

"It's the first time you've said my first name. It's important for our friendship."

Mikeš beamed a big smile at Jonny and patted him on the shoulder as they walked.

"Honza, the answer to your question is running. Yes, I am a runner! Not so fast now, of course, but I still run. Maybe jog is a better word."

"Very impressive. I don't think I have run since school. The last time was running for the bus."

Mikeš looked at Jonny smiling, realising the joke. "Ha ha, very good. It's an English joke, I think. I like this type of humour. I will teach you Czech and you can teach me some jokes."

As they turned off the side street and onto Old Town Square, still in step, Mikeš gestured to the sight before them with an expanse of his arm. "The Czech people sometimes forget how lucky they are to have such marvellous history. You know, one of the sponsored road races I still run is along the river and around the famous streets at twilight. It is quite magical."

"I think I'll need a bit of practice before I can run a race," countered Jonny.

"It's only 10km, my friend. Some good running shoes and a couple of weeks training, you'll be fine."

Jonny chuckled to himself, unconvinced. The smile on his face was soon wiped off, though, when, his new friend nodded back at him with a deadly serious expression.

As they walked diagonally across the square towards the restaurant, Jonny took in the majestic view. The cobbled stones basked in the spring sunshine, framed effortlessly by the assortment of historic buildings and churches. Tourists were milling around, enjoying the open space, with the customary crowd swelling around the astronomical clock. Relaxing in the restaurant over the past few afternoons, he had fallen under the spell of the square. This day felt different, striding across alongside a colleague with a serious crime to investigate. Some would even say he was working again.

At the centre of the square they passed the Jan Hus Memorial, a dominating statue and popular meeting place. The compelling monument was hard to miss, depicting the defiance of Hus, recognised in Prague as a martyr, and influential philosopher and reformer in the 14th century. Jonny was admiring the pure force of the stone and bronze sculpture, symbolising the strength to not conform to oppressive regimes, when Mikeš stopped dramatically and turned to face him.

"And Honza, one more thing," started Mikeš.

"Yes," prompted Jonny, intrigued by the seriousness.

Mikeš stalled for maximum effect. "You need to contact your daughter."

Jonny was lost for words. He tried to say something, his mouth opening slightly, but stopped himself. Instead he glanced down, to compose himself. "It is that obvious?"

"Yes," stated Mikeš, firmly. "Family is the most important thing."

Jonny was still startled, not sure how to respond to this eccentric but also caring new acquaintance of his. Mikeš continued his encouraging words. "Maybe you have not seen her for a long time. But time does not matter, you need her. And she will always need you because you are her father."

"Thank you, Felix." Jonny nodded respectfully and held out his hand for Mikeš to shake, sealing their new friendship.

Mikeš abruptly snapped into action, something Jonny was getting used to. He put his arm around Jonny's shoulder and lifted his cane to point towards the restaurant. "Come on, Honza, we have work to do."

They approached the restaurant, the coloured police tape bold and prominent. The police presence was never good for the trade of neighbouring restaurants, unless a high profile killing generated morbid interest from locals and visitors. Not following the local news, he did not know how extensive the murder coverage, was, especially on TV. There were no press camped outside the restaurant, so either interest was waning only one day later, or the city had a new headline to follow. Mikeš walked towards the uniformed officer protecting access to the crime scene and spoke to him in Czech. He stepped under the tape being held for him and beckoned for Jonny to follow.

"You go ahead, Felix," Jonny urged. "I just want to take a look at the access to the restaurant from the side. I'll catch up with you." Mikeš waved his acknowledgment and proceeded inside the restaurant to check on the progress of evidence gathering.

Jonny scanned the adjoining restaurants from the edge of the square and then walked through the terrace entrance of the adjacent restaurant. He stopped at the doors leading inside to the main restaurant, instead turning to look over the police tape preventing access into the crime scene at the next-door restaurant. He was now standing under the arches and could see right down the walkway along the row of restaurants.

A waiter from the restaurant approached him, but before he could say anything Jonny firmly stated his purpose. "I am with the police investigation team." The waiter nodded and walked away, clearly confused and not expecting a British person. It was only then Jonny realised he had no police identification – in fact he didn't even have his passport on him. He could be anyone. But maybe Mikeš was right, he had the look. Once a detective, always a detective.

Jonny studied the connecting restaurants carefully. It was an odd set-up for adjacent, competing businesses, but it was enforced by the frontage of the historic buildings and was probably similar in other old European cities. The four restaurants shared an open frontage under the arches, allowing a clear walkway through. This gave each restaurant a small roofed terrace area which they had extended, under awnings, onto the edge of the square using plants and rope to separate from next door. Some of the restaurants used the terrace space under the arches for storing serving items such as menus, serviettes and cutlery, but the walkway was still accessible by pedestrians from one end of the row of buildings to the other.

It was time to put himself in the shoes of the murderer. In his later years as lead detective on murder cases, he had developed a habit of imagining himself to be the killer and retracing steps as much as possible. In truth, the results from it were mixed, but he felt the greatest benefit was getting into the mindset of being a hunter tracking his prey. The best outcome would be to discover an escape route with incriminating evidence, vital to the prosecution, but most attempts ended in failure, with no rewards to further the investigation. He doubted he would find anything this time, especially as he was both in a foreign country and rusty after a few months out of the game. But whatever happened, attempting to retrace the killer's steps had never failed to stir his blood, giving him a natural energy kick and heightening his desire to solve the case.

He stood peering over the police cordon into the restaurant where the murder had been committed. He tried to visualise the criminal fleeing the restrooms moments after killing Neil Robson, and then entering the walkway. Which way would they go? He knew he was now standing in the busier restaurant, having intentionally avoided it himself for that very reason. Being busier it provided greater cover than the other restaurants, and also had large potted plants lining the terrace.

Jonny instinctively turned and started to stride away from the crime scene, along the walkway through the adjoining restaurants. At the end of the arches where the row of restaurants finished, he stopped. He unconsciously knew turning right was the only option; the killer would have wanted to get away from the busy square as quickly as possible. He turned right down the narrow side street, stepping across the cobbled stones slowly, scanning the ground for any clue wanting to present itself. After fifty metres he came to a junction. Left would take him back to a busy main street he had walked around a few days before. Straight on was to another cobbled courtyard with access out the other side, but Jonny knew a busy Irish bar was situated there. His gut feeling was to go right, knowing it headed into a series of smaller streets, providing maze-like options for doubling back and losing someone, if required. He was now walking parallel to the square and behind the Gothic church. The street widened halfway along, providing car parking space, and another junction. Right was out of the question as it went back to the corner of Old Town Square. He turned left and continued cautiously, noting the slightly wider road and the parked cars on both sides. A few tourists were watching him intently, but he was in the zone and too preoccupied to notice anyone.

He proceeded slowly, slightly bent over, watching the ground closely and examining each doorway and drain. Despite scanning for them, there were no public litter bins in view, probably due to the security risk given the close proximity to the square. He walked another thirty metres until he came to a left turn. It was inviting because the entrance to the street was smaller, however Jonny knew from walking the city in the past few days that it led to an area of busy cafés and bars. He rejected the option and kept walking straight ahead on the same road, past a restaurant and a picture gallery, before coming to another junction. This time the choices were only left or right. The street was narrower and quieter, car parking only on the far side, with only one way through by car. That way was left; another junction was visible seventy-five metres away, all roads leading from it in a one-way system out of the old town. By contrast, going right led to what appeared a dead end, but in fact was a small pedestrian passage leading under the overhead buildings. On the other side of the passage, Jonny knew, was a pedestrianised road, a busy thoroughfare with many tourist attractions and souvenir shops.

As he stood at the junction, looking left and right, he noticed a couple of small craft shops and also a small gated garden on the opposite side of the street. Otherwise all the buildings on the narrow street were for residence or small businesses. He felt pressed to go right, believing the killer would want to re-join the busy tourist route at this point and blend into the crowd. As he walked through the passage he realised how busy the other side was, the pedestrian road being used by a vast number of people, tourists and locals, as a main route to connect parts of the old town.

On impulse, Jonny turned around and returned to his position at the junction to start again. If the killer wanted to re-join the crowds, they certainly wouldn't want to do it carrying the murder weapon. Maybe the killer had decided to dump the weapon and then double-back to the passage to join the crowds. Following his instinct, Jonny crossed the narrow road and stood in front of the gated garden. Attached to a building, probably serving a business, the small garden comprised of only one tree, some shrubs and various waste and recycling bins on a paved area. He stepped slowly around the perimeter of the garden, peering through the metal railings, looking closely at the soiled area under and around the shrubbery. Around the far side of the garden he bent down to look under a bush when, out of the corner of his eye, he saw the glint of the sun against metal. Taking his pencil out of his jacket pocket, he was able to reach in through the railings and lift the leaves enough to uncover a silver coloured, metal penknife, about 7-8cm long and shaped like a fish. The knife was closed, blade folded in, and it appeared to have been dropped only recently, sitting proudly on top of the earth. It was too dark under the shadow of the plants to see if there was any blood, but Jonny knew it was a job for forensics anyway.

Jonny lifted his head to the sky, taking in a deep breath of fresh air. He could feel the energy in his fingertips, hear the blood fizzing around his body. The exhilaration he felt was impossible to explain, even to himself; it was a raw, primal feeling of joy. He had tried to kid himself over the past months that he didn't miss the job, but this moment confirmed how much he needed the rush of the chase in his life. They could stuff the boring parts of the job, the paperwork and tedious reporting to superiors, but this feeling was what policing was all about and it couldn't be beaten.

He relaxed his shoulders and took stock of the situation. Deep down he knew he had found the murder weapon, but patience was required for the blood and DNA tests to be completed on the knife. In his experience, coincidences were often cited as possible explanations, usually by suspects and their legal teams, but they rarely happened. The discovery of the murder weapon, if proven correct, also provided valuable information about the route taken by the killer when they fled the scene of the crime.

Walking around the garden perimeter, he tried the fence door but it was locked. Considering his options, he only then realised he did not have mobile numbers for Mikeš or Boukal. Jonny certainly couldn't leave the scene of his discovery. He had only one option, wait it out until someone came by.

The street was empty for a few minutes so he filled the time taking photos with his mobile phone: the street location, the garden and the fish-shaped penknife under the plants. Scanning the street again, he saw a middle-aged couple walking toward him from the passage.

"Excuse me, do you speak English?" he shouted.

The couple came closer but stopped a safe distance away. "We are from the Netherlands. We speak some English."

"Great. I am a policeman. I need you to take an urgent message for me. I cannot leave my position. Can you do this for me?"

The couple looked at each other before the man confirmed, "Yes."

"Okay, thank you. Please go to the restaurant on Old Town Square with police tape around it. Pass a message to Detective Chief Inspector Mikeš. Tell him Honza is on the street called Templová. Tell him to come here as quickly as possible. I will wait here until he arrives."

"Right," repeated the man. "Mikeš, Honza, Templová."

"Perfect, thank you. You are really helping a police investigation."

The couple walked away rapidly, following the street Jonny had walked down. He saw the lady smiling at the man, thrilled to have the added excitement of being brought into a possible police chase whilst on holiday.

Jonny waited another ten or so minutes before Mikeš and a uniformed police officer hurried down the passage towards him. "Honza, we thought we had lost you. Are you okay?"

"Perfect, thanks. And the good news is that I think I've found our murder weapon." Jonny gestured to the garden spot through the fence, bending down to lift the plant leaves with his pencil.

Mikeš squatted next to Jonny and peered through the railings. "Ty vole!" he exclaimed.

Jonny looked at Mikeš quizzically. "It means something like 'bloody hell'."

Mikeš took another long look at the knife and turned to Jonny, smiling. "Well, well, Honza… You are quite a special detective, aren't you!"

10

The Crime Scene

Mikeš led Jonny at pace through the terrace and inside the restaurant. He stopped dramatically in the middle of the floor, took off his hat with a flourish, and tapped his cane loudly on the tiled floor. A cluster of police officers, including Boukal, were gathered around the room, clearly waiting for their arrival, some still dressed in forensic protective suits.

With a cough to grab everyone's attention, Mikeš made his announcement in his characteristically booming voice. "Dámy a pánové. Podívej, Mr Fox našel nůž!"

Mikeš brought a plastic bag out of his trouser pocket and held it up, high and proud, as the crowd launched into applause.

Mikeš ushered Jonny forward, to stand next to him. "Honza, I've just made an announcement that you have found the murder weapon. The knife."

"No, no, please don't. I don't want a fuss."

"Too late, my friend!"

"Anyway, we can't be certain it's the murder weapon yet. Forensics need to process it."

"Honza, both you and I know it is the murder weapon."

With that assured endorsement, Mikeš pushed the bag containing the penknife into Jonny's hand and gave him a celebratory slap on the back, pushing him forward to take the ovation. Although stunned, Jonny kept his composure, scanning the faces surrounding him and mouthing "Děkuju" to each one.

Jonny was used to compliments and congratulatory words throughout his career, but he found himself overcome by this reception. He was, after all, a foreigner, and unknown to them all until this week. Now he was being lorded as a hero. The delight being shown for him and for the breakthrough in the investigation was genuine and touching. Jonny knew Mikeš' backing had given him status within the group, but now he had the pleasure of being warmly accepted for proving his own worth.

The clapping continued unabated and Jonny, blushing now, tried to pacify the crowd by hand signals. Sensing Jonny's discomfort, Boukal walked over and shook his hand. "Congratulations, Honza. Finding the knife like that was inspired."

"Thank you. But there was a fair amount of luck involved."

"Don't listen to him, Marek," interrupted Mikeš. "He is a special detective and we are the ones lucky enough to have him helping us."

Boukal took the plastic bag and turned it over in his hand. "I don't know if Felix has explained, but this knife is symbolic of the old Czechoslovakia. It was first produced in the early 1900s and is still popular now. It's called a Rybička; Ryba means fish, hence the shape of the outer casing. But, actually, it's more commonly used for mushroom picking in the forest."

Jonny took back the plastic bag and was examining the knife inside closely when, abruptly, Mikeš clapped his hands loudly for all to hear. As quickly as he started the party, Mikeš put his hand up to indicate the show was over and everyone should get back to work.

Less interested in the history lesson, Mikeš was quickly back into the planning mode. "Marek, we need to get a team of our best people to check the roads on the escape route for any signs of evidence. Can you please co-ordinate with Sergeant Dvořáková? Honza will give you the route he took. We'll take the knife because we are going to the Pathology Lab next to get the autopsy results. The first thing we need to do is get confirmation from forensics that it is the murder weapon."

"We particularly need to focus on the garden area where the knife was discarded," added Jonny, "especially the gate and fence. Forensics need to check meticulously for DNA, fibres and fingerprints. If the killer made one mistake dropping the knife there, they may have been distracted and made another mistake. Maybe they caught themselves on one of the railings."

"Yes, sir," confirmed Boukal, directed at both of them, and scampered off, immediately calling out to one of the uniformed officers to demonstrate the urgency.

"See Honza," Mikeš smiled, "you are becoming quite famous already."

"I'm not really one who likes all the attention."

"I know. But I do!" Mikeš winked and pulled Jonny away, arm around the shoulder. "Now let's show you the crime scene."

***

Wearing plastic gloves and with plastic covers over their shoes, Mikeš and Jonny stepped over the taped threshold into the restrooms. The two forensics staff were carefully checking the tiles by the sink; they stopped and stepped outside to give them improved access.

Boukal had been right; the restroom layout was unusual by UK standards, but was probably common in the Czech Republic. The entrance room was approximately four metres squared, tiled floor to ceiling, and only housed four sinks, mirrors and two hand drying machines on opposite walls. The only other furniture in the room was a bin screwed to the wall and a radiator. On the opposite wall to the sinks were two doors, one labelled 'Ženy' and the other 'Muži'.

On the floor was a taped outline of where Neil Robson was lying when he was found. Without a word, Mikeš passed a folder to Jonny, inside of which were photos fresh from Monday when the body was discovered. Jonny turned over the first photo, matching it with the outline on the floor, and studied carefully the shape of the pool of blood around the victim's head and upper torso. The next photos showed the blood splatter on both the wall next to the entrance door and on the ceiling, the stains of which were both still visible.

Jonny pointed to a close-up photo of the dead body on the tiled floor. "The body position is not natural. My guess is he was unconscious when he hit the floor."

Mikeš nodded his agreement. "The high amount of blood would indicate it was a deep wound. We will find out more from the autopsy."

"Also," Jonny continued his analysis, "the wound looks like it was on the upper left-hand side of his neck and he fell this way." He pointed towards the door. "So, it seems likely he was turned towards the sinks when he was stabbed. Maybe he was looking in the mirror."

"That was my thinking as well," confirmed Mikeš.

The scene of any murder was always tragic, but Jonny had been unfortunate enough to witness many scenes ghastlier than this. He had come to learn what evil looked like, often staring it right between the eyes. He knew he would never get used to the harsh reality of what a human could do to its fellow man, especially if children were involved.

As a young policeman he had been first on the scene of a family massacre, and had seen everything in between: a pensioner beaten to death over £20 in their purse, unreported domestic violence ending in tragedy, all the way to the signature murder of the serial killer, Bill Sutherland, a true monster. Jonny had come to understand, through experience, some of the sadistic workings of a deranged murderer's mind, and could recognise their desire or need to kill. But to mutilate a body afterwards was depraved, beyond any rational comprehension, and something he would never understand.

Most murders were straightforward, just needing to be

framed around motive and opportunity, and supported by concrete evidence to build a solid case. Often it was an iterative process rather than a dramatic discovery, small steps in sensible directions to help identify motivation, requiring the search for evidence to ratify the theory or prove it unlikely, or simply impossible. Working the process hard, without jumping to conclusions, had always appealed to Jonny, driving him on to find the right piece of the puzzle for the next move, not letting the killer get too far ahead. The paralysis of analysing one situation was not acceptable, instead he preferred putting together the full picture through informed action and reviewing the outcomes as they progressed.

This scenario was certainly less gruesome than many he had observed, but was still somewhat baffling. Before Jonny vocalised his thinking to Mikeš, he wanted first to take in the space from all possible angles. First, he went into the men's toilets and let the self-closing door shut behind him. Inside were two urinals and two toilet cubicles, all along the same wall, the small space only being four metres by three metres. There was a window for ventilation, but it was small, impossible for an adult to squeeze through. Jonny stood outside one of the cubicles and replayed stepping to the exit door, opening it quickly, to surprise the victim at the sinks.

Back in the main restroom area, the door closing behind him, Jonny looked around for inspiration. "Felix, stand over there, in front of the sink. Bend over slightly."

Mikeš did as Jonny suggested.

"Can you see me in the mirror now?" Jonny asked.

"I can see a shape from your shadow, but I can only see you clearly if I lift my head slightly. My body in the mirror is blocking the view."

"As I thought," Jonny started to explain. "If Neil Robson went to the toilet, presumably the urinals, the killer could have been in one of the cubicles and followed him out. Then he could have attacked him from behind, like this." Jonny made an overhead movement, bringing his hand down on Mikeš' neck.

Jonny turned and next opened the door to the ladies' toilets. The door again closed itself behind him. The room was the same size as the men's, with the opposite layout for ease of plumbing. Four cubicles were lined up on the wall, with only a narrow corridor in front of them. The ventilation window was the same size. He exited the toilets, as before, and stood in the main restroom area with his arm up above his head, pretending to hold a knife.

"Same," he confirmed to Mikeš. "The toilet doors are so close together."

After a few minutes looking around the space again, Mikeš was the first to share his thoughts. "In many ways it appears to be a clean murder. The killer waits in hiding somewhere, probably in the cubicles, and follows the victim out. The stab of the knife is quick and to the back of the neck. Neil Robson falls quickly after the stabbing and the killer steps over him and leaves the restrooms, careful to stay composed and not attract any attention."

"And motive?" Jonny pushed.

"It looks more and more to me like an organised killing. Maybe someone paid to have Neil Robson killed."

"I understand why you say this, Felix. It is certainly possible. It's odd though why they didn't try to make it look like a robbery. And…"

"Yes?" prompted Mikeš.

"I'm a little surprised Neil Robson didn't put up a fight. He was a tall guy, well built. If I was standing at the sink, I think I would have recognised someone coming out of the toilets fast, even if I couldn't see them clearly. I would have instinctively turned or tried to duck out of the way. But it looks like he was just stabbed and then fell over."

"But Honza you are a detective, trained to sense danger. This is a restroom and many people will enter and leave."

"Yes, I suppose you are right," Jonny admitted.

Jonny and Mikeš looked at each other, exasperated that

the killer's modus operandi was not presenting itself.

"Motive is what we need to find," Jonny spoke aloud. "Then it will all fall into place."

Mikeš put his arm around Jonny once more. "Let's go and see the body. Maybe that will tell us something."

11

The Other Half

If the smell and atmosphere of the police station had stirred a feeling of home away from home, spiking Jonny's senses and triggering many good memories, the morgue had an equal and opposite effect. If truth be told, he had a weak stomach. On a few occasions in the past he had even resorted to using the diversion of a vital, but ultimately fictional, phone call to excuse himself from the examination room during a particularly gruesome autopsy.

    Jonny never knew if the horror of the initiation on his first criminal case had caused this fragility, or merely pushed it along, but it was certainly carved in his memory. His DCI at the time had organised the rite of passage, the pathologist cutting open the chest of the deceased right in front of them. Without any warning. All just to shock him and be able to tell a humorous story back at the station. How times had changed. He couldn't imagine anyone even trying a stunt like that now for fear of Human Resources knocking on their door. After that traumatic experience, he had made his own personal decision never to inflict such a test, or any other initiation ceremony for that matter, on any new recruit, even if they happened to be his worst enemy.

    His most painful experience though had been his last autopsy, the body of fifteen-year-old Alison Bryce laying on the examination table. She had looked so peaceful and angelic, but the rage inside him had been close to exploding, his feeling of anger mixed with the guilt for not catching the serial killer earlier. The image of her face had stayed with him for months, appearing frequently in his nightmares. Although it affected him deeply and caused him sleepless nights, he had been able to cope by using his experiences from the previous cases that had also touched him personally. But when Alison's face started to interchange with the face of his own daughter, Charlotte, in his nightmares he knew he needed desperately to make a life change and leave the police.

The outside of the hospital was imposing but weathered, apparently in need of some love and modernisation. However, the exterior was deceiving because the wards and the outpatient departments were modern and bright. Mikeš briefed Jonny on the redevelopment programme, explaining that some departments were leading in their field, many with state of the art equipment installed.

Walking towards the morgue, Jonny felt like he was in the presence of a minor celebrity. Mikeš, hat and cane in hand, greeted all the staff with gusto, seeming to know everyone's first name. The staff's reaction to Mikeš' arrival, all waves and beaming smiles, confirmed Jonny's growing impression that he was a deep-rooted member of the establishment and loved by all.

Mikeš briefed Jonny as they walked down the hospital corridor to the morgue. "Honza, Dr Králová is a truly great doctor with amazing knowledge of medical science. A real expert in forensic pathology, respected across the world. We have worked together on many important cases."

"I look forward to meeting them."

Mikeš smiled at Jonny. "As well as a true friend and partner in crime."

Jonny couldn't help noting the odd choice of words, but knew Mikeš was prone to making exaggerated claims about almost everyone he had been introduced to so far. In fact, he guessed that Mikeš probably did the same when talking to other people about him.

Mikeš pressed the intercom and the access buzzer

sounded almost immediately, unlocking the door. On pushing open the door, Mikeš and Jonny were greeted by a nimble, fit looking lady doctor in a white coat. She was in her late fifties with medium length, brown hair and intense, almost piercing eyes.

"Hello Mr Fox. Felix has told me a lot about you."

"Really good to meet you." Jonny shook her extended hand.

"My name is Dr Králová, but you can call me Ella. Please come in."

Mikeš placed his hat and cane on a table inside the entrance and Králová led them across the room towards the body of Neil Robson, laying naked on a standard metal examination table. Jonny was pleased to note the forensic work seemed to have been completed, no surgical instruments or, more importantly, blood in sight. However, the aggravating smell of formaldehyde and cadaverine was still lingering in the air, hard to escape in such an environment.

"Thank you for speaking English, Ella," offered Jonny. "Sometimes I feel such a fraud, being here in Prague and everyone speaking English to me."

"It is no problem at all," she replied with a smile. "Secretly we like to try out our English on British visitors. I have travelled quite extensively with my work so I've had lots of practice. Plus it is hard to exist in the medical profession without good English and Latin."

"Of course," acknowledged Jonny.

"Mind you, Felix still needs a bit of work," Králová stated with a devilish look in her eye. "But he's trying hard."

Jonny turned to Mikeš, who, whilst smiling, was being strangely quiet. In fact, Jonny realised, Mikeš had not said a single word since arriving at the morgue. Jonny had got used to Mikeš' dramatic, talkative manner, always seeking to be centre of attention. This performance seemed out of character.

Jonny decided to keep the conversation flowing. "By

the way Ella, please call me Honza. Felix has given me the Czech nickname and it has kind of stuck."

Králová looked at Mikeš with an affectionate shake of her head and big, smiling eyes. "That sounds like Felix."

The chemistry between the long-standing colleagues, doctor and detective, had some underlying history he couldn't fathom. One thing was clear though – Králová was definitely in charge. Jonny chose to press on and ignore the awkwardness. "Felix has told me all about your experience. He told me you have helped solve many important cases."

Králová looked at Mikeš with a wide, mischievous smile. "Honza, I think he's just trying to flatter me."

Jonny looked from Králová to Mikeš and back again, deciding now was the time to stop talking before he well and truly put his foot in it.

Králová lent slightly towards Jonny. "I bet he didn't tell you we were married for close to twenty years."

Jonny looked at Mikeš in astonishment. Mikeš just shrugged his shoulders in acceptance, the missing jigsaw piece of his shared history with Králová now clearly apparent.

"Yes, I am 'the other half' I think you say in the UK," Králová teased. "But it's quite sweet really. He still asks me out for dates every couple of weeks and we go out for dinner, a glass of wine or a classical concert. But living with him was a nightmare, you can imagine. No, it's better this way. It allows us both to live our own lives but remain good friends."

Jonny was truly stunned and found himself muttering out loud. "Well, I never expected this."

Králová ignored the comment and looked straight at Mikeš with a penetrating stare. "So Felix, before we start are you going to tell me why you were an hour late?"

"Well..." stammered Mikeš. "Yes, my dear, I'm sorry. But we have good news. Honza found a suspicious knife in the streets behind the square." Mikeš pulled the plastic evidence bag from his pocket and held out the penknife.

Králová stared intently at Mikeš for a few moments.

She then turned to Jonny with a smile on her face. "You know, he always has an excuse ready. I can never catch him out."

Jonny felt the need to support his friend. "Well, Ella, actually it's true. I suppose it's sort of my fault. But it is good news. Hopefully the knife I found will turn out to be the murder weapon."

Králová laughed softly to herself, finding the situation amusing. "I see you boys are sticking together already."

She took the plastic bag and turned it over in her hands, studying the silver fish-shaped penknife casing and the single blade tucked into the frame. "A Rybička. That is unusual. The blade is about the right length, though. I will need to test it, of course. I'll also check any blood samples, DNA and fingerprints."

Mikeš coughed subtly to get her attention. "My dear, I'm sorry to push you, but can we go through the findings from the autopsy. Boukal is picking us up soon, we have another witness to interview."

"Okay, my dear." Králová winked at Jonny.

"Right," she started, moving closer to the examination table. "The victim, Neil Robson, was healthy and relatively fit for his age of thirty-four. Other than the knife wound there are no bruises or other cuts on the body. The toxicology tests did not show up anything unusual, other than an increased level of alcohol after his weekend of drinking. The contents of his stomach were consistent with what we have been told he had for lunch and he had emptied his bladder. So having examined the body, there is, in my opinion, no reason for him to die other than the stab wound he received to the back of the neck." She bent down and, with a pen taken from a coat pocket, indicated around the wound. "He was stabbed only once with a blade about 5-6cm in length. The incision severed the carotid artery and would have caused a significant spurt of blood, consistent with what I found at the crime scene. Once he was stabbed, he would have fallen quickly, consistent with the unnatural position in which he was found on the floor."

Jonny concurred. "Yes, we noted that earlier from the photos from the scene."

"Have you found any other DNA samples on the victim?" ventured Mikeš.

"Hang on Felix, I haven't finished yet." Králová paused to make her point. "The interesting aspect of this case is the angle of the blade entry." Králová turned the shoulder of the corpse for Jonny and Mikeš to get a better view. "If you look here, you can see the blade punctured the skin at almost a right angle to the back. So, if the assailant was holding the knife up at head height, necessary to get the right purchase for stabbing someone, they would be shorter than the victim, maybe up to 20cm shorter. Neil Robson was 187cm, or just over six feet and one inch tall, so the killer may be only 167-172cm tall, or about five feet eight inches."

Jonny interrupted. "But couldn't the killer have been bending over the victim, for example if Neil Robson was leaning over the sink?"

"Yes, of course. I am assuming both were standing in this calculation. Any bend in the back of the victim, for example when using the sink, would reduce the difference in height between them. When the crime scene was discovered the tap wasn't on, hence we have to assume the victim had not started to use the sink properly. But we cannot be sure how bent over the sink he was, if at all. Sorry, it is not an exact science."

"But the killer definitely stabbed him from behind?" Jonny probed.

"Yes," Králová confirmed. "The incision was relatively clean; the blade was in and out quickly. If the killer and victim were face to face, wrestling, it would have been virtually impossible to get such a clean strike. Plus, as I said before, there was no bruising or other injuries on the deceased, indicating there wasn't a struggle."

"So," Jonny surmised, "Neil Robson goes to the urinals and returns to the main restroom area to wash his hands.

There appear to be three possibilities. Firstly, the killer enters the restrooms through the main entrance door to surprise him. Secondly, the killer is waiting there when he comes out from the men's toilets. Or thirdly, the killer is hiding, either in the men's cubicles or the ladies' toilets, and surprises him from behind when he is approaching the sinks."

"They must be the only possible options," Mikeš agreed.

Jonny continued hypothesising. "It seems to me there are two possible modes of kill here. If the killer jumps out and attacks Neil Robson as he is standing at the sinks, it would indicate a planned or organised killing. We know it wasn't a robbery because his wallet and phone were not taken. However, there could also have been some sort of confrontation, after which the victim turns away towards the sinks and is attacked." He paused. "Maybe Neil Robson knew his killer."

"Both are certainly feasible," confirmed Králová. "The knife attack was not frenzied. If it was there would be multiple wounds and the body would be messy. It was instead a single stab to the neck and the seriousness of the injury would have been obvious straight away from the amount of blood. A professional killer would probably go for the neck when attacking from behind, to disable the victim at least. The neck is however also the obvious point to stab if the killer knew the victim and was lashing out when he turned to the sinks. Unfortunately, I can't help you more than that."

Mikeš nodded in agreement at the logic, but looked confused. "But if it wasn't planned, why was the killer carrying a knife in the first place?"

Králová smiled at Mikeš, putting her hand gently on his forearm. "Well, my dear, I suppose that's your job to work out."

"With Honza's help, of course." Mikeš winked at Jonny.

Mikeš coughed gently again. "So back to my earlier question, dear, did you find any DNA on Neil Robson's body?"

"So far, no DNA other than from the victim and his

friends. They are still checking the scene, but any findings could be difficult to isolate because the restrooms were used by many people. It looks like the football shirt the victim was wearing was new, probably bought here in Prague, and we've found various fibres on it. We're working through samples of the clothing worn by the victim's friends so we can isolate them."

Jonny looked confused. "If the murder was committed by a professional, I can understand why no DNA would be left at the scene. But wouldn't you expect DNA to be left if the murder wasn't planned and the victim knew the killer?"

Králová thought for a moment. "Possibly. But from what I understand, the victim had only just gone to the restrooms. Therefore, the murder must have happened quite quickly. If there was a confrontation or stand-off as you suggest, the point of the stabbing may have been the first time the killer was close to the victim."

Jonny nodded, deep in thought. "And I suppose the killer's clothes would have had blood on?"

"Yes," confirmed Králová, "but unfortunately I can't tell you exactly how much."

Mikeš' mobile phone started to ring. "Boukal?" He listened for a moment. "Pět minut. Diky."

Mikeš turned to Jonny. "Boukal will be here in five minutes."

Králová gestured towards the door and they all walked across the room together. "It was a pleasure to meet you, Honza. Hope to see you again soon."

"Thank you, Ella." Jonny and Králová shook hands again.

Králová then turned her attention on Mikeš. "And Felix, I'll see you tomorrow night for dinner. Don't be late again."

"Yes, my dear."

12

Interview 1 – James Hopkins

The following is a transcript of the recorded interview conducted with James Hopkins (JH) on the afternoon of Tuesday, 16th March 2010. The interview was held at the home of JH in Prague 3.

    Present at the interview were Chief Warrant Officer Felix Mikeš (FM), Chief Sergeant Marek Boukal (MB) and Consultant Jonathan Fox (JF).

MB: Interview commenced at 16:32. Please state your name for the record.
JH: James Hopkins.
MB: This interview is to help us with the on-going investigation into the murder of Neil Robson, yesterday, 15th March 2010. You have agreed for the interview to be recorded so we can refer back to it if we need to. You are not under caution nor at this present time suspected of being involved in the murder. The purpose of the interview is to gain important background information and to rule you out of our enquiries. Do you understand?
JH: Yes.
MB: Present with us at this interview are Chief Warrant Officer, Felix Mikeš, Jonathan Fox and myself, Marek Boukal, Chief Sergeant. Mr Fox is a consultant working with the Czech Police team on this murder investigation. Do you understand?
JH: Yes.
MB: Thank you for being flexible to our late request and leav-

ing your job a bit earlier to meet today.
JH: No problem.
MB: First of all, can you tell us how you found out about the murder?
JH: Martin called me last night to tell me.
MB: Martin Wilson?
JH: Yes.
MB: What time?
JH: I think about 8pm. I can check on my phone if you need to know the exact time.
MB: Okay, maybe later.
JF: Were you surprised?
JH: Yes, of course. Neil wasn't my favourite person, as I'm sure you are aware, but nobody expects anyone to be murdered.
MB: Can you give us some background on how you know Neil and Martin?
JH: We all went to school together. Adrian (Scott) as well. I was really only friends with Martin. We were both not cool enough to be in the gang.
JF: You sound bitter.
JH: Well not everyone looks back at their school days with pleasure. I was one of the kids, like Martin, who took a few beatings. Neil and Adrian never seemed to suffer the same fate, they were always in the popular group.
JF: Was there a significant event involving Neil that happened during your school days? Something maybe involving Adrian, Martin or you?
JH: No, I cannot remember anything.
MB: After you left university we understand you started working at the same company as Neil. How did this happen?
JH: We all went to separate universities. Neil and I both studied Biology degrees, or rather I think his was Biochemistry. Adrian was something else, maybe History. During the time I was at university I was not in touch with Neil, but I saw Martin when I came home during the holidays and he was still in touch with Neil. In my last year I applied to pharmaceutical

companies and decided to take the offer of a company relatively close to where we lived.

MB: In Bishop's Stortford?

JH: That's the town we lived in. The pharmaceutical company was about fifteen miles away. After I had accepted the job offer, Martin told me Neil had got a job on the same graduate scheme. So we started together in the September.

JF: And were you pleased about this?

JH: No, not really. I didn't really like him much.

MB: And we understand you left within a year or so of starting the job.

JH: Yes. In truth, it wasn't really the right job for me. I'm now a teacher.

MB: But what happened?

JH: On the graduate scheme we were given different assignments, usually in groups, in order to expose us to different parts of the company. You know, strengthen our understanding of every part of the organisation, from product design to manufacturing to marketing. I was doing ok, not brilliant but I wasn't the worst performer on the scheme. By contrast, Neil was standing out, a high flyer. He was a bit of a natural, and had the confidence and competitiveness you need. After about nine months he and I were assigned to work together on a new project in Operations. I won't go into detail but it involved calculating the quantity of raw materials we needed. The bottom line is we made a mistake. It was a genuine error and both of us were involved. Our line manager, who checked our work, also missed it. I obviously wasn't happy with the mistake we made, but we were all interviewed afterwards and I believed it was an honest, shared error. However, once the post-implementation review was completed, it turned out I got the majority of the blame. I found out Neil and our line manager had concocted a story which was simply not true. As a result, I got put on disciplinary and eventually I resigned after four or five months.

JF: Did you appeal and also confront Neil?

JH: Yes and yes. Neil was a slippery weasel, always has been, and got all the important people on his side. The appeal stood no chance really.
JF: So what did you do?
JH: I looked at applying for other jobs in the same sector, but the disciplinary record was going to be a problem unless I waited it out for a few years. I decided to take some time out, went travelling, and then applied to go on a PGCE. Sorry, that's a teacher training course.
JF: And you never confronted Neil?
JH: I had strong words with him, but he just deflected it away. He said it wasn't anything to do with him.
JF: Were you never tempted to get him back for what he did?
JH: Do you mean, did I wait to kill him in Prague over ten years later? The answer is no.
JF: I actually wasn't implying that. I was just thinking a lot of people would have punched him at least.
JH: I'm not really a physical type of guy.
JF: Okay, but you still saw him around?
JH: Yes, I saw him around town, sometimes down the pub. But it was fairly easy to avoid him.
JF: But you kept in contact with Martin?
JH: Yes, off and on. We weren't great mates, but Martin is one of those people who is very good at keeping in contact. That's the reason we're still in contact today.
MB: Can you explain how you ended up in Prague?
JH: I passed my teaching probation and taught in the UK for three years. But the travelling I had done had given me the appetite for more, so I decided to look for teaching posts abroad. I didn't want to just teach English and waste some years abroad, I wanted to follow a career. I eventually got the job of a science teacher at one of the International Schools in Prague. It works because the science lessons are in English. I've been there for six years now and am now Head of Biology.
JF: Sounds like you've achieved something positive out of it.
JH: Thanks. Yes, I'm happy here.

MB: Thank you for explaining. And Martin told us you helped him get the tickets for the football match.

JH: Correct. Martin would message me frequently, as I've said before, but I haven't seen him for three or four years. He explained in one message they wanted to see Sparta vs Slavia and I know someone that goes to see Slavia regularly. Anyway, I checked with my friend and told Martin I would be able to help.

JF: You didn't go with them?

JH: No, I'm not a football fan. I organised the tickets and Martin transferred the money to me.

JF: What happened when you met them on Saturday night?

JH: I had been out for drinks with friends locally in Prague 3. I had agreed with Martin to meet him in the centre later, near Wenceslas Square. He sent me a message to say they were in the Lucerna pub. It was all friendly at the beginning, everyone thanking me for helping with the tickets. But Neil and Adrian were pretty drunk, more than the others, and Neil started talking about the pharmaceutical company.

JF: What did he say?

JH: He said I should have stayed. It seems he's been there for over ten years and has done well. I think he's even got some shares now. I'd had a couple of drinks myself and didn't take it well. I told the rest of the group that I didn't have much choice at the time because Neil had got me sacked. He then said something back and it went from there. Adrian jumped in, calming Neil down. It was nothing really, but I regret it.

JF: Why?

JH: I wanted them to see me as doing well, living and working here in Prague. I really don't care about what happened at the pharmaceutical company, it's all in the past. But I was stupid, I reacted when I should have just ignored him.

MB: And you left soon after?

JH: Yes. I think Martin came back from the toilets and I said I was going. I left about 11:30pm (23:30) and got the metro back home.

FM: And where were you on Monday afternoon?
JH: I was at school. I had a mix of lessons and free periods, but I was at school until I left about 6pm.
FM: Did other people see you at school in the afternoon?
JH: Alibis, you mean? Yes, of course, I was in school all afternoon.
FM: And where did you go after leaving school?
JH: I got the metro back here. I only stopped to go for some food shopping between the metro and my apartment. I was back by 6:45pm (18:45) latest. And Martin called me at 8pm (20:00), as I said earlier.
FM: Can you please give Chief Sergeant Boukal details of the people at school who will have seen you and also your route home.
JH: Sure.
JF: Can you think of any reason why any of the group would want to kill Neil?
JH: I only knew Neil, Adrian and Martin. I was aware of Gary (Needham) from when I was younger, but I never really knew him. The others, Darren (Kozma) and Richard (Weston), I don't think I've even met before. Neil and Adrian were always thick as thieves and it seems that nothing has changed. Sorry I'm waffling. No, I don't know anything really. I only know what Martin has told me and it's not much.
JF: Do you know why Martin was friends with Neil and Adrian? In some ways it seems an unlikely combination.
JH: I've never really understood it either. Martin is a nice guy, but a bit righteous. When I asked him before, he just said they had been friends since school, and friends were friends. He said the same about me and him.
JF: Do you think he was jealous of Neil and Adrian?
JH: Martin? Yes, maybe. He always seemed to know a lot about them. He would sometimes mention Neil and I'd tell him I wasn't interested. But he'd keep mentioning both of them, like he had nothing else to chat about. I think Martin was probably just a bit boring, maybe wanted more from life but

was too scared to go after it himself. Instead, he was living his life through them.

JF: Anything else?

JH: I know Sophie (Wilson), Martin's wife, didn't really like Neil. But only because Martin told me once.

JF: Did you meet up with Martin when they came over to Prague with their wives last year?

JH: No. Martin mentioned they were coming, but I didn't think it was really appropriate. Plus, I didn't want to see Neil.

MB: Okay, thank you. Any more questions?

JF: Have you ever seen Martin get angry with Neil before?

JH: When we were at school, yes. But Neil was a pretty annoying person, arrogant and always in your face. Since then, I remember messages from Martin where he was definitely annoyed with Neil but I can't remember any details. Sorry.

JF: Okay, thanks. But please let us know if you remember anything else.

JH: Sure. But there's no way Martin could do anything like this, he isn't the type. I've never seen him hurt a fly.

MB: Thanks for your time, Mr Hopkins. I will remain with you after the interview is finished to take fingerprints and also a DNA swab. Just to rule you out of our enquiries, as I explained at the beginning. We will contact you again if we have any further questions. Interview terminated at 17:07.

13

The Aerial Jigsaw

Jonny and Mikeš stood next to the car, both silent and deep in thought, waiting for Boukal to emerge from the apartment building. The late afternoon sun had plunged the street in golden light, the only shade coming from the budding blossom trees lining the pavement on both sides.

Mikeš stood slightly hunched, looking down in concentration, the wide brim hat protecting his eyes from the low sun. Jonny made a mental note to treat himself to a pair of sunglasses; whilst he had never really been a shades man, the spring weather in Prague appeared to make them almost a necessity.

The restlessness was radiating from Mikeš' body. Out of nervous habit or boredom, probably both, Mikeš was tapping his foot and his cane in unison, to the tune of some beat in his own head. He made quite a picture – the eccentric older gentleman who had lived life to the full but was still impatient for adventure.

As they continued to wait, Jonny scanned the buildings to distract himself. So far during his stay he had walked down many streets, mainly in the centre and Prague 2, but had not taken as much time as he should to just stop and look up. He knew Prague had not been bombed in the war and the buildings in central Prague were a testament to this wonder. Although he didn't exactly know where he was, having just been told it was a residential area in Žižkov, Prague 3, the architecture was as captivating here as in the centre of the city.

The buildings lining both sides of this particular street were all colourful but different, with varying porticos and cornices, some with balustrades accessible through single panel glass doors. They however retained an architectural style that was both charming and slightly hypnotic, built around the symmetry of the similar-sized, rectangular windows. The grand entrance doors were large, heavy wooden double doors, their carved frontages gleaming in the sunshine. These doors provided access to the numerous apartments inside, but also gave the buildings majesty and a historical timestamp.

Mikeš was tapping his cane on the pavement more persistently now, implying how frustrated he was. The day had been useful in terms of background information, starting the process of piecing together the lives of the victim and his friends. But Jonny knew progress had been slow and they were no nearer establishing any element of motive. Finding the knife had been a blessing, but it was their only lead at the moment, and he knew the outcome of the forensic analysis was crucial.

"I find it hard to believe James Hopkins had anything to do with the murder," Jonny suggested as a conversation opener.

Mikeš glanced up and nodded his agreement.

Jonny continued. "He would have needed to take all afternoon off from school and follow Neil Robson and his friends around the centre. There is no way he would know what restaurant they were going to. Anyway, I'm sure the alibis will confirm he was in school. I didn't recognise any signs to suggest he was lying."

"Unless he hired someone to kill him," Mikeš offered.

"It is possible. But I can't believe he would wait over ten years for revenge. Initially, when we interviewed the others, I thought the argument between Neil and James was serious. But now it seems fairly trivial. Unless there is anything from forensics or the alibis, I think we have to move on."

Mikeš concurred reluctantly. "I agree."

"When we interview the friends again tomorrow we need to lean on them," Jonny stated.

Mikeš was confused. "Lean on them?"

"Sorry, Felix. I keep forgetting. It means to push harder on them. Especially Martin Wilson and Darren Kozma. Let's see if we can make them crack, find something we missed today."

"Yes. We will play bad cop and bad cop."

"Perfect," Jonny laughed.

"Also, the victim's wife is arriving tomorrow," Mikeš added. "After the identification of the body we should talk to her."

"Yes, it will help us with the background information."

After a brief silence, Jonny delicately changed the subject. "Ella is a very competent forensic pathologist. Lovely lady as well. You did shock me a bit, though."

"I'm sorry about that, my friend," Mikeš snorted. "The truth is she is my Achilles' heel. I have loved her from the first moment I saw her, and I always will."

The building door opened and Boukal emerged, carrying a folder of papers and a capsule with the DNA sample. He clicked open the car with his key and walked around to the driver's side.

Mikeš stepped a pace towards to Jonny and held out his hand. "Honza, I know neither of us are satisfied with our progress today; it has been frustrating. You are an excellent detective, I knew it as soon as I saw you. I have really enjoyed working with you so far."

"Thank you," Jonny replied.

They shook hands and stood facing each other, both in a sombre mood.

Mikeš suddenly beamed, inducing positive energy into the conversation as Jonny knew he liked to do. "But, tomorrow is another day! We will catch this killer, I am positive of it."

"Yes, we will," confirmed Jonny.

Boukal pushed open the passenger door. Mikeš held open the door and signalled for Jonny to get in the rear door. "Honza, we can drive you back."

"Actually, I think I'll walk," Jonny stated. "It's a beautiful evening again. How long will it take to walk back to Náměstí Míru?"

"Oh, it's not far," considered Mikeš. "Maybe forty minutes. Depends how many pubs you stop at on the way."

Jonny laughed. "Not tonight, Felix. But we'll have a party when we catch the killer."

"That's a certainty, my friend. And a Czech tradition!"

Mikeš got into the car, closed the door, and wound down his window. "Have a good walk, Honza. See you tomorrow."

"Let's rock n' roll, Marek," Mikeš boomed. The car pulled off hastily and sped down the road, Mikeš waving his arm out of the still open car window.

After checking his smartphone to confirm the route, Jonny set off energetically; his mission was to stretch his legs, clear his head and explore a new part of Prague. As age had crept up on him, he had found walking more and more satisfying, especially after a day of meetings. It certainly helped him sleep better with some tiredness in the limbs.

Although he hadn't yet researched this area of the city, he knew Žižkov afforded great views of the city, right across to the other side of the river. As he strode through the maze of similar tree-lined streets in the residential area, he caught only brief glimpses of the view. When he finally came to the main street named Seifertova, he was able to truly appreciate the elevation of these surrounding hills, the road falling away at a significant incline towards the centre. He stopped to take in the fresh new aspect of this unpretentious but grand city, balancing everyday urban life with a rich, historical heritage.

The enthralling perspective gave him the sudden urge to get higher before the sun set over the city. He knew from his guide book that Vítkov hill was on his right, hosting the National Monument, but it was both a long hike and in the wrong direction. Deciding to leave it for another day's sightseeing, he headed towards the former Žižkov Television Tower, now open to the public and a major touristic attraction, hoping to get access to the 360-degree observation level before the sun gave up for the evening.

As Jonny crossed the road and quickened his pace, he realised the temperature was dropping. He had never been one to feel the cold, and he knew his jacket and shirt would suffice. But tonight would be cold, a clear night sky without cloud cover; there could even be a spring frost.

Within a few minutes he could see the top of the Television Tower as he zigzagged through the streets. His route took him uphill, at one point walking alongside but looking down on the stadium of one of the city's football teams, FK Viktoria Žižkov. Within ten minutes he had arrived and after quickly paying his entrance fee, he took the lifts to the observatory, ninety-three metres up from ground level. He was pleased to note the lack of visitors, nearly 6pm on a Tuesday evening not being the most popular time for tourists.

Walking through the various rooms on the observatory level provided a spellbinding aerial jigsaw of the central areas of Prague. The view was carved out into a pattern of irregular rectangles of connected buildings, each with a courtyard space inside, all topped with uniform red tiled roofs. Jonny spotted many rooftop terraces protruding out over the courtyards and couldn't resist imagining one of them as the perfect spot for a retired policeman. The jewels in the Prague skyline were all visible in the fading light. The flowing nature of the city landscape, from the hills to the basin area around the river, was startling to observe, and so much more enlightening than the view of the city from ground level.

As he settled down on a seat in front of the window, watching the sun setting behind the castle, Jonny realised how fond he was becoming of Prague. His trip here was already proving to be therapeutic, helping him start to explore unresolved personal matters, from his recent retirement to the need to contact his daughter. From somewhere deep inside he also felt the irresistible sensation of the city pulling him forwards towards a new challenge and exploring his Czech heritage. The beautiful view of the sunset behind the famous skyline was only adding to this pull effect.

***

Opening the front door of the apartment, Jonny felt pleased with himself and extremely tired. The full two days of new experiences had really touched him, but now he was feeling the effects.

Many years spent in the police had kept him in shape. The daily hustle and bustle, running to and from meetings, chasing criminals with vigour, drinks in the evenings, had installed in him a level of work fitness, both physical and mental, he had simply taken for granted. Now was different; the months since his retirement had left him unfit. Mikeš had been smart enough to notice it too, demonstrating again that underneath his eccentric exterior was an astute wealth of experience.

As expected, Ivana opened the living room door, but only peered around the door cautiously. "Hi Jonny. Have you had a good day?"

"Yes, it was fun. I'm exhausted now though."

Ivana stepped into the hall tentatively, back to wearing her usual casual house clothes. "I'm sorry about this morning. I was just worried something had happened."

"It's no problem at all. I'm sorry, but I would have explained beforehand if I had known..."

Ivana interrupted, keen to explain. "Look, you can come and go as you want. This is your home for the time you are in Prague. You don't need to explain anything to me. Sometimes I can appear too forward, but I'm really only trying to help."

Jonny smiled. "You are not being too forward. I am enjoying my stay here."

"Oh, good."

"No, I mean it. I really am. I'm also really enjoying my time in Prague. This city is very special."

"That's great." Ivana looked relieved.

"Actually Ivana," Jonny continued. "I was thinking we could maybe have that drink tomorrow. I really enjoyed the Hloupý Honza last night…"

"Yes, I heard," Ivana laughed. "Jaroslav called me earlier. He was checking you were okay."

Jonny put his hand over his face in mock embarrassment. "They are really nice people."

"A drink tomorrow night would be lovely. We can finally have a good talk. But only if you are sure."

"I am sure," Jonny reassured her. "But maybe not too many questions. I'm not great at answers."

Ivana laughed. "Of course, Jonny. I'm not checking up on you."

"Okay, well, I'm off for an early night now. See you tomorrow."

"Have you had something to eat?" Ivana enquired as he walked away.

"Too many questions," he replied, winking back at her mischievously.

"Oh sorry, Jonny," Ivana blushed. "Good night."

"Good night, Ivana," Jonny called out as he climbed the stairs to the attic.

Up in his room he had a prolonged, relaxing shower to make up for the rush in the morning, and changed into his bedclothes. Sitting at the desk he checked his emails briefly, but, as expected there was nothing of interest or for action, only junk messages.

He reached for the iPod and went straight for his favourite Bob Dylan album, *Bringing It All Back Home*. The album always gave him everything he needed, the bridge between Dylan's acoustic and electric days, one side dedicated to each. It also seemed to reflect his current juncture perfectly, coming closer to understanding issues from his past whilst moving forward to the future.

As the first guitar riffs of 'Subterranean Homesick Blues' commenced, Jonny gazed out of the window onto the illuminated church clock on the Náměstí Míru square. He pondered the day's interviews and links between the friends. The nature of the murder was also peculiar. When he thought about the characters involved, he kept coming back to Martin Wilson. He seemed to Jonny to be the central character, the pivotal point of the group. The victim was perhaps the big character, the life and soul of the party, but Martin was the organiser, the confidante to the others and, importantly, the gossip.

Jonny's mobile phone bleeped and halted his train of thought. It was a message from Mikeš.

```
Ahoj Honza, its Felix. Now you have my
mobile number! See you at the station early to
morrow. Dobrou noc.
```

Jonny smiled to himself, realising his new, developing friendship with Mikeš was another reason for his good mood and his enjoyable day.

14

Early Bird

Wednesday, 17ᵗʰ March

Feeling more at home and with a strong sense of purpose, Jonny woke early, refreshed after his best night's sleep in months. He showered quickly and left the apartment promptly, before Ivana was awake. When working he always preferred to get out of the house as quickly as possible, grabbing breakfast on the way, as if he could surprise the day into revealing its secrets.

Based on his research of the Prague transport system before going to bed, Jonny took the A Metro line from Náměstí Míru to Staroměstská. The journey was only three stops from Prague 2 to Prague 1, but brought him out in the heart of Prague Old Town, Staré Město. The ticketing system was an odd concept for him, being based upon the length of travel rather than distance. He had opted for a daily ticket which allowed him to travel on any bus, tram or metro, for any length of time, during the calendar day. And all for the price of a single journey between zones on the London Underground.

Jonny's independence was essential to him and he wanted to get to the station early to demonstrate it, rather than relying on Boukal to drive him around. He had always been his own boss and he wasn't about to change now. In responding to the message from Mikeš last night, he had made it clear he would make his own way in the morning, a small but important personal privilege that he knew Mikeš would respect.

On exiting the Staroměstská station he realised he was very early, the walk to the police station being less than ten minutes. Realising he had time for breakfast, he scanned the street and chose a small, independent café, where he sat outside in the spring morning sun with a coffee and a freshly baked croissant.

Whilst he had always been self-sufficient, never needing anyone to look after him and often pushing away anyone that tried, he was not an adventurous type. Rather than seeking out new experiences, he would stick to his preferred routine; his holidays were both limited and planned for total relaxation, he always went to the same restaurants and rarely had time for casual nights out at the local. In fact his whole routine had been based around work and was referred to as 'safe and repetitive' by the few girlfriends with whom he'd had, usually brief, relationships.

By contrast, at work he had always been one step ahead, adapting police methods to embrace new scientific and technological advancements. Many people feared change, and the police force was no different, but he had never doubted himself, trusting his judgement would usually be right. As a result, he had gained a reputation for pushing boundaries and getting results.

Planning and navigating the metro system in a new city would have been natural and easy for many people. But to Jonny it was a small sign of his new-found confidence to push himself into the new life opportunities opening up to him. Everything seems to be happening for a reason, he thought. As he finished his breakfast and prepared to set off for the station, he resolved to accept the challenges of the day ahead even if they pushed him into what would normally be uncomfortable situations for him.

He arrived at the police station ten minutes before 8am. Not too early to be standing around waiting, but timely enough to make a statement he was here and ready to work the case. After considering who to ask for at the front desk, he decided on Dvořáková; she was ambitious and would make a point of arriving before the men, demonstrating her dedication and making a gender point at the same time. And he was right. After a quick phone call from the night policeman still on duty, Dvořáková arrived in reception to greet him.

"Dobrý den," Jonny said, shaking her hand.

"Hello again," Dvořáková welcomed him. "But because we now know each other, it is better if you say either 'Ahoj' or 'Brý den', a shortened version of 'Dobrý den'."

"Thanks. That's good to know."

Dvořáková organised for him to sign in as a visitor and then led him behind reception, past the interview rooms and access to the cells, and through a security door, upstairs to the main office.

"Detective Chief Inspector Mikeš isn't here yet," Dvořáková explained as they walked across the open plan office to the Incident Room.

"No problem at all. I just wanted to get here early to study the board."

Jonny took off his jacket as they entered the room, making himself at home.

"Would you like a coffee?" Dvořáková asked.

"If you are making one of your special coffees then I would definitely have one." Jonny probed cheekily.

"Sure. I was just going to make one myself. Mind you, don't tell anyone else. It's an honour only granted to visiting guests." Dvořáková smiled back, Jonny's gesture well and truly returned, before leaving the room.

Jonny had always made sure to maintain good relationships with the local sergeant, also bringing them into his plans on a case as soon as he could. He knew from his own experience they were usually overloaded, dealing with a multitude of organisational and management tasks. They appreciated early warning and clear communication, helping their planning and in turn providing focus during the important first stages of an investigation.

The best sergeants were also the next likely promotions into detective roles. Any investment of time in their development provided ample payback when the newly promoted staff wanted to work for you. Jonny always despaired at other senior detectives not willing to invest their time, and then moaning later when the new talent wasn't keen to work for them.

Jonny knew he had already impressed Dvořáková, both by arriving early in the morning and also with his insights on behavioural science the day before. Generating some credits now could pay dividends later. Because of his lack of knowledge of the Czech Police, and the likelihood Mikeš would often be too preoccupied to help, Jonny had a feeling he might need to call in support from Dvořáková at some point during the investigation.

Jonny turned his attention to the murder board, as Mikeš had called it, standing dead centre in front of it and examining the web of connections slowly, from the victim outwards. This was a task requiring silence, no distractions, allowing your mind to wander over every piece of evidence. He had often stayed late in the office for hours letting his thoughts run away with whimsical theories – daydreaming with a purpose. Following his thoughts from the previous evening, Jonny focused on Martin Wilson and why this person was the glue for the group of friends. Dvořáková returned with two mugs of coffee, handed one to Jonny, and stood next to him facing the board.

"I listened to the interview recordings last night before I left," Dvořáková stated, keen to impress. "There didn't seem to be anything obvious jumping out."

"Yes," confirmed Jonny, pleased his instinct about Dvořáková had been right. "But I am convinced there is something not quite right about this group of friends and we need to start with Martin Wilson. I think he knows more than he is telling us."

"And Marek told me there was nothing from the interview with James Hopkins."

"We need to check out his movements and talk to his alibis, but yes, I have to agree. I doubt he had anything to do with the murder. The only other possibility is that something else has happened between Neil Robson and James which we don't know about. Which leads us back to Martin Wilson." Jonny pointed at the photo of Martin on the board.

Both Jonny and Dvořáková turned on hearing a commotion coming from the main office.

"Mikeš?" asked Jonny.

"Yes. He makes a similar entrance every day."

Jonny smiled at the unfolding dramatic entrance. "You can certainly hear him before you can see him."

Right on queue Mikeš bounced into the Incident Room, hat and cane appearing to arrive before him. He was sporting his, by now familiar, tweed suit, paired with a colourful purple shirt and tie combination. "Honza! Ahoj. You're here. The early bird."

"Good morning, Felix."

"See I am learning your English sayings."

"Very good," Jonny complemented him. "But maybe I am just a good teacher."

Mikeš put his arm around Jonny and squeezed him into an embrace. "You absolutely are, my friend."

As Mikeš placed his hat and cane on a table, Boukal arrived, trailing behind his boss and breathing heavily, looking like he was still wearing the previous day's clothes.

"Ok," Mikeš bellowed, the morning fog horn. "We have the morning briefing at 8.30 so let's have a quick recap of where we are."

Boukal put his papers down, scrambled for a marker pen and stood at the board, ready to make notes.

Jonny decided to start, allowing Boukal time to recover his composure. "I have been thinking through all the possible scenarios and there still doesn't seem to be any hint of a clear motive. But all the relationships in the group seem to lead back to Martin Wilson. I would like to interview him again today."

"Agreed," endorsed Mikeš.

"Also," continued Jonny. "I want to interview Darren Kozma again. He was lying about something yesterday. Actually, maybe 'hiding something' is a better way to express it. Either way we need to dig deeper."

Mikeš turned to Dvořáková. "Lucie, can you please organise the interviews for later this morning."

"Yes, sir."

Mikeš continued to lead. "What else do we have?"

"We are still checking the CCTV around the restaurant and Old Town Square, but nothing yet," Dvořáková started. "We are also now extending the CCTV to cover the believed escape route discovered yesterday. This morning we are also sending out uniformed staff to check with residents, shops owners and restaurant staff along the route to see if they saw anyone unusual around 3pm on Monday."

"Excellent," confirmed Mikeš. "Let's hope someone saw something."

Boukal jumped in. "A team of officers searched the escape route for evidence yesterday but found nothing. Forensics are still processing the scene at the small garden, where the knife was found. This work should finish today."

"Will we be able to trace the knife?" questioned Jonny.

"I very much doubt it," answered Boukal. "These Rybička knifes are cheap and available from almost any souvenir or hardware shop. They are even available for tourists on the craft markets in central Prague."

"Almost all children used to be given such a penknife for summer camps," explained Mikeš.

Boukal continued. "The knife looked new. Whilst these knives are freely available, they are also quite distinctive. We can check with shops near Old Town Square and see if any of the shop owners remember one of the friends buying such a knife over the weekend or on Monday morning."

"Good. Have we got confirmed walking routes for Darren Kozma, Richard Weston and Gary Needham?" Jonny asked.

"Yes. They are in the folder there." Dvořáková indicated one of the folders on the table next to the board. "Richard Weston was definitely not near Old Town Square at 3pm Monday because he has a series of photos taken on his mobile phone from the observation deck near the Strahov Monastery; the times on the photos range from 2.47pm to 3.05pm. However, we are still checking the CCTV on all their stated routes and also checking with staff at the places they stopped at, mainly cafés, as well as the pub Gary Needham said he went to."

Boukal stepped in "We have now completed reviewing Neil Robson's mobile phone. As I thought, some older messages have definitely been deleted, as was the call history before the weekend. All the information is in the folder."

"And what about calls and messages made by the friends?" Jonny asked.

"I've also put them in the folder," Boukal confirmed. "There were no unusual calls or messages to Czech numbers from any of their phones and there don't appear to be any messages or call histories deleted."

"Okay, thanks, I'll have a look at them all," confirmed Jonny.

"I have good and bad news from Dr Králová," started Mikeš. "You remember Ella?" he asked Jonny.

"Of course, Felix."

"Well, the good news is that the knife is definitely our murder weapon. The blood was a match to Neil Robson. Unfortunately, there were no fingerprints or DNA on the knife."

Jonny shook his head. "The killer must have cleaned it as they walked away from the scene."

"Unless they were wearing gloves?" suggested Boukal.

"Definitely possible if it was a professional hitman," answered Jonny.

"Dr Králová has also isolated the fibres on the victim's football shirt," Mikeš continued. "Only one fibre is unaccounted for, the rest match back to the friends. This one fibre appears to be from a black sweatshirt or jumper."

"Or a hoodie?" ventured Jonny.

"I suppose it could be." Mikeš nodded.

"It is most likely Neil Robson wasn't expecting to meet the killer in the restrooms," Jonny explained. "It doesn't seem like a planned meeting. So, the killer may have dressed to hide their identity when arriving at and leaving the restaurant."

"Good point, Honza," enthused Mikeš. "I will check with Ella. Her autopsy report is available, but it is only in Czech. There was nothing in it more than she told us yesterday."

"Okay," Jonny acknowledged.

Dvořáková finished making a note on her pad. "I will give the new information about possible outfits the killer was wearing to my officers. It may help with the CCTV tracking and also when trying to jog people's memories along the escape route."

"The victim's wife, Carly Robson, is arriving this morning," Boukal reminded them. "I am arranging for her to identify the body. Afterwards I will arrange an interview here."

"Good, but go gentle," Jonny suggested. "It will be a real shock for her to have to come abroad to identify her husband's dead body. I suggest we talk to her at her hotel first. She's not under suspicion."

Boukal nodded his understanding.

"Did the other wives come with her?" added Jonny.

"I don't know yet," Boukal stated. "We were told yesterday they were flying to Prague together, but we can ask Mrs Robson later."

"Okay!" roared Mikeš, checking his pocket watch and readying to close the meeting in his usual vociferous way.

"Just one more thing," Jonny interrupted. "I would like to visit the hotel where the friends were staying. It's a habit of mine really. I'd like to see the victim's hotel room, just have a look around and see if it stirs any thoughts."

Boukal answered. "The hotel room he stayed in is not being used until further notice. The hotel management left the room untouched as soon as they heard from us. But, as I think I told you yesterday, the room had been already cleaned."

"That's fine," Jonny replied. "I'm not expecting to find anything, just to look around."

"I will organise it with the hotel," confirmed Dvořáková. "It might also be best if I accompany you on the visit because you are not officially with the police. I can also organise for you to see his belongings."

"Perfect," replied Jonny.

"Okay, show over!" hollered Mikeš again. "Let's catch this murderer."

15

Meeting the Fox

Dvořáková led Jonny downstairs to the evidence store in the basement, leaving Mikeš to run the morning briefing with his team of detectives. The basement was gloomy and dusty with no windows, the same as in every police station Jonny had ever worked in. Not only did it serve as a security measure, but also as a reminder to any officer venturing down there that they were entering the foundations of all criminal investigations – where the dirty police work was done. The stale air and nocturnal existence seemed to attract older, idiosyncratic characters who sought to serve their final years of service in isolation with minimal human contact. There'd been a time when Jonny thought it might suit him, but he couldn't stomach the thought of trading a peaceful life for the thrill of the chase, the most treasured part of the job to him.

  This basement layout was also eerily similar to every other one he had been in before. On entering the secure area using the keypad system, they arrived in the main space taken up with a comprehensive filing system along two walls, containing all the police standards handbooks one could ever need as well as extensive reference material. A corridor to one side led to more locked rooms, probably used for a multitude of purposes from study, simple quiet time or disciplinary meetings. Directly opposite the entrance door was the evidence store room.

  Pleased to see another police standard apparently the same the world over, Jonny noted the evidence store was manned like a bunker, with access only through a hatch with a sliding glass window. Next to the hatch was a locked security door with a multiple swipe access and keypad system.

"We store evidence related to open cases here, but once the case is closed we send the evidence boxes off for archive outside the city," explained Dvořáková.

"Same as in UK," confirmed Jonny. "It's amazing how the boxes build up."

As they approached the hatch, Dvořáková smiled at Jonny. "You are now about to meet one of the biggest characters in our department. He is almost an institution here."

"I had a feeling you were going to say that. Bigger even than Mikeš?"

"Similar," confirmed Dvořáková. "They started in the police department on the same day and were partners for a long time."

Through the glass window Jonny could see the profile of a rotund, silver-haired uniformed officer with a plump face and a bushy moustache. He was looking down at some papers on his desk through half eye reading glasses perched low on the bridge of his nose. Classical music could be heard playing loudly from inside the evidence room, and as they approached the hatch Jonny could see the officer was totally absorbed in the orchestral sounds.

Dvořáková stepped up to the window and tapped on the glass. The officer was initially shocked, sharply awoken from his musical daydream, but his face broke into a beaming smile when he looked up and saw her standing there.

The officer opened the sliding window. "Lucie," he exclaimed over the music, even louder now with the window open.

Dvořáková made a signal with her hand to turn down the music. The officer scampered to his side to quickly reach the volume button, issuing an apologetic "Pardon."

"Ahoj Lucie," the officer started again, the music now reduced to a manageable, background level.

"Ahoj Josef. Jak se máš?"

"Dobře," confirmed the officer, smiling.

Dvořáková turned to Jonny. "Mr Fox, can I introduce you to Mr Fox."

Jonny looked puzzled. "So, your surname is also Fox?"

"Yes," confirmed the officer, taking the glasses off his nose. "My name is Josef Liška. But please call me Josef."

Jonny laughed at the coincidence, reaching out to shake Liška's offered hand through the hatch. "Good to meet you. So 'Liška' is Czech for 'Fox'. I like that, it has a nice sound."

"Yes. The fox always makes a good policeman," Liška stated. "We are solitary animals, but good hunters."

Jonny laughed. "I've never thought about that before, but, yes, you're probably right. I'm Jonny by the way, but, as you probably know by now, everyone is calling me Honza."

"Thank you, Honza. Yes, I have been looking forward to meeting you. Felix has told me you are an excellent detective. Congratulations on finding the knife yesterday, it was an inspired piece of police work."

Jonny nodded in respect. "Thank you. But, as you know, it is always part inspiration and part luck."

"I have known Felix a long time and I trust his judgement. If he tells me someone is a great detective, it must be true. Mind you, he has some peculiarities, shall we say, and is not always easy to work with. If you ever need some guidance on Felix, or just someone to talk to, you know where I am. I think I can claim to be the expert after working with him for so long."

"Thank you," confirmed Jonny. "I really appreciate it."

Dvořáková addressed Jonny. "If you want to get anything done around here, you need to keep on Josef's good side."

"No," Liška laughed, waving away the suggestion. "It's only because I'm old enough to know where everything is. The truth is that a few years ago I opted for the quiet life, and I left the chasing of criminals to Felix. Rather than put me on the pension, they instead put me down in this foxhole to keep me out of trouble."

Liška continued as Jonny and Dvořáková laughed. "I do, however, know where most things are and will always help. The only time I ever get angry is when people try to break the rules. The regulations are there for a reason, to keep everything in order, and without control we would have a complete mess."

"Absolutely," confirmed Jonny. "I agree totally."

Dvořáková looked at both men, unshaken in her opinion. "I still think what I said is correct."

Liška gave her a wry, innocent smile, then shrugged his shoulders in acceptance and changed the subject. "Do you like music, Honza?"

"Yes," confirmed Jonny. "I love all music, especially live performances. But Bob Dylan is my hero."

"The Czech people love Bob Dylan," mused Liška. "There was a big connection from the late sixties, during the time of the Prague Spring here."

"Yes, I have read that."

"Down here in the dungeon, it is a classical paradise," Liška declared to Jonny. "Do you know many Czech composers?"

"No not really. Dvořák is the only composer I have heard of."

"Yes, Antonín Dvořák is the most famous, especially his 9th Symphony. His surname is the same as Lucie's family name."

"I am not related," confirmed Dvořáková.

"But," enthused Liška. "There are many more famous Czech composers. Bedřich Smetana is known as the 'father of Czech music' and Leoš Janáček wrote some beautiful pieces of music. There are many more, some not very well known. Come down here anytime and I'll take you through my playlist."

"I would like that. My knowledge of classical music is very limited," confessed Jonny. "Thank you."

Dvořáková cleared her throat. "Ok, back to work, boys. You can talk music later."

Liška winked at Jonny. "Lucie is a top police officer, you know. I think she will end up managing this station one day, maybe all of Prague."

"I think you could be right," agreed Jonny.

"Can we have the belongings for Neil Robson please," continued Dvořáková, smiling meekly, ignoring the attempted flattery.

"Coming up," declared Liška, lifting his heavy frame out of the chair and moving towards the shelf racks at the back of the room.

As Liška sorted through the boxes, whistling to himself, Jonny mulled over how welcoming everyone had been to him. His approach over the past few years had perhaps become too sanitised in his role as a DCI, taking people for granted and not seeing the small human things that made all the difference. He had forgotten about all the characters he had encountered when he first started in the police force, bringing humour and eccentricities with them. Slowly these characters had been forced out as the job became more process-based and focused on results. He relished this second opportunity to enjoy these type of characters, Mikeš and Liška included. Hopefully, he could use their experience and unconventional methods to help close this investigation successfully.

Liška plonked the box down on the table, with a heavy breath and, putting his reading glasses back on, filled in a form which he passed across to Dvořáková for signing. After checking the returned form for accuracy, Liška pushed the box through the hatch. "Good luck."

"Thanks, Josef," Jonny replied.

"Děkujeme," Dvořáková said, and turned away with the box in hand, keen to show her independence by carrying it herself.

Jonny followed Dvořáková down the corridor to an

empty room, opening the door for her.

"What was the word you used just now?" asked Jonny.

"'Děkujeme'? It means 'thank you from us'. I don't think you have such a word in English. The Czech language is very difficult, we have many ways to say the same things."

"I think it's a touching way to say thank you," Jonny commented.

Dvořáková put the box on the table. "I'd better go back upstairs and check everyone knows what they are doing. Will you be okay here?"

"Yes, of course," confirmed Jonny. "Before you go, can I ask if anyone else has been through the evidence?"

"Yes. Marek has reviewed the evidence and a report is in the folder upstairs. I don't think there was much to note in Neil Robson's belongings."

"Okay, thanks. See you later."

As Dvořáková left the room and closed the door, Jonny donned the plastic gloves she had left for him and opened the cardboard box. Inside, the contents were bagged: a flight cabin bag, the clothing worn the day Neil Robson was killed, and the belongings on him at the time of his death. He also took out the itemised list of the box's contents, but noting it was in Czech he put it on the table as it wasn't going to help him much. The only personal item he knew was missing was the victim's mobile phone and Boukal was still processing it.

First, he looked through the clothes and belongings found at the crime scene. He picked up the jeans, out of habit checking all the pockets which were empty. He held up the Sparta Prague football shirt and turned it over in his hands looking for the knife entry point. He smelt the shirt and looked at it closely, before shutting his eyes and trying to re-enact the scene from the restaurant in his mind. He remembered the friends sitting together when he arrived, seemingly happy and enjoying their lunch. It must have taken ten minutes for Jonny to order and be delivered his coffee, during which time nothing of note had happened to make him look over in the direction of their table. But then the heated argument, the exchange of words and the victim leaving the table. But why did Neil back down and walk off to the restrooms? If anything, he was the strong one and his friend, Martin Wilson, was weaker, more yielding and the more likely to storm off in a huff.

Going through the contents of the victim's pockets at the time of the murder revealed nothing unusual: house and car keys, a handkerchief, Czech coins, chewing gum and a brown wallet. He opened the wallet carefully and examined the contents, but again it provided limited insight: mixed Czech and UK cash notes, credit cards, gym membership card, hotel room card, a couple of paper credit card receipts from restaurants, and a family photo, presumably his wife and young children.

The flight holdall was only half full. Jonny found the passport, worn clothes from the trip, a Kindle and a wash bag with men's toiletries – he certainly travelled light. Jonny checked the external zips of the holdall, finding only a few random items, including a small padlock, spare UK coins and more chewing gum. Inside he slid his hand inside the inner pockets of the holdall, all of which were empty apart from the large zip compartment which contained a small black notebook and company branded pen.

Jonny held the notebook in his hand and turned it over. Could it have been missed when the luggage was first examined? Pulling the itemised list of contents towards him he ran his eye down the printed lines. He knew the Czech word for 'black' was 'cerný' and he was sure 'book' began with 'kni...' Ah, there it was on the list: 'Malá černá kniha'. His brief elation had been quickly crushed, soon realising it was not a revealing discovery at all.

He opened and flicked through the notebook, trying to determine the reason for keeping such a book in these days of modern technology. It appeared to be a rudimentary reminder system, the book having only one handwritten item per ruled line, approximately fifteen items per page, and any completed task was crossed through. The notebook was also relatively new, only twenty or so pages having been used; the reminders listed did not have dates but Jonny could see the diary went back only a few months because the first reminders in the book referred to Christmas. Almost all the handwritten reminders were trivial: 'Book car service', 'Phone upgrade when?', 'Birthday ideas.'

Jonny checked the list for open reminders and all seemed unimportant. He returned to the last completed page in the notebook and flicked backwards through the list of prompts. As he skimmed the pages he noticed a handful of listings he did not understand. The last such entry was 'H18-8', the previous one 'H14-2', and then 'H16-26' - all crossed through. Turning back one more page, he found another similar crossed entry, this time with a different letter of the alphabet at the front – 'B16-24'.

Concentrating hard, he sat very still, looking at the open pages, a deep furrow developing on his forehead. He knew Neil Robson was a biochemist working in a pharmaceutical company. Perhaps they just referred to something he was working on; 'H' was definitely the atomic symbol of Hydrogen, but he was less certain on 'B'. But why the date order and also, why cross them out? Perhaps they were a reminder system for some project he was working on, the codes getting replaced by new ones every few weeks or so?

Frustrated, he decided to start again at the beginning. Opening the first page of the notebook he slowly consulted each page, writing down in his own notebook each entry that either he did not understand or appeared to be in some sort of code. Once completed he had a list of fifteen unintelligible entries in date ascending order, all of which had been crossed through, indicating they had been completed, or maybe the reminder date had passed:

B15-5

B16-7
B18O-14
B16-21
B16-28
H20-2
B16-3
H19-9
B15-12
H18-16
H19O-22
B16-24
H16-26
H14-2
H18-8

Finally, he turned the black notebook over in his hand, checking inside the front and back covers and all the empty pages, keen to ensure he hadn't missed something. When he was sure there was nothing else unexplained, he closed the notebook and looked again at the list now written out in his own notebook. He slowly scanned through the list of coded entries he had copied, reading them through slowly forwards, backwards and then again in random order, looking for possible patterns.

Having looked at the list for long enough without any inspiration, Jonny decided to take the evidence box back. He carefully repacked the items as he had found them, keen to maintain high standards. Lastly, he put the itemised list of contents inside and closed the box, before carrying it out of the room and back towards the evidence room.

Liška was pleased to see him again. He turned down the classical music and opened the sliding window. "Find anything, Honza?"

"Not sure. I found a strange list of coded reminders in Neil Robson's notebook. Probably nothing, but I need to have a think about them."

"Interesting," agreed Liška.

"But everything is back in the box as I found it."

"Great. I will of course need to check it and get Lucie to countersign. Rules are rules. But can I ask you to sign here anyway to show you have returned the box."

"Sure," Jonny confirmed, taking the paper and initialling it before passing it through the hatch to Liška with the box.

"You probably don't recognise this composer," Liška stated. "It is Jan Dismas Zelenka. He was much admired by Johann Sebastian Bach. This piece is called 'Missa Votiva in E minor', one of my favourites."

Jonny listened briefly to the choral voices. "It evokes a lot of passion. I like it. It seems I have a lot to learn."

"You certainly do. Prague and the Czech Republic have a rich tapestry of historical music. There's really no need to listen to anything else."

Jonny pulled a fake, shocked face. "But there's no way I can give up my Bob Dylan!"

Both men laughed and shook hands, another friendship established.

16

Interview 2 – Martin Wilson

The following is a transcript of the recorded interview conducted with Martin Wilson (MW) on the morning of Wednesday, 17th March 2010.

Present at the interview were Chief Warrant Officer Felix Mikeš (FM), Chief Sergeant Marek Boukal (MB) and Consultant Jonathan Fox (JF). The reason for the presence of JF was explained at the beginning of the interview; he is continuing to assist the Czech Police team on this murder investigation.

MB: Interview commenced at 09:22. Please state your name for the record.
MW: Martin Wilson. I want to know why I am being interviewed again.
MB: You are not under caution. We just want to ask you some more questions to help us in our investigation into Neil Robson's murder.
MW: Are you interviewing all the others as well?
MB: We will ask to interview the others if we believe it is necessary.
JF: Is it really a problem, Martin? I thought you would want to help. After all, it was your friend who was killed.
MW: Yes, of course. But I don't like this suspicion.
JF: Who said anything about suspicion?
MW: Well, it's obvious.
JF: Is it? If we had a charge to put to you, I can assure you you'd know about it. Can we just ask you some more questions in

good faith, and you answer those questions as best you can?
[Pause]
JF: Is that okay?
MW: [inaudible]
MB: Can you please repeat that for the tape.
MW: Yes. Okay? Yes. But I want to say for the record that my argument with Neil at the restaurant table was trivial. I know it doesn't look good, but, for goodness' sake, I was still at the table when he was murdered in the toilets.
FM: Calm down, Mr Wilson. You have made your point. We just want to ask you some more questions to try and find his killer. Marek, please continue.
MB: Okay, Martin. Now yesterday you told us about your argument with Neil at the table. We would like you to talk through it in more detail so we fully understand. Nothing more. Can you start from the beginning and talk us through how it started and also what Adrian Scott did whilst the argument escalated?
MW: Ade (Adrian Scott) couldn't have had anything to do with this either. He was still at the table with me.
FM: Just answer the question. And please use Adrian's full first name.
MW: Okay. Let me think. When we were walking to the restaurant, we were talking about the cabaret on Saturday night. Neil was telling a funny story from the club. He had paid one of the girls there to give a private dance to Gary (Needham), in secret you know, and they were laughing about the shock on his face when she walked over to him and dragged him off. It was funny, Neil always did good impressions. Anyway we sat down on the restaurant terrace and I think we just talked about Prague and the trip whilst we looked at the menus and decided what to order. As lunch arrived I started to ask them for their thoughts on the next trips. I'm the born organiser, always looking forward, and was suggesting places to go for our next football trip. I was even suggesting cities to visit with the wives. I think Neil was finding it all a bit boring and

wanted to change the subject. He was often like that, more preferred the laddish jokes than serious talk. I suppose we got into a verbal jest, you know, as we ate lunch. I was trying to get some ideas out of them and he just wanted to talk about funny stuff which had happened in the club. Then he started to get angry, calling me a prude for not being interested in stuff like that. You know, he was calling me gay, saying my marriage was just a sham. I know he was just having a laugh, but Neil could be cruel and when he started he wouldn't let up. Adrian tried to deflect him, get him to talk about something else, but Neil just carried on. Then he started saying I'd wasted my life, you know, all the stuff I told you last time. It was all unnecessary, but he kept going. I tried to keep calm but lost it in the end, calling him a liar and then I mentioned the situation with Richard (Weston) and Natasha (Richard's ex-wife).

MB: Thanks. That is helpful.

JF: Is this something Neil would do often? Pick arguments with people, I mean.

MW: Not often, but probably more than most. He seemed to think he was above other people, that he was always right. Classic, spoilt only child. But he'd always apologise about it afterwards, say he was wrong to keep pushing the point.

JF: And why specifically did you bring up the subject of Richard and Natasha when you got angry?

MW: I'm not sure. Maybe it's just because it's one of the few mistakes he's made in his life.

JF: One area of your life you think you've done better than him?

MW: Yes, I suppose so.

JF: And you think it was wrong what he did?

MW: Of course it was wrong. Carly (Robson), his wife, is a lovely lady and she didn't deserve to be treated like that.

JF: But surely he can do whatever he wants to do with his life?

MW: Look, I'm not going to get into this because it's in the past. He made a mistake and he made it difficult for our group of friends for a while. It's maybe one thing I've got on him, and,

yes, I was just using it to attack him back. Okay?
JF: Is this the reason why, in your view, he stormed off?
MW: I'm not really sure. Maybe he just wanted to go to the toilet.
JF: And was there any indication he had organised to meet someone? Did he perhaps look at his watch when you were arguing?
MW: I hadn't thought about that. [Pause] No, I don't think so. Why would you meet someone in the toilets?
FM: Drugs?
MW: Look, I don't know anything about that. I've never seen Neil take any drugs. And I wouldn't want to be involved if he did.
JF: Okay. Back to Richard, do you think there is any possibility he was still holding a grudge against Neil after all this time?
MW: I can't imagine why he would want to come on a trip abroad with him five years later if there was a problem.
FM: Unless he wanted the opportunity to kill him.
MW: I cannot comment. I saw nothing indicating there was a problem.
JF: And was Neil still seeing Natasha?
MW: I don't know. Maybe ask Adrian. There were rumours she was still contacting him after Richard threw her out, but it was just a rumour and it's a long time ago now.
JF: How long? I mean, how long was she rumoured to have been contacting him?
MW: I don't remember. Maybe a few months. Not long probably.
JF: How did Neil's wife take it?
MW: I've never spoken to her about it. Adrian will know better than me.
JF: But your wife, Sophie, is a close friend of Carly Robson?
MW: Yes, but I don't know what they talk about. I only know that Carly blamed Natasha for chasing Neil.
JF: Was Neil having an affair with anyone else in the last few months?

MW: I'm the last person to hear gossip like this. Again, you should talk to Adrian. He's the only one Neil would possibly tell personal information like that to.
JF: We really appreciate you talking to us like this. It's important we explore every avenue of Neil's life. You are interesting because you are central to the group of friends.
MW: It's only because I'm the organiser.
JF: Yes, I understand, but also you are in a trusted position. Maybe people tell you things they don't tell other people in the group. Am I right?
MW: Yes, I suppose so. But not because I ask, only because they know I won't tell anyone else.
JF: This is exactly what I mean. So, my question to you is, has anyone told you anything secret in the last three months?
MW: But I would be betraying a confidence.
JF: I know, but it may lead to catching Neil's killer. We will be very sensitive.
[Pause]
JF: Please think, is there any secret you've been told recently?
MW: Well, I'm not sure it's a secret only I know.
JF: Please just explain. It might help us.
MW: It concerns Darren (Kozma).
JF: Go on.
MW: We both commute into London on the train and I see him a couple of times a week. He was often the butt of jokes at the pub because he's never really had a steady girlfriend. One evening he asked if he could meet me for a drink near Liverpool Street station in London. Anyway he decided to confess to me that he is gay. I told him I didn't think it was going to be a problem for anyone in our group. The world has changed. Years ago would have been different, but now I think most people are more accepting. I told him to tell everyone, but he wasn't so sure.
JF: When was this?
MW: In January.
JF: And has he told the others?

MW: No, not that I'm aware of.
JF: Is there something else about Darren you are not telling us?
MW: Well, it's very sensitive. [Pause] After he'd told me he was gay, I'm sure I saw him looking at Neil more. It's probably nothing, but on a few occasions it did seem he was paying Neil a lot of attention.
JF: That is very useful.
FM: Do you believe Neil knew?
MW: I don't know.
FM: Was Neil's attitude to Darren different on this trip?
MW: No, not really. They were never best friends, but they always got on well.
FM: Did Neil and Darren spend any time alone together on the trip?
MW: I don't think so. Maybe at the cabaret, I wasn't there.
FM: What time are we meeting Darren again?
MB: He is coming in at midday.
MW: Can you please be careful when you are talking to him about this. He's my friend.
MB: We will, of course. But you have to understand it could be important to our investigation.
MW: Okay.
JF: Have you been told any other secrets?
MW: No.
JF: What about arguments? In the last three months have you seen Neil arguing with anyone? Please think, any small piece of information you can remember may be useful.
[Pause]
MW: The only altercation I can remember recently was between Neil and Gary. It was down the pub one Friday, probably three weeks ago. Yes, definitely in February. They were talking inside, at the bar, and it flared up. Richard told them to take it outside, so it was over quickly.
JF: What was it about?
MW: I didn't hear anything they said when they were arguing, but Richard told me later it was about money.

JF: Did you hear anything else about it afterwards?

MW: No. As I've said a few times, that type of confrontation tended to follow Neil around. A bit like my argument with him on Monday. It was almost normal, if that makes sense. And as far as I'm aware, there was no ongoing issue between Neil and Gary afterwards. I certainly haven't heard anything about it on this trip.

JF: Any other arguments involving Neil?

[Pause]

MW: No, I can't remember any others.

JF: Okay, thanks.

FM: We need to talk to Gary again.

JF: Yes.

MB: Can I take you back to the weekend you organised here in Prague with your wives last year. Can you tell us about your schedule whilst you were here, and, in particular, did anything happen involving Neil during the weekend?

MW: Why is this relevant?

JF: Well, your friend was killed in Prague. If it wasn't one of his friends, who else did it? Might it have been something left over from the last time he was here? You must see the logic in this thinking.

MW: Yes, I suppose so. [Pause] It was quite a sedate trip really, no heavy nights. Adrian, Neil and I had planned it ourselves in secret. Well, mostly me, to treat the wives. The wives go out together once a month or so and get on well. We thought it'd be nice to take them somewhere together. We didn't tell them where we were going beforehand, only told them at the airport.

JF: Nice gesture.

MW: Yes, it was a lovely weekend. We arrived late Friday and had a drink in the hotel. Next day we went on a long, historic walk. Later we went on a boat trip on the river with a jazz band playing. That was early evening, and from there we walked to the restaurant I had booked which was overlooking the river. On Sunday we had a lazy morning and then met for lunch. We had some free time after lunch, but only about an hour, and then met back at the hotel for the taxi back to the airport. Obviously we weren't together all the time. We split up into couples and people went together if they wanted to particularly visit something, but most of the time we were sitting down together at a café or lunch, and obviously dinner in the evening.

JF: And did anything unexpected happen? Please think, any small detail could be vital.

MW: Sorry, I don't remember anything unexpected, not just about Neil, I mean anyone. I remember being pleased with myself the plan worked out so well and everyone enjoyed themselves.

JF: There were no arguments at all?

MW: Not that I remember, no.

MB: That seems all for now. Please think back over the things we have talked about. I'm sure you can understand, we are looking for anything unusual or unexpected, however small, that may have happened.

MW: I will. But I still can't see any of his friends doing this. He was an idiot at times, but it doesn't make sense why one of us would want to do this, especially abroad. It must have been a random attack.

JF: Just one more thing, do you recognise these codes?

FM: What are they?

JF: Sorry, I haven't had time to brief you. I'll tell you afterwards.

MB: For the record, Mr Fox is now showing Mr Martin Wilson a series of letters and numbers which have been copied from the victim's notebook.

[Pause]

MW: Sorry, no. Do you know what they relate to?

JF: No, not at the moment.

MB: Okay, thank you. Interview terminated at 10:08.

17

Discovering Links

The Incident Room was strangely quiet, Jonny and Boukal providing the focal point as they sat close together in front of the murder board, flicking through the pages of separate folders. Only Mikeš broke the unending silence, shuffling in his seat out of boredom, crossing his legs and breaking the calm by humming an unrecognisable tune.

In Jonny's experience the vital breakthroughs in an investigation were often only discovered through meticulous paperwork. The key links were found by cross-referencing bank statements, mobile phone records, or even love letters, to uncover seemingly normal, although in fact irregular, behaviours that could relate back to another activity. Every criminal made mistakes. Jonny was patient, often called pedantic in the past by former colleagues who struggled to comprehend his methods. But he didn't care what they called him, his painstaking approach worked and discovering links was his forte.

Whilst Mikeš had a proven track record, and was clearly highly respected, his methods seemed almost the complete opposite. Boukal had mostly likely been right. Mikeš had probably acted differently when he was a tenacious young detective, but now he sometimes seemed like a distracted conductor, unable to keep his attention on one section of the orchestra for longer than the opening sonata of a symphony.

"So, what are thinking?" Mikeš finally relented, unable

to contain himself any longer. "Motive, I mean. It must be love or money."

Jonny took his time to look up and answer, careful to finish analysing the page and mark his place. "I agree it could be either of those. What is clear is that the killer has covered their tracks well. But we need to keep an open mind and not to jump to conclusions. We still don't have any evidence of whether it is a professional kill or someone the victim knew. The clues we need are going to be within all this detail somewhere." He wafted his arm over the folders and the information on the board.

"It's certainly not looking like we're going to solve this case easily," Mikeš stated, sighing loudly. "The killer has been clever."

"Patience, Felix, patience," Jonny smiled reassuringly. "We will get there."

"You are right, Honza. The trouble is, I'm not very patient."

Jonny smiled sympathetically, appreciating the self-effacing honesty. Despite his slightly annoying impulses, Mikeš was still a breath of fresh air, such an improvement on the many egotistical senior detectives he'd had to work closely with over the years.

"I had a case not dissimilar to this about ten years ago," Jonny explained. "There were three couples, all married with children, and everything on the surface appeared happy. My first reaction was love: the couples were very close, had known each other for a long time, even going on holiday together. I thought there must be some undetected love triangle. But I found nothing. Next I moved on to money: each couple had achieved different levels of financial standing, and one of the men had recently been made redundant, borrowing some money from another couple. Again, I found nothing. In the end, it was pure jealousy. One of the women was murdered because of a long-standing envy, unresolved and still growing since university days. Pure jealousy is very hard to detect if the killer can keep their normal reactions under control, and in this case they had been doing it for nearly twenty years so had a lot of practice. In the end, the killer just couldn't take it anymore and something snapped inside their head."

Boukal had stopped checking the pages of information in his folder and was now captivated by Jonny's case recount. "So how did you catch the killer?"

"Well, it was certainly one of my most inventive trappings," Jonny pronounced. "The victim's body was available to view in an open casket in the days before the funeral, for people to pay their respects. With consent from the husband, I organised for a small video camera to be placed in the flower arrangement on top of the casket. The killer, a supposed friend of almost twenty years, visited her and confessed everything on film, spitting out venom at the victim as she lay dead in the open casket. She couldn't resist the last opportunity to recount all the things she felt the deceased had been done wrongly to her and tell her she deserved to die. The tape was inadmissible in court, of course, but we had enough to lead us to the answers and we were able to gather sufficient evidence to convict her."

"Wow, that's ingenious," remarked Boukal.

"Bravo," echoed Mikeš. "Honza, I think in young Marek you have a potential pupil. I have brought him into as many situations as I can, and he is learning a lot, but he could also learn much from your vast experience. Would you be a second mentor to him, teach him about your experience in the UK?"

Jonny smiled at Boukal. "It would be my pleasure. Once we solve this case we can plan some time together."

"Thank you," Boukal replied, looking delighted with the result.

Mikeš suddenly burst into voice. "Katka, my saviour!"

Jonny turned to see Dvořáková approaching the room. Katka trailed behind her, pushing a trolley with morning coffee and biscuits.

"We used to have a morning tea trolley in the UK, but it

was a long time ago now," remembered Jonny.

"It's still a tradition here and Katka is one of my heroines," Mikeš stated. "I think she's the only person who's been here longer than me. Actually she's been here so long we don't know how old she is."

Mikeš opened the door and Katka greeted her bosses with "Ahoj," placing the refreshments on the table. She turned to Jonny and addressed him directly. "Ahoj, Honza."

Mikeš laughed. "My friend, if Katka knows your name, you are definitely, how do you say, part of the furniture."

"Looks like it," agreed Jonny, chuckling to himself.

Katka exited the room to choruses of "Děkuju," with a smile and a departing wave.

As Dvořáková handed out the cups of coffee, Mikeš restored the focus. "So Honza, what were the codes you mentioned in the interview?"

"To tell you the truth, I'm not sure yet. They may turn out to be nothing important. Neil Robson's notebook contained a list of handwritten reminders, which he had crossed through when they were completed. Most of the other tasks in the notebook were easy to understand, but there was a list of fifteen cryptic codes, noted since December, spread out over the three-month period. The codes don't make any sense, but I have a feeling there is a pattern to them."

"Marek, did you spot them?" asked Mikeš.

Boukal looked hesitant. "Yes, but it wasn't clear they had anything to do with the investigation."

"Marek is probably right," Jonny immediately diffused any sign of blame. "I just spotted them in the notebook and wanted to keep them in mind. Just in case something else pops up to link to them."

"Well, Marek, write them up on the board so we are all aware of them," instructed Mikeš. "It's important to record everything we find regardless of whether it appears to be relevant or not at this stage."

As Boukal jumped to the order and wrote up the codes,

Jonny explained his rationale. "The codes each have one letter in them, either a capital 'B' or 'H' at the start, followed by numbers. Two of the codes have an 'O' inserted in the middle; definitely not a 'zero'. They could be something to do with his work. But if they were written to conceal something then cracking the code could help the investigation."

Boukal finished writing up the codes from Jonny's notebook and stood back to review the list. "I assumed they were maybe the victim's method to remember his passwords or security key codes at work. I know I struggle. It's hard to remember them all, so I make cryptic notes to remind myself."

"Could be," agreed Jonny. "I was just now reviewing the calls and messages to and from Neil's phone whilst he was in Prague. One thing I spotted was that the messages sent and received by him over the past few days were all to men apart from his wife and someone called Heather Davis. The messages to her did not reveal anything particular; they were about work, but were also slightly flirtatious. But it did make me think of the 'H' in the codes. I'll complete the check and maybe give her a call later to confirm how she knows him."

"Back to Martin Wilson," Mikeš said, checking the time on his pocket watch. "He seemed much more genuine today. He is obviously upset he is under suspicion, but I felt he was mostly telling the truth."

Jonny nodded. "Yes, I agree. We pushed him quite hard and now we have two leads to follow up. We have an interview with Darren Kozma next, but what about Gary Needham?"

"We are organising a follow-up interview with Gary for this afternoon," confirmed Boukal.

"The thing I don't understand about Martin is why he was so angry today," Jonny offered. "He is an intelligent man and must understand we need to ask the questions. He fought back at the start and then folded easily, giving us the information we wanted. Slightly odd behaviour. I detected fear on his face a few times when we put pressure on him. Perhaps he is just worried he is going to get the blame from the wives for what has happened. He did organise the trip after all. But, yes, I do believe he was telling the truth."

"Lucie, is there any progress on Darren's movements on Monday afternoon?" enquired Mikeš.

"We are still checking, but nothing at the moment," summarised Dvořáková. "The route he said he took was mainly small streets in the old town and the CCTV coverage there is not extensive. We have checked at the café and fast food restaurant he told us he stopped at, but unfortunately they don't have CCTV and nobody there remembers him from his photo."

"Let's see what he has to say about it when we challenge him," Jonny concluded. "There was definitely something he was hiding in the first interview. Hopefully we've now found what it is and he'll open up when we test him. If we don't find an alibi for him, I might go and walk the route myself, to see if it's possible to get from The Lennon Wall to the restaurant, and then back to the hotel, in the time available."

Mikeš snorted. "You love your hunting, don't you, Honza!"

"It takes extra time and effort, but I would always recommend it. When you walk the street, following the actual routes taken, it sharpens your instinct and helps get inside the mind of the person you are tracking."

"You sound like another 'Fox' I worked with." exclaimed Mikeš.

Jonny laughed. "Yes, I met Josef earlier. You must have made quite a team."

"Yes, yes," mused Mikeš, clapping his hands together in excited memory. "Those were the days – the Black Cat and the Fox."

Sensing Mikeš slipping into reminiscing about his detective past, Jonny picked up the folder ready to restart the dig for connections. "Back to the grindstone, I think. Marek and I will check all these phone calls and messages thoroughly."

"Is there anything else you want me to do?" asked

Dvořáková.

"Not right now," Jonny confirmed. "Depending on what we find, we might need to submit information requests to the UK Police, or even seek orders to check their mobile phone signals whilst they were in this country. It may be the only way we'll definitely know where they all were on Monday afternoon."

18

Interview 2 – Darren Kozma

The following is a transcript of the recorded interview conducted with Darren Kozma (DK) on the morning of Wednesday, 17th March 2010.

    Present at the interview were Chief Warrant Officer Felix Mikeš (FM), Chief Sergeant Marek Boukal (MB) and Consultant Jonathan Fox (JF). The reason for the presence of JF was explained at the beginning of the interview; he is continuing to assist the Czech Police team on this murder investigation.

MB: Interview commenced at 11:07. Please state your name for the record.
DK: Darren Kozma.
MB: Thank you for coming in again. We just want to ask you more questions to help us in our investigation.
DK: Okay.
MB: Firstly, I'd like to go through some practical points. Let's start with the route you took after leaving Richard (Weston) and Gary (Needham) on Monday afternoon. We have the route here, put together by Sergeant Dvořáková based upon the information you gave her.
DK: I'm sorry, but I couldn't remember exactly which small streets I walked down in the old town, but it's approximately right. Also, the timings are estimated because I wasn't checking my watch all the time.
MB: Sure, I understand. But, according to the route you were at The Lennon Wall at 14:22.

DK: Yes, I took a photo on my phone at this time. I showed it to the sergeant.
MB: And you stayed there for about twenty minutes?
DK: Yes. I took the photo in the middle of the stay, so I probably left at 2:30pm (14:30).
JF: Can you explain what was happening at the wall?
DK: Not a lot. It was Monday, so less busy after the weekend. We all walked there on Saturday and it was much busier then. There were a few couples writing on the wall, some Japanese tourists as well. Also, there was a busker playing Beatles songs.
MB: And from there you walked back to Charles Bridge and crossed back to the other side?
DK: Yes. After crossing the bridge I turned right and walked alongside the road next to the river for about fifty metres. Then I crossed the road and went down a narrow, cobbled street back into the old town. From there I walked through the narrow streets, roughly as I've indicated, and I remember coming to The Bethlehem Chapel.
FM: On Bethlémská Náměstí?
DK: Yes. I remember getting slightly confused on the circular road. But it finally led through to the small square.
MB: And you said you had a coffee at the Chapel Café?
DK: Yes.
MB: But we've checked with the people there and they don't remember you.
DK: Well it was quite busy. I just had a quick coffee on my own.
MB: And the time was in the range 3-3:15pm (15:00-15:15)?
DK: I think so.
MB: Is that when you sent your message to Neil Robson?
DK: Yes, I think so.
MB: The message saying, and I quote - 'Wished I'd come for lunch with you!"
DK: Yes.
JF: Why did you send the message?
DK: I was getting hungry.
JF: But why to Neil?

DK: Why not? I was closer to him than the other guys.
JF: And he didn't reply?
DK: No. But I now know he... well...
[Pause]
MB: And after leaving the Chapel Café you walked slowly around the streets, towards Národní?
DK: Yes, our hotel is on the other side of Národní, towards Wenceslas Square, so I was walking in that direction. I was walking slowly, killing time I suppose. I stopped to look in a few shops, but didn't buy anything. I bought a takeaway baguette just off Národní and ate it as I walked back to the hotel.
MB: We've checked with the fast food place and they don't remember you, either.
DK: Well, I was there for probably less than thirty seconds. I'm not surprised they don't remember me.
MB: And at the moment we haven't been able to pick you up on CCTV on the route you've given.
DK: That's not my fault. I know I might have got one or two streets wrong, but I've definitely given you the right information.
JF: Darren, the problem we have is that we know you've not been totally upfront and honest with us. And now some of us are starting to doubt the accuracy of some of the other information you've given us.
[Pause]
JF: Do you understand what I am saying?
DK: No.
JF: Okay, let's start again. What was the nature of your relationship with Neil?
DK: He was my friend.
JF: Nothing more?
[Pause]
DK: Martin (Wilson) has been talking to you, hasn't he?
JF: Look, it is in everyone's best interests you tell us everything. Then we can quickly eliminate you from our enquiries and move on to finding out who committed this horrible

crime. Isn't it what we all want?

DK: Of course. But it's a private matter.

JF: I appreciate the sensitivity and we are not pressing you. I am just asking you to tell us the whole truth to help the investigation. When we first properly talked to you yesterday, it was clear to me you were hiding something.

DK: What do you mean?

JF: When you were talking yesterday your body language was very defensive. Guarded I would say, implying there was something you didn't want to talk about. Your arms were crossed most of the time and you were looking down when talking. Also, occasionally you were biting your lip which is a sign of underlying anxiety.

[Long pause]

DK: Okay. But will what I tell you remain confidential?

JF: If it has nothing to do with the case, yes of course. But I can't promise it if it turns out to be relevant to how Neil got murdered.

DK: I don't understand what is happening here.

JF: I think it is better if you just tell us everything. I give you my word we will not tell anyone else without talking to you first.

DK: But you are probably not even in an official capacity with the Czech Police.

JF: Felix?

FM: I promise, as the equivalent of a Detective Chief Inspector on the case.

[Long pause]

DK: It is complicated. I've always been very secretive about my personal life because people are so quick to judge, and they can be cruel. I just want to live a normal life, enjoy time with my friends and family.

JF: I understand.

DK: For a long time I thought I was bisexual. From university I had girlfriends, none of which lasted long, but I also felt a secret attraction to men. It's been okay to live with it up to now because I've just been a single guy, my excuse being that I just haven't found the right woman yet. It's growing more difficult now because people see me at thirty-five and keep asking me if I want to settle down and get married. Sometimes it becomes a difficult conversation to stop. People are trying to set me up on dates with their single girlfriends.

JF: I can imagine. Did any of your friends guess?

DK: I don't think so. Only Martin knows because I told him a few months ago, but you know it anyway. I'm no different to any other guy. I like beer, football and lads talk. Normal stuff. I've even brought girlfriends to the pub before.

JF: I don't want to pry, but has anything else changed? You said you were getting pressure about not getting married. But is there anything else?

DK: No. But I want to get it out in the open. I want people, my friends, to know me for who I am.

JF: Honesty is always the best route and people appreciate it. When this is all done, I would encourage you to tell everyone. You might lose a few people along the way, but they're probably not the right friends for you anyway.

DK: I know.

JF: But I have to ask this. Is there any other connection between what you have told us and Neil?

DK: How do you mean?

JF: Well, you must be able to see why I need to ask. You have a burning secret, Neil gets killed whilst on a friend's trip abroad and you have no alibi. Well, not yet, anyway.

DK: I don't like your insinuation. I wouldn't kill Neil. He was always nice to me. We would talk a lot when we met down the pub. He was generous and kind, he even paid some of Gary's costs for this trip.

JF: And did you ever see Neil outside of the pub?

DK: You can meet people wherever you want, it's not a crime.

JF: Please just answer the question. Did you ever see Neil outside of the pub?

DK: Not much. A few times down the town, I suppose. If we

did bump into each other he'd always invite me for a coffee. He was a kind person.

JF: What did you talk to Neil about on this trip? Did he tell you anything important?

DK: It was just normal stuff. He was fun, always having a laugh. We got on well.

JF: And did you speak to the others the same?

DK: We all got on well. But I suppose I'd always talk to Neil more because we shared the same sense of humour.

JF: I appreciate this is delicate situation, but you are not really telling us much.

DK: I don't know what to say. I really don't think anything unusual happened or was said on the trip.

FM: Yet your friend is dead.

DK: I know. But we all think it must have been a random attack.

JF: But it wasn't a mugging. His wallet and belongings were not taken.

[Pause]

JF: Going back to the cabaret on Saturday night, did anything unusual happen? Think hard.

DK: I don't remember anything unusual. Neil was quite drunk but apart from being loud he was okay.

JF: He didn't get into an argument with anyone?

DK: No.

JF: Did he take any drugs that evening?

DK: I didn't see any.

JF: Have you ever seen him taking drugs?

DK: On a few of the trips we've bought some weed and shared it, but not for a while now. Neil and Adrian (Scott) were always the drivers if we ever did buy any, but they've not been interested in recent trips. Maybe it's because both of them have settled down.

JF: And a delicate question, again, I'm sorry. Why did you decide to go to the cabaret?

DK: Why wouldn't I go along?

JF: I'm asking why you decided to go to the cabaret.
DK: It's not a crime. I've been before. I always thought it was funny.
JF: Did you want to go because Neil was going?
DK: Look, four of us went. Richard and Gary were as involved as me.
JF: You haven't really answered the question.
DK: I went because I wanted to.
JF: Okay, let's change the subject. If Neil spoke to you a lot, did he tell you in recent months if he was having an affair?
DK: No, I don't think he would tell me this type of information.
JF: Did Neil, Adrian and Martin talk much about the romantic weekend they had with their wives here last year?
DK: There was some mention of it, but it was all positive.
JF: Nobody mentioned any trouble Neil got into whilst on that trip?
DK: No, I don't remember any.
JF: And you cannot think of any reason why someone would want to hurt him?
DK: Sorry, no.
JF: Final thing, do you recognise these codes?
MB: For the record, Mr Fox is now showing Mr Darren Kozma a series of letters and numbers which have been copied from the victim's notebook.
DK: No. What are they?
JF: It doesn't matter for now.
[Pause]
MB: Thank you. Please try to remember if anything unusual happened on the trip. Even the smallest thing might help us, even if you didn't witness it yourself. Interview terminated at 11:42.

19

A Confession to Complete Strangers

The Lennon Wall was busy with tourists, but with an air of calm and humility. Secreted under the soaring trees, acting the part of nature's sentries, the wall was a blaze of graffiti colour and candles burning in respect. Jonny had already stood at this famous tourist spot in Malá Strana during his short stay, it being high on his list of places to visit in Prague. But this return visit felt just as profound. If he lived in the city, he imagined he would visit the wall regularly, a shrine of sorts, with its unwavering support of peaceful actions and free speech.

Taking a few moments rest before his task in hand, Jonny took time to re-read the plaques describing the history of the living monument. He closed his eyes and tried to evoke the energy and dreams of the suppressed youth who created the wall back in the 1980s, ultimately a key symbol towards the Velvet Revolution in 1989. John Lennon had long been a symbol of world peace from his actions, demonstrating and protesting for people to follow. He had become a hero to many more after his death, inspiring people to storm the wall and rewrite the graffiti. Initial anti-communism slogans quickly progressed to ones of hope and peace, continued attempts by the police to whitewash the walls failing miserably. It was a small, ongoing war, but the people had won.

Jonny stepped back to take in the expanse of the wall and the combined scream of youthful colour, as representative today of its intended symbolism as ever in its near thirty-year history. He was shaken from his reflections by two young, female Japanese tourists standing close, smiling at him infectiously. Laden down with backpacks, maps and guide books, the young ladies appeared more kitted out for a mountain hike than a city tour.

"Excuse me, sir, can you please take photo?" asked one in broken English, using her hand to indicate a profile of them and then pointing towards the wall behind.

"Of course," responded Jonny.

He stood holding the mobile phone they had given him, and waited for them to take off their baggage and arrange themselves in a suitable pose. Their youthful exuberance was so fresh. He so admired their burning desire to travel halfway around the world on a sightseeing trip. Here he was, well into his middle years, and only now was he exploring a new city. He'd never had the urge before, choosing instead the traditional route of career and family. But standing there, playing a bit part in their adventure, he couldn't help wonder what route he would choose if he was eighteen again, especially given the wealth of options now available to the young.

"Ok, smile," shouted Jonny as he snapped away. He took a number of exposures to hopefully compensate for his inability, proved frequently over the years, to take a good photo.

The young ladies huddled together around the phone when he handed it back. They seemed pleased, laughing together as they flicked through the camera gallery.

"I hope they are ok," Jonny started to explain. "Sorry, I am not very good."

"No, no, thank you," the ladies said excitedly, almost in unison. "Can we have a selfie with you?"

"Me?" Jonny looked startled.

Before he knew it, the young ladies had bunched around him, one either side, trying to squash all of them into the shot. With shouts of "Cheese!" and excited laughter, he found himself immortalised in the photo collection from the European leg of their tour.

"Do you live here?" asked the bolder lady, shyly.

Jonny stopped, momentarily stumped by the question. After a brief pause, all he could muster was, "I wish I did."

He smiled at them and watched as they put their touring armour back on. They bowed to him in respect and skipped away, happy at the interaction, towards the busker singing 'Imagine' for the crowds.

Rooted to the spot after the chance meeting, confused by his subconscious confession to complete strangers, Jonny watched the young ladies with a sense of awe. They first circled the busker, dropping some coins in his hat. Pushing their way forward into the small crowd, they stood together, arms around each other, moving to the music seemingly without a care in the world.

Jonny was technically also on holiday. However, the events of the last two days had pulled him into resolving a murder. It was a sobering responsibility and the thought snapped him into action. He looked at his watch, mentally synchronising it to 2.26pm, mid-point between the timestamp on the photo taken by Darren Kozma and the time he said he'd left the wall on Monday afternoon. Jonny again checked the map application on his smartphone to memorise the shortest route and directions. Time to test if Darren could have murdered Neil Robson. Was there enough time for him to get from the wall to the restaurant by 3pm, commit murder, and then return to the hotel before 4pm?

Declining the offer of sandwiches in the office, Jonny had left the police station with Mikeš and Boukal but parted company with them almost immediately. Mikeš and Boukal were scheduled to meet the deceased's wife for the body identification. Never keen on dead bodies, Jonny instead wanted to use the available time productively, as well as get some fresh air after being stuck in interview rooms almost all morning. He had already decided to test Darren's claim the only way he knew how: by physically imitating the steps he would have had to take in order to be in the frame for murder, only this time against the clock.

The butterflies in his stomach reminded him how this type of task had been his first love on the job: tangible action, usually on foot, to track down the criminal. From his first job in uniform, he had always looked forward to being drafted onto a team searching for missing evidence or persons, retracing the known steps and elaborating on them by thinking ahead. Desk work was for others, this was real police work. As he had followed the promotion path, he had found it more difficult to stay involved in field work, often leaving him feeling frustrated. To compensate, he had developed the habit of undertaking such hunts on his own. Or rather, just him and the shadow of the killer.

As Jonny stepped out, heading back in the direction of Charles Bridge at a swift pace, he smiled to himself recounting Josef's reference to their shared surname. *Ha, Mr Fox the killer catcher!* Having always been so engrossed in the job, it was slightly disconcerting to him how it had taken a visit to another country and a chance meeting with another, almost retired, policeman to point out the link. He seemed to be learning so much about himself on this trip, as if a sort of unconscious homecoming was stirring reflection and analysis on a level he had never experienced before.

Feeling good for whatever was happening to him, his soul more alive than he remembered, Jonny strode away from the wall. The first landmark to cross was the Water Wheel Bridge spanning the Čertovka stream flowing from River Vltava. The narrow streets took him past the John Lennon Pub and up the steps from the side street, to join the bridge road.

But this task allowed no time to dwell and enjoy the delightful views. Instead, he snaked across the bridge as fast as he could, between art stalls where artists were offering live drawing sessions, a jazz band in full swing and the usual throng of mid-week tourists. It amazed him how many sightseers there were and they all shared the ability to dawdle, stop and change direction without any signal. Once over the bridge, he turned right to follow the river, as Darren had intimated, but then crossed the main road before disappearing into the old town's side streets. Trusting his instincts rather than following Darren's given route, Jonny headed down a narrow, cobbled street in the direction of Old Town Square, being careful to avoid visible CCTV cameras.

Darren had started to open up in the second interview, his body language less tense. Jonny knew though that the interview had only really confirmed what Martin had already told them, not provided any real insight into the relationship Darren had, or wanted, with Neil Robson. Darren had also used distancing language when answering key questions, indicating he was probably still not telling the whole truth. Jonny's conjecture was that Darren had been in love with Neil, but it was only a potential lead. The real question was what had happened between them and was it enough to push the spurned, desperate party into some form of jealous revenge.

By snaking his way through the old streets, he managed to meet the busy street called Melantrichova, joining the bottom of Wenceslas Square with the alley entering Old Town Square, opposite the astronomical clock. However, rather than joining the thoroughfare heading towards Old Town Square, he crossed straight over the street, following the maze of narrow, cobbled streets with the aim of entering the square from the far corner. Hitting a dead end, he doubled back. Taking another street, he eventually found an alley that brought him to his intended corner, under the watchful gaze of the Gothic church, and with the restaurant visible less than 100 metres away. Walking quickly across the pedestrian street meeting the square, Jonny approached the restaurant along the walkway under the arches. He checked his watch, 2.42pm. So Darren could definitely have made the journey in time, with plenty of time left to find the right restaurant, stake out Neil and follow him to the restrooms when the opportune moment arrived.

Jonny consulted his smartphone again, checking the route from the restaurant back to the hotel. Even allowing for a tortuous escape route behind the Gothic church, heading initially in the wrong direction and then having to weave back along the small streets to avoid CCTV, the walk would only take twenty minutes at normal walking pace. The knife could have been purchased beforehand, even in the days before, and the time available would have allowed for the purchase of a hoodie, discarding it on route back to the hotel. Jonny knew he had a potential suspect. The key now was to establish the motivation. What had happened between Neil and Darren over the weekend?

Checking his watch, he estimated he still had at least thirty minutes before Mikeš called him to arrange the rendezvous before walking to the hotel to talk to Carly Robson. Taking a back street called Železná, away from the square, he found an expresso bar and ordered a coffee and baguette. Keen to fill the time proactively, he opened his notebook and reviewed the outstanding points. The codes were still a mystery, perhaps just an innocent personal code, but he needed to push the boundaries and at least try to unravel them. The conversation with Carly would maybe enlighten them, but he knew they needed to tread carefully. To try and get ahead of the game, he decided there and then to call Heather Davis, the only female, based on the messages on Neil's mobile phone, to have communicated with him whilst he was in Prague.

Dialling the number whilst sipping his coffee, the irony wasn't lost on him that he was in a foreign capital city, investigating the death of a British person and calling back home to conduct background checks.

"Hello."

"Hello, is this Heather Davis?"

"Yes. Who is speaking?"

"My name is Jonathan Fox. I am a consultant with the Czech Police. Have you heard the news about Neil Robson?"

"Yes, it's terrible. We were told yesterday. I think a family friend, Sophie Wilson, called the office to let us know. Everyone is in shock."

"Do you mind if I ask you a few questions?"

"Of course."

"How did you know Neil?"

"We were work colleagues. I am a Marketing Manager. We worked together a lot on new product and campaign developments."

"I see. And do you know the family? His wife, Carly?"

"We have met a few times. On work parties, dinners, that type of thing."

"Can I ask why Neil and you were sending messages to each other over the weekend? He was on holiday with friends in Prague."

"No real reason. We just got on well together. Neil was always laughing and joking."

"And flirting?"

"Yes, I suppose so. Innocent fun. Neil was a good laugh."

"But you were the only female he shared messages with whilst he was away. The rest of the messages were to his male friends."

"I'm sorry, I can't explain that. He sent me a message and I responded."

"I'm sorry to ask this, but was there more between you and Neil?"

"What do you mean?"

"Were you in a relationship of some sort with Neil?"

"Look, I don't see how this question can have anything to do with your investigation. I've been in the UK all the time he was away."

"This is a confidential phone call. I will not tell anyone else. It's important because it might just help us solve part of this murder investigation."

"How?"

"I'm sorry, I cannot say."

"Neil was a good friend of mine."

"Is that it?"

"I'm sorry, I don't see the relevance of this. I need to go

now."

"Hang on, please. Can I just ask one more question? Did Neil say anything to you about his trip to Prague? Maybe he was meeting someone, or he had a problem from his last visit here? Is there anything at all you can remember him saying?"

"I'm sorry, he never mentioned anything to me. I really have to go now."

"Okay, thank you for your time."

"Bye."

Jonny slowly finished his lunch, mulling over the conversation. Whilst he couldn't prove it, he knew there was a high probability Neil Robson had some sort of relationship with Heather Davis. They worked closely together so had opportunity, plus Neil had history with his supposedly one-off night with Richard Weston's wife. Probably not the first time either; Jonny knew the type.

Leaving the coffee bar, he strolled back towards Old Town Square, stopping outside an old fashioned souvenir shop, the attractive frontage drawing him in. So far he hadn't bought any souvenirs, but he knew he still had plenty of time left on his trip. He walked around the shop, half interested, when he saw a Rybička penknife. It was the same as used in the murder, for sale in a small, presentation boxset. The blade was half open, sitting amongst the silky material, presenting the engraving of 'Praha' on the near side. He didn't need the knife, but wanted it on him to know how it felt in the hand, to understand its mechanism, ease of opening and closing, anything to jolt his understanding of how this crime happened.

The shop was busy and Jonny had to wait to be served. Holding the box, he idly scanned the cheap merchandise and confectionary crowded around the till for last minute purchases. His gaze fell on the postcards: two tall racks of varied cards, ranging from photos of Prague a century ago to beautiful views across Charles Bridge in snow. Remembering what Mikeš had wisely advised him, he flicked the cards and, unable to decide, chose a postcard showing a selection of views from across the city. He had no idea how he was going to describe to his daughter in such few words what had driven him to come here, but he knew he needed to make contact. Mikeš had shown him how easy it was to form new relationships, and now he needed to be brave, not worry about rejection, and try to re-establish his most important relationship in the world.

20

The Inner Circle

Mikeš was waiting under the Powder Tower, looking resplendent in his tweed suit, hat and cane. As Jonny approached, out of the shadows of the historic buildings, he was able to study Mikeš undetected. The elegant stance and warm, open expression, were attracting curious looks from passers-by. Topped with the slightly nervous tapping of his cane, Mikeš resembled a coiled spring ready to burst into life. Jonny smiled to himself, recognising how much warmth he already felt for this man, a natural return for the affinity he had been shown during his welcome. Clearly the relationship was a two-way street, with Mikeš gaining from Jonny's expertise on the investigation, but on balance he felt he was getting more than his fair share from the association.

When Mikeš finally spotted Jonny weaving through the crowd, his face curved into a beaming smile. Before Jonny could even greet him, Mikeš was straight into tour operator mode, his cane raised loftily in honour of the tower behind him. "Honza, welcome to my favourite spot in this city of mine. This tower was one of the thirteen original gates to the original Prague Old Town. Built in the 1400s, it was used to store gunpowder in the 17th century, hence its name – the Powder Tower. I have always thought about it as a great-grandfather, looking over us all, keeping us safe."

Jonny stood and looked up at the imposing Gothic tower. The walls above the arch appeared from distance to be embroidered on the stone, the carvings were so intricate, leading up to the slate roof spire. "It's magnificent," he agreed.

Mikeš nodded in appreciation. "It's a privilege to work every day amongst such history."

After a brief moment of respect, Mikeš put his arm around Jonny's shoulders and led him away. "So, tell me, what did the fox find?"

Jonny smiled at his friend. "Well, Darren Kozma could definitely have done it. He had plenty of time to walk from the Lennon Wall to the restaurant, I timed it."

"I could have told you that," Mikeš chuckled. "Remember, Honza, I know this city like the back of my hand."

Undeterred, Jonny pulled the penknife boxset out of his pocket. "Look what I bought along the route."

Mikeš looked down at the Rybička. "I hope you bought something for your daughter as well."

Jonny smiled knowingly and pulled the postcard out his jacket pocket.

Mikeš slapped him on the back. "I'm glad, my friend. Say hello from me when you write to her."

As they walked to the hotel where the wives were staying, Mikeš briefed Jonny on the body identification. Naturally, Carly Robson had been distraught, needing the support of her close friend, Sophie Wilson. The ladies, also including Lizzie Scott, had arrived in Prague late morning. Carly had not wanted to stay in the same hotel her late husband had been staying, so Adrian Scott and Martin Wilson were changing hotels to stay with their wives. The three other friends were remaining at the other hotel. Mikeš informed Jonny of the bubbling resentment from Carly and Sophie about, in their opinion, the excessive interviewing of Neil Robson's friends when, again, in their view, it seemed to obviously have been a random, mindless attack.

On entering the hotel foyer, they spotted the group sitting quietly together in a corner with numerous pots of tea on the table, their rooms probably not yet available. Jonny observed Adrian and Martin looking over towards them with stern faces. He knew from experience, an inner circle often pulled together and exhibited aggressive behaviour towards the police during the initial stages of an investigation; they could not believe someone within their family or group of friends could have committed such a crime, or at least been involved in it.

Mikeš made a quick detour to reception before re-joining Jonny as they approached the group together. "Mrs Robson," Mikeš commenced. "I have asked reception to prioritise your rooms. Hopefully they will be ready soon."

Carly turned to face them, speaking quietly. "Okay. Thank you."

Jonny quickly assessed the group. Carly and Sophie looked drawn and tired, probably having been crying together on-off for two days. Both ladies, he reminded himself, were mothers and would naturally bond over such an emotional situation. Sophie was clearly protective, sitting with her arm around Carly. The other wife, Lizzie, was sitting on the other side of Carly. She also looked tired and drained from the emotion, and was being comforted by her husband, Adrian. Although they were all similar ages, Lizzie looked much younger, although Jonny knew it probably had more to do with the physical effect of raising young children on the others than anything else. Martin made up the inner circle. He was sitting next to Sophie to provide support to his wife, but as Jonny expected, he did not look integral to the party, instead sitting slightly on the outside looking in on the action.

"Mrs Robson, would it be possible to speak to you?" Mikeš continued. "We understand this is difficult for you, but there are some things we need to understand."

Carly nodded in response, wiping her eyes with a tissue. Sophie took control, ushering Martin to move up and make space for Mikeš and Jonny to sit down next to her.

Mikeš coughed politely. "I'm sorry, but we need to talk to Mrs Robson alone."

Sophie turned on Mikeš, her short blonde hair flaring

and her face raging. "Can't you see she is upset? My god! We are not from this country. It's your job to protect us and catch whoever did this. Instead, all you seem to want to do is interview our friends…"

"Sophie, please stop. They are just trying to do their job." Martin lent over and put his arm around his wife, calming her enough to stop her rant. Her angry eyes however told a different story, still burning into Mikeš.

"It's okay, Sophie, I need to do this," Carly gently said to her friend, kissing her on the side of the face.

"Thank you," said Mikeš. "The hotel are allowing us to use a room just along the corridor."

Carly was rising from her seat slowly, reassuring Sophie, when a receptionist appeared next to Jonny and addressed the seated group. "Hello. I just wanted to let you know all your rooms will be available in ten minutes. We are just getting them ready now. Thank you for choosing to stay in our hotel again and we are here to help if you need anything."

"Thank you," replied Adrian on behalf of the group.

The receptionist smiled and retreated back to reception.

Sophie called out to Carly as she walked away with Mikeš and Jonny. "Carly, Martin and I will put your bag in your room. Call me when you are finished."

Seated in the room, Jonny took the initiative to explain his presence. "Mrs Robson…"

"Please, call me Carly." She was slim with long brown hair, slight in frame, some would say delicate, probably the most naturally attractive of the three wives. But Jonny could see she had a sturdy and resolute constitution and wondered to himself how much it was natural and how much it had been developed by what the victim, her husband, had put her through.

"Okay, Carly. My name is Jonathan Fox, I am working as a consultant with the Czech Police. Until recently I worked in the Homicide and Serious Crime unit within the Metropolitan

Police in London. Detective Chief Inspector Mikeš has asked me to advise his team on the investigation. And may I just say I am very sorry for your loss. It's a terrible thing to have happened. I can assure you we are doing everything we can to find who did this."

Carly paused to wipe her eyes, before looking slowly at both men. "I have some questions I want to ask."

"Go ahead," prompted Mikeš with an encouraging smile.

"Mr Fox, why were you at the restaurant when Neil and his friends were having lunch?"

"Carly, it was pure coincidence. I am here on holiday and I had just stopped for a coffee. I was sitting on the terrace admiring the view when everyone in the restaurant heard the commotion inside."

Mikeš injected to take control. "I asked Mr Fox to be involved in the investigation to help speed up solving the case. He is a very experienced detective."

"But why are you interviewing all our friends over and over?" Carly declared. "Martin has told us he's already been interviewed twice. Surely…"

Jonny held up his hands to pacify her. "I understand why you are thinking this. Completely. But can I just explain a few things. If you are not satisfied after our explanation, we can discuss it further."

Carly nodded, lacking the energy for a fight and content to be led.

Jonny composed himself, preparing to provide a clear explanation. He was aware of the sensitive situation and did not want to give away uncorroborated information which might hurt her unnecessarily.

"The first point is that when your husband was murdered, nothing was taken from him. If it was a random act, you would expect his wallet or mobile phone to have been taken, like a robbery. The second point is there was not a struggle. These points lead us to believe the person who murdered Neil was either a professional, and I'll come back to this, or someone he knew. These are the two areas of focus for our investigation. They are also the reason why we need to talk to you, your friends, anyone who was connected to your husband. We need to understand his life, put together a picture of any arguments, resentment, money problems, etc. Basically, all the things which could lead us to a motive. I know it is very difficult for you to accept at this testing time, but I believe you or your friends know some information which will lead us to his killer."

Carly sniffed and wiped her eyes. "You really think someone in our group killed Neil?"

"I'm not saying someone did," Jonny answered cautiously. "But I do believe there is a reason why he was killed and someone in your group knows why, even if they have not yet made the connection. It is possible, as I mentioned before, a professional committed this terrible act. If this is right, I still believe someone in your group has information which will help us explain the reason why and help us find the killer. Think about it – why Prague? Neil has been here twice in the last year, once on a trip with the wives and again now with the boys. There must be some significance as to why he was killed here."

Carly looked down, wiping away the tears rolling down her cheeks, distressed but taking in the information being provided.

"I know it feels intrusive for everyone," continued Jonny, "but this is why we have to talk to all of your friends, sometimes over and over about the same thing. We are trying to jog their memories about something they maybe didn't consider significant before."

Jonny waited for Carly to raise her head and show her understanding.

"Before we ask you some questions, I would like to ask something else of you," Jonny stated. "At this time it is very important to maintain confidentiality. I notice Sophie is a close friend, but please do not even tell her, or anyone else, about what we discuss. It is vitally important nobody jumps to conclusions or tries to pre-empt our enquiries. We just want straightforward, honest answers to our questions. In return, we promise to keep you informed on a daily basis about what we find."

After a pause, Carly blew her nose, looked at him and agreed. "Okay."

Jonny started cautiously. "Carly, we know Neil worked at a pharmaceutical company. What about you?"

"I worked at the same company before. We met there. But for the last four years or so I've been at home looking after the children."

"Okay. I'm sorry to have to raise such a personal issue now but it's something we need to ask you about. We know what happened between Neil and Natasha, Richard Weston's wife. Although it was over five years ago, how long after you found out did Natasha keep trying to contact your husband?"

Carly sat up in her seat, suddenly defensive. "That bloody stupid woman! I could never work out what Neil saw in her. But he was so sorry about it after, said he was drunk and she trapped him. She carried on sending him messages for two to three months, he showed them to me. It was a difficult time, but then our first son was born and everything has been happy since."

"So," ventured Jonny with care, "you did not suspect Neil of having any other affairs since then."

"No."

"That's good. Sorry we have to ask."

After a brief pause, Jonny continued. "Going back to Richard, did you suspect he held a grudge against Neil for what happened?"

"No, not at all. Neil told me they sorted it out. Richard has never treated either of us badly because of it and he is actually happier now with Hana."

"Okay, thank you. Moving on, do you know if Neil had

any money problems, maybe involving Gary Needham? We have been told they were arguing about money in the pub a few weeks ago."

"No, I don't know anything about an argument," she confirmed. "I checked our finances before I came over here, just in case something had happened. Everything was as I expected."

"That is very wise," endorsed Jonny.

"Do you know what money the argument was about?" Carly asked.

"Not yet. We are talking to Gary again later today."

Mikeš interjected. "I'm afraid we need to keep your husband's belongings for a bit longer, certainly whilst the investigation is ongoing. We will return everything to you in due course."

Jonny took his notebook from his pocket. "When we were going through Neil's notebook we found some reminders which do not make sense to us. Do you recognise these?" Carly studied the list briefly, but shook her head.

"The reminders seem to be from the last three months," Jonny explained. "There are fifteen entries in total, all crossed out like they had been completed."

Carly shrugged. "He liked to keep a notebook of reminders. But I'm not really sure why. I always thought he just liked crossing things off."

"Do you keep a shared calendar at home?" suggested Jonny. "Maybe a calendar in the kitchen you write key events for both of you and the children?"

"Yes, we do. It's on the kitchen wall."

"Would you be able to get a copy of the last few months, say from December to March?"

"My mother is at home looking after the children. I'll ask her to take some photos and send to me. But why do you need it?"

"Thank you," said Jonny. "Maybe it's nothing, but, as I said, we have to try and piece together all the information we have. It would be useful to see the family calendar."

Jonny looked down at his notes before continuing. "Neil had a message over the weekend from Heather Davis. Do you know her?"

"Yes. She works with Neil. Is there something wrong?"

"No, not at all," Jonny reassured her. "We are just trying to establish links for all the people who were contact with your husband whilst he was in Prague."

Carly relaxed. "I've met her a couple of times, with her partner, on company events."

"Okay, that's all I wanted to know."

Jonny flicked through his notebook and looked up at Carly. "There is just one more thing I would like to ask you about. When you all came over to Prague in the middle of last year, did anything unusual happen to Neil? Please think. Any small detail may be really important."

Carly paused. "No. All I remember is a lovely weekend. Really amazing. It was great surprise from all the guys, although we knew Martin arranged most of it. Everyone got on so well, no arguments, and we had a very relaxing time."

"And how was Neil on the trip?"

"He was really romantic. Of course, we were with friends a lot of the time, but we fitted in a walk by ourselves on the Saturday afternoon. And it was nice just to have some time on our own, away from the children."

"And what did you and Neil do on the Sunday afternoon after lunch?"

"I sat with Sophie chatting. We were tired so we grabbed a coffee and sat on a bench. The weather was lovely. Neil…" Carly paused to think. "Yes, Neil wanted to go to the Mucha Museum. Nobody else wanted to go with him, so he went on his own. He brought back some postcards, one of which is on the fridge at home."

"And can you remember what everyone else did?"

"Not really. We only had just over an hour before we had to get back to the hotel for the taxi. Lizzie probably went shopping. Martin and Adrian... no, sorry, I can't remember."

"That's okay," confirmed Jonny. "But nothing out of the ordinary happened to Neil over the weekend? He didn't go out on his own for a long period?"

"No. Neil was happy and, for me, it was a lovely weekend with my husband and good friends."

"Thank you, Carly. We appreciate how difficult this has been for you. Detective Chief Inspector Mikeš and I will do everything we can to catch the person who killed your husband. Please get some rest and we will update you with progress on a daily basis."

Carly nodded and lowered her head, wiping away her tears.

21

Interview 2 – Gary Needham

The following is a transcript of the recorded interview conducted with Gary Needham (GN) on the afternoon of Wednesday, 17th March 2010.

Present at the interview were Chief Warrant Officer Felix Mikeš (FM), Chief Sergeant Marek Boukal (MB) and Consultant Jonathan Fox (JF). The reason for the presence of JF was explained at the beginning of the interview; he is continuing to assist the Czech Police team on this murder investigation.

MB: Interview commenced at 15:26. Please state your name for the record.
GN: Gary Needham.
MB: Thank you for coming in again. We just want to ask you more questions to help us in our investigation.
GN: Okay.
FM: During the interviews with the other people in your group, we have found out you were not totally honest with us last time.
GN: What do you mean?
FM: We have been told you have had an argument with Neil Robson over money in the last few weeks.
GN: So what? It was nothing.
FM: It didn't sound like nothing to us. We have been told you were arguing in the pub, and it got so heated you were both told by the landlord to go outside.
GN: Who told you?

FM: It doesn't matter.

GN: It does to me.

FM: I repeat, it does not matter.

JF: Gary, please calm down. This is a serious matter and we need you to be honest with us. We know you had an argument with Neil. There are witnesses. Now, we can do this one of two ways: you can tell us everything and save us time, or alternatively, we will charge you for withholding information and conduct our own investigation into the matter to find out what happened. The second option will take longer, but I can assure you we will find out. Much better for you would be to comply with our request, tell us the truth, so that, if you are not involved, we can eliminate you from our enquiries.

GN: But this is stupid. How can a private matter between Neil and I have any bearing on your investigation?

JF: Your friend, Neil, was murdered. Isn't that a good enough reason for you?

GN: Do I need a lawyer?

FM: We can arrange for you to have legal representation if you want.

JF: There is no trick here, Gary. Detective Chief Inspector Mikeš will definitely organise a lawyer if you want one. But, it's important for me to repeat, we just want to ask you some questions and get to the truth. You are not being charged and we do not have a reason, at the moment, to suspect you were involved in the murder. But we need information about the argument and the money so we can rule you out. Isn't that what you want?

GN: Of course.

JF: Can we just ask you some questions and get this over and done with quickly?

[Pause]

GN: Okay.

JF: Good. In the interview yesterday, you said, and I quote: 'I've been going through a difficult time recently'. You also mentioned the separation from your wife, Grace, six months ago,

and the divorce proceedings you are currently going through. Finally, you were kind about Neil, saying he had been good to you – 'generous' was the word you used. You said he had helped you by paying some of the costs of the trip here. Given all of these points, am I right in assuming you borrowed money from Neil to help pay your divorce costs?
GN: Yes and no.
JF: Please explain.
[Pause]
GN: It's actually more to do with my business. I run a small building firm, with only three staff now. We have done well over the years, mainly doing smaller jobs in the area like extensions and patios, but also the occasional bigger job like a loft conversion. All the jobs were local with recommendations by word of mouth. About two years ago it started to get harder. A couple of bigger building firms began focusing on the area because it's an affluent commuter belt, plenty of cash. It would have been fine if they'd just taken a share of the work because there is plenty, but they went in hard, undercutting me to the extent that I'm hardly making any money on the jobs I do get. I had to reduce the number of builders from six to three and reduce my costs by taking on younger, less experienced staff on apprentice schemes.
JF: Very sorry to hear that. How have you coped?
GN: Not very well. I've been stressed, not sleeping well, my blood pressure has shot through the roof. I've not been much fun to be around, no spare money, drinking too much when I did have some cash. In truth, Grace took the brunt of it. In the end she couldn't take it anymore and left me. I've tried to get her back, begged her, but she's made her mind up.
JF: And so Neil helped you out financially?
GN: Not at first. Money was tight, but I could survive. But Grace started the divorce proceedings and, even though we don't have any kids, the legal costs are ridiculous. I went to the bank but they wouldn't lend me any money when they saw the business accounts.

JF: So you asked Neil?
GN: No, he offered. As I told you last time, he was being really kind to me. He listened when I wanted to talk, always asked how I was. He knew I was going through a difficult time and he wanted to support me. I suppose one night down the pub I had one too many and told him the plain fact that I might go bankrupt. That's when he offered to lend me some money.
JF: How much?
GN: £10,000.
JF: When was this?
GN: In the middle of January.
JF: And when did he say he wanted the money paid back?
GN: He said £3,000 in three months, another £3,000 in another three months, then the balance three months later.
JF: So £3,000 in April, £3,000 in July and £4,000 in October.
GN: Yes. We didn't set exact dates, but it's about right. He was flexible.
JF: And I'm guessing there was a problem with the first payment?
GN: I was really confident when we agreed the schedule. I had a couple of jobs lined up, but I lost them to the other building firms. I was stuck, had no way of being able to pay him anything with the divorce costs racking up. I barely had enough money during February for diesel for the vans.
JF: So you told Neil you couldn't pay him the first instalment?
GN: Yes. That's when we argued. He thought I was doing it on purpose, but it was genuine. I promised to get the money back for him, but told him I needed more time.
JF: What did he say?
GN: He was angry because he had just paid the balance on the trip here. He had agreed to pay some of my costs on the basis I'd pay him back the money. He said he felt cheated, but there was nothing I could do.
JF: But you still decided to come? You could have cancelled.
GN: Once Neil had calmed down, he said I should come. The hotel and flights had been paid for. I've just tried to take it easy

on spending money.
JF: And interestingly, none of your friends seem to have noticed any problem between you and Neil on this trip.
GN: I know, he's very good at separating things. He got angry when I told him, but then he was able to put it to one side and not worry about it. I asked him about it once and he said he had learned to do it at work. I think it's more to do with the fact he can afford it. He would probably react differently if he needed the money.
JF: He has a lot of money?
GN: Well, I think so. His house is big enough, I built the extension for him. Plus he seems to always have a flash car. I think he's done well at work.
JF: Did his wife, Carly (Robson), know about the money he lent to you?
GN: He told me not to mention it to her.
JF: Why?
GN: I don't know. I needed the money, so I did what he told me to do.
JF: How did he give you the money?
GN: In cash.
JF: Isn't that a bit unusual?
GN: I didn't really think about it. Money is money, right?
JF: Sure.
[Pause]
JF: Did Neil say anything else to you about the money? Maybe he said something else when he mentioned Carly, or maybe he mentioned somebody else. Please think hard, anything could be important.
GN: All I do remember is him referring to it as his 'fun money'. It was during our first conversation about it, when he offered to help.
JF: Can you remember exactly what he said?
GN: Something like 'I have some fun money, but I need it back'.
JF: Do you know what he meant?
GN: No, sorry. I just needed the money.

JF: Can you remember anything else?
GN: No.
JF: Did you ever see Neil write down any codes like these? Maybe in relation to the money he lent you.
MB: For the record, Mr Fox is now showing Mr Gary Needham a series of letters and numbers which have been copied from the victim's notebook.
GN: No, sorry. We just talked, it was a verbal agreement.
FM: What would you have done if you couldn't pay him back?
GN: I don't know, I hadn't thought about it. I have some jobs at the moment, but I do need more. I need to get the divorce sorted and then just work hard, I suppose.
FM: It would be easier if you didn't need to pay it back at all?
GN: I don't like what you are insinuating. I had nothing to do with Neil's death. He was my friend. I knew this would happen. You ask me to tell the truth and then twist it.
JF: Look Gary, you must understand there is motive here. Especially if Neil's wife didn't know about the money. Let's talk instead about the route you took on Monday afternoon, before you got back to the hotel. If we can prove you were not in the vicinity of the restaurant then we can eliminate you.
[Pause]
JF: Okay?
GN: What do you want to know?
MB: We have your route here, put together by Sergeant Dvořáková based upon the information you gave her. You told her you walked through the streets in the old town after leaving Darren Kozma and Richard Weston and went to a pub called U Valentů.
GN: I think that was the pub. I just saw the Pilsner Urquell sign and walked in.
MB: And you believe you were there about 2:15pm? (14:15)
GN: Yes.
MB: The good news is the bar staff there remember you.
GN: See.
MB: The bad news is they say you only stayed for about thirty

minutes.
[Pause]
GN: Shit, that's right. I remember now. There was a pub I wanted to go to whilst I was in Prague. A friend told me about it, but the others didn't fancy it. It's a small microbrewery. Yes, I went there as well.
FM: Why didn't you tell us this before?
GN: Sorry, I forgot. There was a lot going on.
FM: Was it the brewery pub at U Pivovaru?
GN: Yes.
FM: You would have had to walk close to Old Town Square to get there. Close to the restaurant.
GN: I didn't know where I was, I just followed the directions on my phone.
MB: And what time did you get there?
GN: Sorry. I can't be sure. Maybe 3:15pm (15:15) or just after.
MB: And how long did you stay there?
GN: I was there until just after 4pm (16:00). I had forgotten the time and had to rush back to the hotel.
MB: We will check with the pub.
GN: They should remember me. It was a Monday afternoon and it wasn't busy. A few people there were eating, but I sat near the bar and was just drinking. I wanted to sample the beer.
FM: Changing your story is not very helpful.
GN: Apologies for forgetting. But what I've told you now is the truth.
FM: Can you remember any part of the walk to U Pivovaru?
GN: Sorry, I don't remember. I know I got a bit lost, but I definitely didn't go to Old Town Square.
FM: You must have been drunk.
GN: I had a couple of beers in the first pub. Like I told you last time, I was sad to be going back to the UK and having to face reality.
FM: How many beers did you have?
GN: In total, probably five.

JF: Gary, you must see how this looks. It is very important you review the route with Chief Sergeant Boukal after the interview. We need it to be as accurate as possible, especially the times, so we can contact the brewery pub and also check CCTV along the route. But you need to accept we might need to talk to you again in the morning. Do you understand?
GN: Yes.
[Pause]
MB: Interview terminated at 16:07.

22

Anger Management

Mikeš stormed into the Incident Room, threw down his book and pen dramatically, and stood in front of the murder board with his arm crossed and a deep frown on his face. Jonny entered a few moments later, having been left behind in the walk from the interview room. Obviously angry and keen to get back downstairs to home territory, Mikeš had bounded down the stairs, taking two steps at a time, almost in flight. Jonny decided to let him go.

    Jonny's experience told him it was time to keep his own counsel. He slipped into the room silently and sat down on a chair, taking out his notebook to review. He had worked with many people who needed time to regulate themselves, to calm down or blow off steam, especially when investigations got tense or progress was being obstructed. He had only known Mikeš for a few days and now he was seeing a different, maybe truer, side of this usually affable character. Up until now Mikeš had acted as the genteel statesman, cajoling his troops with energy and panache, never letting his mask slip. But now Jonny could see the steely resolve of the seasoned detective, the never-say-die attitude needed to be successful in the job.

    Everyone had a different tipping point and personal method of anger management. Jonny knew his own threshold was high – more than most; unlike many colleagues, the usual setbacks and challenges never phased him. Instead it had the opposite effect, instilling in him a renewed tenacity to come out on top. However, when he blew he really blew.

Calming himself down was best achieved on his own, away from the office. He had learnt this the hard way early in his career, and hence a few times in recent years he had gone completely AWOL to save himself and others. Thankfully for him he was also unable to sleep during these times of tension, and he often headed back to the office under the cover of night to continue his work undisturbed. These night sittings were therapeutic, allowing him to clear his head of the unnecessary day-to-day distractions and challenge the conventional thinking on the case. The unbroken focus often prompted valuable insights into the investigation and, in some cases, breakthroughs that led to the perpetrator being brought to justice. Without these advances in the case and the ever-important results they brought, he would probably not have survived the wrath of his commander-in-chief who often lost patience with his unconventional methods and prolonged absences from the office.

The Sutherland case had been a prime example and, it being in retrospect his last case, no doubt had a significant toll on him, both mentally and physically. When the body of Alison Bryce had been found, the knot used for strangling her was immediately recognised as Sutherland's signature. Jonny had flown into a fury, at the killer, but mostly at himself, for not catching him earlier and preventing the serial killer's fourth victim.

For two days and night he had locked himself in his office with all the material from the investigation: going over statements, photos from the crime scene, the map showing the locations of where the bodies had been found, everything, all for the umpteenth time. He mostly ignored the food and drink provided by worried members of his team, and only caught a few hours of sleep when his eyelids could stay open no longer, collapsing over his desk in exhaustion. At dawn on the second morning, the sun rising through the far window of the office, his mind suddenly connected the symbolism of the knot to the killer's modus operandi.

Jonny quickly established that all the girls had attended the same guide movement and the net was closed on the volunteers running the group. Sutherland's wife had run the group over the five years, Sutherland providing help with van driving and other menial jobs. The catalyst for his killing spree had been the end of his marriage, tipping him over the edge when he couldn't have contact with the girls in the guide movement. His sick revenge was to track and kill the girls he had loved over the years. Alison had been the youngest of his victims, only having left the group recently, and had been saved until last.

Mikeš moved abruptly, Jonny's deep memories suddenly broken. Mikeš appeared to have calmed, shifting his standing position at the board to look around the room. Despite having been accepted into the hub of the team, Jonny remained silent, acutely aware he was still an outsider and knowing this was not the right time for him to lead.

"I want these so-called friends all locked down," started Mikeš, an angry tone in his voice. "Gary Needham, Darren Kozma, and also Richard Weston. They are trying to run us around in circles."

"You have their passports already," stated Jonny.

"Yes, I know. But I want them reporting to us every morning, afternoon and evening. If any of them get out of the country we will have trouble extraditing them back here. The paperwork will be complicated and will take a long time."

"I agree."

"If one of them wants to run for it, they can get over the border easily on a train or in a car. I will position a uniformed officer at the hotel and I want these friends checked at 8am, 1pm and 8pm."

"What about Adrian Scott and Martin Wilson?" Jonny enquired. "They are now in the other hotel."

Mikeš paused to consider the threat. "I know, but they have their wives here now. I do not think they will run."

"They might if we get close to solving the case and they are involved."

"Honza, you really think it might be them?" Mikeš looked shocked. "Gary," he continued, pointing at the board, "he is definitely my prime suspect."

"Felix, I really don't know at the moment. We are slowly finding out more, but I think there is more to come. Remember, even if we have a suspect, we need to find the evidence to convict them." Jonny paused to make his point. "I want to talk to Adrian Scott again tomorrow morning. He was the closest to the victim and might know more about what we found out today."

Boukal walked in with a sigh. "That Gary is so difficult. He can't remember any clear details."

"He remembers what he wants to remember!" snapped Mikeš.

Boukal exchanged a look with Jonny, then continued his update. "I now have an updated route for Gary, and approximate times he left the first pub and arrived at the second pub. I'll liaise with Lucie to check the CCTV and personally go to the pubs myself to verify potential alibis. The only trouble we might have is that some of the staff working there Monday afternoon may not be in right now. I'll go and check with the pub and get contact details as soon as I can."

Mikeš, still angry, spoke, almost mumbling to himself. "These friends are not friends."

Jonny and Boukal again looked at each other, not sure how to react, their eye contact agreeing it was best to let Mikeš continue when he was ready.

Eventually Mikeš posed his question.

"Honza, please tell me. What is keeping these friends together? Something is not right."

Jonny stalled, keen to convey his rationalisation as clearly as possible. "I think the group is a reflection of the person at the centre, Neil Robson. We don't know everything about him, but he definitely had secrets. I mean, who has £10,000 spare cash, money his wife doesn't even know about? I also think he was still cheating on his wife, but we can't prove it at the moment. Felix, you are right. These are mostly poor examples of men, all circling around another bad example of a man, but one who has confidence, money and charm."

"Honza, you are exactly right," Mikeš exclaimed. "A perfect description."

Jonny decided to use the opening to present his current thinking. "Of the friends, only Richard has an alibi by way of the photos he took from the observation deck around 3pm – this evidence is hard to fake. But Darren and Gary do not have any alibi at the moment. Also, Adrian and Martin are right in the centre of all of this chaos and must have known roughly where they were going for lunch. It would have been fairly easy for either of them, maybe even working together, to arrange for someone to kill Neil if they wanted to."

Boukal jumped back into the conversation. "There is also James Hopkins. We have confirmed sightings of him in his school at lunchtime and when he left for home. But between 2pm and 4pm he had no lessons. He says he was working alone on lesson plans for the next day, but it would have been possible for him to sneak out, get to Old Town Square and then back to the school within two hours."

Jonny screwed up his face, unconvinced. "I don't see it. How would he know what restaurant they were going to?"

"Maybe Martin told him," suggested Boukal.

"It is definitely worth checking out," Jonny agreed. "But it must be a long shot."

"It would be good to eliminate someone at least," huffed Mikeš.

"I will check the CCTV at the school," stated Boukal. "I'm sure they will have CCTV on the gates to deter intruders during the school opening times. It would show whether he left the school premises."

Silence again descended over the room. Dvořáková entered, closing the door gently behind her. Sensing the tension, she sat down, papers on her lap, waiting respectfully for the opportunity to brief the senior detective team.

"We need some evidence," remarked Mikeš, showing his frustration.

"Stay patient, Felix," commented Jonny, reassuringly. "The killer will have made a mistake. We just need to follow all the leads and I'm sure we will find it."

Sensing an opening in the conversation, Dvořáková presented her progress report. "The door-to-door check along the escape route is continuing. We are repeating the exercise now for businesses, restaurants and shops where the owners or staff were not in this morning. Also, we have found some CCTV footage of Richard and Gary, but nothing so far to disprove the routes they gave us."

"Gary's route has changed slightly," Boukal added. "I'll take you through it afterwards."

"Okay," Dvořáková acknowledged. "Also, I have checked with our UK Police Liaison team and we can get authorisation to track the mobile signals for all the group but it will take two or three days to process. We will also get confirmation of the calls and text messages made from Neil Robson's phone over the past few months."

"Make the request," stated Mikeš. "We can't wait, time is running out."

"Yes, sir."

Dvořáková opened her folder, took out a plastic badge and handed it to Jonny. "I have produced an identification badge confirming you are a consultant with the Prague Police Department. The card also provides swipe access to this building."

Jonny turned the card over in his hand, a smile emerging as he looked at the photo. "You used the photo you took on Monday when I was a potential suspect."

"It was the only photo I had," explained Dvořáková with a smile.

Jonny laughed. "And it says – Jonathan (Honza) Fox."

"Yes, that was my little joke," she teased. "But actually I think it is necessary. Everyone in this station knows you as Honza now. Jonathan would mean nothing to them."

Mikeš lent in to look at the badge, then slapped Jonny on the back. "You are official now, my friend!"

"Seems like it," Jonny smiled, feeling like the new boy in the class.

"And to celebrate," continued Mikeš, "Ella and I would like to invite you to dinner tomorrow night."

"We'd better solve this case soon then," Jonny declared.

"Looks like it. Now, everyone, let's rock n' roll, we've got a killer to find!"

23

Room Service

Observing the city sights out of the passenger window as the car moved slowly in the early evening rush hour traffic, Jonny tried to map out in his head the convoluted route they were taking. Passing first the State Opera on the inner-city dual carriageway, and then the National Museum at the top of Wenceslas Square, he had the feeling they were now travelling away from the city centre, in the wrong direction.

"Don't worry. I'm not going to kidnap you," Dvořáková joked, sensing his unease. "The traffic in Prague city centre is particularly bad at this time of day. The only way to get from Old Town Square to the hotel is to take a big loop. We're turning right up here and then we'll drop down to a side road."

"It would have been easier to walk," suggested Jonny.

"Probably," she agreed. "The Czech people find it hard to live without a car."

"It's just a shame so many of the main roads go right through the city centre. It sort of encourages people to keep driving."

Dvořáková nodded in agreement, her eyes on the road as the traffic started to move.

"Back in the UK, I gave up my car two years ago," Jonny explained. "I was living in London, working in central London and had access to a driver when I needed it. But being conscious of the growing level of traffic, I always tried to get around on public transport if I could. I found I didn't have any real need for a permanent car. When I did have one it was just sitting outside my apartment block most of the time."

"That would be hard here," commented Dvořáková. "The public transport is not good enough. Plus, many people leave the city at the weekend so need a car. The lifestyle in Prague is very much work and live in the city during the week and go to your cottage, or *chata*, at the weekend."

"I'm not saying people shouldn't drive," clarified Jonny, still looking out of the car window. "But I do think there is a different way, with less cars and less pollution."

Dvořáková looked across quickly, tested by the thought, before turning back to concentrate on the road. As she had promised, she indicated and turn the car right at the next traffic lights, before taking another quick right, looping back towards the other side of Wenceslas Square. Within a minute they were parked outside the hotel.

She turned off the engine. "I just wanted to say I really welcome the different approach you have brought to this investigation. The way you look at a situation from every angle is so refreshing."

"It is not really so different," Jonny claimed. "I just always try to challenge my own thinking. I am usually harder on myself than anyone else. It can make you introverted, not great for your personal life, but definitely helps in chasing criminals."

"And Honza, can I ask what are we looking for here, at the hotel?"

"I really don't know," admitted Jonny. "If you poke about as much as I do, something might present itself."

As they entered the foyer, Jonny's badge clipped proudly to the breast pocket of his jacket, he was reminded how much he disliked the impersonal, airless feel of large hotels. He had always veered away from these chain hotels, not feeling at home in the staged atmosphere of faceless smiles and detached politeness. It was only when forced, during early family holidays or rare conferences, he had accepted a stay full of false welcomes, lift journeys and stuffy corridors.

Dvořáková walked over to reception to announce their arrival and to get the room key. A few customers nudged each other at the sight of a uniformed officer in their hotel. Jonny surveyed the lobby area but noticed nothing out of the ordinary: the concierge desk in the corner, an area of soft seating, directions pointing down a corridor to the bar and restaurant, no doubt where breakfast was also served, and straight ahead, up some steps, three lifts leading to the floors above.

"Room 226," she stated, holding up a room card.

As the waited for the lift, Dvořáková seized the opportunity she had been waiting for. "The behavioural science course I took at university left a big impression on me. Actually, it was one of the key reasons I chose a career in the police force. I am very interested to learn the ability to read facial expressions."

The lift arrived and they got in, Dvořáková scanning the room card and pressing the button for the second floor. "Don't forget, seventy-five per cent of all communication is non-verbal," Jonny quantified. "Until recently, the focus was just on body language. It's still a very useful tool and I always watch to see what impression the interviewee is giving me. But it can be faked fairly easily. The great thing about facial expressions is they are natural. You have to watch very closely because they happen so fast. Studying a video recording is much easier."

"It is so powerful," she affirmed.

The lift door opened and they followed the signs through the fire door and down the corridor. Jonny felt a slight shiver down his spine; dimly lit hotel corridors were one of his pet hates. It was almost like an allergy to plain painted walls, badly chosen carpets and a seemingly endless succession of doors.

Outside Room 226, Dvořáková handed him a pair of plastic gloves and opened the door with the key card. Jonny stepped inside and surveyed the room. In truth, he could have been standing in any hotel room in any city across the world.

Even the framed abstract prints on the wall had nothing to do with Prague.

"So, the room hasn't been used since Sunday night," he stated.

"That's right. The room was cleaned Monday afternoon, after they all checked out. But the room has been left vacant since."

"And where were the other friends staying?"

"The six rooms were spread across different floors," Dvořáková said, consulting her paper. "Two of them were on the first floor; Gary Needham is still there. Three were on the second floor; only Darren Kozma is left. Richard Weston was the only one of the group on the third floor, and he's still there."

"And Adrian Scott and Martin Wilson?"

Dvořáková consulted her paper again. "Martin Wilson was on the first floor. Adrian Scott was on the second, just a few doors down from here. Do you think it is relevant?"

"I don't know," he confessed. "I just like to have an accurate picture in my head."

Jonny walked across the room to the window. The view was mostly of the opposite buildings, but he could see the street below if he craned his neck. Moving around the room, he sat at the desk, swivelling around to survey the dimensions, next sat on the one armchair, before laying down on the bed.

Dvořáková broke into a smile. "You are almost as eccentric as Felix."

"You're probably right. These are the quirks of the job you develop. You'll be the same when you're a DCI."

Dvořáková continued smiling, clearly enjoying the compliment.

"I wouldn't recommend the bed, it's a bit lumpy," he joked as he jumped off and proceeded to work his way around the room. He coolly checked every piece of furniture: he opened all the drawers, looked inside the cupboards and wardrobes, before laying on his stomach to check under the bed and mattress. He then checked behind the pictures and went into the bathroom.

She stood watching him closely, as if his methods were going to reveal some secret policing technique not in the manuals.

"It's okay, I'm not mad," Jonny offered. "It's just a habit I've got. About ten years ago I found a small, but vital, piece of evidence after my team of about fifteen officers had already checked the murder scene. It helped find the killers of a defenceless old man. Ever since then I have this compulsion to check everything again myself."

"I agree, it's important to be diligent and thorough," she acknowledged.

"But, there's nothing here!" Jonny declared. "Let's talk to reception."

As they waited for the next descending lift, Dvořáková took out her notebook and flicked the pages. "Do you think the symbolism of the fish shaped penknife has any meaning in this murder?"

"The Rybička? It's a good thought."

"Last night I was looking up the symbolism of the fish. According to astrology, the fish symbolises a number of maybe generic things including fertility, feelings, creativity, rebirth and good luck. But there is also the connection to the water element, representing the deeper awareness of the unconsciousness or higher self."

"Interesting," mused Jonny. "There's also the Pisces star sign, in March I think."

"Yes, February 19th to March 20th," she stated confidently.

"Very thorough, Lucie," he encouraged. "We should definitely keep it in mind. Something might connect to it."

Reception was quiet; late afternoon in the middle of the week, before the early evening check-in rush. Dvořáková spoke to one of the receptionists in Czech, who scuttled off into the office behind. When the manager emerged, looking smart and upright, Dvořáková switched to English to introduce herself and Jonny, all shaking hands across the counter.

Jonny took the lead. "Thank you for your time. I just wanted to ask your reception staff about the person who was murdered on Monday. And also about his group of friends. It will only take a few minutes."

"Of course," confirmed the manager. He approached the three reception staff: two women and one man. After having the situation explained to them in a lowered voice, the reception staff followed their manager to the end of the reception desk.

"Hello," Jonny started. "We would like to know if any of you noticed anything unusual about Neil Robson, or the people in his group, over their initial stay from Friday to Sunday night."

The reception staff looked at each other, pulling perplexed faces. The man, short and well built, spoke for them. "The group were a bit drunk on the Saturday night. Our night porter told us one fell over in the foyer here. But otherwise they were well behaved, no problems. I would actually say, probably better behaved than most groups of men we have staying here."

"And did you notice any arguments involving Neil Robson? Either people in his group or maybe another guest."

The reception staff all shook their heads. "No," confirmed the taller of the female receptionists.

"And how did the group pay for the booking?" continued Jonny.

The manager took the question. "Martin Wilson paid the booking for all six rooms online when he booked. However, since Monday we have been maintaining separate invoices for the extra nights. Martin Wilson and Adrian Scott paid when they left today. The other three men will pay when they leave."

"Has Gary Needham said anything to you about paying

the bill?" Jonny probed.

"No," the manager confirmed. He looked at his staff for any further contribution, but they shook their heads.

Jonny kept the questions flowing. "Have there been any problems with the remaining guests who have stayed here since Monday night?"

Again, the receptionists looked at each other for inspiration. "They have been very quiet, spending a lot of time in their rooms," confirmed the man. The taller female receptionist added "Mr Needham sat at the bar most of Monday night on his own. I understand he had quite a lot to drink, but he was no trouble."

"Thank you," stated Jonny. "And please think hard about this question. Was there anything unusual at all about Neil Robson during his stay? Did anything at all happen, however small, which is not usual for a tourist staying at your hotel?"

The manager spoke first. "I was not on reception much, but I didn't hear anything from the other staff." He then looked towards his receptionists. The man and the taller woman shook their head and shrugged respectively. The other, smaller receptionist remained quiet, but looked at her manager nervously.

Jonny noticed her hesitation. "Do you remember something?" he encouraged her.

"Well, it wasn't 'unusual' as such," she started, "but he had a letter hand-delivered to him."

Jonny looked surprised. "That's interesting. Did you take delivery of it?"

"No. I think Leo, the concierge, took the envelope," she answered. "Leo passed it to me and I gave it to Mr Robson."

"Leo is not working today," explained the manager.

"And when was this?" Jonny continued, keen to maintain the focus.

"The envelope was delivered sometime on Saturday afternoon. I had just come onto my shift at 15:00 and Leo gave it to me soon after. Mr Robson came back with his friends around 17:00 and I gave him the envelope."

"Was he expecting it?"

"No, I don't think so," confirmed the receptionist. "I gave him the envelope when they passed reception. I remembered them from when they checked in on Friday."

"How did you know which one was Neil Robson?" asked Jonny, looking confused. "You must have a lot of people staying here."

The receptionist blushed and looked down. The taller receptionist intervened on her colleague's behalf. "He was quite a good-looking guy."

"So," Jonny continued, undeterred, "you called out to him and he came over to reception."

The smaller receptionist nodded.

"And what did he say when you handed him the envelope?"

"He initially looked confused. I told him the envelope had been delivered for him. He opened the envelope straight away, looked at the page inside, and then folded it up and put it in his pocket."

"And did you see the page inside."

"No, but it looked handwritten."

"Can you remember what was on the envelope?" asked Jonny.

"It was just his name 'Neil Robson' in capital letters."

"Would you say it was a man's or woman's handwriting?"

The receptionist shook her head. "Sorry, I don't know."

"This next question is very important," Jonny pushed. "What did he do after reading the letter?"

"As I said, he folded the page and put it in his pocket with the envelope. Then he thanked me and re-joined his friends who were waiting for him at the lifts. He didn't seem like he was expecting a letter, but also he didn't seem to react at all when he opened it. Does that make sense?"

"No reaction at all?" Jonny looked surprised.

"No. He read it like it was a shopping list. He didn't react at all, said nothing and folded it up."

"That is really useful," Jonny confirmed. "But if you remember anything else, can you please let us know immediately."

Dvořáková stepped in. "I will give you my contact details. We will also need to speak to Leo to get a description of the person who dropped the envelope with the concierge. And we will also need to review your CCTV footage for the entrance and foyer on Saturday afternoon."

"Yes, sure," confirmed the manager. "I will get the CCTV to you in a couple of hours. I will also call Leo immediately."

"Thank you all very much," Jonny added enthusiastically, smiling at the smaller receptionist. "This information is really helpful to our investigation."

Jonny turned away from reception, leaving Dvořáková to make the practical arrangements. He stood in the middle of the hotel foyer thinking through all the reasons why Neil Robson might receive a handwritten letter whilst on holiday in Prague.

Dvořáková sidled up to him. "Your instinct was right."

Jonny smiled back. "Just following a lead. But now we need to sieve through all the rubbish the cleaner collected from the rooms she cleaned."

Dvořáková pulled a face. "The manager just told me she cleaned thirty rooms on Monday."

"Great!" Jonny shook his head ironically. "But I want to check the rubbish myself tomorrow morning. We can't miss anything."

"Sure," confirmed Dvořáková, "I'll arrange it with Josef."

"Thanks. Let's hope the letter and envelope are in there."

24

Park Life

Pleased to be out in the fresh air, with a potentially important breakthrough in the case to brighten his spirits, Jonny had already decided to walk when Dvořáková offered him a lift. "No, but thank you," he replied. "The weather is too good to jump back in the car."

"Okay. I'll get on with those checks back at base."

"Thanks, Lucie."

There was a slight hesitation as they stood at the car. "And thank you, Honza."

Jonny looked confused. "For what?"

"For including me in this. It means a lot to me."

"You are a very competent police officer and have a big career ahead of you. If I can help in any way, I'm happy to do so."

Dvořáková smiled at him warmly.

"Actually, there is something you could help with me," Jonny countered. "If you wanted to walk back to Náměstí Míru from here and see some greenery, maybe some trees in bloom, which way would you recommend walking?"

"There are plenty of nice parks in Prague 2," she explained. "The best route would be to walk up Vinohradská, behind the Museum, and take a left into Riegrovy sady. It's a lovely, hilly park and you get great views back over the city."

"I think I walked past an entrance to that park last night. Great, thanks."

"Another park to visit when you have time is Havlíčkovy sady," enthused Dvořáková. "They have their own vineyard there, called Grébovka. It's like going back in time. I think it's been there since the 14th century."

"Sounds perfect for a weekend walk," Jonny said, shaking her hand. "See you tomorrow, and don't work too late."

Dvořáková laughed out loud. "I can only imagine how you would have replied to that when you were a hungry, ambitious sergeant."

Jonny laughed with her. "That's a good point."

He instinctively headed off in the direction of Wenceslas Square, a spring in his step, enjoying the sensation of being respected in a new environment. His involvement was considered central to solving the case, but had the benefit of being detached enough to be excused from the paperwork and the late nights during a serious investigation. He was realistic enough to know this might be a one-off, but he was enjoying himself fully for the first time in a long while, and actually starting to look forward to what his future had to bring.

The top of Wenceslas Square was busy. Workers on their way home after a long day mixed in with people meeting up for a mid-week drink or meal, the weather attracting people outside for the last sun. The bronze statue of King Wenceslas on his horse, flag raised proudly and riding gallantly in front of his people, leader of the Czech lands, was a popular and symbolic meeting point for locals and visitors alike.

Seeing the people meeting up, embracing and sharing humorous stories, made Jonny think of Ivana. He knew he had to make it back to the apartment in time for a shower and change before going out for dinner. He quickly got out his mobile phone and sent her a message

```
Hi Ivana, I'll be back at 7pm.
```

Putting the phone back in his jacket pocket, Jonny started striding out, across the traffic lights in front of the museum, bearing left, through the underpass and out onto Vinohradská. His bearings were noticeably starting to improve, and whereas a few days ago he was wandering aimlessly, happy to eat up the time exploring and open to where he ended up, now he felt confident in his direction to travel, even if the street names were still alien to him. At the street called Italská he turned left and after ascending 100 metres or so, he met the entrance to the park, Riegrovy sady.

The park was impressively landscaped, the path rolling around the perimeter, lifting and dipping with the natural hills. The grassed areas were expansive and populated by impressive shrubbery and trees, new foliage growing with the season. At an intersection in the path, he followed the break taking him uphill towards the centre. The gradient of the path was severe and as he reached the top he stopped to catch his breath – the summit revealed a mass of people sat out on the grass bank overlooking the early evening picture show of the sun setting over the city. Although the view was not as expansive as the Television Tower the day before, the trees and grass provided a contrasting frame for the city skyline. Jonny found the contrast in urban topography captivating, an idyllic but unfamiliar vision of park life. He stood watching the sun descend over the horizon in the setting of friends sat talking in groups, parents playing ball games with their children, and numerous dogs chasing each other with unbridled enthusiasm.

Jolted by the inspired setting, particularly the screams and shouts of happy children having fun, he pulled the postcard out of his jacket pocket and sat down on a vacant bench. He wrote the address with his pen and then hovered over the left-hand side of the postcard, waiting for the words to come. For a full five minutes, pen poised, he composed words in his head, rewrote them and eventually discarded them; too funny would be seen as flippant, serious and needy would not be appealing to a teenager. And only a little space to fill. In the end he went for the factually correct with a twist to show his true feelings.

Dear Charlotte
I have decided to visit Prague and explore your grandmother's birthplace. It's a beautiful city, full of culture and history.
I would love to show you around some time.
Thinking about you lots.
Dad x

The moment was broken by his mobile phone beeping twice in short succession. The first message was from Ivana.

```
Ok, see you later. I've booked us dinner at
the pub.
```

The second was from Mikeš.

```
Honza, where are you? Coffee?
```

Not one for long exchanges of phone messages, Jonny immediately called Mikeš back, agreeing to meet him for a quick coffee at a café on the square at the almost unpronounceable Jiřího z Poděbrad. Jonny was pleased to see Mikeš had also sent him a message with the address, the map application on his smartphone more reliable than his memory of the slightly garbled instructions provided over the phone.

Descending the rolling hills on the other side of the park, past a crowded and noisy beer garden, he made his way out of an exit and along a street called Polská. He noted the street names in the area seemed to be heavily dominated by country and capital names. The end of the road met the corner of a large square, dominated by a large, modern church with an imposing round clock on the brick tower. He spotted a post box and quickly dispatched the postcard with a small kiss, before heading down the side of the square in search of the café. A sprawling, celebratory crowd were drinking wine on the pavement outside a Vinotéka, forcing Jonny to dodge his way through.

The café was a popular spot, mostly frequented by locals, full both inside and on the limited seating outside. He stopped at the door and scanned the interior. The café décor was a mixture of modern, bright colours with traditional furniture, old photos and memorabilia hanging on the walls. Mikeš and Boukal were sitting at a window table, the hat and cane hanging up like they belonged.

Mikeš rose to his feet when he saw Jonny, shouting "Honza!" across the busy café and waving his arms expansively. Jonny had already become so used to his new friend's exuberant behaviour, he thought nothing of it. The other customers seated around them on tables did not flinch, almost expecting it from the vibrantly-dressed gentleman. The men all shook hands and sat down, Mikeš waving for attention from a waitress.

"I'm sorry, I don't have long," Jonny explained. "I'm meeting a friend for dinner."

"Another friend!" boomed Mikeš, laughing and slapping him on the back. "You are settling in to the city."

"Well, actually it's my landlady," Jonny clarified.

"Say no more, my friend," Mikeš smiled, tapping the side of his nose. "If you go missing in action we know where to find her."

Jonny laughed, knowing how futile it was to defend himself without suffering further ridicule. Best quit now, rather than dig a deeper hole, he thought. In truth he could do without going out tonight, but he didn't want to let Ivana down when she had been so helpful, keen to make his stay as pleasant as possible. He was aware of the strong possibility she was attracted to him, and, whilst she was both attractive and charming, he wasn't sure he was ready for a relationship yet. He put it to the back of his mind, deciding instead to deal with it later, whatever happened, and just enjoy himself.

The waitress came over to the table and Mikeš ordered a cappuccino for Jonny.

"So," Mikeš started, "Lucie has updated me about the letter. What do you think it means?"

Jonny paused before answering. "It opens up the possibility that someone from outside the group knew Neil Robson was coming to Prague over the weekend. Maybe it relates to something left over from his visit to Prague last year?"

"Like what?" Mikeš posed.

Jonny hesitated. "Drugs? Sex? Money? I don't know, maybe all of them. We need to find out more about their schedule on the so-called romantic weekend with the wives. Neil's wife, Carly, gave us an insight earlier, but I want the organiser of the trip, Martin Wilson, and also his wife, Sophie, to detail what they did on each day. We need to find out exactly how much free time Neil had and what he did."

Silence fell over the table, as each of them considered the implications.

"The letter also could easily have been from someone within the group," Jonny declared. "Maybe Darren Kozma was in love with Neil and wanted to meet him somewhere secret?"

"But why a handwritten letter?" asked Boukal, looking confused.

"More romantic? Mysterious? I don't know really. Also, Gary Needham could have wanted to put the record straight with Neil about the money."

"A builder would be unlikely to write a letter," suggested Mikeš.

"I agree," stated Jonny. "Also it could have been Richard Weston, still holding a grudge after five years and luring Neil to his death by organising for someone to kill him. Unlikely, but possible."

"I was looking over the first interview transcripts again," announced Boukal. "Richard said his new girlfriend or partner, Hana, is originally from Czech Republic. It seems like a strange coincidence."

"You're right, I'd forgotten that," agreed Mikeš. "Well done, Marek."

Jonny nodded, showing his appreciation. "Looks like we need to talk to them all again. First, I want to speak to Adrian Scott and find out more about Neil's personal life. He has been his close friend since school. If anyone will know about a secret life, it will be him."

"It could also have been James Hopkins who wrote the letter," Boukal added. "We are still waiting for the school CCTV tapes to check so we can eliminate him from the investigation."

"Very true," confirmed Jonny.

Mikeš put his head in his hands dramatically. "I thought we were getting somewhere, but actually we are still no closer."

Jonny put his hand reassuringly on Mikeš. "I actually think we are closing in. We need to find the letter and envelope, and hopefully also get a good description of the person who delivered it."

"Yes, we need that," Mikeš confirmed.

"Also," Jonny continued. "I think the codes are linked in some way. I was looking at them again after the interviews today and I'm beginning to think the date order is significant. At first, I thought they were related to money, but I'm not so sure now. I called Heather Davis earlier. She is the woman who Neil was exchanging messages with over the weekend. She was very defensive about how she knew Neil, and I detected she was hiding something. I want to check the actual notebook again, to study the other reminders listed around these codes to try to understand their context before deciding what else to do."

The waitress delivered the coffee. Jonny thanked her, "Děkuju."

The distraction seemed to perk Mikeš up. "This is Ella's favourite café. We often come here in the morning when we are both free. They have a food market on the square which she likes looking around."

"I didn't know you lived here," ventured Jonny.

"We both live further out now, but we had a flat here when we first got married. This café has sentimental meaning for both of us. And great cakes as well – the best Honey Cake in

Prague!"

Jonny sipped his cappuccino, considering Mikeš' personal admission. "I'm learning fast how this city can take hold of your heart. It has a power which is hard to describe."

"I'm glad you feel it, Honza. This city is special."

25

Tempting Questions

Entering the Hloupý Honza pub with Ivana, Jonny had felt like a returning, long-lost son, such was the warmth of the welcome. He knew Czech people were convivial, keen on a party, especially if alcohol was involved, but the level of hospitability he had received from these members of the local community was unexpected.

When he commented on the friendliness, Ivana gave him a glimpse into the national psyche. "You need to understand: we love the British. You are like a visiting celebrity and everyone wants to know you, to practice their English on you, and then tell their friends about you."

"No wonder people from the UK come back here time and again."

"It's odd, though," she continued. "Czech people are not so open and friendly to each other. It's changing with the new generation, but older people are still naturally reserved, taking time to trust each other."

Ivana had dressed up for the evening out, wearing a halter-neck dress, exposing her shoulders and accentuating her figure. With her hair worn up and held with combs, complemented by long earrings and only a little makeup, she looked natural and stylish, fit for any occasion. Having seen her preparing for a night out before, Jonny had expected her to dress up, but was still surprised at how attractive she looked. She had merely blushed when he had complimented her, waving away his flattery. He had also made his own, modest effort, wearing a clean, open-necked shirt, paired with chinos and a jacket.

After shaking hands with the landlord, Jerry, Jonny waved to Monika behind the bar, then greeted the ever-present Štefan and his canine companion, Viky. Jonny and Ivana sat at their reserved table, two large beers arriving almost immediately.

"That's impressive service," praised Jonny.

"The benefits of being a regular," Ivana chuckled, and raised her glass for a toast. "Na zdraví."

Štefan raised his glass in response to their invitation across the tables. Viky barked, keen not to be forgotten.

"I'm starving," Jonny declared. "Do they have any specials tonight?"

"Actually, I have a confession to make," Ivana responded, lowering her eyes timidly. "I took the liberty of ordering for us. They have an amazing speciality of a whole roasted duck, but you have to order it twenty-four hours in advance. I arranged it with Jaroslav yesterday. The food will come soon."

"No need to apologise," he assured her. "It sounds perfect."

Jonny sat back and relaxed, pleased that Ivana had taken care of everything. She smiled bashfully, apparently delighted at having made the right choice.

They sipped their drinks, Jonny ruminating on all the kind-hearted gestures coming his way over the past few days. There was a time in the past, defensive after lost love or missing his daughter, when he would revert to an introverted, gruff persona, either rejecting offers of kindness or accepting them ungraciously. The sincere tenderness being shown to him by Ivana and others felt positively alien, but he resolved to accede to it, and return it with benevolence and openness.

"You were talking just now about the older generation of Czech people," he started. "Well, I do know what you mean. My mother was Czech, she was born in Prague. But she moved to UK in her early twenties. She was an amazing woman, but she could be very tough. She was also suspicious of people who were over-friendly."

"I knew it," declared Ivana, putting her hand to her mouth. "I didn't want to ask, knowing you're a private person, but you do have something of a Slavic look."

"Do I?" Jonny looked surprised.

"Yes. It's the shape of the face, quite broad. Also, you have quite prominent cheekbones."

Jonny suddenly felt self-conscious, not used to talking about himself, and quickly moved the conversation along. "My father was Scottish, but I don't remember him. He left us when I was only three."

"Have you seen photos of him?"

"Not really. My mother was very bitter after he left and decided to live life pretending he'd never existed. I think I only saw one photo of him when I was very young. I found it in a drawer when looking for something. When my mother realised what it was she quickly snatched it away. She probably burnt it."

"But weren't you ever interested to find your father?"

"No, not at all. When he left, he left both of us. It would have been easy for him to find me, my mother was stilling living in the same small house they moved into together. But he never wanted to find me so I am not interested."

The swing doors of the kitchen burst open, curbing their conversation. Jerry appeared, lavishly carrying a roasting tin in one hand, a tea towel over his other arm. The steam and mouth-watering aroma reached them first, followed by the tin laid on the table between them, revealing perhaps the most sumptuous looking meal Jonny had ever seen. "Wow!" was all he could muster, shocked but also ravenous. Ivana smiled at his reaction.

"Dobrou chut," Jerry said, giving a small bow and retreating back to the kitchen.

"I did say it was a speciality," Ivana reminded him. "And

you should carve."

Jonny pensively picked up the carving cutlery and started to dissect the duck, placing the first portion on Ivana's plate.

"So, Jonny..."

He interrupted her. "Please call me Honza. Everyone at work is, and it seems kind of fitting here."

She looked stumped, speechless for a moment. "Honza! Really?"

Jonny smiled, nodding his approval, as he continued cutting up the bird.

"Ok, Honza," Ivana started tentatively, rolling the name around on her tongue. "Are you here in Prague to trace your family?"

"No," he replied firmly. "My mother never kept contact with them. I just wanted to see the Prague she told me stories about."

"But why not?" she appealed to him. "Maybe it is your destiny to find some of your mother's family. You might be able to build some bridges over the generations. Your cousins, or even your aunts and uncles? Family is more important than anything else."

Jonny laughed. "You are not the first person to say that to me over the last few days."

"Well, I won't push any more. But, and this is just an offer, if you want to trace your family, I might be able to help. I have a good friend who works in the government department looking after registrations: births, marriages, deaths. I could introduce you to her."

Jonny looked at Ivana, his carving job finished, again feeling touched by the tender and generous offer to help him. "Thank you very much, Ivana. I will need to think about it. It's more than just searching for family, it's about what my mother would want. But it is really kind of you."

Ivana looked at the plates, admiring the knife work, smiled at him and said "Dobrou chut."

Jonny smiled back. "Thank you for inviting me tonight and organising all this. Dobrou chut."

They both started eating, silence descending as they focused on the meal. Ivana looked at him, waiting for the verdict with baited breath. Jonny, knowing she was waiting for his reaction, could not stop the wide grin. "This duck is amazing."

"I thought you'd like it."

They looked at each other across the table, unable to stop grinning. Eventually, the temptation of the tasty food overcame Jonny and he resumed eating, reflecting on the radiance of the evening so far.

"Honza, I promised myself not to ask you lots of questions tonight, but I can't resist just one. Am I allowed?"

"Ok, just one," Jonny joked.

"Just now you said 'everyone at work'. I didn't know you were working here."

"That isn't a question," Jonny replied, teasing her.

"Okay, cheeky," she mock slapped his hand across the table. "My question is – what work are you doing here in Prague?"

Jonny prepared his revelation. "I am a retired policeman, nearly twenty-five years in the UK Police. It's a very long story, but I have somehow got dragged into investigating a murder here in Prague."

"I knew it!" declared Ivana again, more excited this time. Jonny couldn't help laughing at her girlish reaction.

She quickly continued the questioning. "Is it the murder which happened in Old Town Square earlier in the week?"

Jonny smiled. "Yes." He put his finger up to his lip, "But you can't tell anyone."

"How exciting!" Ivana said loudly, dropping her cutlery and clapping her hands together. He put his finger to his lip again, "Shhh..." looking around the pub for something or someone unknown that might be lurking in the shadows, trying to overhear their conversation.

Monika arrived at the table uninvited, holding two fresh beers. Only then did Jonny realise Ivana had already finished her first beer, his beer glass still a quarter full. Jonny, taking the initiative, said "Děkujeme" to Monika. Both Ivana and Monika were shocked.

"What?" Jonny exclaimed, looking puzzled.

"Nothing," Monika replied. "We are impressed with your Czech."

"Diky moc."

"Now you are just showing off," Ivana said. Monika laughed, collected the spare glass, and walked back to the bar.

"My mother used to speak to me in Czech when I was young," Jonny offered. "But I rebelled when I went to school and would only speak to her in English. A lot of words sound familiar, but it was a long time ago."

"Don't worry, you are already doing better than most British people who visit."

Jonny looked at the new beers on the table in front of them. "I have a serious question for you, Ivana. How do Czech women drink so much beer and stay so slim?"

"For us it's like medicine," she proposed, jokily. "The famous saying we have is whenever you go to the doctor they will tell you to drink more beer whatever is wrong with you!"

Jonny laughed loudly, enjoying himself immensely.

Jerry appeared at the table, ghosting into the space whilst they were engrossed in each other's company. "So, Honza, how's the duck?"

"I don't know the Czech word for it, but it's fantastic."

"Výborný," Ivana said. "It means 'excellent'."

"Výborný," Jonny echoed.

Jerry bowed his head. "I am so pleased you are enjoying it. It is a special dish for me because it is cooked to my grandmother's recipe."

"Thank you," said Jonny. "I feel very privileged to be able to try it."

Jerry put his hands together in a prayer like gesture,

thanking Jonny with earnest pride, and backed away from the table, leaving them alone again.

"So, are you famous?" asked Ivana, looking around quickly to make sure nobody else was listening.

"I think that's another question!" Jonny pounced, smiling suggestively, before relenting and continuing. "No, I'm not. But do you know Felix Mikeš?"

"The Black Cat?" squealed Ivana in delight.

Jonny laughed out loud. "Yes, him. Well I'm assisting Mikeš with the investigation."

"You must be famous then," Ivana clapped again in excitement. "He is famous across the Czech Republic after catching so many criminals. But he is old now. He must be nearly eighty."

Jonny laughed so much he almost choked on his food. "I am going to enjoy telling him that."

Ivana gasped, suddenly aware of her faux pas. "No, no, no. Honza, you can't. Promise me you won't say anything."

Jonny laughed, enjoying himself immensely, and raised his glass to Štefan on the nearby table. "Na zdraví." Štefan raised his glass in toast and winked back at Jonny. Viky joined in, barking his approval.

The walk back to the apartment was meandering and peaceful, the back streets quiet apart from the few revellers making their way home after closing time. Ivana held onto his arm tightly, her head sometimes leaning on his shoulder, looking up at the sky in wonder.

"Honza?"

"Yes?"

"I have heard you playing Bob Dylan."

"Is this another question?" he teased.

Ivana laughed and slapped him arm lightly. Slightly drunk now, she ignored his point and carried on. "Czech people love Bob Dylan. He is in the heart of people here. Did you know he is playing a concert here soon?"

"Yes, I already have tickets. I'm a big fan. I bought the

tickets on impulse and it's one of the reasons I'm here in Prague now."

"Václav Havel, our famous President, is a fan. They met at Bob Dylan's last concert here."

"Yes, they are both great men!" Jonny replied.

Ivana put her head on his shoulder and squeezed into him as they walked.

Back at the apartment Jonny opened the door with his key, holding it open for Ivana.

"I like a British gentleman," she said, leaning in to kiss him fleetingly.

Before Jonny could say anything she was disappearing through the living room door, beckoning him in after her with instructions to make himself comfortable on the sofa.

Ivana reappeared after a few minutes carrying two nightcaps, and placed them on the coffee table in front of the sofa. Looking deep into his eyes, she started to unclasp her dress from behind her neck, eventually working enough to wriggle free, the dress falling to her ankles.

"Ivana..." Jonny started.

"Shhh," she whispered, softly. "I'm not asking anything of you. It was just a perfect evening and I want to do this."

Jonny sat on the sofa speechless, slowly looking Ivana up and down in her lingerie. Standing over him, allowing him time to feast with his eyes, she slowly ran a finger along his cheek. Jonny gulped, trying to catch air, caught in her seductive spell. She gracefully sat down next to him, thigh to thigh, and picked up both shot glasses, handing one to him.

"Na zdraví" she said. He repeated the toast and they drank in unison. The liquor tasted extra strong, making his head buzz, but he took her glass and placed it with his on the table. Looking into her eyes, he took her face delicately in his hands and leaned forward to kiss her wet lips. As they kissed passionately, her fingers running through his hair, their tongues twirling in foreplay, he ran his hand around her lacy bra, over the soft skin of her stomach and onto her inner thigh, passing tantalisingly over her silky knickers.

Ivana broke off and looked into his eyes, her hand on his cheek. "I think we should go somewhere a little bit more comfortable." Jonny could only nod his approval, his voice failing him in the heat of desire.

She rose from the sofa, hand outstretched.

He stood, now towering over her, and took her hands. "Are you sure?"

Her only response was to reach up and kiss him, curl her hand into his, and lead him off in the direction of the bedroom.

26

The Big Test

Thursday, 18th March

Jonny woke early to the feel of warm, soft skin against him, a faint smell of perfume filling the air. The alarm he'd set the night before continued to beep, but Ivana remained asleep beside him, her hair tousled over the pillow and her delicate features moving in time with her shallow breathing. As he lay there readying himself to start the day, his eyes adjusting to the half-light, everything felt alien, but oddly calm and comforting.

He wasn't one for one-night stands; the balance of pleasure and guilt didn't equate for him. The few times alcohol had blocked his usual sense of reasoning, he had only panicked, trying to extricate himself from the situation as soon as was practical. Preferably without the standard embarrassed conversation, full of fake interest in each other and hesitant promises to call.

But this was different. He sensed no blame was there to apportion, given the way the evening had evolved and the comfort on both sides. As she had said, it had just felt right. But he also knew he wasn't looking for a serious relationship right now, and if he worried about anything it was how they would dance around the new deeper bond between them.

Even though he still hardly knew Ivana, he already felt protective of her. Her kindness was almost crushing for someone like him, not used to receiving support and goodwill. Watching her breathing lightly next to him, he knew how special she was and resolved to keep making her feel special whatever happened. It was another part of his new, ever-growing challenge in the heart of this great city.

Although he had a lot of thinking to do, he also knew that he couldn't just lay there, let alone fall back to sleep. He needed to stir himself into action because people in Prague were relying on him now; this murder case had to be solved soon.

"Ivana," he whispered softly.

He repeated her name slightly louder, running his hand gently over her hair. She opened a sleepy eye and smiled at him. "Ahoj."

"I have to go now. I'm needed on the police investigation."

"Okay," she murmured in return, her eyes struggling to stay open.

Jonny kissed her on the lips and pulled the sheet up to her neck, before sliding quietly out of bed and picking up his clothes strewn over the bedroom floor. Looking back to see Ivana, now turned over, going back to sleep, he smiled to himself and tiptoed out of the room, picking up his shoes on his way back up to his attic room.

He showered quickly, dressed and left the apartment in double-quick time, keen to arrive early at the police station before the morning briefing. With coffee and croissant in hand, picked up at the same café on the walk from the metro, Jonny tested his new key card, gaining access to the building. The night duty policeman greeting him like a member of the establishment. "Ahoj, Honza."

Settling himself in the Incident Room, eating his breakfast whilst reappraising the outline evidence and connections on the board, Jonny found himself thinking about the restaurant. Maybe it was pure chance the friends decided to have lunch there. They were just wandering and selected the venue for lunch based on similar criteria he had himself used. After all, it had become the favourite spot for his afternoon coffee. But maybe it was planned, or at least that area of Old Town Square had already been chosen. And, if so, who else knew about it? He wrote a reminder in his notebook to ask in the interviews planned for the day ahead.

Dvořáková walked into the room holding some papers and a coffee. She saw Jonny consuming his breakfast. "I see you don't need my coffee today."

"I didn't want to push my luck," he joked, smiling wryly.

Ignoring his quip, she sat down next to him and opened her folder. "We have good news and bad news. I have spoken to the concierge at the hotel and he has given us a description of the person who delivered the letter. The bad news is that he did not see their face."

"CCTV?" he offered.

"Unfortunately not," she said. "The person delivering the letter is caught on both the CCTV camera at the hotel entrance and also inside the foyer. However, we cannot get a clear view of their face. They are wearing a black hoodie, as you thought, black trousers and white trainers. They walk in quickly, hand the letter to the concierge and then leave, but all the time the hoodie is concealing their face. It is so fast, they must have known exactly where they were going."

"They clearly didn't want to be identified," Jonny stated. "The question is who by?"

She looked puzzled. "What do you mean?"

"Well, they clearly didn't want to be identified by the hotel staff. But maybe they were also worried about being seen by Neil Robson and his friends. Perhaps the person delivering the letter didn't know where they all were and was maybe worried they would bump into them in the hotel foyer."

Dvořáková paused in thought, considering the permutations.

"And," Jonny continued, "I suppose the person delivering the letter didn't touch any other surface on their way in and out of the hotel?"

"No. They had the envelope in their hand, walked in and handed it straight to the concierge. They didn't touch anything. Even the hotel doors open automatically."

He sighed at the information. "The only chance of getting a fingerprint is if we can find the letter and the envelope in the hotel rubbish."

"I am getting still photos produced from the CCTV video," Dvořáková informed him. "I have watched both videos a few times and the person is of average height with a medium build. But it is hard to tell anything more distinctive because they are wearing baggy clothes."

Jonny nodded. "Dr Králová said there was a possibility the killer was smaller than the victim, so that information is consistent. I would like to see the videos myself. We can also show the still photos to the friends in the interviews later. Maybe we should show the photos around Old Town Square again to see if they jog any memories with shopkeepers."

"I'll organise it," Dvořáková confirmed. "Also, a shop owner along the escape route, near where you found the knife, remembers someone acting suspiciously near the small garden on Monday afternoon. They couldn't be sure of the exact time, but one of my officers took a statement. I'm arranging for her to come into the station and give us a more detailed description. She did not see the face of the person, but she verified they were wearing black clothes. The slight difference is this witness remembers the person wearing a dark hat, like a baseball cap."

"A cap," Jonny mused. "I suggest you put out a call to your uniformed officers to check if a black cap was found on Monday afternoon. Anywhere along the escape route and beyond in the old town. It's possible the killer dumped it on their getaway. If so, we would have some DNA."

"Yes, sir."

"Lucie, please. Just call me Honza. I'm not your boss."

"Ok, Honza," she said, smiling.

Jonny hesitated, deep in thought, a frown developing on his forehead. "We are definitely closing in. But we still have nothing to indicate whether the killer was a professional, hired to murder Neil Robson, or was someone he knew."

Both looked at the board, hoping the mystery would reveal itself.

"We need to find the letter," Jonny muttered. "My next task."

The commotion of Mikeš' arrival in the office reached them in the sanctity of the Incident Room. Although they had only worked together for a few days, Jonny instantly recognised Mikeš' entourage of noise and bustle. But this day's arrival was different, the uproar reaching them filled with less morning jollity, instead it was dominated by a lot of angry huffing and cursing. Mikeš burst into the room, a whirl of hat and cane, erupting into an irate monologue. "I knew it, I knew it. Never trust anyone with money troubles. I should have trusted my instinct and locked them inside the hotel. No, no. Nobody would listen to me. Damn him. He could be anywhere by now..."

Jonny stood up, concerned. "Felix, what has happened?"

Mikeš stopped ranting, but his eyes were still livid, roaming around the room menacingly, looking for something on which to take out his anger. He drew a deep breath to calm himself, then looked directly at Jonny. "I will tell you what has happened. Gary has run off. Exactly what I was worried about."

"Really?" Jonny looked stunned.

"Yes, really," Mikeš confirmed anxiously, a tight frown on his brow. "The officer watching the hotel went up to Gary's room this morning to check him, but he was not there. The bed had not been slept in. His mobile phone is also switched off. He's gone and we've no idea where he is."

"I can't believe it," Jonny added. "He didn't seem the

type to run."

"Well, he has!" Mikeš barked, the irritation written on his face. "And we've lost our prime suspect."

Unable to mask his evident fury, Mikeš was in a state of perpetual motion. He was not able to sit down but also unsure of what to do with himself, oscillating from one foot to the other in his own giddy ritual. The day's choice of a bright yellow shirt/tie combination, paired with his tweed suit, gave the impression of an angry, caged lion.

Dvořáková looked between the two men, transfixed by the rising tension in the room.

Jonny wasn't sure if the anger was directed at him or not. Mikeš was clearly an exuberant character, prone to deep swings in mood, but this felt different. His strong emotional response was making it difficult for Jonny to read which way he was going to react. Jonny was also aware that his own lack of experience of the culture was not helping.

Jonny's role on the team had its obvious benefits, being able to stay involved in a meaningful project whilst not being fully responsible. But the obvious flipside was the potential to be the easy choice of fall guy. He had never had a consultant or similar working on his own teams, it being a role his nature would fight against, but he could imagine the inclination to apportion blame unfairly on non-permanent members when things didn't go to plan. In Jonny's experience these equipoises in the police were usually driven by work politics, taking the easy way out, apportioning blame to save face and maintain good PR regardless of the impact on catching criminals.

Jonny knew the only way was to fight for justice, whatever else happened around him. In the full realisation that the situation could go one of two ways, he made a snap decision to push on with what he believed to be right. He'd enjoyed himself immensely so far on this little adventure, but everything happened for a reason, and the preservation of his own role was not an excuse to hold back.

"Felix, is there anything you want me to do?" Jonny enquired, starting tentatively.

"No, Honza. Marek is over at the hotel now co-ordinating the search. Gary was out drinking last night, but the hotel staff are not sure whether he returned or not."

Doing what his first boss had taught him, Jonny decided to push on, fronting up to the key issue. All or nothing. "By the way, Felix, I don't think it was Gary."

Mikeš looked at Jonny, nonplussed.

Jonny clarified. "I don't think Gary Needham killed Neil Robson."

"Why?"

Jonny knew this was the big test. "In my experience Gary is the type of person who would pay back every pound of what he owed to a friend. He would pay late, he would be a pain in the arse about it, getting drunk when you expected him to meet you, but he would pay you back eventually. I know I can't prove it, but I feel it in my bones."

Sensing the concentrated audience, he continued. "Gary is a small-time builder used to earning enough money to go to the pub every week and put food on the table. He likes and respects Neil too much. He would never cheat him, let alone kill him."

Mikeš looked directly at Jonny, unwavering. "Money problems drive people to desperation. I have seen it many times. Just look at Gary, he was in a terrible state when we interviewed him yesterday."

"Yes, that's true," Jonny countered. "But I think he is more emotional about his divorce. He clearly still loves his wife and wants her back. The money problems caused their relationship to dissolve, but that's got nothing to do with Neil. If anything, Neil tried to help Gary by lending him some money."

Mikeš remained silent, considering the points made. His head was clearly telling him to stay calm, but his body was tense, coiled like a spring.

Jonny resumed. "Also, Neil only gave the money to Gary in January. Yes, he is struggling to make the first payment, but it doesn't feel like it was a desperate situation yet. Certainly not enough to kill someone."

"I am not convinced," Mikeš stated flatly, unable to mask his evident fury. "Gary could be lying. Neil maybe needed the money for something else and was demanding it back from him."

"Also possible," Jonny conceded. "But I still don't think it was Gary. We need to find him, of course, but mainly because he might have other information which could help us. For example, he might recognise the person who delivered the letter. But, I think, the killer is someone else and we need to dig deeper to find them."

"You had better be right," Mikeš snapped, shaking his head in anguish. "If Gary turns out to be the murderer and we let him get away, there will be big trouble for all of us!"

"Just trust me on this, Felix," Jonny pleaded.

27

The Rubbish Job

The basement was eerily empty when Jonny entered, now navigating the building alone using his key card. The only activity was the sound of classical music playing loudly behind the window hatch of the evidence room. Liška, a whirl of animated arm movements, was conducting his own imaginary orchestra. Fresh from the tension in the Incident Room, Jonny approached cautiously, not wanting to intrude on a private moment. To his relief, Liška saw him out of the corner of his eye, beckoning him over with a vigorous wave of his hand and a beaming smile.

Liška quickly turned down the music volume and opened the hatch. "Sorry, Honza, I was completely lost in the moment. Josef Mysliveček's violin concerto in D major does that to me!"

"Stirring music, Josef."

"He is much underrated. Mysliveček was friends with Mozart and his father. Tremendous musicality." Liška closed his eyes to listen as the solo violin played to a crescendo, finally opening his eyes when the movement had finished, shaking his head in disbelief at the emotion invoked by the music.

"Seeing someone so passionate about music is almost as good as enjoying the music itself," Jonny commented.

"You understand it, Honza. I can see it," Liška asserted. "I do not understand how some people can operate without music in their lives. It's like living without beauty."

"Very poetic, Josef. I agree wholeheartedly with the sentiment."

Conscious of his imposition on valuable investigation time, Liška snapped back to reality. Reaching across his desk, he grabbed a form and opened it after putting on his half eye reading glasses. "I have taken the liberty of preparing the rubbish from the hotel room in Room 1, just down the corridor."

"That's great. Thank you."

"No problem. It's Lucie you should thank, really. She called me yesterday. Here's the key for the room and I just need you to sign the form. She has already authorised it."

Jonny took the form, signed it and pushed it back through the hatch. Liška counter-signed and torn off the copy page for Jonny.

"But, I should tell you," Liška confessed, pulling a contorted face, "the rubbish is starting to smell a bit. The bags contain all the rubbish the cleaner took from the rooms she cleaned on Monday, from papers to banana skins."

Jonny laughed, holding up a small plastic bag. "Don't worry, I was expecting it. Lucie has given me a mask, as well as some tweezers, plastic gloves and evidence bags."

"She is always so well prepared!" Liška glowed with admiration.

"I'll probably be able to ask for a transfer to forensics after this," Jonny joked, and Liška laughed with him.

"How are you finding working with Felix?" Liška enquired.

"Well it was all going great until just now," Jonny shrugged his shoulders. "One of the suspects has disappeared from the hotel and Felix has gone into orbit. He's not happy at all, like a bear with a sore head."

Liška chortled to himself. "That sounds like Felix."

"Yes," Jonny agreed. "I find him hard to read sometimes. Especially now, he's very angry and is not really listening."

"I understand, I've seen it lots of times before. But the greatest thing about Felix is that he never holds grudges. He can get mad, go into a sulk, but he'll always return, holding no resentment at all, whatever has happened. I think it's a great strength."

"You are right," Jonny concurred. "When I get mad it can take me days to recover and I'm not fun to be around."

Liška continued, a serious look on his face. "It is not for me to say, but life has not always been kind to Felix. But he always bounces back, he's an optimist."

"He is certainly very emotional," said Jonny, a hint of frustration in his voice.

Liška chuckled softly. "He certainly is."

"I'm more of a detail man myself," Jonny admitted. "I'm not high maintenance, just charge my batteries and I just keep going, following all the leads until the investigation is over."

"It's the reason why you get on so well with him. You complement each other," Liška said, knowingly. "In many ways, you are like me. I used to balance out Felix's overbearing characteristics, being solid and reliable when he could sometimes be pompous and pretentious. The difference is you are probably a much better detective than me."

Jonny modestly waved away the suggestion. "I doubt it."

Liška took off his glasses, holding them limply in his hand. "Honza, just be patient. In a very short time, Felix will be back to the person you know best. Trust me."

"Thank you, Josef. It is good to hear some reassurance."

"Anytime, my friend." Liška reached out his hand and they shook.

Jonny started to turn away, plastic bag, form and room key in hand, when he remembered something and quickly circled back. "Actually Josef, there was one other thing. Can I have Neil Robson's black notebook out of the evidence box? I want to keep it on me, use it on the investigation. I've made my own notes of the information from it I'm interested in, but I'd like to have the full notebook on me when comparing it to his schedule, if I can get it, and also his phone records. I might even show it to his wife. I think there are clues in the book, but I need to get inside the victim's head and understand why he wrote them."

"It's an unconventional request, but the notebook has already been processed by forensics so I don't see any reason why not," Liška confirmed. "I'll check with Lucie, and also Felix if I need to, then get the paperwork ready."

"Thanks, Josef."

Jonny opened the door of Room 1 and was momentarily halted in his tracks, the scale of the task ahead of him clear to see. On the floor alongside the table were six large, sealed, dustbin-sized bags of rubbish to be searched by hand. The clear plastic allowed a glimpse of the varied nature of the items thrown away in hotel bins or left behind in the room; used tissues, old socks, newspapers, and various items of food items, all decomposing, from fruit to half-eaten pizza slices.

Never one to shirk a tough job and always willing to roll up his sleeves, Jonny took off his jacket, donned the plastic gloves and mask and laid out the disposable paper sheets left for him on the table. He knew the odds were against him, the envelope having been delivered Saturday and the room cleaned on Monday. The only hope was that the letter was meaningful enough for Neil to have held onto it over the weekend, or he was too hungover on Sunday and refused the room cleaning service. This was either going to be a monumental waste of time and effort, time he could ill afford to lose, or a hallelujah moment for the case.

The first bag, when emptied onto the table, added a pungent fragrance to the task, matching the sense of smell to his vision. The smell was an odd mixture of a damp basement, human flatulence and the contrasting, and almost pleasant, sweetness of strawberries from the rotting dairy products.

Jonny dived into the task, held open the emptied plastic bag and, precisely but quickly, placed all non-paper items back inside the bag. On the few occasions he had to open up a tissue or unidentifiable item of rubbish, he acted quickly, sometimes gagging at the contents, before determining it was not going to aid his search and throwing it swiftly back into the plastic bag.

The first two bags of rubbish were of no interest all, the only paper items being newspapers and flyers picked up by guests on their travels around the city. His eyebrows raised at a leaflet for the Sex Machines Museum in Prague, but, like the other rubbish, he screwed it up and threw it aside.

The third bag contained reams of paper, seemingly from a conference, and took him a painstakingly long time to sift through, the paper having become damp in the bag. Jonny was just starting to lose his patience, when the door opened behind him and Dvořáková entered carrying two mugs of coffee.

"I thought you might need some caffeine and a helping hand," she announced.

"My saviour!" Jonny held up his plastic gloves, smeared with dirt and liquid. "I would give you a hug, but I don't think you'd thank me."

Dvořáková laughed, backing away from his outstretched hands.

"I'm on bag three," Jonny explained after a sip of coffee, indicating towards the remaining bags on the floor.

"I have come prepared," she declared, pulling plastic gloves and a mask from her pocket and holding them up dramatically.

They worked as a team with minimal interaction, Dvořáková holding open the plastic bag and Jonny sorting through the items shaken out on the table. Jonny controlled the process, again first discarding the non-paper and working meticulously through the remaining debris. Bag three revealed nothing, the same for bag four. Halfway through bag five, Jonny froze, holding a small piece of torn paper up to the light. "Hang on," he muttered.

Dvořáková, her interest suddenly piqued, rested the half full plastic bag on the floor and moved in closer to get a better look. Jonny picked up the torn corner of a page with the tweezers, holding it up for both of them to examine the handwriting written on it.

"This piece must be the top left-hand corner," Jonny stated. "The writing is in capital letters, it says 'WE NEED TO TA'."

Dvořáková lent in further. "Maybe 'talk'?" she offered.

"Could be," he agreed. "The question is whether it is *our* letter. Let's keep going."

Back to their silent teamwork, the torn paper now inside an evidence bag and laid separately on a chair, Jonny continued to carefully sort through the rubbish of bag five.

"The cleaner would be very unlikely to put the waste from one room in two separate bags," Dvořáková suggested.

"You never know," he replied without stopping. "The dustbin bag may have been full between emptying the bin from the bedroom and then the bin from the bathroom, or vice versa."

Jonny suddenly halted again, picking out from the debris another piece of paper. He held the paper up to the light with the tweezers, examining it in detail and then holding it next to the first piece in the evidence bag.

"This is the piece underneath," he stated. "It says 'MEET ME AT'."

Spurred on by the discovery, Jonny worked faster but still concentrating hard on each item he picked up. With only a few items left on the table he discovered another piece of the jigsaw. "This must be the top right-hand piece. You were right, the first line of the letter says 'WE NEED TO TALK ABOUT THE FUTURE'."

Dvořáková looked pleased with herself, enthused by her involvement in the discovery.

Jonny checked all the remaining items laid out on the table, but found no further segments of the letter. "I must have missed the other piece, or pieces. We need to check the bag again."

They poured the contents of bag five back onto the table and restarted the painstaking process. After another ten minutes the table was clear but they hadn't found anything.

"We need to check the final bag," Jonny insisted.

The sixth bag was unloaded onto the table and checked using the same rigorous process. They found nothing even close to another portion of the letter, only general rubbish and a lot of food waste.

Jonny put the three parts of the letter, all in separate evidence bags, on the table and studied them. He recited out loud the words as Dvořáková looked over his shoulder:

WE NEED TO TALK ABOUT THE FUTURE
MEET ME AT

Jonny pointed to the space left by the missing piece of the letter. "Looking at where the sentences were started on the left-hand side of the paper, there was definitely something written after 'MEET ME AT'. Probably either a venue or a time, or maybe both."

"Do you think you missed the last piece of the letter?" Dvořáková questioned him.

"I'm sure I didn't. We even checked bag five twice."

"But where could it be?"

Jonny paused to consider the options. "My guess is he tore off the bottom of the letter. Either it meant something to him and he wanted to keep it, or it contained some important information."

"The location to meet?"

"Could be..." His voice trailed off, his attention consumed by the message.

"And the murderer then took the piece of letter after they killed him?" she posed.

"Possible. But it would have been slow and messy to check all his pockets and wallet. Maybe Neil Robson just threw it away another time. Also, the envelope is not here either." Jonny shook his head, irked by getting so close. "Damn!" he muttered in frustration.

Jonny sealed the three plastic evidence bags. "We need to send these pieces of the letter to forensics to check for fingerprints and DNA. But we need a photo taken before they are sent off. Also, I want to be very careful how much we tell the potential suspects about this letter. Let's see if we can catch someone out."

Dvořáková nodded and looked at her watch. "Honza, Adrian Scott was booked for interview at 10am. Felix said he was going over to the hotel to check the search for Gary Needham. I also doubt if Marek is back. Shall we conduct the interview together?"

"Fine with me," Jonny agreed. "But let's reseal the bags and ask Josef if we can leave them here. We might need to check them again later."

"No problem, leave it to me," she assured him.

28

Interview 2 – Adrian Scott

The following is a transcript of the recorded interview conducted with Adrian Scott (AS) on the morning of Thursday, 18th March 2010.

Present at the interview were Sergeant Lucie Dvořáková (LD) and Consultant Jonathan Fox (JF). The reason for the presence of JF was explained at the beginning of the interview; he is continuing to assist the Czech Police team on this murder investigation.

LD: Interview commenced at 10:14. Please state your name for the tape.
AS: Adrian Scott.
JF: Thank you for coming in again. We understand it is a stressful situation for all of you. Since we spoke on Tuesday, some information has come to light and we need to ask you more questions to help us in our investigation.
AS: Where is the leading detective, the one who came with you to talk to Carly (Robson) yesterday?
LD: Chief Warrant Officer Felix Mikeš is out of the office at the moment. I am leading the interview with assistance from Mr Fox.
JF: Adrian, do you know Gary (Needham) has not been seen at his hotel since evening last night?
AS: Darren (Kozma) called me and told me something was going on. He told me there are lots of police officers at their hotel.

JF: Yes. Do you have any idea where Gary would go?
AS: No, sorry. I am as surprised as you.
JF: No problem, I wasn't expecting you to know. As we are talking about Gary, I would like to ask you some questions about his relationship with Neil Robson.
AS: Okay.
JF: Did you know that Neil had loaned Gary some money?
AS: No, I didn't know. Well, actually I suspected something.
JF: Please explain.
AS: I first suspected something when they argued down the pub back a few weeks ago. Richard (Weston) dealt with it, but told us all the argument between Neil and Gary was something about money. I asked Neil about it and he just said Gary was tight with money and wasn't buying his share of the drinks.
JF: And you didn't believe him?
AS: It was just that I saw them huddled together a couple of times after the night of the argument, always deep in conversation. They weren't really close so it was a bit unusual. But there were no further arguments between them after that time in the pub.
JF: Didn't you ask Neil if anything was wrong?
AS: No.
JF: But I thought you two were close, best friends?
AS: We have known each other since school, he's like a brother. We used to share everything, but it's different when you settle down. We're both married, he's had two kids recently with Carly, it changes how much time you can spend together. If he wanted to lend Gary some money it is not my concern.
JF: And do you know if Neil had a secret stash of money?
AS: How do you mean?
JF: Money his wife did not know about. Cash.
AS: When we first met our wives, girlfriends back then, and respectively settled down we used to hide money away for beers down the pub, trips into London, and also for trips abroad like this one. It was silly really, but it made us feel like we could be

free. We called it the Party Fund.

JF: Was it for drugs?

AS: We went crazy a couple of times, mostly on trips abroad, but drugs was never our thing. Alcohol was our drug of choice, always has been.

JF: How much did you keep hidden away?

AS: A couple of hundred pounds.

JF: And did you stop it?

AS: Yes. It just died away after a few years of settling down.

JF: And Neil?

AS: I think so. He's never mentioned anything to me since we stopped.

JF: Did you ever have any suspicion that Neil was on drugs?

AS: No. Neil was never really into it. It was usually me pulling him along to buy some weed. He was more into beer and chasing women.

JF: I'm getting the feeling you weren't as close to Neil as you wanted to be. Am I right?

AS: We saw each other every week or so, sent a lot of messages but mostly jokes and football chat. It's not that we weren't as close as I wanted, it just gets more difficult when you settle down. I had more free time than him because Lizzie (Scott) and I don't have children yet, but he was pretty good at getting out when family and work allowed.

JF: Thanks. Do you know if Neil was having an affair with anyone?

AS: No.

JF: Do you know if he has ever had an affair whilst he's been married?

AS: Will the information I provide be treated as confidential?

JF: What we say to everyone is we'll treat it as confidential if it is background information, but we cannot promise if it turns out to be pertinent to the investigation. You must be able to understand.

AS: Yes.

JF: So please tell us what you know.

AS: In the first years of his marriage to Carly, Neil had a few flings. He always told me they were one-night stands.
JF: Including Richard's wife, Natasha?
AS: Yes.
JF: And after Natasha?
AS: I don't think so. That situation caused him a lot of problems, with Carly obviously, but also within his group of friends. He wasn't allowed in the pub for a while.
JF: Yes, we know. So you think he learned his lesson?
AS: I think so. He always claimed afterwards that he was being a good boy, a family man.
JF: And did you believe him?
AS: I had no reason to doubt him. He seemed devoted to Carly and the kids.
JF: Do you know Heather Davis?
AS: No. Who is she?
JF: It doesn't matter. Going back to Natasha, do you think it's possible that Richard could hold a grudge against Neil after all these years?
AS: No.
JF: Why so certain?
AS: They got on well, I think it was in the past. Richard is happier now, with Hana, than he was before.
JF: We have found out somebody delivered a handwritten note to Neil at the hotel on Saturday afternoon. Do you remember it happening?
[Pause]
AS: Actually I do remember something. Neil was called over to reception and a receptionist handed him something. It looked like an envelope. He laughed it off, said it was a mistake.
JF: Neil didn't say anything else about it?
AS: No.
JF: Did you see Neil open the envelope?
AS: Only from a distance.
JF: So you didn't see what was inside the envelope?
AS: No.

JF: Didn't you think it was a bit odd?

AS: At the time, yes, I suppose so. But he said it was just a mistake and nothing more was said about it.

JF: Didn't you or one of your friends think it might be important to tell us about it?

AS: I'm sorry. It was such a small thing, over in a matter of seconds. I didn't think anything of it.

JF: We have an image on CCTV of someone delivering the envelope. Unfortunately their face is not distinguishable.

AS: Really? [Pause] That's odd, isn't it?

JF: I think so. Who would know he was here in Prague?

AS: I don't know.

JF: Here is a photo of the person who delivered the envelope to the hotel? Do you recognise the person?

LD: For the purposes of the tape, Mr Fox is now showing Mr Adrian Scott a still photo taken from the hotel CCTV recording.

AS: It's impossible to recognise anyone from this photo.

JF: Please look closely, you might recognise something.

[Pause]

AS: No, sorry. It could be anyone.

JF: Please think carefully, do you remember anything out of the ordinary happening to Neil in the last few weeks, or over the weekend? Maybe he said something to you?

AS: I have thought long and hard about this. I assumed what happened in the restaurant was just a random attack, but clearly you don't think so. I can't think of anything.

JF: In Neil's weekend holdall we found a notebook of reminders. Some of the entries do not make sense to us. Do you recognise these at all?

LD: For the purposes of the tape, Mr Fox is now showing Mr Adrian Scott a series of letters and numbers which have been copied from Neil Robson's notebook.

[Pause]

AS: Sorry, no.

JF: Let's go back to the weekend you spent here in Prague last year with your wives. Do you remember anything unusual happening to Neil?

AS: No. Martin (Wilson) told me you had quizzed him about that weekend. We spent almost all the time together with our wives, walking the city, on the boat, at lunch or dinner.

JF: And Neil didn't go missing for any period of time?

AS: I don't remember anything unusual. You should ask Carly.

JF: On Sunday afternoon after lunch, you and Martin went off somewhere. Can you tell me where?

AS: I'll be honest and say I couldn't remember. It was Martin who reminded me we went to see the Kafka Memorial.

JF: You couldn't remember?

AS: No. For me, it was just a little walk after a heavy lunch. Martin had wanted to see the statue all weekend, but our walking route on the Saturday had missed it. Being honest, I can't remember a lot about it. We walked to the memorial, looked at it and then took a walk back through the Jewish Quarter.

JF: Why didn't you go with Neil instead of Martin?

AS: Again, I couldn't really remember this either. Martin reminded me that he went to an art museum which is definitely not up my street.

JF: Okay. But you don't remember Neil acting any different when you all got back together?

AS: No.

JF: Can I ask you about Darren and Neil? What type of friendship did they have?

AS: I'm not sure what you are getting at?

JF: Were they close?

AS: I don't think so. Neil and I really only saw Darren down the pub.

JF: Has Martin talked to you about Darren?

AS: No. I don't understand what you mean.

JF: Did Neil and Darren spend a lot of time together on this trip?

AS: Now you mention it, they were talking quite a lot. Darren

can be a bit odd sometimes, a bit too intense for me. Neil liked him more than I did.
JF: Neil went with Darren to the cabaret.
AS: So what? Richard and Gary also went.
JF: Were you jealous Neil spent a lot of time with Darren over the weekend?
AS: Are you joking? I don't understand what you are suggesting.
JF: Well it does seem they spent a lot of time talking.
AS: I don't like your line of questioning.
JF: Let's change the subject. I want to take you back to the argument at lunch between Neil and Martin. In your opinion, why did it start?
AS: I don't know.
JF: Look, I am asking the questions. You might not like some of them, but I am just trying to get to the truth. I am asking you again, why did the argument start between Neil and Martin?
[Pause]
AS: I'm not sure. Martin was just being his usual pernickety self. He finds it hard to relax and just enjoy the moment. All I remember was him talking about where to go on our next football trip and also possible cities to go away again with the wives. Neil could be quite explosive at times and he just lost patience with Martin, turning on him.
JF: Do you think Neil was under stress about something?
AS: I have also thought about this since he was killed and I do think there was something wrong. Even though we didn't see as much of each other as before, I still know him very well. We spent so much time together when we were young, it felt sometimes like we actually were brothers. I've seen Neil react badly before to people, but his reaction to Martin was unusually strong. I tried to calm him down but he just carried on. It was like he flipped. With everything that happened afterwards I didn't get time to reflect on the argument, but now it does feel wrong. An overreaction definitely.
JF: And why pick on Martin?

AS: This is what I mean. Martin was just suggesting places like Budapest for taking the wives away, and also talking about going to Seville for the next football trip. Martin can be pedantic but he certainly didn't mean anything bad.
JF: And I understand Neil got very personal with Martin?
AS: Yes, it was odd. Neil would usually just tell him to shut up, but he launched into an attack about Martin's life: how he'd wasted his youth in our town, and hadn't seen the world. It was very personal.
JF: And what was Neil's reaction to you when you tried to calm him down?
AS: He was quite rude to me as well, accusing me of siding with Martin. I remember him accusing Martin and I of pushing him to go to the restaurant for lunch. It was odd.
JF: Hang on, please explain. Why did you go to that restaurant?
AS: It was nothing really. It was just the restaurant we all went to for lunch on the Sunday of the trip last year with the wives.
JF: And Martin and you wanted to go there again?
AS: It was Martin's suggestion. I went along with it, I thought it was a good idea. Nice memories, something to tell the wives about. Plus the food was excellent.
JF: And what did Neil say when Martin suggested it?
AS: He said we should go somewhere else, but Martin and I outvoted him.
JF: So Neil went to the restaurant reluctantly?
AS: Yes I suppose so. But I really didn't think it was a big deal. We sat down on the terrace, got a drink and ordered our food. The conversation was flowing and I thought we were having a good time, but then Neil starting acting strange.
JF: Can you remember seeing anyone else enter the restaurant? Or maybe Neil looking in the direction of someone whilst you sat at the table?
AS: I've also thought about this and, no, I can't remember anything. Neil didn't seem to spot anyone unusual there. Anyway, I think he would have said something to us.
JF: And why did he go to the toilet?

AS: I just think he needed to go. It was also a good way to get away from the argument with Martin.

JF: Okay. I have no further questions at this stage.

[Pause]

LD: Thank you, Mr Scott. We are going over to the hotel soon to see Mrs Robson again. If you remember anything else after the interview please let us know. Interview terminated at 10:53.

29

Good Friends

The Powder Tower looked resplendent in the late morning glare, standing tall and proud, watching over all the visitors coming in and out of Prague Old Town. Jonny and Dvořáková walked under its arch onto Náměstí Republiky, the square alive with activity. The wide walkway was flanked by the renowned Hybernia Theatre on one side and the striking Municipal House on the other, an Art Nouveau building hosting galleries, small concert rooms and restaurants. The cobbled strip between the two prestigious venues was the place for street-level eating and drinking during the day, transforming itself into the hub for musical concerts in the evening.

Perhaps inspired by Liška's musical passion, Jonny accepted a leaflet on upcoming classical concerts pushed at him by a tout. He stopped to have a quick glance at it, noting the advertisement for Czech composers, and folded it for safe keeping inside his jacket pocket.

The bright sunlight was suddenly obscured by a dense cloud passing overhead, a reminder that the spring sunshine should not be taken for granted. Jonny turned around to see the Gothic tower now looming over them as defender of the historic city, the blackened walls and stone roof looking angry and threatening to any approaching enemy. He chuckled to himself at how an innate object could superficially change its mood with an alteration of the light.

Dvořáková had also stopped and was waiting for him, her arms crossed, looking stern and impatient.

"Lucie, are you ok?"

"Yes, but we need to hurry," she replied quickly, appearing harassed. "There's just a lot of activity going on and I need to get back to the station as soon as I can."

Jonny nodded his understanding. "I can go alone if it's better for you. I'm sure Carly Robson won't mind."

"No, it's fine. I just don't want Felix coming back to the station before me and causing havoc."

She started to walk off briskly, deep in thought. Jonny caught up with her and, aware of the increased tension at such a delicate stage in the investigation, said nothing, instead just matching her stride for stride.

His experience in the police force had taught him how busy the role of sergeant could be, with many tasks to organise and oversee across a multitude of ongoing investigations. It could also be lonely; you were never truly in the pool of uniformed officers, having been promoted from the ranks, and also whilst involved with the senior detective team, not yet considered to be part of the inner sanctum. This meant a sergeant needed double the eyes and ears, keeping tabs on the information flowing up and the orders needing to be channelled down. It was also a role for the thick-skinned because catching some element of blame was hard to avoid when something went wrong. Mikeš was an inclusive and supportive man manager, with significant experience, but Jonny was sure a sergeant in the Czech Police would be under exactly the same pressure.

The square opened up past the Municipal House, the new shopping centre opposite hemmed in by the curving tram track. Following the tramline they walked at pace past a small farmers' market with homemade Czech delicacies including cheese, sausages and wine. Despite the intense walking pace, Jonny's senses couldn't avoid being grabbed by the appealing waft of roasting pig in the middle of the market.

Dvořáková's mobile phone rang and she stopped when she saw the screen. "Felix," she mouthed to Jonny before talking into the phone in Czech. Jonny watched her face for any sign, trying to gauge both progress with the search for Gary Needham and also the accompanying team mood. Jonny's shoulders relaxed when Dvořáková finished the call and smiled.

"Honza, they have found Gary. He was in a non-stop casino."

Jonny laughed with relief. "I should have guessed. The place someone with money problems would definitely go to!"

"Yes," she tutted. "Felix will see us back at the station after we've interviewed Mrs Robson."

"Don't worry, we'll be quick," Jonny reassured her.

Inside the hotel, Carly was standing near reception with Sophie. Jonny acknowledged them as they approached and introduced Dvořáková.

"Carly, we would like to talk to alone again please," Jonny requested.

"Fine," she said.

"And Sophie," Jonny started, "we would also like to talk to you and Lizzie afterwards, if that's okay?"

"Sure," Sophie confirmed, looking pleased to be involved at last. "I'll call Lizzie."

Carly was first to speak as soon as they entered the room. "Is it true Gary has run off?"

Dvořáková took the question. "I have just spoken to DCI Mikeš and he confirmed Gary has been found in Prague."

"Do you think he killed Neil?" Carly continued whilst sitting down.

"We are keeping an open mind," Jonny answered. "It's important we follow all the leads we have. But we do have some questions about your husband's involvement with Gary."

"Neil and Gary?"

"Yes. We now know Gary has been having some money problems, resulting from his business and also his divorce from Grace. He told us he confessed to Neil one night and your husband agreed to lend him £10,000 in January this year."

Carly looked puzzled. "That can't be right. As I told you yesterday, I checked the finances before I came out here. Everything seemed in order."

"Also," continued Jonny, tentatively, "Gary told us Neil gave him the money in cash."

"In cash!" she said, shocked. "I don't believe it."

"Well I can assure you we are going to get to the bottom of it. But now you know what Gary has told us, does it stir any memories at all? Maybe something your husband said about Gary?"

Carly paused in thought. "No. Neil always liked Gary, stuck up for him. But I don't think it can be true. Gary must be making it up."

Jonny concurred. "You could be right. We will follow up with Gary, but I would strongly advise you to check your finances again. Can you do it from here?"

Carly nodded but said nothing.

"There is one other development," Jonny continued, "We now know that someone hand delivered a note to the hotel for your husband on Saturday afternoon."

Carly sat back in her chair, staggered. "This is all starting to sound very strange."

"I understand you," he accepted. "But we have a statement from the receptionist who gave Neil the envelope, handwritten with his name on the front. We also have CCTV footage showing someone delivering the envelope to the concierge at the hotel."

"Who was it?" she asked hurriedly.

"We don't know," Jonny confirmed. "The concierge did not see the person's face, nor is their face visible on the CCTV video recording. However, we have a still photo from the video. Can you please take a look and see if you recognise the person?"

Dvořáková took the photo from her folder and placed it on the table.

Carly looked intently at the photo, but shook her head. "And what did the note say?" she asked.

"We have only found part of the note," Jonny explained. "The person who delivered it, or had it delivered, wanted to meet your husband."

"But why? I don't understand any of this." Carly put her face in her hands and started crying softly.

Jonny allowed her time to compose herself. "Carly, there is some reason your husband was killed in Prague. I don't know what it is yet, but I promise you I will find out. But, please think hard. Is there anything about what we've told you today that jogs even the smallest memory? Anything at all?"

Carly continued to weep. "I'm sorry," she whispered between sniffs. "None of this is making any sense."

Dvořáková leaned forward over the table. "Mrs Robson, can I get you anything?" Carly shook her head.

Jonny continued, aware of the time. "Did you manage to get photos of your family calendar from home?"

"Yes," Carly whispered between sniffles.

"Thank you," Jonny encouraged. "If the sergeant gives you her phone number can you please forward them to her?"

"But why do you need them?" Carly pleaded.

Jonny took Neil Robson's black notebook from his jacket pocket and placed it on the table. Carly looked at it and started crying again, taking a tissue from her pocket.

"I have been through your husband's notebook in detail," Jonny explained. "As I told you yesterday, most of the entries are simple reminders. But there are about fifteen entries which I cannot fathom." Jonny opened the book and pointed out the entries, in reverse order from the latest. Carly looked at each item closely, but after being shown seven entries she shook her head in puzzlement. "They could be anything, probably to do with his work," she stated, frustrated.

Jonny spoke calmly, seeking to reassure her. "You're probably right. We also thought they might be something to do with his work. But I just want to cross-check them against his diary. As you can see, the items were definitely written in date order and I want to make sure there is no correlation with his work schedule."

"But how could they be connected to Neil being killed?" Carly looked lost.

"I don't know yet. We are just following every lead we have."

Jonny turned to Dvořáková. "Sergeant, can you please see if Sophie Wilson and Lizzie Scott are available to talk?"

Dvořáková put the photo back in her folder. Once the door had shut, Jonny lent forward and spoke softly. "Carly, can I ask you again not to say anything about our conversation to anyone else. It is very important."

She nodded in mute agreement, dabbing her eyes.

Dvořáková re-entered the room. "I spoke with Mrs Wilson. They will come here in a few minutes."

"Also, Carly," Jonny continued, "before the others come in I would like to ask you about the restaurant. We have only found out today that the restaurant your husband was killed in was the same restaurant you all went to for lunch on the Sunday of your trip to Prague last year." Jonny paused for effect. "Don't you think it's strange?"

"I suppose so," Carly replied in a strained voice. "But I asked Martin and he said it was his suggestion. Ade told me the same. But, how could they be involved when they were both sitting at the table when Neil was killed. Oh, I can't stand this." Carly started crying again.

Sophie entered the room and immediately went to comfort Carly.

"Lizzie is not feeling well," Sophie explained, "but she said she'll be down in a minute."

"No problem," Jonny reassured her. "I just wanted to ask you all about the schedule you had when you came over to Prague last year with your husbands."

"Martin told us you were asking him about it. I really can't see how it can be connected to what's happened here."

"Well, the restaurant that Neil was killed in on Monday was the same one you all went to on the Sunday of that trip," Jonny asserted. "Is that enough reason for you?"

Sophie looked unconvinced. "What do you want to know?"

"Everything you can remember," Jonny confirmed with authority.

"Right," Sophie started, sighing heavily. "On Friday we landed late, about 10:30pm, and stayed in the hotel for a drink when we arrived."

"So, you didn't go into the city centre?" Jonny probed.

"No," Sophie asserted. "On Saturday morning we woke late, had breakfast, after which we all went for a long walk together. Martin and I had planned out the walk in order to see most of the main sights. We didn't have lunch because we'd had a late breakfast, instead just grabbed a snack with a coffee along the way. Then we all walked back—"

The door opened and Lizzie walked in, looking pale. "I'm really sorry. I've think I've picked up a stomach bug."

"No problem." Jonny offered her the seat next to Sophie.

"I was just running through the schedule for our weekend in Prague last year," Sophie explained.

"Ok, please carry on. I'll add anything else I can remember," Lizzie said.

"Yes," Sophie continued, "so we all headed back to the hotel about 4pm, changed and met again in reception at 5:30pm because the minibus was picking us up for the boat trip. We got off the boat at 7pm and walked along the river to our restaurant, where we had a table booked for 8pm. After the meal we walked back to the hotel. We were together all day. On Sunday, we again had late breakfast and met at 11am for a leisurely walk. We didn't walk far though and stopped for lunch in Old Town Square. After the meal we only had about 90 minutes free, before we had to go back to the hotel for the taxi to the airport."

"This detail is very helpful," Jonny justified. "And what did everyone do in this spare time?"

"Carly and I walked a little bit, but we were both tired so we bought a takeaway coffee and stopped on a bench just off the square. Martin wanted to see the Kafka memorial and Ade went with him, but only because Neil wanted to go to the Mucha Museum. He was the only one interested in art and kept talking about it all weekend. Lizzie, I think you went shopping..."

"Yes, that's right," Lizzie confirmed. "I bought a few souvenirs. It was such a lovely weekend, I wanted everyone to have a small reminder. I bought fridge magnets and embossed notebooks for us girls, and also bought those identical t-shirts for the guys, the ones with 'Prague Drinking Team' on the front. Do you remember, they all wore them down the pub when we got back home?"

Carly smiled at the happy memory. Sophie hugged Carly, also pulling in Lizzie.

"Thank you for taking me through the weekend schedule," Jonny affirmed. "I know how difficult this is for all of you. But it helps paint a picture for me, even if it's not directly connected to what happened here on Monday. It would actually be very useful if you could write down the schedule in as much detail as you can, also asking Martin and Adrian to contribute. It might prompt some more thoughts. Would you be able to do this for us?"

Sophie exhaled heavily. "Yes, I will organise it. But, one thing I can tell you, Mr Fox, is that we are all good friends. We are always looking out for each other, like friends should. You need to start questioning local people about what happened to Neil because it wasn't one of us."

"Thank you, we are," Jonny declared.

30

The Theories

On the walk back from the hotel Jonny was quiet and concentrated, his calm exterior concealing his internal conflict. The tangled knot of information was swirling in his head: key facts, circumstantial data, opinions and explanations, as well as the intonation of the voices, body language and facial expressions. As often on complex investigations, he found the new evidence mixing in his head with details and testimony from other major cases he had worked.

The urge to hide away in a dark room was strong, giving him the peace and quiet he sought to ponder all the angles of the case. He had always tried to portray himself as a team player, but in truth he was more of a leader and with that came quirky methods, including the need for time for just him and the killer.

Jonny also couldn't help but feel a panic creeping up on him, the repercussions of the Sutherland case still raw and unsettling his usual methodical contemplations. The likelihood was that the killer of Neil Robson was not going to kill again, it likely being a one-off revenge murder over love or money. But there was only one way he could make sure: catch the killer.

Dvořáková sensed his ruminations. "Honza, are you ok?"

"Yes," he replied slowly, preoccupied. "But there's something not right. The core group of friends have closed ranks. They are not even entertaining the possibility that it could be one of them. And Sophie Wilson is the leader. It's too perfect."

"I know exactly what you mean," she concurred. "I haven't attended all the interviews but their behaviour today was not what I was expecting. Only Carly Robson seems to be open to the possibility that someone she knows killed her husband."

"That's right," he replied, ardently. "And something else is bothering me. Of everyone we've talked to so far, the only person I've sensed was lying to us was Darren Kozma."

"Maybe he did it," she suggested. "Perhaps he delivered the letter to lure Neil Robson to meet him."

"But why go to all the drama of delivering it to the concierge? He could have just put a letter under Neil's door, or even found a way to anonymously drop it at reception when it was busy. And why a letter, anyway?" He shook his head. "He could have just bought a pay-as-you-go phone and sent Neil a message."

"Well Darren's next interview is organised for 2pm, so you can ask him soon."

"Yes. I suppose so," he pondered, eyes fixed ahead in concentration.

Back at the station, Mikeš and Boukal were inside the Incident Room, updating the team in the absence of the morning briefing. Seeing Jonny and Dvořáková approaching across the open plan office, Mikeš brought the meeting to a halt with his characteristic flamboyant arm gestures. He shooed his team out and stood waiting at the door with a wide grin, reminding Jonny of an eccentric old teacher he once had for Science.

"Honza, you have been busy!" he bellowed, putting his arm around Jonny and leading him inside the room.

"Are you feeling more relaxed now, Felix?" Jonny enquired.

"Yes, yes. I'm sorry about earlier. I just go into a complete spin when I lose a suspect. It happened to me early in my career and it left a big impression on me. I can still remember the feeling of raw anger and embarrassment."

"I understand completely," Jonny assented.

"You also need to understand that Czech Republic has only land borders," Mikeš explained. "It is so easy for a suspect to get into Germany, Austria, Slovakia or Poland." He wagged his finger in warning. "And if this happens it's a big headache, my friend."

"I'd never really thought about that before now," Jonny acknowledged. "Much easier to put border checks in place in UK because we're surrounded by sea."

Mikeš turned to Dvořáková. "Lucie, thank you for supporting Honza in the interviews. I know you have a lot to organise. Great job."

"Thank you, sir." Dvořáková looked more relieved than pleased.

Boukal's mobile phone rang and he took a short call, talking in Czech. "The casino have all the CCTV from the time Gary Needham entered and are sending it over. I want to check he didn't meet anyone there."

"What happened to him?" Jonny asked.

"It seems he had a bit of a wild night," confirmed Boukal. "It was difficult to understand him because he was still quite drunk when we found him, but he says he went drinking on his own last night then walked to the casino between 1am and 2am. He was still there when we tracked him down at about 11am this morning."

"I wonder how he could afford to play at the casino," Jonny mused.

"That's what I was wondering," Boukal said. "The casino management have verified he was winning at the start, so maybe he just got lucky."

Mikeš interjected, keen to move on. "Well, we can interview him later when he sobers up. In the meantime, let's review where we are."

Jonny took the initiative, moving in front of the board, pointing at the murder victim. "When we found out about the letter at the hotel, I began to believe it was possible that Neil had some business dealings in Prague. This was backed up by the fact that he had substantial spare money. Gary told us he was given £10,000 by Neil, in cash, and Carly Robson has confirmed she knew nothing about it. I started to think it was possible Neil was part of a UK group of people investing in an illegal activity in Prague: maybe gambling, drugs or prostitution. If there had been problems with the return on his investment, Neil might have met up with someone on his trip here last year and threatened them. We know Neil could be confrontational. If the business continued to have problems, maybe Neil was causing more trouble and he was killed to keep him quiet. It would have explained why someone wanted to meet him."

"Interesting theory," Mikeš exclaimed.

"Yes," Jonny continued. "But today we found out that the restaurant where Neil was killed was the same venue for the Sunday lunch on the trip here last year with their wives. This is maybe a coincidence that can be explained, in this case by Martin suggesting the restaurant for lunch on Monday, supported by Adrian. The trouble is I just don't believe in coincidence on this scale; one large capital city, so many restaurants in the centre, and the victim is killed in the same restaurant he went to with his friends last year. I don't buy it."

"Sorry, Honza, what don't you buy?" Mikeš asked, puzzled.

Jonny laughed. "Sorry, Felix, it's slang. It means I don't accept it can be true."

Mikeš considered the explanation. "So what is your theory now, Honza?"

"The murder was planned by someone in the group of friends," Jonny stated conclusively.

"Only planned?" Mikeš tested.

"Maybe they also committed the murder," Jonny proposed. "However, because Martin and Adrian were sat at the table when Neil was killed, the number of possible suspects is low."

"And you still don't think it was Gary?" Mikeš followed up.

Jonny shook his head. "No, my thoughts are still the same as this morning. I really don't think he is capable of doing it. Neil lent him some money, but the fact Gary was having problems paying Neil back is not relevant in my opinion. The more important question is where did Neil get the money and where did he keep it? But we should definitely interview Gary again later. He might also know something about the letter delivered to the hotel."

"What did this letter say?" Mikeš asked.

Dvořáková pulled out A4 prints of the letter pieces and handed them around. "We found three parts of the letter and I've sent them off to forensics to check for fingerprints. We haven't found the envelope yet. The letter was written in capital letters so checking the handwriting will be difficult."

Mikeš read out the words. "WE NEED TO TALK ABOUT THE FUTURE… MEET ME AT… but where?"

Jonny shrugged his shoulders. "Or what time? We couldn't find the last piece of the letter. Lucie and I went through the bag twice."

"Maybe we should try once more," Dvořáková suggested.

"We could," Jonny accepted, "but I don't think it's the priority at the moment. It's not going to tell us who the killer is."

"I don't mind having another look," Boukal declared, moving across to the board, pen in hand, to write up the words in the letter.

"Good idea, Marek," Mikeš declared. "Maybe the luck is on your side today. You have already found Gary."

"Yes, congratulations," echoed Jonny. "Great work."

"Thanks," Boukal replied, looking chuffed. "By the way, we've checked the CCTV from the school and James Hopkins is not on camera either leaving or returning between 1pm and

4pm on Monday afternoon. I think he's in the clear."

Jonny realised he was starting to see Boukal in a different light. Although still not dressed smart, again wearing a poorly fitting suit and less than pristine shirt and tie, he was proving both efficient and organised in his work. And most important he was getting results, finding Gary quickly saving a lot of stress and wasted time.

"Another one down," Mikeš declared. "If we assume Richard couldn't have done it because of the time of the photos he took at the observation deck, there are only four friends to go, including Gary."

"Well…" started Jonny, an unconvinced look on his face.

"What is it, Honza?" Mikeš pressed.

"I'm starting to believe it could be the victim's wife, Carly," Jonny put forward. "She looks very upset, but it could also be a good cover. What if she knew her husband was having affairs and was hiding money from her? Also, what is the money for? Another child by a different woman? She knew what hotel he was staying in and also could have subtly suggested to Martin, maybe via Sophie, the idea of taking Neil to the same restaurant for lunch."

"Wow," Mikeš looked shocked. "So you think she organised for him to be killed?"

"Maybe," Jonny paused, careful to select his words. "She was very relaxed when I suggested to her it was strange her husband was killed in the same restaurant they all went to last year. She just said Martin had told her it was his suggestion to go there. She didn't seem to be questioning why at all. I think most people would be freaking out."

Dvořáková reaffirmed the argument. "I thought it was a strange reaction as well."

Boukal became animated. "Maybe Carly knows what the codes in the notebook mean!"

Jonny continued quickly. "I was wondering that. Carly is sending us the Robson family calendar for the past few months. I want to study this closely and compare it against the coded reminders in her husband's notebook. Maybe it won't tell us the killer, but I have a strong feeling it's going to tell us something important."

"Do you think we need to check out the finances for Neil and Carly Robson?" Boukal asked.

Jonny nodded. "If we cannot find the vital piece of information to solve this case within the next twenty-four hours, I think we will need to involve the UK Police on this. Carly has already checked their joint accounts and she's confirmed their finances seem in order. The key question however is where her husband kept the spare money, and where did it come from? The UK Police will advise us, but through them we will definitely be able to check financial information, bank accounts etc."

"The next interview is with Darren," stated Mikeš. "Any more on the CCTV?"

Dvořáková shook her head. "I have updated the route he gave us to show the places we have made positive sightings on the available CCTV. It does not, however, rule him out getting to the restaurant and then back to the hotel by 4pm on Monday. I have also chased the information request to the UK mobile phone providers, but nothing yet. The UK Police Liaison team thinks realistically we will not get anything back until tomorrow at the earliest."

Jonny looked directly at Mikeš. "It is very likely in my opinion that Darren loved Neil. The question is whether he would kill over rejection? Time for the tough questions. Let's see his reaction."

Mikeš nodded, rubbing his hands together in glee. "Agreed."

"Also," Jonny continued. "When we interview Darren and Gary, we should be careful when we talk about the letter. When interviewing Adrian earlier, and also when talking to Carly, I did not explain what was in the envelope or what was written inside. I want to see the individual reactions when we mention it."

"Clever, Honza. I like your thinking." Mikeš slapped Jonny on the back.

Boukal cut into the conversation. "Uniformed officers have now checked with all the souvenir shops around Old Town Square and unfortunately nobody remembers anyone buying either a Rybička knife or a black hoodie. Those shops are just too busy this time of year to remember an individual customer."

A silence descended as they all looked at the board, internally pushing their own theories.

"Anything else?" Mikeš prompted, snapping open his pocket watch.

Dvořáková handed around more A4 sized photos. "Honza and I have looked at the CCTV from the hotel. These are still photographs of the person who delivered the envelope. We also have an artist's impression of the person a shopkeeper saw acting suspiciously on the escape route, near the garden where the knife was found. We don't have an image of the face, but as you can see from these photos, they are very similar; the body shape and height is about the same, and the clothing matches. The shopkeeper thought the person was also wearing a black cap, but she is not 100% sure."

"Honza, you were right about the hoodie," Mikeš stated.

"It's the best outfit to hide the face," Jonny explained. "It seems likely the killer and the person who delivered the envelope are the same, but are they one of the friends or were they hired to kill him?"

31

Interviews 3 & 4 – Darren Kozma

The following are the transcripts of the two recorded interviews conducted with Darren Kozma (DK) on the afternoon of Thursday, 18th March 2010.

Present at each interview were Chief Warrant Officer Felix Mikeš (FM), Chief Sergeant Marek Boukal (MB) and Consultant Jonathan Fox (JF). The reason for the presence of JF was explained at the beginning of the interview; he is continuing to assist the Czech Police team on this murder investigation.

Interview #1

MB: Interview commenced at 14:03. Please state your name for the record.
DK: Darren Kozma. Before you start asking me questions I want to know a couple of things.
MB: What are they?
DK: Why am being interviewed for the third time?
MB: We have found new evidence relating to Neil Robson's murder and want to ask you further questions.
DK: Am I under suspicion for Neil's murder?
JF: Darren, let me try to explain for you. Your friend was murdered whilst on a trip abroad with friends, including you. In the first interview you didn't tell us the whole truth...
DK: Yes, but...
JF: Let me finish please. I understand why you withheld information about your sexuality, I really do, but it is our job to keep asking questions until we get to the truth. Now, further

evidence has come to light and we want to ask you some questions about it. That's all.
DK: So, do I need a lawyer?
JF: Detective Chief Inspector Mikeš will arrange a legal representative for you if you want. But you are not being charged with anything at this stage. We are still just fact finding and want to ask you more questions.
FM: Mr Fox is correct. If you want a legal representative at any time you just need to tell us. But we will still ask you the same questions.
DK: I understand. And does this interview have anything to do with Gary (Needham) disappearing?
FM: We have nothing to say about it, but Gary has been found now.
DK: Is he back at the hotel yet?
FM: No, not yet.
DK: When will he be back?
FM: We don't know.
[Pause]
JF: Darren, is it okay if we proceed? The quicker we ask you the questions, the more time we have to look for Neil's murderer.
DK: Okay.
JF: On Saturday afternoon, do you remember coming back into the hotel after your walk together?
DK: Yes. We got back about 5pm (17:00).
JF: Do you remember Neil being called over to reception and being handed an envelope?
DK: Yes, I do. It was slightly odd because we already had our room key cards.
JF: What did you think when he was called over by the receptionist?
DK: I don't know, really.
JF: Please think.
DK: Well, I suppose my initial reaction was that reception had a message for him. Maybe from his wife?
JF: Why his wife?

DK: I don't know really. One of the kids could have been ill and maybe he wasn't answering his phone. Carly (Robson) knew where we were staying.
JF: Why did you jump to that conclusion? It could just have been a simple note from the hotel about the room.
DK: Yes, of course. It could have been anything, I suppose. Well apart from the hotel booking because Martin (Wilson) had handled all of it.
JF: But why did you think it was from Carly?
DK: Nothing really.
FM: Please answer the question.
DK: It's just when we are away, or down the pub, she does keep calling him and sending him messages.
FM: This is what we want, Darren, the truth. Please tell us everything you know. Let us decide what is important or not. Okay?
DK: Right, sorry.
JF: What happened after Neil opened the envelope?
DK: We had all stopped in the foyer whilst he walked over to reception. I remember he opened the envelope, looked at the letter inside and put it back in the envelope. Then he folded up the envelope and put it in his pocket.
JF: And walked back to you and the group of friends?
DK: Yes. We were all interested and I think Adrian (Scott) asked him what it was.
JF: And what did Neil say?
DK: He just said it was a mistake. But…
JF: Yes…
DK: But it was odd he didn't throw the envelope away, he put it in his pocket.
JF: And you walked together to the lifts?
DK: Yes. Neil was getting teased about it being another message from Carly, but it was all light-hearted. We took the lift and went up to our rooms.
JF: And you later met up for dinner and drinks. Was the envelope mentioned again?

DK: Yes. I think someone raised it at dinner, but Neil just waved it away. We were all having fun, it wasn't the time for a detailed Q&A.
JF: And was it mentioned again on the trip?
DK: No, I don't think so.
JF: And final question, did you see what was written inside the envelope?
DK: It could have been anything. We were too far away.
JF: Right Darren, I want to stop here and give you some feedback.
DK: About what?
JF: Because you are not telling us the truth.
DK: I am.
JF: First point, when I asked you just now if you saw what was written in the envelope you said and I quote 'It could have been anything'. This is classic distancing language. You could have just said 'No' but you didn't, instead you deflected the question away so you didn't have to lie to us in your answer. This indicates to me you saw what was written inside.
DK: But...
JF: Secondly, just now I asked you what happened when Neil opened the envelope. You said, he opened the envelope and I quote 'looked at the letter inside'. Darren, we did not say anything about a letter. That was the word you used, unprompted by us. We have now found pieces of the letter inside the envelope, but we haven't told anyone outside of the investigation team. It could have been lots of things inside the envelope: a postcard, a compliment slip, a cheque, anything. You were too far away to see Neil opening the envelope, but you know it was a letter. Can you explain to us how you knew it was a letter?
[Pause]
JF: Do you want to know what I think, Darren? You have seen the letter. But you were all standing too far away when Neil opened the envelope in the foyer, so therefore you must have seen inside the envelope at a later date. Either that or you

wrote the letter yourself and had it delivered to Neil at the hotel.
DK: No.
JF: I seriously suggest you start telling us the truth. Otherwise you could be in big trouble here.
[Long pause]
DK: I feel sick. Can I go to the bathroom?
FM: Yes, but we will continue with the interview after a short break.
MB: Interview terminated at 14:23.

Interview #2

MB: Interview commenced at 14:44. Please state your name for the record.
DK: Darren Kozma.
JF: I hope you have had time to reflect on what happened in the last interview? We know you saw the letter inside the envelope and it is vital you tell us everything now.
FM: Mr Kozma, if we don't get the truth the situation is going to be a very serious for you.
JF: Let me explain to you, Darren. You have either withheld vital information or lied to us across three interviews. These actions are blocking our pursuit of the person who killed Neil Robson. If you don't comply with our request and tell us everything you know, we will be forced to bring charges against you and you will face trial here in Czech Republic. At the very least you will be charged with withholding vital information, but my expectation is that you will be charged for attempting to pervert the course of justice.
DK: I haven't done anything.
JF: It doesn't matter if you haven't done anything, you are standing in the way of justice. You need to tell us everything. It is your responsibility to tell us the truth and our responsibility to solve the crime.
[Long pause]

DK: Okay, I will tell you everything. But I want to make it absolutely clear I had nothing whatsoever to do with Neil's death. Absolutely nothing! Do you understand?
JF: Darren, it is better if you just tell us what happened. It is the only way to convince us you are innocent.
[Pause]
DK: When Neil was called over by reception and opened the envelope, we were all too far away to see what was in the envelope. You are right. Neil had his back to us anyway, none of us could have seen. Neil put the envelope in his pocket quickly and re-joined our waiting group as if nothing had happened. I think Adrian asked Neil what had happened, but Neil just laughed it off, saying it was a mistake. Neil started talking about something else, we went to the lifts and nothing else was said.
JF: So it wasn't mentioned later at dinner?
DK: No.
JF: What you have just told us fits with Adrian Scott's account of Neil receiving the envelope. But you need to explain to us how you came to see what was inside the envelope.
DK: Later on Saturday night, after the pub, we went to the cabaret. Martin and Adrian headed back to the hotel, but the remaining four of us went in together. I spent most of the time with Neil. Gary was his usual self, walking around exploring, whilst Richard (Weston) spent all the time talking to a dancer. We all left the club at about 3:30am (03:30), as I told you before, then we got some food on Wenceslas Square. Neil was in quite bad shape. I thought he might be sick, so I told Gary and Richard we'd walk ahead and they followed when they'd finished their food.
JF: Why weren't you as drunk as the others?
DK: I was quite drunk, but I had stopped drinking in the cabaret. Neil had kept on drinking bottles of beer.
JF: You were looking after him?
DK: Yes, I suppose so.
JF: Please continue.

DK: We walked back to the hotel. I was holding him up most of the way, he was difficult to move in a straight line. Neil started singing in the hotel foyer and I had to shut him up. I got him upstairs to the second floor and helped him open the door to his room by getting the key card out of his wallet.
JF: So you helped put him to bed?
DK: Not really, I just pulled off his jeans and shoes. He collapsed onto the bed. I tried to get him to drink some water, but he was asleep already.
JF: And you saw the letter?
DK: Yes. [Pause] I thought it was strange when Neil got the letter from reception earlier in the day. It could have been a mistake, as Neil explained, but it was also possible it was something else, maybe a love letter. I was intrigued I suppose and had been thinking about who knew him here in Prague. I wasn't looking for the letter, but it was just there on the desk. The letter had been torn up and then put back together in four pieces.
JF: What did you do?
DK: I read it.
JF: What did it say?
DK: It said something like 'We need to talk about the future'. Underneath it said 'Meet me at the tower 11am Sunday'.
JF: Did you recognise the handwriting?
DK: No. It was written in nondescript capital letters.
JF: And what did you do?
DK: I took one piece of the letter, the piece that said 'at the tower 11am Sunday'. I put the rest of the pieces in the bin. Then I left the room.
JF: Why did you take that particular piece of the letter?
DK: I don't know. I was drunk. It was a stupid thing to do.
JF: You were jealous, weren't you?
[Pause]
JF: Darren?
DK: Yes, probably.
JF: Please continue. I think there is more you need to tell us.

DK: I didn't sleep very well. In the morning I was awake before 10am (10:00) and decided to look online at towers in Prague. There are quite a few, but I just assumed it must be the tower at the astronomical clock on Old Town Square. So I went there for about 10:45am (10:45).
JF: Why?
DK: It was stupid. I suppose I was hoping to find out who sent the letter.
JF: And who did you see?
DK: Nobody I knew. I was there at 10:45am (10:45) and stayed until about 11:30am (11:30). It was very crowded, but I didn't see anyone I recognised either approaching or leaving the entrance to the tower.
JF: But you didn't go up the tower?
DK: No, there was a big queue and I didn't have time. I was nearly late getting back to the hotel because we had planned to meet at midday, to go for brunch before the football match.
JF: And where was Neil all this time?
DK: In bed, I suppose. I didn't see him at Old Town Square. I actually got back to the hotel before Neil woke up. Adrian had to go and bang on his door to wake him up.
JF: So when your friend was drunk and asleep, you looked at the letter he had received, took a piece, put the rest of the pieces in the bin, and the next morning you went to see who wanted to meet him. Isn't that intruding on his personal life?
[Pause]
DK: Yes. I am sorry.
JF: I think you need to explain a bit more than just saying 'sorry'.
DK: I was very confused. I tried to talk to Neil when we were in the cabaret, but he just thought I was joking.
JF: You told him you loved him?
DK: No. I just tried telling him what I was going through. I wanted him to know. Trouble was we'd both had too much to drink; I was explaining it badly and he thought I was joking.
JF: And you were jealous when you found the letter and so de-

cided to try to find out who wanted to meet Neil?
DK: Yes.
JF: What did you do with the piece of the letter?
DK: I threw it into a bin on the street when I was walking back to the hotel.
JF: And what happened to the envelope the letter was sent in?
DK: I don't know. I didn't see the envelope in his hotel room.
JF: And did anything else get mentioned about the letter on Sunday or Monday? Did Neil say anything to you about the letter, maybe ask you what happened on Saturday night?
DK: No, nothing at all. I was worried someone might have seen me at the tower so I kept out of Neil's way as much as possible. After the football he said something to me like 'You were saying some weird stuff last night', but I just waved it away, telling him to ignore it. I felt stupid. It was clear Neil wasn't going to like me.
JF: Darren, this is not the issue here and you know it. We don't care what you do in your personal life, but the fact is you've withheld vital evidence for three days after your friend was killed. We might have been able to catch the killer by now.
DK: Oh no, don't say that. I was just scared.
FM: This is a serious matter and you will have to stay in Prague until I confirm you can leave. It is still possible charges will be brought against you, we will have to review the matter. You will be escorted back to the hotel now and will stay there at all times. The hotel has a twenty-four-hour police presence and you will be checked regularly in your room. Do you understand me?
DK: Yes. But I didn't have anything to do with Neil's death, I promise.
JF: Before we finish, I have two more questions. Firstly, why didn't you go for lunch on Monday with Neil, Adrian and Martin?
DK: I just wanted to stay out of the way. I was embarrassed.
JF: But you sent the text message to Neil because you wanted him to know you were thinking about him?

DK: Yes, I suppose so.

JF: Second question, is there any other reason you went to the astronomical clock on Old Town Square rather than to one of the other towers? Maybe Neil or somebody else had said something about a tower during the trip?

DK: No. I just looked online. I didn't know which tower to go to. I only chose the one on Old Town Square because I thought it was the most famous one.

JF: And did you see anyone at the tower wearing a black hoodie? Maybe someone trying to hide their face?

DK: I don't remember anything. It was very busy.

JF: And do you recognise this person?

MB: For the purposes of the tape, Mr Fox is now showing Mr Darren Kozma a still photo taken from the hotel CCTV recording.

DK: Where is this from?

JF: Darren, I'm asking the questions. Do you recognise the person in the photo?

DK: No.

JF: Please have a hard think about what you saw at the tower. Also, try to remember if you saw someone dressed in a black hoodie over the weekend. Maybe someone hanging around the hotel, someone you saw when you went out to the pubs and restaurants, or even at the tower.

DK: Okay.

MB: Interview terminated at 15:22.

32

Cracking the Code

Knowing he had only an hour or so before the next interview with Gary Needham, Jonny left the station seeking solitude, somewhere quiet to gather his thoughts and study Neil Robson's notebook. After the furore caused by Gary's disappearance in the morning, Mikeš was now back to his flamboyant best, prowling around the office encouraging his troops to increase their efforts in solving the case. Whilst Mikeš' finest quality was vital to running an effective team, it brought excessive noise and high spirits that made desk work almost impossible. In the past Jonny would dive into the sanctity of his own office, but he didn't have one here. The only other option was hiding in the basement, but the disruption of music discussions with Liška, whilst usually engaging, were definitely not what he needed right now; he needed peace and quiet to allow him space to think.

    Seeking a welcoming, known atmosphere, somewhere he felt comfortable, Jonny headed off across Old Town Square in the direction of Staroměstská metro station, back towards the small café he had found the previous day for breakfast. Although the spring sunshine had been replaced by cloud, the air temperature was still enjoyable for the time of year, making being outside much preferable to inside. Despite this, Jonny could feel bad weather threatening, mirroring the onset of a storm brewing on the murder case.

    He strode purposefully across the square, past the memorial statue of Jan Hus, intent on maximising his isolation time. To his annoyance his mobile rang and looking at the phone he saw Mikeš' name on the screen. He decided to let it ring out, muting the ringtone.

When the call disconnected, Jonny noticed an earlier message from Ivana

Hi, hope you're having a good day. Drink later?

Jonny quickly typed out a reply.

Sorry, I'm out for dinner with the famous Czech detective! I'll pop in to say hi when I come back to get changed. Honza

He promptly turned off his mobile. Now nobody will be able to find me, he thought.

Jonny lifted his gaze, ready to restart his walk, and found himself momentarily taken aback by the unassuming splendour of St. Nicholas' Church on the corner of the square. Even during his short stay in the city, he'd already walked this way a dozen times without noticing the old Gothic parish church. With only a few steps before encountering the simple entrance door, it was as if the church did not want to make a fuss, instead blending in modestly amongst the architectural riches around the square. Craning his neck, he observed the white, almost innocent façade, leading up to three towers, the central dome connected to the belfry. Above the entrance was an elegant tall arch window, flanked by pillars and statues and crowned by a striking, gold cross.

Jonny shook his head in wonderment; this city had such a collection of treasures, it was able to serve up surprises every day. Suddenly conscious of the limited time available, he put his head down and walked away, the spell broken. He didn't have time to be hoodwinked again by the city.

Arriving at the café, he quickly found a quiet corner and ordered a coffee and baguette for lunch. The smiling owner, recognising a returning and possible regular customer, wanted to engage in a conversation about the weather, but Jonny brushed him off gently, quickly opening the folder containing the black notebook and prints of the Robson family calendar. To close off his surroundings completely, he took his iPod out of his jacket, put in his headphones and selected Bob Dylan's *The Times They Are A-Changing*, an album which always managed to transport him to another place. The songs of hypnotic storybook tales had helped soothe his rages, provided a backdrop scenery to another world when he had wanted to escape, and 'One Too Many Mornings' could even untangle his thoughts and let him sleep when his head was spinning.

He'd instinctively grabbed his iPod on leaving his room in the morning, for no specific reason other than he'd had no free time the day before to listen to his music. The habit of diving into Dylan's world of poetry was close to obsessive and one day without his daily dose left a hole he felt almost physically. His iPod had been a regular and indispensable accessory on his investigative work over the past few years, his team acutely aware of his dedication and wary to interrupt him if he had his headphones on. From the time when he'd got his own office, his desk had always been adorned with a portable CD player or, before that, an old tape cassette machine.

With the music soothing his senses, allowing his thoughts to travel uninterrupted, Jonny reflected on the true story finally prised from Darren Kozma in the last interview. It never failed to amaze him the web of lies people concocted to protect themselves and their pride. The net was closing in on the inner circle of friends: Darren, he believed, was innocent, Gary Needham he knew could never do it, Richard Weston had an alibi by way of photos he'd taken on his phone, and James Hopkins had never left his school on Monday afternoon. Somehow, despite all the other people in Neil Robson's close group having alibis or not even being in the country at the time of the murder, one of them had either killed Neil or organised his killing.

Jonny turned his focus to the coded reminders. He opened up his own notebook with the fifteen illegible entries written in date ascending order and placed Neil Robson's notebook next to them. Finally, he placed the printed copies of the Robson family calendar on the table. It was a compulsion of his to be able to see all the evidence in front of him, to take it in collectively, drawing together conclusions or theories, testing them, and then starting again if necessary. The key to cracking the code, if in fact it did relate to anything at all, was to prove some semblance of logic in relation to the dates and then be able to extrapolate the meaning of later entries, proving any assumptions made.

His hunch was telling him the codes were date driven because the last number increased and then always reset without getting beyond the normal 30 or 31 days in a month, or 28 days for February 2010. Because the first reminders in the relatively new notebook were just before Christmas, he started on the assumption the first entry 'B15-5' was related to the 5th January 2010. Using this assumption, he rewrote the coded entries out again on a separate page in his own notebook, this time by month:

January
B15-5
B16-7
B18O-14
B16-21
B16-28

February
H20-2
B16-3
H19-9
B15-12
H18-16
H19O-22
B16-24
H16-26

> March
> H14-2
> H18-8

Flicking through the family calendar photos, Jonny noted down the handwritten entries for the calendar for 14th January: 'Neil – Pharmaceutical Awards (London)' and for 22nd February: 'Neil – Work Strategy Day/Overnight.' Could the 'O' refer to an overnight stay for Neil? He checked all the other corresponding dates in the coded reminders against the family calendar and the only other one with mention of a possible hotel stay was 2nd February: 'Neil - Marketing Agency dinner (London)'.

He sat staring at his notes. If both entries with 'O' referred to overnight stays, either genuine or faked, could it be he stayed away from home with different women; 14th January was 'B' and 22nd February was 'H'. The numbers after the letter were an unknown at this stage, but if the codes were Neil's reminders for meetings it had to be assumed they were related to meeting times in a twenty-four-hour format.

Deciding to take a chance and only knowing one 'H', he turned on his mobile phone and dialled Heather Davis' number. She was still the only known female to be in contact with Neil Robson over the weekend in Prague, other than his wife, and Jonny had found no evidence to disprove his first reaction that Heather Davis was involved in some way.

"Hello," she answered tentatively.

"Hello, Ms Davis. This is Jonathan Fox, we spoke yesterday."

"Yes, I remember. But I don't have anything else to say to you."

"I completely understand. Can I just take two minutes of your time to explain something to you? I hope you will then allow me to ask you a question. If, however, you don't want to I will respect your decision and leave you alone."

"Ok. But I don't have much time."

"Thank you. Ms Davis. This is a delicate situation, but I want first to assure you of my absolute discretion. Anything you say to me will remain between you and me, confidential. Even if I taped this conversation, which I am not, I wouldn't be able to use it in court. The only thing I care about is finding out who killed Neil Robson. It is my belief that someone close to him, actually someone in his close circle of friends, planned to have him killed whilst he was on the trip to Prague. I am certain you are not involved. What I do have, however, is a list of coded reminders in Neil's notebook. At the moment I cannot understand what they mean. But, and this is really important, if you were willing to answer one personal question about the codes, it might help me crack it and be able to track down the killer. And I repeat, this is my only interest."

The line remained silent.

"Ms Davis, are you there?"

"Mr Fox, I really want to help you, but I can't. Sorry."

Before Jonny could say anything else the line went dead.

Jonny slammed his fist on the table in anger, attracting the gaze of the café owner and the few afternoon customers. Realising his indiscretion, he raised his palm in apology to all around, then, when the staring had subsided, buried his head in his hands in pure frustration. What now? He had been sure he was on the right track. But if Heather Davis didn't want to help the investigation he had no way to force her, unless the UK Police got involved and that would be a long, drawn-out process.

After composing himself, he realised the only logical next step was an interview with Carly Robson. He reviewed the family calendar again against his assumed date code, making notes for each entry. Returning to the original notebook, he flicked through checking entries both before and after the coded reminders to see if there was anything he had missed.

Realising he had done everything he could for now, he started to sort the photos back in order for the folder when his mobile rang. His first thought was Mikeš chasing him again, but his heart jumped when he looked at the screen – it was the same UK number he had just called.

"Hello, Jonathan Fox."

"Hello, it's Heather Davis."

"Hello, Ms Davis. Thank you for calling me back."

"Mr Fox, I really want to help catch the person who killed Neil. Will this question really help with your investigation?"

"I believe so, Ms Davis."

"And are you sure I won't get dragged into this?"

"I promise you this call cannot be used as evidence. I can only use it as information to further the investigation and hopefully find Neil's killer. And I think this is what you want as much as I do."

"Yes, I do."

"Does this mean you will answer my question?"

"Yes, but quickly please."

Jonny looked to the heavens in thanks.

"Ok. It's quite a long question. Did you and Neil have an affair, starting on 2nd February this year, meeting again on 9th and 16th February and also staying overnight together on 22nd February?"

The line went very quiet.

"Ms Davis, this is so important to the investigation."

"Yes. Hang on, I am just checking."

"Sorry, take your time. I'm just keen to know if I'm right with all the dates."

"Yes. I started working with Neil a few years ago and we grew very close. The relationship started before 2nd February when we had a drink after a meeting off-site in January, but 2nd February was the first time we met up in secret. I always told him I didn't want just an affair, I wanted a future with him. He promised me he was going to leave his wife and we would live together."

"And what was on the 22nd February?"

"We had a strategy day, but Neil pretended to his wife it was an overnight stay so we could be together. We stayed in a hotel."

"And did you meet Neil on 24th or 26th February?"

"Only on the 26th. Neil faked a meeting with a supplier and we checked into a hotel for a few hours."

"Was the meeting at 4pm on 26th?"

"Yes, I think so. How did you know that?"

"The coded reminder gives the date and time. But please don't worry, nobody will be able to work it out. It's only because I have studied the entries for hours. I will not tell anyone else."

"Okay."

"Using these codes I assume you also met with Neil on 2nd and 8th March?"

"Yes."

"Ms Davis, can I ask you just one more question? Did Neil ever mention another woman liking him? Maybe someone pursuing him, someone who wanted to be with him?"

"No, I don't remember him saying anything. He told me he'd been faithful to his wife, but they'd fallen out of love."

"Do you mean they had both fallen out of love? Or had he fallen out of love with her? Please think, it's important."

"I don't know. The way he explained it sounded like they were both having problems, but it could have been just him. Sorry, I don't know any more."

"Ms Davis, thank you so much for helping me. You have been very brave answering my questions. You have really helped the investigation and I promise you I will do everything I can to find Neil's killer."

"Thank you. I loved him, you know."

"Yes, I understand. Thank you again."

The call disconnected and Jonny punched the air, his emotions taking him by surprise; solving this case meant more to him than he realised. The net was tightening and he felt sure they were getting close. Carly Robson was the important cog now, time to lift the lid on their true marital relationship. Gulping the last of his coffee, he idly scribbled down in his notebook: Who was 'B' and what happened to her in February?

33

Interview 3 – Gary Needham

The following is a transcript of the recorded interview conducted with Gary Needham (GN) on the afternoon of Thursday, 18th March 2010.

Present at the interview were Chief Warrant Officer Felix Mikeš (FM), Chief Sergeant Marek Boukal (MB) and Consultant Jonathan Fox (JF). The reason for the presence of JF was explained at the beginning of the interview; he is continuing to assist the Czech Police team on this murder investigation.

MB: Interview commenced at 17:02. Please state your name for the record.
GN: Gary Needham.
FM: Your situation is very serious. We have interviewed you twice before today regarding the murder of Neil Robson. During these interviews, firstly, you did not tell us about the loan he made to you...
GN: Not relevant!
FM: If you interrupt me and continue to behave badly during the investigation, I will charge you with obstructing a police investigation...
GN: You probably will anyway.
JF: Gary, don't make this worse for yourself. Just listen to Detective Chief Inspector Mikeš and answer the question. Let's all get out of here as quickly as we can.
[Pause]
FM: As I was saying, first you didn't tell us about the loan. Sec-

ondly, you failed to remember correctly the route you took on Monday afternoon whilst Neil was being murdered. And then you tell us you went to two pubs instead of one. And finally, you disappeared from the hotel when you have been told to check-in with the police officers there at 8am, 1pm and 8pm.
GN: What does it matter anyway?
JF: Why do you say that?
GN: My life is really not worth living. A stint in jail in Czech Republic might actually be better, I could start again afterwards.
JF: You don't mean it.
GN: I found out yesterday I have to pay another £1,000 in legal costs for the divorce. I can't work because I'm stuck here so my building business is suffering. And now I'll probably get a court order to pay Carly (Robson) back the £10,000 that Neil lent to me on a verbal agreement.
JF: I can assure you, going to jail will not help you. The sooner you answer our questions, truthfully, the sooner you can get back to the UK and sort out your difficulties. Stop feeling sorry for yourself.
[Pause]
JF: Well?
GN: What do you want to know?
JF: Why did you run?
GN: I didn't run! I just got drunk and went to the casino. My brother transferred me £200 and I was stupid enough to gamble it. Ok?
JF: It sounded like you were winning.
GN: Yes I was, but then I blew it.
JF: Well Chief Sergeant Boukal has had confirmation from the casino that the chips you were left with were worth about £150.
GN: Really?
MB: Yes. I have the money in Czech Korunas for you.
JF: See, it's not all bad. But I suggest you use this bit of luck to rethink your approach to the situation.

GN: Why are you being so nice to me?
JF: I'm not really. I just happen to believe you had nothing to do with the murder. But we need some answers so we can eliminate you from our enquiries.
GN: Okay. And thanks.
JF: So tell us for the record what happened last night?
GN: I went back to the small brewery I told you about.
MB: U Pivovaru?
GN: Yes. I went there to see if anyone remembered me from Monday. I wanted to prove my innocence. The stupid thing was that none of the staff from Monday were working last night.
MB: That's because they have two shifts of staff and work a rota of a long and a short week. This means every week Monday and Wednesday have different staff.
GN: Typical. Anyway I had a few beers there then walked to the Old Town Square and stood outside the restaurant a while to pay my respects to Neil. Afterwards I went to an Irish Bar around the corner for a few more and someone told me about the casino.
MB: Luckily for you, we've picked you up on CCTV when you came close to Old Town Square last night. The CCTV from the casino also verifies that you didn't meet anyone there.
GN: That is what I told you.
MB: And we have spoken to the staff working at U Pivovaru on Monday and they have verified you visited the brewery pub during the hours you stated, including the time of the murder.
GN: My luck is in.
FM: This is a serious matter.
GN: Sorry.
JF: Gary, last time we talked extensively about the money Neil lent to you. I am not in any way doubting what you told us, but I want to ask a couple of direct questions again. Please think hard about them. Okay?
GN: Yes.
JF: You said Neil had called it, and I quote, 'his fun money'.

We have suspicions Neil may have been involved with other women and kept some money hidden from his wife to support this lifestyle. Finding out more about this is really important to solving the case. I know you don't want to say anything bad about your friend, but is there anything at all you can tell us about this side of Neil's life?
GN: Well, it's quite a long time ago now...
JF: Doesn't matter, anything you tell us will be very useful.
GN: About four years ago I was building Neil and Carly's house extension. It was quite messy so Carly had taken their child away, probably to see her parents. They only had one kid then. Anyway it was Sunday morning and we weren't working, but I popped around some time in the morning to tidy up an unfinished job ready for when the boys came back into work on Monday morning. I had keys for the gate so just went round the back. As I started working I heard a noise and looked up to see Neil having sex with another woman in his kitchen. I left quickly, but he saw me.
JF: What did he do?
GN: He sent me a message asking to have a chat. When I came round early on Monday he caught me and wanted to talk about it. I told him categorically it was nothing to do with me and I wouldn't say anything to anyone. As far as I was concerned he could do whatever he wanted.
JF: Did he believe you?
GN: I think so. We weren't best mates, but we'd known each other for a long time. Anyway, I never said anything. You are the first people I have ever told.
JF: And did you ever suspect him of other affairs?
GN: I think it's just the way Neil was. I never heard about any other women, but I did suspect it. And, yes, when he said 'fun money' it was clear between us what he meant.
JF: Did Carly know about his affairs?
GN: I really don't know. But she must have suspected Neil, especially after what happened with Natasha.
JF: And is this why Neil was always generous with you?

GN: Yes, probably. But he never mentioned it again. I think he just valued my loyalty.
JF: And the reason he lent you the money when you needed it?
GN: Again, yes probably. He said I'd been good to him and so he was returning the favour by helping me out.
JF: You told us Neil got angry and you argued, a few weeks ago, when you told him you couldn't pay him the first instalment. During the argument, or at any time after, did Neil indicate what he needed the money back for?
GN: No. He never said anything.
JF: Okay, thank you. The second thing I wanted to ask you about is Saturday. Do you remember an envelope being given to Neil when you all returned to the hotel late on Saturday afternoon, after your walk around the city?
GN: Sort of. We all walked in and the receptionist called Neil over. I thought it was funny because it seemed she just wanted to talk to him. But I think she handed him an envelope.
JF: And can you remember what happened?
GN: I couldn't really see, but he definitely opened the envelope and looked inside.
JF: And when he re-joined the group?
GN: Someone made a joke but I can't remember who. Neil said it was nothing and we all walked off.
JF: And it wasn't mentioned again?
GN: No, I don't think so.
JF: This is a photo of a person we are interested in. Do you recognise who it is?
MB: For the purposes of the tape, Mr Fox is now showing Mr Gary Needham a still photo taken from the hotel CCTV recording.
GN: Sorry, no.
JF: Okay. Back to Saturday night, do you remember Darren (Kozma) talking with Neil?
GN: Darren?
JF: Yes.
GN: He can't be involved.

JF: I'm not saying he is. But do you remember Neil and Darren talking in the cabaret?
GN: Yes.
JF: What was happening between them?
GN: It's a bit fuzzy really. I remember thinking they were being a bit boring. Darren seemed to be talking to Neil about something serious.
JF: And when you left the club?
GN: We all walked out together, the three of us plus Richard (Weston). But Neil and Darren walked ahead back to the hotel. I think Darren was holding Neil up because he was quite drunk.
JF: And at the hotel?
GN: Richard and I were about 50 metres behind them, but Neil was still singing in the foyer when we got to the hotel. Darren persuaded Neil to stop and we all went to the lifts. I got off at the 1st floor and left the others in the lift.
JF: And nothing else, either at the hotel or in the club, was unusual?
GN: No, I don't remember anything.
JF: And when did you see Neil and Darren the next day?
GN: I was in the foyer at midday having a coffee when Darren walked into the hotel. I asked him where he had been and he said he'd been for a walk. Neil was last to surface, I think Adrian (Scott) had to go and bang on his door.
JF: Thanks. But if you remember anything different from Saturday night between Neil and Darren can you please let us know.
GN: Sure. And thank you for helping me.
JF: We just want to catch Neil's killer.
GN: It's all I want as well.
MB: Please note you need to remain at the hotel until further notice and make sure you are available to check-in with the police officers at the agreed times. Is that understood?
GN: Yes.
MB: Interview terminated at 17:31.

34

A Time for Change

Boukal stood in front of the murder board with pen in hand and, on instruction from Mikeš, put a large cross through the photographs of Darren Kozma and Gary Needham. "So everyone is agreed?" asked Mikeš to unified nods of agreement, including Jonny and Dvořáková.

"And so," clarified Boukal, "with Richard Weston and James Hopkins ruled out we are back to the inner group of friends: the husbands and wives who visited Prague together last year, on the so-called 'Romantic Weekend'."

"Yes," agreed Jonny. "After I talked to Heather Davis, we now have confirmation that Neil Robson was having an affair with her. But the timing here is important. The affair only started in February even though they had worked together for a while. If I am right, he was having an affair with someone else before Heather – the person marked as 'B' in the notebook reminders. The big question is who was she and how long was the affair going on? And, perhaps more importantly, did Carly Robson finally find out about her husband's secret life?"

"Do you think this 'B' could have come to Prague and killed him in revenge?" probed Mikeš.

"It is possible," Jonny concurred. "But without a phone number and no face identification from the CCTV, we are going to need the UK Police involvement to track the potential suspects. They will need to track all the phone calls and messages to and from Neil Robson over the first few months of this year."

"The call history before the weekend and some older messages on his phone were definitely deleted," Boukal stated. "When we get the information back from the UK mobile phone providers we will have the calls and messages made over the past few months, but we'll still need to involve the UK Police to produce a definitive list of possible suspects."

"Neil Robson was certainly used to hiding his double life," Mikeš murmured.

"My gut feeling is still that Neil's murder is connected to the group of people we have here in Prague," Jonny explained. "As well as the coincidence of the same restaurant, we also have the letter delivered to the hotel. The letter suggested meeting Neil at a tower in Prague. The tower isn't named in the letter so it implies the writer of the letter and Neil both have history connected to the tower in question. It must have meant something special to both of them."

"I will prepare a list of all the towers in Prague," Boukal added.

Mikeš nodded in praise. "Good thinking, Marek."

"We need to formally interview Carly Robson," Jonny declared. "The state of her relationship with her husband and what she knew about his secret life are crucial to finding the killer. She needs to understand how serious the situation is, so I suggest the interview is held here at the station and is recorded."

Boukal wrote 'secret life?' along the line linking Neil and Carly Robson on the board. "I will organise the interview."

Dvořáková entered the conversation in support. "Carly Robson is the key in my opinion. I also think the choice of the murder weapon is symbolic. The Rybička penknife is only famous in Czech Republic and Slovakia. Why would a British person pick it out without prior knowledge or some research? It must mean something."

"Lucie could be right," Mikeš acknowledged. "Remember Dr Králová's summation from the post-mortem: no struggle, clean wound and the potential the victim knew the killer.

We just need to find the link."

A thoughtful hush descended on the group as they all studied the board, seeking out some form of inspiration to break through the guarded web of friendships staring back at them.

Jonny broke the silence. "We also need to interview Adrian Scott and Martin Wilson again. So far every piece of information they have given us has taken us away from the killer. Why is that? I can't work out if they are totally innocent or up to their necks in lies and deceit, maybe even working together."

There was no answer, just quiet contemplation.

Jonny stood up. "I'm going over to the hotel. I asked Sophie and Martin Wilson to write down the schedule for the husband and wife trip to Prague last year. It might tell us something more about the tower. Are you coming?"

"No," Mikeš shook his head. "Take Marek. I've got a few things to tidy up. Don't forget dinner tonight. The table is booked for 7:30pm."

"It seems wrong to be going out for dinner when we have a killer on the loose," Jonny stated.

"Honza," Mikeš clarified, "nobody is going to stop me having dinner with the most beautiful woman in the world and my new best friend."

Jonny laughed nervously. He had always been totally focused on a case until it was solved. Any thought of social events, especially dinners, were almost beyond comprehension. It was however a trait peculiar to him, his colleagues in the force proving much better able to manage the difficult balance between their work and personal lives. Those closest to him had been worse affected: cancelled evenings out, parent's evenings and school shows he had failed to attend. Being too stubborn to change, he had barged on with the same methodology all these years, batting away offers to help and pleas to open his eyes and see other people's needs. Perhaps now was the time to change? Everything else seemed to be changing, why not this as well.

"Don't worry, Honza, you will solve this case. I know it! It is your fate, the reason you were here in Prague when Neil Robson was murdered." Mikeš put his arm on Jonny's shoulder reassuringly.

"I wish I had your faith." Jonny smiled reluctantly.

The walk to the hotel with Boukal was quiet and reflective. Jonny felt on edge, as he always did at this stage of an investigation, and sought solace in the passing grand architecture. The walk through The Powder Tower arch was tranquil, the only noise challenging the thoughts in his head coming from people bustling around on their daily business. Perhaps this was the tower with a secret? The proud gatekeeper of the city kept its resolve and remained mute, focused as always on the role of grand protector.

Nearing the hotel, Boukal broke the silence. "Isn't life strange? We only met you on Monday, but here we are three days later and you are central to the investigation team."

"Yes. And remember, I've only been in Prague for one week. Maybe Felix was right about fate."

"By the way, I'm really enjoying having you with us on the team. Your contribution has been vital and I'm learning a lot from observing your different investigation techniques. Being truthful, I don't think we'd have been able to solve this case at all without your help. I think Felix knew this from the start, that's why he was so keen to get you involved."

"Thank you, Marek, I'm enjoying it as well. But I'll be a lot happier when we do actually solve it."

"You're talking about the fat lady."

Jonny laughed. "You'll need to explain that one to Felix. It's right up his street."

***

Inside the hotel foyer, Martin and Sophie Wilson were sitting quietly at a corner table with a bottle of water. Jonny noted the distance between them but knew it was hard to read anything into it with the level of stress surrounding all the friends, especially if one of them or both was holding a confidence.

Jonny coughed gently to announce their arrival. "May we sit down?"

"Of course." Sophie was still in charge, although her tough exterior appeared to have softened from earlier.

"How is Carly?" Jonny enquired delicately. "We'd like to arrange an interview with her."

Sophie gave a tired sigh. "She's gone to bed with a migraine. I bought her some pills."

"We can arrange for a doctor to see her," Boukal offered.

"Thank you. I'll see how she is later."

"And how are you both?" Jonny asked, his gaze moving between Sophie and Martin.

Sophie answered first. "We are all very tired and I'm worried about our young daughter. When do you think we'll be able to go home?"

"I'm sorry, I don't know at the moment," Jonny answered sincerely.

"Lizzie is struggling as well," Martin ventured. "She needs to get back to work. I think she has an important case. Ade has taken her out for a walk to calm her down."

"We all understand it's a difficult time," Jonny confirmed. "We believe we are getting closer, but we need to speak to Carly again first."

Sophie sighed again and turned away in disgust. Martin reached out to comfort her.

Sensing the rising tension, Jonny decided to pursue his line of questioning whilst the opportunity was still available. "Did you get a chance to write down the schedule for your weekend visit last year?"

Taking the initiative, Martin picked up the two sheets of paper on the table and passed them to Jonny. "My wife has been very tired this afternoon so I wrote down what I could remember. Sophie has just reviewed it and added a few items."

"Thank you. Can you talk me through it? I'm particularly interested in what towers you visited whilst you were in Prague."

Suddenly enthused, able to contribute something positive, Martin pointed to the top of the first paper. "Sophie and I worked out the walking route to see as many sights as we could on the Saturday. We walked from Wenceslas Square to Náměstí Republiky to take in the newer parts of the town, then we went through the Powder Tower into the Old Town."

"Did you go up the tower?" Jonny probed.

"No," interjected Sophie, apparently keen to take control. "We were aiming to go up the Old Town Hall Tower, next to the astronomical clock, but it was too busy. I think we'd have waited if we were staying for a few more nights, but we really only had one full day of sightseeing."

"I understand," Jonny smiled reassuringly. "Where did you go from there?"

Martin picked up the narrative. "We walked to Charles Bridge. There are actually towers on both sides of the bridge: Old Town Bridge Tower and Lesser Town Bridge Towers on the other side."

"I hadn't thought about those towers," added Boukal.

"Yes," Martin continued. "Richard's girlfriend, Hana, used to live in Prague and helped us put the route together."

Jonny looked surprised. "Hana?"

"Yes," replied Martin. He turned to his wife for support. "Sophie, you remember her helping us?"

Sophie nodded. "Of course, she was very helpful. She used to work in the centre of Prague so knows it well. We wanted to maximise our time on Saturday afternoon and so her knowledge was invaluable."

"Makes sense," Jonny encouraged.

Martin continued the story. "The bridge was still busy but I think most of us went up the towers on the other side of the bridge; the queue was shorter."

Sophie interjected, annoyed. "Martin, we all went up together. I remember. We got lots of good photos."

"Okay," Jonny acknowledged, pausing to studying the schedule written on the papers. "Please continue describing the walking route."

"We walked up to the castle," Martin continued, "then across to the observation deck. I remember everyone was getting tired so we stopped at the Lookout Tower on Petřín hill. We all had a drink on the terrace. Afterwards we looked around the museum and went up the tower."

"This is important," Jonny looked directly at Martin and Sophie. "Can you remember who went up the tower?"

"I don't think Carly went up," Martin said, looking at his wife for confirmation.

"Yes she did," Sophie reacted angrily. "She said she was tired and wanted to rest a bit longer. But she definitely went up, everyone did. Don't you remember the photo of all of us on the lower observation level of the tower?"

"Oh yes, that's right," Martin ratified, "I remember now."

"So," Jonny summarised, "you all arrived at the tower together and rested for a while on the terrace. Then you all went up the tower, but maybe at different times, Carly going up last."

"Correct," Martin agreed.

"And do you remember who went up the tower first?"

Martin shook his head. "No." Sophie shook her head reluctantly, still irritated to be answering questions.

Jonny looked again at the written schedule. "And do you remember anything else unusual happening when climbing any of the towers, on Charles Bridge or on Petřín hill?"

"No," Sophie stated flatly. "It was a beautiful day, everyone was getting on so well. I don't understand why you are asking these questions."

Jonny looked directly at Martin for an answer. "Sorry, no, I don't remember anything," he replied.

"And after Petřin hill?" Jonny encouraged.

Martin picked up the storyline to spare his wife. "We waited for the funicular railway to descend the hill, then walked to the Lennon Wall. We were all beaten by this time so we strolled back across Charles Bridge and made our way back to the hotel."

"And what hotel did you stay in?" Jonny asked.

"We stayed in this hotel," Sophie confirmed. "I know it might seem a bit odd booking the same hotel this time, but I had to book quickly for Carly, Lizzie and I. I didn't have any time for research so I just checked availability at this hotel because it was good last time."

"Perfectly understandable." Jonny nodded sympathetically.

"Do you still have some of the photos from the day?" enquired Boukal.

Martin nodded. "I have some on my phone definitely, but I'd need to go through the gallery. Sophie and I have taken a lot of photos of Olivia, our daughter, and I can't remember what I've kept on my phone from that Prague trip."

"Can you have a look and send all the photos you have to me," Boukal asked. "I will circulate them to Mr Fox and the other detectives in the team."

Sophie put her head down and started to cry softly. "I just want to go home. This is a nightmare."

35

What's in a Name?

Jonny had headed back to his temporary Prague home to get changed, his head spinning from the day's revelations and the untangling web of deceit. He knew they were missing one simple connection, after which everything would fall into place. Where would they find it?

Despite reassurances from Mikeš about dinner, he was finding it difficult to fight his natural inclination to focus on the evidence. Leaving the office before dark at such a critical stage of an investigation was unheard of for him, and with dinner looming he felt anxious. In truth, it was another indelible mark left by the Sutherland case. Only through his meticulous approach over two nights, locked in his office, had he found the missing link needed to catch the serial killer. He wanted to do the same for this case; to find somewhere away from distractions and revisit every bit of evidence to find an opening to the truth.

Now standing in front of the apartment door, he knew he had to face Ivana. Until the day before she had just been his landlady, albeit a slightly flirtatious one, but now the equilibrium was unknown and the potentially tricky relationship ahead scared him. He knew his track record in these delicate situations was poor; time and again he had proved to be inept at handling the emotional side with sensitivity and he had even been known to hide away, never to return calls or messages.

The previous evening had had a magical quality and

felt like the culmination of all the deeply touching experiences to seek him out during his short time in this city. But now real life was about to face him when he opened the door and he could feel the tension in his neck muscles. If he wanted a new start, now was the time to relax, enjoy his relationships with other people, especially Ivana, and be honest with them, and in particular himself. The eternal weak excuse of being overwhelmed by a high-profile murder case was totally unacceptable and he knew it.

He stepped tentatively into the hall expecting the living room door to swing open in greeting. But there was no reception, nothing. He stood still, temporarily disarmed by the unexpected silence, contemplating his best move. Eventually, with a deep breath and taking care to get the right depth, he knocked on the living room door. Within moments the door opened to a beaming and slightly breathless Ivana, her hands covered in flour.

"Hi, Honza. Did you have a good day?"

All Jonny could do was laugh out loud, his apprehension evaporating in an instant.

"What are you laughing at?"

"Well, I knew you had some talents," he teased, "but this is a new one."

"Cheeky!" She shook a white, dusty fist at him in jest. "Maybe I'm making you a cake for when you solve this important case."

"Wow, I can't remember the last time anyone baked me a cake."

"I said, maybe," she repeated sternly but with smiling eyes. "Now go and get changed for your dinner with the famous detective."

"Yes, ma'am," he gave her a mock salute and a smile before starting to walk off to the stairs.

"And Honza?"

Jonny stopped and turned to face her.

"I had a wonderful time last night," she started. "We

both know we aren't kids anymore and we don't owe each other anything. But if you need anyone to celebrate with when you catch the killer, just let me know."

Momentarily taken aback by the sensibility and kindness, Jonny had to compose himself before he could reply. "Ivana, you are a very special lady and I would be delighted to celebrate with you. I just have to catch him first."

"It could be a her!" she replied, laughing. "Now go and enjoy your dinner, Mr Fox."

"Thank you." Jonny skipped up the steps in a positive mood, all stress and hesitation dissipated.

***

With a spring in his step, he had showered and changed quickly before taking a tram from Náměstí Míru to the river, getting off at the National Theatre, the grand theatre for ballet, opera and drama. The tram had been packed and he'd struggled to push through the crush to validate his ticket by timestamping it in the machine. Although he was a seasoned traveller on the London tube network, the tram movement made him unsteady, the seemingly high speed on the straight sections of track followed, without any warning, by the need to hold on for dear life on the curves.

His feet back on solid ground, he walked to the river's edge and looked across at the three islands dominating this wider stretch of the Vltava. The reflection of the building and street lights on the far bank were twinkling on the water amongst the swaying shadows of the trees. The early evening boat trips were in full swing, guests eating and drinking to music as the bows broke through the river top, sending rhythmic pulses of waves towards the shore.

With time to spare, Jonny walked leisurely along the east bank opposite Kampa Park on the far shore. The afternoon cloud had passed, leaving an evening of clear skies. With darkness dropping its cloak over the city, he was pulled along by the icon of Charles Bridge, its arches lit up and reflecting in the water, with Prague Castle illuminated and sitting majestically up on the hill above.

The beauty of the view made him want to share it. His thoughts turned to his daughter and he smiled to himself, imagining her reaction when she saw the postcard. He knew already that he wanted to show her around Prague, show her the sights of her grandmother's birthplace, but he couldn't be sure what her reaction would be. He had so much to tell her that had been stored up for years, not excuses but an honest assessment of himself and how much he loved her, and only now did he feel ready to open his heart and tell her. He resolved to call her in a couple of days to tell her how much he missed her.

On reaching the restaurant he had started to worry he was underdressed. Never one for lavish clothing choices, he was once again wearing his stock choice of simple jacket, fresh plain shirt and clean chinos. The restaurant reception was sumptuous, the walls lined with gold wallpaper and drapes, leading to a window-fronted restaurant with an almost exclusive view over the bridge. He first caught sight of Králová at the table, wearing a stylish, plum silk dress and her hair elegantly worn up. As he was led to the table he almost choked when he spotted Mikeš wearing a black embroidered velvet smoking jacket and silver cravat.

Mikeš sprung out of his seat and reached out his hand. "Honza!"

Králová stood up elegantly and accepted Jonny's hand and kiss on the cheek. "Ella, you look lovely."

The head waiter pulled out the spare chair at the table and Jonny sat down. "I feel like I'm having dinner with Prague royalty."

Mikeš roared with laughter.

"Yes, I suppose it must look a bit odd," Králová explained. "The truth is Felix and I have always dressed up for dinner, even when we were married. We're a bit old fashioned like that. Aren't we, dear?"

"Yes, dear," Mikeš replied, looking lovingly at Králová before taking up the story. "This is our favourite restaurant and we always have the same table. We first came here in 1992."

"It was very different then, mind you," added Králová. "The Velvet Revolution had just occurred and Czechoslovakia was trying to build its own identity and culture."

Jonny nodded, looking around to take in his surroundings fully. "It must have been a fascinating time."

"And the food here is tremendous," enthused Mikeš.

"In that case, you can order for me, Felix," Jonny encouraged. "Last night the food was selected for me at dinner and it was wonderful. I'm sure you will do the same."

Mikeš did not disappoint: a traditional soup starter of chicken broth, mushrooms, a poached egg and dill, followed by veal schnitzel with potato puree and seasonal asparagus. As they ate, the food accompanied by a Moravian dry white wine, the conversation turned to the murder case.

"Felix says this murder case is frustrating him, but that doesn't take much," Králová started. "What is your notion?"

"We are definitely closing in," Jonny summarised. "In my opinion Neil Robson was killed by his wife or one of his close friends. And based upon his extramarital behaviour, my feeling is the motive is connected to love; possibly jealousy or revenge. We will have to interview his wife, Carly, formally tomorrow and try to find a connection to the clues we already have: the letter, the suggested meeting at the tower, and also the coded reminders in her husband's notebook."

"Marek called me and told me Richard Weston's new partner, Hana, had helped Martin and Sophie Wilson create their walking schedule last year," Mikeš stoked the debate. "Do you think it is connected?"

"I think it is unlikely," Jonny confirmed. "The one obvious question is whether Hana was having an affair with Neil. But we haven't found any evidence that would suggest this and so I doubt she is the 'B' in the coded reminders. Anyway, it will be easy to check tomorrow if she has been in the UK all this time; Richard told us she was running the pub in his absence. If she wasn't in Prague, she would have had to hire someone to kill him. But it doesn't seem to fit in with what Ella found at the post-mortem. If Neil did not know the person who killed him surely there would have been more of a struggle?"

"It was certainly one of the cleanest wounds I have seen for a long time," Králová declared. "It was almost as if the victim had stood there and let someone stab him from behind."

Stillness descended on the table as they ate, the incongruity of the murder disturbing them. Jonny looked out of the restaurant window at the serene view, the dark river moving slowly in silent shapes, edged with the glimmer of golden, refracted light.

Jonny finished his schnitzel and put his cutlery together on the empty plate. "I do believe there is another reason why Carly Robson has come to Prague. Of course, she has come to identify the body of her husband, but it's interesting that she has come with friends rather than a family member. There seem to be enough hints about her husband's behaviour over a long time and she must have known he wasn't faithful, even if she couldn't prove it. Also, their marriage doesn't seem as happy as she and Sophie have told us. It's almost as if she is here to find out the truth. And we need to find out what she suspects, or at least what she is expecting to find out."

"Honza, that's very perceptive," Mikeš stated, looking impressed. "This is exactly why I wanted you to help us on this case. My detectives are good, especially young Marek, but nobody, including me, would have been able to understand this group of so-called friends like you do."

"Thank you, Felix," Jonny accepted.

Mikeš suddenly became animated, unable as usual to control his arms. "I have a strong feeling we are going to solve this case soon!"

"Ever the optimist, that's my dear Felix" affirmed Králová, patting Mikeš' arm gently.

The dessert was served: boiled cottage cheese dumplings with fresh strawberries and sprinkled with icing sugar. Mikeš stared at the plate, transfixed in reverence.

"His favourite," Králová explained, smiling kindly.

"I would never have thought of ordering dumplings for dessert," confessed Jonny after tasting the first sumptuous mouthful. "Delicious."

"Felix tells me you have a daughter," Králová gently enquired.

"Yes, I have. Charlotte is fifteen now. It's been difficult in the last few years because she's got to the teenage stage and blames me for everything, much of which she's probably right about. Her mother and I got divorced when she was seven so it's been hard for her."

"Divorce is difficult for a child of any age, "Králová agreed. "Felix and I wanted children at one time, but it just never seemed to happen. We were always both too busy with our respective careers. But we still have each other, in our own little strange relationship."

"And you don't think you'd ever live together again?"

Králová shook her head vigorously. "No, no. Our relationship was very bad at one point, but somehow we've pulled it back to this nice middle ground. We have, however, agreed we'll move into the same old people's home when the time comes."

Mikeš' captivating smile gave his love away and he reached over to hold Králová's hand.

"And you, Honza?" Králová delved deeper. "I mean, have you had a serious relationship since your marriage broke up?"

"There was one lady about five years ago. But it was the wrong time, the wrong place." Jonny paused, caught in reflection. "The one that got away."

Mikeš lifted his wine glass for a toast. "To love. To

Prague. And to Honza, our new friend."

They clinked glasses and drank after the mandatory "Na zdraví."

"So, are you getting used to being called 'Honza'?" Králová enquired.

Jonny laughed. "Not really. A few times people at the station have called out to me and I haven't even reacted. They must think I'm either rude or deaf."

Mikeš and Králová laughed, enjoying the self-effacing humour.

"We have a saying in the UK," Jonny continued. "'What's in a name?' The people here, including you both, have been so nice to me, I'm happy to be called anything."

"It will take a while," Králová assured him. "I had the same problem during and after school. My first name on my birth certificate is Isabela, but only my family still call me that. I couldn't stand it; for me it always sounded like an old woman's name. At school I made all my friends call me Bela. But once I'd left school I thought it sounded a bit girlish, so I changed it to Ella at university. Anyway it's been my name now for thirty years so I've had lots of practice. It's not very Czech and many people are surprised, but I like it."

Jonny had frozen halfway through her story and didn't react at all when she finished. He sat still, his face pale, looking directly ahead into the space between his dinner companions.

Mikeš and Králová looked at each other, concerned.

"Honza, are you ok?" Králová asked gently.

"What's happened, my friend?" Mikeš half-shouted.

Jonny remained fixed in his trance like state, eyes wide in concentration, his brain working in overdrive. All eyes on him now, he put his thumb and forefinger to his forehand and pinched it tight in shock realisation.

Struggling to contain his excitement, he lifted his head to look across the table at Mikeš. "I know who killed Neil Robson."

36

High Drama

Friday, 19th March

The day's priority was to take quick and decisive action to solve the case. The murderer had to be caught at all costs, so Jonny chose to forego autonomy and was collected by Boukal, the car journey to the station far quicker than any other option. The atmosphere was serious and business-like, with the day only to be judged a success if the killer was caught. The only conceivable currency was justice, the trade being imprisonment for a long time. Jonny trusted his instinct; he knew the killer's identity, now he had to prove it before they could slip away.

"Dobré ráno," Boukal greeted him, extending his hand. Jonny shook it. "Dobré ráno."

"I bought you a caffe latte and croissant again. I hope that's okay."

"Perfect, thank you, Marek. But you don't need to buy breakfast for me. I'm not your boss."

"I know. I just wanted to." Boukal smiled respectfully, before turning his attention back to the road and pulling the car into traffic on the Náměstí Míru square.

Jonny picked up the coffee and took a sip, stealing a sideways glance at his companion.

"Marek, I think I misjudged you," Jonny started. "If you don't mind me saying your appearance is not the smartest."

Boukal laughed. "Yes, it's not one of my strong points."

"But first appearances are very important in this line of work. Like many people, I made an initial judgement based upon how you look. But, and this is the important part, you have proved to be organised, efficient and also smart. Felix is lucky to have you as his right-hand man."

"Thank you, Honza. I respect you and those comments mean a lot to me."

"Prosím," Jonny replied. "You are a good detective. But when we spend some time together after this case is solved, I am still taking you to get two new suits, five clean shirts, some matching ties and a smart but functional pair of shoes."

Boukal laughed, his eyes on the road. "Yes, sir!"

The rest of the journey was quiet and reflective, Jonny taking the time to go over his supposition once more in his head. The Prague sights slipped by almost unregistered as he gazed out the passenger window, sipping his coffee, his thoughts elsewhere.

As they turned off the inner-city dual carriageway towards the old town, it suddenly dawned on him he'd been in Prague for over a week already. The story of the first seven days would have been inconceivable a week ago, but here he was, feeling thoroughly at home, settled, and chasing down a murderer. Some things never change, he thought.

One delight of his first week had been getting familiar with this great historic city. The unfolding events had taken him around the centre in cars, taxis, trams and the metro, as well as his own style of hunting on foot through the cobbled streets. He now felt acclimatised, comfortable in his new environment, and with a great fondness for the people and their culture. A thought crept up on him and metaphorically hit him with a slap in the face, something he had not considered since he was a young boy. *I'm half-Czech*. He'd only really thought about his mother being Czech and he believed the reason he was here was to explore her country of birth. He'd never considered it might, in fact, be his own personal journey. He shook his head in reflective disbelief at how the mind could close doors on such key data, only the unconscious keeping it alive and kicking.

He was brought back to reality by Boukal saying something blurry and indistinguishable.

"I'm sorry Marek, I was away with the fairies. What did you say?"

"I was just saying the weather forecast is cloud and maybe some rain, but clearing with sun expected late afternoon."

Jonny smiled to himself. "Let's hope it turns out to be a beautiful day."

Mikeš was sitting in the Incident Room looking studiously at the murder board when Jonny and Boukal arrived at the station. In his customary tweed suit, the day's tie/shirt combination centred on a lime colour, he looked like a gamekeeper plotting his next expedition through uncharted territory.

"Honza!" he boomed, standing up to greet Jonny in his usual effervescent manner. "I've just been thinking about your hypothesis. Are you convinced you're right?"

"Yes, I am," Jonny assured him. "Everything fits together for me, but I think we should run through it from the top and test it before we take any action."

"By the way," Mikeš clarified, "I've told Marek you think you've solved the case. But I haven't told him who you think it is."

"This will be a good test," Jonny joked, enjoying the theatrical staging. "Where's Lucie?"

"She's chasing up your hunch," Mikeš explained. "She's contacting the airlines and the hotel, as you requested. But we should start without her. She will join us as soon as she has some information."

Relinquishing control of the board, Mikeš sat down next to Boukal, eager students ready for the master lesson. Jonny stood in front of the board and composed himself, preparing to outline his reasoning and have his surmise verified.

"Yesterday we made great progress. We eliminated Darren Kozma, Gary Needham and James Hopkins, adding to Richard Weston, who we'd already established could not have been at the restaurant at 3pm on Monday afternoon. Adrian Scott and Martin Wilson, despite not really helping us during the investigation, were always long shots in my opinion. Both were still sitting at the table on the restaurant terrace at the time Neil Robson was murdered. To have their friend killed whilst they remained at the table would have been an illusion worthy of a magic show. Also, we didn't find any unusual calls or messages on their phones so it was hard to see how either, or both if they worked as a team, could have organised a professional killing. And throughout the interviews this week we have found no motive for why either of them would have wanted Neil dead. The whole concept was implausible."

"Agreed," Mikeš bellowed, enjoying the high drama.

"So, my sights were set firmly on Carly Robson and the 'B' mentioned in the coded reminders. I know Hana's name came up yesterday because she helped Sophie and Martin Wilson put together the walking tour for the married couple's trip to Prague last year, including visits to the towers. But there is nothing we have found to connect her with Neil."

Dvořáková entered the room discretely, nodding respectfully to everyone in the room, and sat down next to Boukal. Jonny's gaze was taken by the wad of notes on her lap, his eyes almost burning holes in the paper. He collected himself and prepared to continue; he wanted desperately to know if his hunch was right, but it was correct to do this in the right order.

"Carly must have been aware, or at least strongly suspected, her husband was having affairs with other women. Adrian has told us Neil was seeing other women early in his marriage. Neil was caught with Richard's ex-wife, Natasha, about five years ago. Gary also saw him with someone else at the marital home after Neil and Carly's first child was born. And finally, we know about the recent affair with Heather

Davis. But interestingly, Carly claimed she did not know what the coded reminders were in her husband's notebook, and, in a strange way, I believe her. I think she knew in her heart her husband was unfaithful, probably cheating on her continuously, but she was lacking any tangible evidence. She wanted to know, but at the same time she was scared of what she would find out. This is why I think she has come to Prague – to find out the truth. Deep down, she probably still loved him, so the exposure of her husband's obsessive double-life and the damage to her family is proving too much for her right now."

"But she could have had him killed," Mikeš offered.

"It was one possibility I was seriously considering. If Carly found out about the multiple affairs, she could have hired someone to kill him on a trip abroad to reduce the potential of the suspicion coming back on her. However, when I asked her about Heather Davis she definitely didn't know about their affair; she would have reacted differently if she knew, more aggressive. In contrast, when I asked her about Natasha she defended Neil, blaming Natasha for chasing her husband; she hated Natasha for what happened. Clearly we were going to interview Carly today, and we still can, but I think she has no concrete evidence of her husband's cheating and hence no strong motive for having him killed."

Boukal interrupted. "So, you don't believe it was a professional killer, hired in the UK or Prague, to follow Neil Robson and murder him?"

"I have nothing to conclusively rule it out at this point. But the more I have thought about it, the post-mortem findings suggest Neil knew the person who killed him, even if they weren't close. This is why a few days ago I started to think about the possibility of Neil having underground business contacts in Prague. If Neil didn't know the killer at all surely there would have been more of a struggle?"

"And the other woman, 'B'?" Mikeš prompted keenly.

"The mysterious other woman," Jonny paused, sighing. "Well, this is where I was stuck. In theory, it could have been anyone in the UK, someone unknown to us. But the important point, the trigger, is that their affair seems to have stopped recently, in late February. In my opinion, Neil got bored and moved on to his next conquest, Heather Davis."

Mikeš shook his head in disgust.

Jonny continued. "The mystery woman, 'B', would probably have known all the details of the Prague trip, including the hotel where Neil and his friends were staying. 'B' could have flown over to Prague, delivered the letter to the hotel, and then, after he didn't show up to meet her at the tower, followed Neil and his friends around Prague on Sunday and Monday. But if she is a person unknown to us, how do we explain the tower and the restaurant? The tower is easier to explain; maybe she had been to Prague recently and they'd talked about their shared favourite tower in the city centre. The restaurant is more difficult to fathom, the only conceivable explanation being she followed them Monday afternoon, not knowing about the significance of the restaurant, and pounced when Neil went to the restrooms after lunch."

Jonny paused and took a sip of water. The tension in the room was electric, the finale approaching.

"I was lost," Jonny stated. "To identify the killer we would need to work closely with the UK Police to track Neil's phone activity in January and February, matching it against the list of women who flew to Prague last Friday or Saturday. This would take a long time." He paused. "But it all changed at dinner last night. When Ella relayed the story about how she had changed her name since school, I knew the killer was one of Neil Robson's friends. Ella told me that the name given to her by her parents is Isabela, but she changed it first to Bela at school and then, at university, to Ella, the name she still uses now. As soon as she had finished the story I knew the identity of the murderer."

Boukal was engrossed, mouth wide open in concentration, his tongue protruding.

Mikeš interrupted the monologue, frustrated. "Come

on Honza, we're going crazy here. How did you know?"

"Many people also shorten or change their name in the UK, retaining some element of their full name. Like my name. I am christened Jonathan and this is the name my mother always used. At school some people called me Jon, but I've always preferred Jonny. Elizabeth is the same. Some people liked to be called Liz or Lizzie... or Beth."

"It was Lizzie?" Boukal said, stunned. "She always looked so feminine, fragile almost. It's hard to believe she killed a tall man like Neil Robson."

"But as soon as I twigged..." started Jonny.

"I remember 'twigged' from our first meeting," Mikeš said excitedly. "It's slang for 'worked out'."

"Yes, yes, well remembered, Felix." Jonny smiled, remembering their strange first meeting, only four days before.

Jonny paused ahead of his conclusion. "As soon as I twigged the name possibility, everything fell into place. Firstly, although nobody else calls her Beth, I think it was Neil's pet name for Lizzie when they were having the affair. This is why it appeared in the coded reminders; 'B' for Beth. Secondly, I believe their affair originates from the trip to Prague last year; something romantic happened between Neil and Lizzie in one of the towers. I cannot be sure, but it was probably one of the observation levels on the Petřin Lookout Tower. Also, on the Sunday of that trip, after lunch, they had some spare time and Neil went to the Mucha Museum. It is my belief Lizzie either followed him there or agreed to meet him there. Their affair seems to have lasted until February this year, when Neil swapped her for Heather Davis."

"It's hard to believe someone could be so desperate," Mikeš muttered.

"Actually I believe she had reason more than just love to follow him to Prague," Jonny presented. "When Lucie and I interviewed Carly yesterday, we asked to speak to Sophie and Lizzie afterwards. Lizzie arrived late and said she had a stomach bug, but I think she is pregnant with Neil's child."

"Wow!" Boukal blurted.

"So, the knife was symbolic," stated Dvořáková, excitedly.

"Yes, Lucie, you were right," Jonny confirmed. "I think she walked around the shops on Sunday after Neil didn't meet her at the tower. Remember the friends had tickets to the football match so she had plenty of time on her own. I believe she saw the Rybička penknife in a shop, just like I did, and was caught by its symbolism for fertility and good luck. She bought the knife as a present for Neil, hoping the symbolism and the fact it comes from Czech Republic would make him realise their destiny was to be together."

Mikeš patted Dvořáková on the back. "Well done, Lucie."

"Thank you, sir."

"The choice of restaurant was a big coincidence. It was Martin's idea to go there and Adrian supported him. Neil only fought the suggestion because it brought back bad memories about Lizzie. When Lizzie followed Neil, Adrian and Martin, she must have been surprised they went to the same restaurant, but I think she took it as another sign of their destiny to be together. She knew the layout of the restaurant, and so it was relatively easy for her to watch them and sneak in from the walkway under the arches when he went to the restrooms. She must have been angry he had ignored her letter, but she knew it was probably her last chance. He would have been surprised to see her, and even more surprised when she told him she was pregnant with his baby. She could have told him anytime, but he was probably ignoring her messages in the UK; following him to Prague was supposed to be a romantic gesture, a reminder of how it had all started."

"So," Mikeš took up the story, "he rejected her and she stabbed him out of frustration or jealousy. A crime of passion, here in the heart of Prague!"

"Yes," Jonny agreed, glumly. "But I don't think she intended to kill him. This is why there wasn't a struggle. She presented the penknife as a gift, a sign of their shared fate, wanting him to accept her and their baby. Judging by the testaments about Neil's character we have witnessed, he probably told her to stop being stupid. After all, Adrian is his best friend. Maybe he told her to get an abortion and just forget about their affair – for him it was over. Whatever was said effectively killed off their future together. He dismissed her and turned away to wash his hands. She was angry, feeling completely rejected and she lashed out, stabbing him fatally in the neck with the penknife she had bought for him."

"Why did she run?" Boukal posed.

"I don't know, Marek. She was probably just scared. And the disguise of the black hoodie to conceal her face was only so she would not be seen by her husband, Adrian, or one of the other friends. I don't believe she intended to lure Neil to the tower to kill him. She wanted to tell him she loved him and was pregnant with his child. But when he didn't show up at the tower, her only option was to follow him on Monday."

"Whatever the reason, she killed another person," Mikeš stated blankly.

"Well, that's what we now need to prove," Jonny agreed solemnly. "Hopefully beginning with Lucie. What did you find out?"

All eyes turned to Dvořáková and her wad of papers.

She lifted up the top paper from her lap and read from it, eager to ensure accuracy. "Lizzie Scott, full name Elizabeth Scott, flew from London Stansted to Prague at 07:15 on Saturday morning. She flew back on Tuesday afternoon. She then flew back to Prague with her friends on Wednesday morning. All flights were with the same airline."

"Ty vole! You were right, Honza!" Mikeš clapped excitedly and punched the air.

Jonny smiled, pleased to be proved right. As always in these situations, his pleasure at uncovering the tangle of lies and deceit was tinged with sadness at the stupidity and waste, for everyone involved including the unborn child.

"That's a good start," stated Jonny. "Any information from the hotel?"

Dvořáková shuffled her papers, pulling out the next sheet. "I spoke to the hotel the wives are staying in now and, after initial confusion, the hotel management have confirmed Lizzie Scott stayed at the hotel Saturday to Monday, checking out Tuesday morning, and then again from Wednesday with her husband. The confusion was because Mrs Scott tried to get one of the receptionists to delete the first booking and fold it into the current booking. She basically tried to hide the first booking."

"We've got her!" exclaimed Boukal.

"Felix," Jonny looked at his friend, "do you remember when we first went to the hotel to see the wives? They were sitting in the corner with Adrian and Martin, who had just moved from the other hotel. You asked reception to speed up their rooms and a receptionist came over to tell them their rooms would be ready soon, also thanking them for using the hotel again. Well, it was true they had all stayed there before because they used the same hotel for the trip to Prague last year. Adrian replied because he thought the receptionist's smiles were intended for all of them, but in fact the receptionist was smiling at Lizzie, sitting next to him, because she had only recently stayed in the hotel. If we check, I bet that receptionist didn't even work at the hotel last year."

"We have more good news," started Dvořáková. "Forensics have confirmed that the letter we found in the rubbish bag yesterday has three different fingerprints on it. Two are surely to be Neil's and Darren's. Let's hope for evidence purposes the third fingerprint is Lizzie Scott's."

Jonny looked pleased now. "Yes, fingers crossed. We have lots of circumstantial evidence, but I'm sure your version of the Crown Prosecution Service will want more physical evidence. If you remember, Ella found a fabric strand on Neil's football shirt. Maybe we'll be able to trace this back to Lizzie. Along with the fingerprint on the letter it might be enough evidence. The best, however, would be to get a full confession."

Mikeš checked his pocket watch. "Time for the chase. Let's rock n' roll, team!"

37

The Photo Collection

Boukal had turned into a Formula One driver, the car slipping through the traffic, siren on and lights flashing. Mikeš seemed relaxed in the front passenger seat, twiddling the top of his cane in anticipation but generally unmoved by the slick manoeuvres. Jonny meanwhile remained glued to the back seat, his heart in his mouth every time they overtook a line of cars or took a blind corner. The cars on the road had seemed to respectfully freeze when they heard the siren, obediently carving a series of swerves and chicanes to be negotiated. The screeching tyres and loud rattle of the car's wheels over the cobbled stones played an appropriate soundtrack for a dramatic pursuit through the narrow streets of the old town.

Jonny laughed nervously. "This is a new way to see Prague."

"Marek was a junior racing car champion," Mikeš declared proudly.

"I'll just be pleased when we get there," Jonny shouted back over the noise.

Boukal didn't flinch, remaining silent, eyes firmly on the road. Leaning slightly forward in his seat, elbows raised, he moved the Skoda Superb smoothly between obstacles with minimal effort.

The car skidded to a stop directly outside the hotel entrance. Mikeš and Boukal jumped out, flashed their badges to the doorman and sped inside through the revolving doors. Jonny emerged slowly from the back seat, fumbling for his badge and, legs wobbling slightly, followed as quickly as he could.

Mikeš was already talking to the hotel manager when Jonny arrived at the reception desk. "I've asked the manager to contact Mr and Mrs Scott and request they come down to reception," Mikeš explained.

Whilst they waited, Jonny recognised the same receptionist who had addressed the group of friends on Wednesday. "Excuse me," he beckoned her over. "Can I ask when you started working at the hotel?"

The receptionist was startled by the question and turned to her manager for reassurance. Speaking in Czech, he told her to answer the question.

"Sir, I started working at the hotel in September last year, after my studies finished."

Jonny smiled to himself, pleased for the ratification.

"You were right, Honza," Mikeš stated. "Again!"

Jonny continued talking to the receptionist, undeterred. "I remember you came over to the group on Wednesday, when they were sitting over there in the corner, and explained that their rooms would be ready soon."

She nodded. "Yes, sir."

"And I think you recognised Mrs Scott from her stay over the weekend?"

"Yes, sir," she replied, nervously. "At first, I was confused because Mrs Scott had checked out the day before, on Tuesday. But then I realised she was back at the hotel on Wednesday with a group, including her husband. Over the weekend she had been staying at the hotel alone."

"And was it you she approached to ask about changing the booking on the system?" Jonny continued.

"Yes, sir," she confirmed. "I was again confused. I asked my manager because it was an unusual request. We couldn't delete the first booking because it had already completed; she had paid and checked out. But she was very insistent, so we compromised by making a comment against the first booking on the system. The comment simply stated that the two bookings were linked for one stay in Prague. It was just a comment on the system, but Mrs Scott seemed satisfied with the solution."

"Don't worry, you did an excellent job," Jonny assured her. "Without knowing it, you really helped us with our investigation."

The receptionist blushed. "Thank you, sir."

Adrian exited the lift, followed by Martin and Sophie, and approached reception.

"Where's Lizzie?" Jonny asked.

"I don't know," Adrian answered. "She said she was going for a walk. Why?"

Without answering, Jonny ushered them all over to a quiet corner of the foyer, followed by Mikeš and Boukal.

When they were all sat down, Jonny addressed Adrian directly. "Can you try to call her please?"

"What is this all about?" Sophie interjected in a stern voice. "We are getting fed up…"

"Madam, quiet!" Mikeš rebuked her.

All eyes were on Adrian as he unlocked his smartphone and dialled Lizzie's number. He waited, phone to his ear, then stopped the call and tried again. "She is not answering. Actually, the phone is switched off, it's going to voicemail."

Jonny quickly directed him. "Leave a message. Tell her to call you immediately."

"Hi Lizzie, can you call me as soon as you get this message. Love you."

Boukal put his hand out for the phone. "Can you show me her number? I'll try from my Czech mobile." He entered the number, copying it from Adrian's screen, and put the phone to his ear. "Same," he confirmed.

"Don't leave a message," Jonny instructed. "We don't want to spook her."

Sophie flashed an angry glare at Jonny. "Can you please tell us what the hell is going on here?"

"Yes, I think I deserve an explanation," added Adrian.

"First thing, I want everyone to calm down," Mikeš stated flatly, his tone grave. "Getting angry is not going to help anyone. Also, this is a police investigation and I must remind you that interfering with our enquiries in any way will be considered a serious offence."

Allowing a few moments for everyone to compose themselves, Jonny took centre stage. "We believe Lizzie was involved in Neil's murder in some way."

"What?" Adrian was stunned.

"That's ridiculous," Martin added.

"Let him finish," Mikeš interrupted, raising his voice to quell the unrest.

"Adrian," Jonny continued, "the only way we can resolve this matter is for us to find Lizzie so we can talk to her. Okay?"

Adrian nodded pensively.

Sophie prepared to say something but Mikeš put his palm up to halt her. Martin reached across and put his hand on his wife's forearm to calm her.

"Did she say where she was going?" Jonny asked Adrian.

Adrian shook his head. "She hardly slept and we had another argument this morning."

"What have you been arguing about?"

"I don't know, it seems like everything. We are all under a lot of stress from this situation, but it's been worse for her because she's not been feeling well. She's been sick a number of times from the stomach bug she picked up."

Unable to contain herself any longer, Sophie erupted. "The poor girl is ill. Can't you see? With all the stress we are under I'm not surprised they are arguing. This is absurd."

"Mrs Wilson, I am reminding you for the last time. Let us do the talking." Mikeš stared at Sophie hard, making his point. "Thank you."

"Adrian," Jonny continued, "did you speak to Lizzie over the weekend, whilst you were here in Prague?"

Adrian paused to think. "No, we just exchanged messages. She said she was going to have a relaxing weekend at home, sorting out some of her old stuff and just taking it easy."

Jonny, confused, turned to Martin and Sophie. "I thought she told you she had a lot of work at the moment. An important case, I believe you said."

Martin looked towards his wife. "That's what she told you, isn't it?"

Sophie had a puzzled expression on her face, trying to piece everything together. "Well, I sent her a message on Saturday and asked her to come over for a drink in the evening. Mainly because the guys were away, I didn't want her to be on her own. Carly was bringing her children over. Yes, she definitely told me she couldn't come because she had loads of work. On Tuesday night she called and told me she was still finishing off one part of the big case. So Carly and I met her at the airport on Wednesday morning."

"That doesn't make sense," Adrian added, now looking troubled.

"Let's focus on finding Lizzie now," suggested Jonny, changing the focus of the discussion. "We can sort out the story of the weekend later when we talk to her."

"Mr Scott, are you sure you don't know where she has gone?" Mikeš asked.

Adrian shook his head, remaining silent.

"I believe that one of the towers here in Prague is vital to what happened," Jonny explained. "Please think hard. On your trip to Prague last year which towers did Lizzie climb up, either on her own or with the rest of you?"

Adrian remained silent, trying to process what was happening to him.

Martin took the lead. "Sophie and I talked about this again after you left yesterday. We all went up the small tower on the other side of Charles Bridge, as I told you yesterday. But we were all together when we climbed up and it only took a few minutes; we were just taking photos of the river and back across the bridge. On Petřin hill we spent quite a lot of time at the tower, well over an hour. Because we were initialling having a drink on the terrace under the tower, we went up individually or in pairs. Lizzie and Neil were definitely one of the first to head up the tower, but we still can't remember exactly what order people went up. Some went up to the top cabin which is enclosed, whilst some just stayed on the lower observation level. But we were all on the observation level at one point because we have the photo of all of us together. We asked another tourist to take the photo."

"So, Lizzie and Neil could have been up the tower on their own for a while?" Jonny enquired.

Adrian suddenly jumped in, having thought of something. "Well, there's a reason for that. Neil and Lizzie had agreed to be in charge of the photo collection. Together they were going to collate everyone's photos from the trip and select the best ones to show on the projector at the Prague Evening we held when we got back..." Adrian's voice trailed off as he realised the enormity of what he had just said. He went pale, the blood draining from his face, the web of lies he had been told over the past ten months all coming back to haunt him.

"I think we'd better get to the Petřin Lookout Tower as quickly as we can," Jonny proposed.

"I want to come," Adrian stated firmly. "She is my wife."

Mikeš exchanged a look with Jonny before speaking. "Okay, but Mr Scott you will only observe and you will follow our instructions at all times. I don't want any trouble from you."

Adrian nodded his understanding.

Sophie started to cry softly. "What about Carly? She's still in bed with a migraine."

Martin put his arm around his wife.

"Somehow I think she has already worked this out," Jonny confirmed. "Best leave her, she needs rest. I will come back later to talk to her."

38

View from the Tower

The car sped away from the hotel, tyres spinning, leaving the doorman in a cloud of dust and fumes. Boukal flicked on the siren and the accompanying red and blue flashing lights, and settled back into racing driver mode, the outside world blocked out.

Jonny opted for holding onto the hanging rear door strap as the car hurtled through the red lights at a junction and turned sharp left, right in front of an oncoming tram. For a few inescapable seconds, Jonny thought his Prague adventure had come to a sticky end when, glued to the back-door window, he was able to look directly into the tram driver's alarmed eyes only a few metres away from him.

Sitting next to him, Adrian Scott was also holding on, grateful to have something else to worry about other than his exploding personal life. With his free hand he was trying to call Lizzie again. Jonny knew from experience that her mobile would remain switched off until this matter was resolved for her, one way or another.

Exiting the old town the car accelerated, now appearing to be in cruise control as it followed the central tram tracks, passing near stationary cars on the outside lane. Approaching the city's inner highway, Boukal suddenly braked and cut back left, following the road towards the river, zigzagging through the traffic.

The road alongside the river was wider and straight, the journey becoming slicker with the greater visibility, both for Boukal but especially for the drivers of the other cars, now able to see and hear the approaching police car with good notice. Adrian was now speaking animatedly to Lizzie's office on his mobile, his voice hardly audible above the car noise as they flew along at high speed, his head hitting the car roof intermittently without the use of the steadying handle.

As they slowed to turn onto Čechův most, the arched art nouveau bridge crossing the river, Adrian confirmed his worst fears. "I have just spoken to Lizzie's manager. He told me Lizzie booked Monday and Tuesday as holiday. Then she called on Tuesday and extended the holiday for the whole week. And..." He stopped to compose himself, rubbing his forehead with his palm. "And, her manager confirmed she has no big case she is currently working on."

Jonny grimaced, knowing it was impossible to provide any appropriate words of sympathy in these situations. But he always felt especially sorry for the innocent party, especially in infrequent cases like this where they had been let down not only by their spouse, but also by their best friend. And he didn't even know about the baby yet. "I am truly sorry, I really am," was all he could offer.

Once across the bridge, the car veered left and followed the circular road around the Royal Garden, skirting the perimeter of the castle grounds. The road surface was smoother now and Jonny was beginning to feel settled when, without warning, Boukal swung the car into a sharp left, effectively a U-turn but turning off onto an almost parallel road, before repeating the manoeuvre almost immediately, this time swinging the car right by 180 degrees. The car now roared alongside the top edge of Petřin hill, weaving between the cars, Jonny catching his breath in the back seat and rubbing the bump on his head from the car window. Boukal abruptly braked hard and turned the car into the park, entering through the gates at a more cautious pace due to pedestrians.

Mikeš turned to Jonny in the back seat. "Lucie is already here with an armed response unit. She is waiting for us."

"Good," Jonny confirmed, still rubbing his head. "We'll need to approach with caution because I am concerned for her mental state."

Adrian looked at Jonny but said nothing, his big gulp revealing his trepidation.

The summit of Petřin Lookout Tower was visible now and Boukal drove across the gravel to the gathered police cars, the siren switched off but lights still flashing. Dvořáková was waiting for them with her uniformed officers, all gathered together and awaiting instructions.

Boukal and Mikeš exited the car swiftly and walked over to join Dvořáková, Jonny again lagging behind as he recovered his composure. Adrian also opened his rear car door to exit, but Mikeš barked at him. "Mr Scott, please remain in the car until we give you further instructions. It's for your own welfare." Adrian nodded and complied passively with the order.

Firmly in control, Mikeš commenced the emergency briefing. "Lucie, please update us. Is Mrs Scott in the tower?"

"Yes, sir, I believe she is. One of my officers is sitting with the security guard on the ground floor of the tower. A lady fitting Mrs Scott's description is standing alone on the lower observation level. She is standing at the rail, looking out over the city. Another officer is manning the inner entrance to the tower steps and we are not allowing any new visitors up, only letting visitors come down. I decided to approach the situation with caution in case she was armed, awaiting further orders."

"Excellent work," Mikeš enthused.

Jonny stepped forward. "I doubt she is armed, but you are right to be cautious. I do think, however, there is a good chance she is going to jump. She thinks her life is over in every way and she doesn't believe there is any other way out."

"She will know we are here," added Boukal, back in plain clothes detective mode. "The lower observation level is twenty metres high and encircles the tower. She will definitely have seen the approaching police cars."

"Good research, Marek," Jonny remarked. "You are certainly revealing your hidden talents today!"

"Thanks, I was checking last night," Boukal replied, missing or ignoring the humour. "The overall height of the tower is about sixty-four metres. The observation cabin is near the top, but it's enclosed in glass, and the only way out is back down the same staircase."

"I think she'll stay on the lower observation level," Jonny commented. "If I'm right and she's pregnant, I'm not sure she'll have the energy to climb to the top. But twenty metres is still high and she knows it; she can kill herself and the baby if she jumps from there."

"We need swift and decisive action," hollered Mikeš. "I want her alive. This is a prime tourist spot and I don't want any trouble."

Everyone nodded their acknowledgment.

"Right, this is the plan," Mikeš commanded. "Lucie, clear the terrace and inside the ground floor of the tower. Cordon off the tower and get the public back fifty metres. All visitors returning to the bottom of the tower should immediately be moved to outside the cordon."

"Yes, sir," Dvořáková replied briskly.

"Marek, I want you to go to the security room and take over monitoring of the security cameras for the tower. Keep watch on Mrs Scott's movements and inform me immediately if she starts to move. Honza and I are going up the tower. Lucie has police radios for all of us and this will be our only mode of communication. For the purposes of the operation we will assume she is armed, but I don't want any officer to act unless they receive direct orders from me. Is that clear?"

"Yes, sir," Boukal replied.

Dvořáková handed out the radios.

The ground floor entrance to the tower was ghostly quiet when Mikeš and Jonny stepped inside. The only audible noise was footsteps down the inner spiral staircase as visitors descended, eyes wide in surprise when they spotted the uniformed officers and the police cordon being erected outside.

"Honza, follow me," Mikeš instructed. "And stay close."

They started climbing the inner staircase, part of a double-helix structure allowing visitors to travel up and down the tower concurrently. As they ascended, they passed many visitors descending on the other staircase. "What's happening?" a concerned father shouted across. Jonny smiled to provide reassurance. "Sir, there is nothing to worry about. Please take your time getting down, don't rush. You will be shown where to go when you reach the bottom of the stairs."

After climbing for four minutes they reached the last steps under the lower observation level. Marek's voice came over the radio: "The target is still in place. The lower observation level is otherwise empty. Over."

Jonny put his arm on Mikeš' forearm for attention and whispered. "Felix, I think I should talk to her. Why don't we split up? You go around the other side of the deck and I'll keep her talking for as long as I can."

"Good idea," Mikeš agreed.

Stepping onto the observation level, hands signals between them agreeing their respective directions, Jonny walked around until he could see Lizzie. She seemed calm, her hands on the rail, looking forlornly out over the city. Mikeš, bent down low, started to shuffle along the deck the other way around the tower, careful not to make a loud noise and reveal his presence.

"Hi Lizzie. I'm Jonathan Fox. Hopefully you remember me."

She turned. "Yes. I've been expecting you."

Jonny stepped a few paces forward. "It's a lovely view."

Lizzie reprimanded him, raising her voice. "Stop there, or I will jump."

"Okay, okay," Jonny stopped, arms out in peace. "I just want to talk to you."

"What about? Nothing matters any more. The whole

stupid charade is over."

"Lizzie, I know you didn't mean to kill Neil."

She looked at him with tired, sad eyes. "I loved him. I was willing to give up everything for him. But he was only interested in the next woman to fall for him. I was so stupid." Tears filled her eyes, rolling slowly down her cheeks.

Jonny couldn't see or hear Mikeš.

"So the relationship started here, at the tower, last year?"

Lizzie composed herself. "Yes. He kissed me. He had always been flirtatious, but I knew this was different. He said he wanted me. He told me he'd loved me since the first time her saw me."

"I understand, I really do." Jonny shuffled forward unnoticed.

"The first six months were a dream. We made each other so many promises. I was so happy." She smiled at Jonny, happy in the memory, juxtaposed to the tears streaming down her face. "I didn't think I could have children. Ade and I had tried for over a year. It was almost a joke with our friends. But then, it just happened with Neil. It was a sign."

"Lizzie, this is why I want to talk to you. I guessed about the baby. You cannot think only about yourself now, you must think about both of you."

Jonny shuffled forward again unnoticed. Over Lizzie's shoulder, Jonny saw Mikeš crawling around the deck floor on his hands and knees.

Lizzie was focused on Jonny and her story, tears streaming down her face. "I didn't mean to kill him. I just wanted us to be together. He had told me so many times it was our destiny, but then he just dumped me. And when I told him about the baby he just told me to have an abortion. An abortion! I mean, how could he say that to me?"

"You must have been devastated," Jonny proposed gently, trying not to look at Mikeš, now about five metres behind her.

Lizzie cried some more, wiping her eyes roughly with the back of her hand. "I couldn't help it. I had bought him the penknife as a sign of our love. I thought he would like it. The fish is a sign of fertility. But... but he just dismissed me. I'm so sorry..."

She turned flush against the railing, taking in her last view of picturesque Prague. Her sobbing was audible, her body shaking.

"Lizzie, Lizzie," Jonny extended his arm. "Don't do this. Just think of your family."

"I'm sorry, it's too late," she mumbled to herself, seeking forgiveness from unknown witnesses.

Lizzie's body suddenly burst into action, responding to her decision that now was time. She wrapped her arms over the high rail and started scrabbling her left foot up the protective railing, attempting to get a foothold. The sole of her trainers slipped initially, but she managed to get a toe hold by pressing her trainers hard into the small holes in the railing. She swiftly started to pull up her right knee, placing it on top of the railing, her torso starting to topple over the edge precariously.

Jonny sprung forward, his arm outstretched, but Mikeš was quicker, pouncing like a cat from his low, crouched position. Mikeš' full length dive enabled him to catch her left foot still pressed hard into the railing for leverage, hanging on with a claw grip. Jonny seized her right foot on the top rail and held tight, supporting her body in case she toppled backwards.

"Let me go!" Lizzie pleaded.

"You are not going anywhere," Jonny shouted, the adrenaline pumping around his body.

All three stood locked in position, catching their breath and planning their next move. Lizzie's eyes were still fixed on the city landscape. Jonny spoke calmly. "Lizzie, we have you. Move this foot down slowly and we will support you."

Lizzie remained tense, her body fighting the human

chains on her legs. She tried to kick free, her gaze remaining fixed on the urban view from the tower. Eventually, her energy sapped and she released the tension in her body. Jonny brought her right foot down to the deck level slowly. Lizzie slumped to the floor, crying, Jonny on one side and Mikeš on the other, each still holding one of her ankles.

Mikeš, breathing heavy, looked across at his new friend with a big, beaming smile.

"Honza, that was close!"

39

Cathartic Action

Boukal and Dvořáková ran around the deck of the lower observation level, responding to the backup call from Mikeš over the police radio. Mikeš was now standing up, dusting down his tweed suit with irritated frustration. Jonny was still seated next to Lizzie, his hand on her forearm, providing both reassurance and prevention in case she tried to jump again. She was crying softly, her face obscured by her hair, her head bent forward over her hugged knees.

"Everyone's okay," Jonny announced. "But Mrs Scott will need an ambulance."

"An ambulance is already here," Dvořáková explained. "I'll get the medics up here to check her over." She immediately used her radio, speaking in Czech.

"Lizzie?" Jonny waited for her attention, but nothing. "Lizzie, please listen to me." She tilted to head slightly to get a sideways view of him through one eye. "Sergeant Dvořáková is going to look after you now. The ambulance staff will be up here in a few minutes. Do you understand?" She nodded her head with the slightest movement and returned to her former posture.

Mikeš and Jonny descended the staircase in reflective mode, their aching muscles slowing them. The ambulance staff passed them on the other staircase, carrying medical equipment up to the lower observation level. Mikeš briefed them across the gap in the open steel framed stairwells.

Back on ground level, Mikeš turned to face Jonny close

up, hand extended, mischievous grin on his face. "Honza, you and I make quite a team."

Jonny shook the extended hand, smiling at this infectious character. "Not bad for two old guys." They both laughed, the joy of their joint arrest tinged with relief.

Mikeš slapped Jonny on the back. "I knew you would solve this case. I knew it when we first met on Monday."

"That seems like a very long time ago now," Jonny stated.

Mikeš chuckled. "I think you British say 'Time flies when you're having fun'."

"Very good, Felix. It sounds about right. Now, I'm going to have a walk, I need to clear my head."

"I thought you might say that. Enjoy your 'Honza Time' and I'll see you back at the station." Mikeš put his arm around his shoulder and walked him out of the tower.

Jonny took the direct route down the hill via the pathways. The queues for the funicular railway going down were deep, everyone keen to get off the top of the hill with the heavy police presence at the tower. The views were stunning, the city sights awakening with the brightening light and clearing clouds.

At a junction in the path he stopped and turned to look back up at the tower. With only sky behind it viewed from below, the steel framework loomed large, the majestic landmark recalling the design of its big brother, the Eiffel Tower.

Keen to put distance between himself and the tower, he strode down the hill at pace. He almost lost his footing once, walking directly across the grass under the blossom trees, the incline deceivingly steep. At the bottom of the hill he kept right, following the river, feeling the intense need to keep moving.

His thoughts kept returning to the Sutherland case. But not the usual sensation of failure, believing he hadn't acted fast enough to save the serial killer's last victim, Alison Bryce. No, this felt different. He felt relief passing through him, and a sense of healing – the power of redemption. The murder of Neil Robson was not preventable, but his prompt actions had helped Mikeš and his team solve the case and prevent any further damage to the people involved.

Jonny knew the difficult cases from his past would probably always haunt him, such was his sensitive nature, but the pain from the Sutherland case was definitely duller. And the future a little brighter.

Given his role as consultant on the investigation, most would assume his work was done. But he instinctively knew he had one more job to do, a cathartic action he felt was necessary to close the loop. But first, he needed food, his stomach reminding him loudly he was ravenously hungry.

Crossing the river, he walked back towards the old town and, being a creature of habit, returned to his new favourite café and ordered lunch and a coffee. Settled in his favourite corner, he took out his mobile phone, switched it on and sent a message to Ivana

Caught HER! Celebration drink later? Honza

Almost immediately he received a reply

YES!!! and YES!!! x

***

At the hotel, Jonny approached reception, showed his badge and asked if they would call Mrs Robson.

The receptionist used the telephone on the desk. "Sir, Mrs Robson has asked if you will go up to her room. It's Room 313."

"Ok. Thank you."

He turned to walk away, but stopped. "And has Mr Scott returned?"

"Yes, sir. He returned to the hotel, quickly packed and checked out."

Jonny nodded to himself, understanding the reaction. After the day's revelations, Adrian wouldn't want to face anyone.

On the third floor, he knocked gently on the door of Room 313. Carly came to the door. "Come in, Mr Fox."

"Thank you for seeing me," he started. "I just wanted to check how you are."

"Thank you. It is very kind of you." She offered him the only armchair in the room and perched on the side of the bed. Her small suitcase was open on the bed, half packed.

"Are you leaving today?" he asked.

"Yes. I can't stay here any longer. I have to get back for the children. Sophie has booked tickets on the early evening flight, I'm going back with her and Martin."

"That's good. It's where you should be now."

"Yes."

An uncomfortable silence descended, both reluctant to begin the obvious conversation subject. Eventually Jonny succumbed. "I'm terribly sorry you had to find out everything this way. But I think you had worked it out somehow before I did."

Carly nodded and lowered her head, composing herself. "Having had two children, I know the signs. It was clear to me Lizzie was pregnant. I asked her, but she denied it, of course. Then I asked Adrian and he knew nothing about it. That's when it all fell into place. I didn't know how she did it, but I knew she was involved in Neil's murder. It was too much for me and I just collapsed, I couldn't get out of bed."

"You have been very strong," he reminded her. "I know you loved Neil, but he couldn't have made life easy for you at times."

She lowered her head, tears coming now. Jonny passed her a tissue from the desk.

"He was such a wonderful father. We had our best times as a family. But..." She couldn't finish the sentence.

"I understand."

Carly looked down again, dabbing her eyes.

"Is there anything you want to ask me?" Jonny enquired.

She hesitated. "Do you have enough evidence to charge her?"

"Yes, I believe so," he confirmed. "We will have to wait for the physical evidence tests. But we already have two confession statements from when DCI Mikeš and I apprehended her."

Carly nodded. "Thank you, Mr Fox."

Jonny stood up. "You take care of yourself and your children. Goodbye." He walked out of the hotel room and closed the door softly behind him.

Jonny took the lift to the ground floor and walked across the foyer. As he neared the exit he heard someone call his name behind him. "Mr Fox."

Sophie and Martin Wilson were standing at reception with their suitcases. Sophie walked over to him, her features more relaxed and softer than before. "I want to thank you and apologise."

"There is really no need. It was a difficult situation."

"Yes, true. But I should have trusted you and supported your lines of enquiry. Instead, I'm afraid I made it difficult for you."

"Not really," he assured her. "The truth was going to come out one way or another. It was just a matter of time."

"Thank you again." She held out her hand and they shook.

"Have a good flight home and make sure you support your true friends. Life is too short to waste time on bad people."

Jonny smiled at her, then turned away and left the hotel, leaving her standing in the middle of the foyer.

40

Looking for Honza

When Jonny arrived at the police station, all was quiet. He entered the building using his key card, and walked up the stairs to the open plan office expecting noise and excitement. Instead the office was empty, every desk vacant. The only person on the floor was Katka, the tea lady, pushing her trolley around and clearing desks of used mugs and crockery.

"Ahoj, Honza," she greeted him with a discrete wave and a smile.

He made a gesture with his arms, asking her where everyone was. She only pointed towards the Incident Room at the end of the office.

The door was open, but the room empty. Jonny stepped inside and immediately noticed the murder board had been cleared of all photos and scribbles related to the Neil Robson case, instead replaced by an A4 photo of him with a message written underneath in large letters.

> *Hledá se Honza!*
> *Čekáme na tebe v mojí oblíbené hospodě*
> *Felix*

Jonny smiled to himself. Another riddle to solve. Mikeš knew him so well already.

Relishing the challenge, he took out his smartphone and opened up the translation application. He already knew 'hospoda' was Czech for 'pub', but he couldn't be sure of the rest of the words.

Looking for Honza!
We are waiting for you in my favourite pub
Felix

He sat down and using the map application searched for local pubs. Not recognising anything immediately, he stopped to think. What was it Mikeš had said about his name when they first met? A famous black cat character from children's books. Typing 'black cat pub prague' into the search engine solved the mystery; the Černá kočka (*Black Cat*) pub was only a short walking distance from the station.

***

Walking into the old, traditional Czech pub, Jonny was greeted by erupting cheers and clapping. Mikeš stepped over and extended his hand in greeting, an impish grin on his face. "So you solved my little puzzle."

"Yes, very clever, Felix."

Mikeš laughed. "It's the start of your Czech lessons."

Keen to get on with the salute, Boukal thrust a glass of Pilsner Urquell into Jonny's hand. Dvořáková waved across at him from the bar, a beer also in her hand.

Felix led the toast. "To Honza. Thank you and na zdraví." Everybody drank in toast and the clapping recommenced.

Even though this was his second ovation in almost as many days, Jonny still felt uncomfortable in the limelight. He knew his contribution to solving the case had been important, but his natural inclination was to celebrate as a team, not singling anyone out for special treatment. But the compassion of these people, many of whom knew nothing more than his given Czech name, was so authentic, it was almost hard to believe. He nodded and said "Děkuju" to everyone, as members of the team approached him and shook his hand or clinked his glass in a sign of respect.

After the crowd had settled, Jonny found himself back in the more usual huddle of Mikeš, Boukal and Dvořáková. Sensing the value of the occasion, Jonny cleared his throat and scanned the small group. "I want to thank you all for making me feel so at home. You are very special people."

"Hear, hear," shouted Mikeš and slapped Jonny on the back.

"Actually," Dvořáková started, "we decided to get you a little gift."

"No, please," Jonny protested, looking embarrassed. "I don't want anything."

"Just open it," Boukal declared.

Jonny took the gift and opened the wrapping paper deliberately. When he saw inside he burst out laughing. It was a miniature model of the Petřin Lookout Tower. "That's brilliant. Thank you so much."

"Something to remind you of your first detective adventure in Prague," Dvořáková explained.

Jonny kissed her on the cheek and shook the men's hands. He held the tower model aloft as a trophy and people standing around cheered.

Jonny's mobile phone started ringing. His first reaction was to ignore it, but, with the others now looking at him, he took the phone out of his pocket and glanced at the screen. *Charlotte.* Shocked and also, like any parent, slightly concerned something had happened, he made his excuses and stepped outside the pub.

"Hi, Charlotte," he answered.

"Hi, Dad. What are you doing in Prague?"

"Ha. So, you got my postcard?"

"Yes, it came today. I was shocked. Are you okay?"

"Yes, fine. Prague is an amazing city."

"What are you doing there?"

"I just wanted a holiday, haven't had one for a while.

And I suppose I've always wanted to explore the city where your grandmother was born, see some of the places she told me about when I was young."

"And how's it going?"

"Well, it's certainly been an adventure. I can't explain it all in one phone call. You'll have to come and visit me."

"I'd like that."

Jonny was smiling so much passers-by were looking at him oddly. His luck was certainly changing.

"How long are you staying in Prague?"

"Three months initially."

"Three months!"

"Yes. Lots of time to visit me. Maybe in the Easter holidays?"

"Sounds good. I'll need to do some revising during the holidays for my exams, but a few days away will be fine."

"Of course, we can plan a short trip. I'll agree something with your mum."

"Great."

"Anyway, what about you? I don't think you've ever asked me so many questions before."

"Well, Dad, that's because you never do anything interesting. Prague is cool."

"You have a point there." Jonny laughed.

"Charlotte," he continued, "I'm so sorry I missed your parent's evening this week."

"It's okay, Dad, I didn't think you'd come."

"Yes, your mum said. But it's not good enough. I'm sorry."

"Look, I've got to go. I'm going over to my friends soon."

"No problem. And Charlotte, thanks for calling. It's lovely to hear your voice."

"You too, Dad."

"I'll call you in a few days and we can make some plans for Prague."

"Great, Take care."

"Love you."

"You too. Bye, Dad."

"Bye, Charlotte."

The call disconnected but Jonny remaining looking at the screen of his phone, dazed and overwhelmed, his eyes welling up. A week ago the probability of his daughter coming to visit him in Prague was a faraway fantasy, but now it might just possibly happen. His shook his head in amazement at the unexpected curveballs of life.

Mikeš grabbed him as soon as he re-entered the pub. "Honza, where have you been? I thought you'd gone on another walkabout."

Jonny laughed. "It was my daughter calling me."

Mikeš stopped and looked directly into his eyes, realising the significance of the event. "Excellent news, I'm so pleased for you. Now you have a happy family in the UK and a new family in Prague."

"Yes. It feels good."

Mikeš ushered over Boukal and Dvořáková. Jonny picked up his beer ready for the next of many toasts.

"And here's to our next case." Mikeš bellowed.

Jonny looked confused. "Next case?"

"Yes, Honza. I've asked the Police Commissioner in Prague if we can put you on a contract and he has agreed."

"But Felix, I might not want a contract."

Mikeš laughed out loud, putting a compassionate arm around Jonny's shoulders. "You know you do. You are definitely too young to retire, my friend."

41

Leave it to Chance

Saturday, 20th March

The afternoon sun was shining, an open bottle of local red wine and two glasses sat between them on the table. Jonny couldn't remember a time he'd felt more relaxed, at peace with himself.

Deciding to take a stroll after lunch, he had remembered Dvořáková's recommendation and suggested walking to Havlíčkovy sady, one of the local parks in Prague 2. They were in no hurry today. They had meandered around the Italian Renaissance city park, visiting all the fountains and statues. At the pond they had sat and watched the many fish swimming around and then walked the perimeter of the Grébovka pavilion, stopping to look out at the urban spectacle across the rolling hills of the Prague suburbs.

The wooden replica Vineyard Gazebo offered tables on the terrace, overlooking the restored hillside plantation of grapevines, a remnant of the winery's former glory. The vines were starting to bud with the season, mottled green shoots appearing on the haggard looking old plants.

Ivana was first to break the silence. "Do you have any plans for next week?"

Jonny chuckled to himself, remembering the events of the week. "You know, I think I'll leave it to chance. My luck seems to be in at the moment so I'll take whatever life throws at me."

"You are getting very philosophical, Honza."

He shrugged his shoulders. "Not really. But I do believe, now more than ever, that things happen for a reason."

He took a sip of the wine, letting the dark flavours of fruit and flowers, with a spicy aroma, wash around his mouth.

"Actually, there was something I wanted to ask you," he said.

"Yes."

"When we had dinner this week, you mentioned you had a friend who worked in the government office for registrations."

Ivana nodded, watching him closely.

"Well, I've decided I would like to trace my Czech family tree. I've thought about it hard and I think my mother would want me to. Whatever happened to her here is a long time in the past. My life is different to hers and it would be nice to find out what other family I have here in Prague."

Ivana smiled. "I'm pleased for you."

"I brought some documents of hers with me to Prague, but they are very old. I don't even know what they are about."

"It doesn't matter. The only important point is that you want to try searching for your family. I am sure we can work out the rest. I'll call my friend and arrange for you to meet her."

"Thank you."

Jonny gazed out over the city. He had enough life experience to know he couldn't predict what was going to happen to him in the coming weeks and months. But one thing he knew for sure was that he was going to be in Prague for longer than he'd originally planned.

Printed in Great Britain
by Amazon